"One of the happiest . . . books in this series." —*Locus*

"Avid Deryni readers will rush to this book, and novices to the series will not be disappointed." —*VOYA*

"A rich and romantic tale sure to please lovers of fantasy, romance, intrigue, and the Middle Ages."

—*Realms of Fantasy*

"Excellent book. Deryni fans, enjoy."

—*Billings (MT) Gazette*

More praise for Katherine Kurtz's

Deryni novels

"An incredible historical tapestry of a world that never was and of immensely vital people who ought to be."

—Anne McCaffrey, award-winning author of the Dragonriders of Pern series

"A rich feast of medieval chivalry, romance, and magic—the book that all Katherine Kurtz fans have been awaiting."

—Marion Zimmer Bradley, author of *The Mists of Avalon*

"At her best, Kurtz's love of history lets her do things with her characters and their world that no nonhistorian could hope to do." —*Chicago Sun-Times*

"Kurtz has created a fascinating idealization of the Middle Ages and infused it with a kind of magic one can truly believe in." —*Fantasy Review*

Deryni books available from Ace

DERYNI RISING
DERYNI CHECKMATE
HIGH DERYNI
KING KELSON'S BRIDE
IN THE KING'S SERVICE
CHILDE MORGAN

Childe Morgan

KATHERINE KURTZ

ACE BOOKS, NEW YORK

THE BERKLEY PUBLISHING GROUP
Published by the Penguin Group
Penguin Group (USA) Inc.
375 Hudson Street, New York, New York 10014, USA
Penguin Group (Canada), 90 Eglinton Avenue East, Suite 700, Toronto, Ontario M4P 2Y3, Canada
(a division of Pearson Penguin Canada Inc.)
Penguin Books Ltd., 80 Strand, London WC2R 0RL, England
Penguin Group Ireland, 25 St. Stephen's Green, Dublin 2, Ireland (a division of Penguin Books Ltd.)
Penguin Group (Australia), 250 Camberwell Road, Camberwell, Victoria 3124, Australia
(a division of Pearson Australia Group Pty. Ltd.)
Penguin Books India Pvt. Ltd., 11 Community Centre, Panchsheel Park, New Delhi—110 017, India
Penguin Group (NZ), 67 Apollo Drive, Rosedale, North Shore 0632, New Zealand
(a division of Pearson New Zealand Ltd.)
Penguin Books (South Africa) (Pty.) Ltd., 24 Sturdee Avenue, Rosebank, Johannesburg 2196,
South Africa

Penguin Books Ltd., Registered Offices: 80 Strand, London WC2R 0RL, England

CHILDE MORGAN

An Ace Book / published by arrangement with the author

PRINTING HISTORY
Ace hardcover edition / December 2006
Ace mass-market edition / February 2008

Cover art by Matt Stawicki.
Hand lettering by Pyrographx.
Cover design by Annette Fiore.
Interior text design by Kristin del Rosario.

For information, address: The Berkley Publishing Group,
a division of Penguin Group (USA) Inc.,
375 Hudson Street, New York, New York 10014.

ISBN: 978-0-441-01554-2

ACE
Ace Books are published by The Berkley Publishing Group,
a division of Penguin Group (USA) Inc.,
375 Hudson Street, New York, New York 10014.

PRINTED IN THE UNITED STATES OF AMERICA

10 9 8 7 6 5 4 3 2 1

The Eleven Kingdoms
Northern Sea
Atalantic Ocean
Gulf of Northarch
Claibourne
Stevenham
Kheldish Riding
(Old Kheldour)
Marley
Rhendall
Cassan
Gulf of Kheldour
Kilshane
Tolán
Tiegre
Czalsky
Jándrich
Kierney
Iomaire Plain
Truvorsk
Transha
Meara
The Purple March
Llyndruth Plain
Kulnán
Torenth
Beldour R.
Ratharkin
Gwynedd
Sasovna
Brustarkia
Cloome
Culteine
Valoret
Carcashale
The Fertile Crescent
Arjenol
Arx Fidei
Rhengarth Plain
Beldouria
The Connait
Rhemuth
Lendour
Beldour
Sostra
Cashien
Jenas
Desse
Haldane
Csorna
Komnene
Danoc
Concaradine
Beldour R.
Corwyn

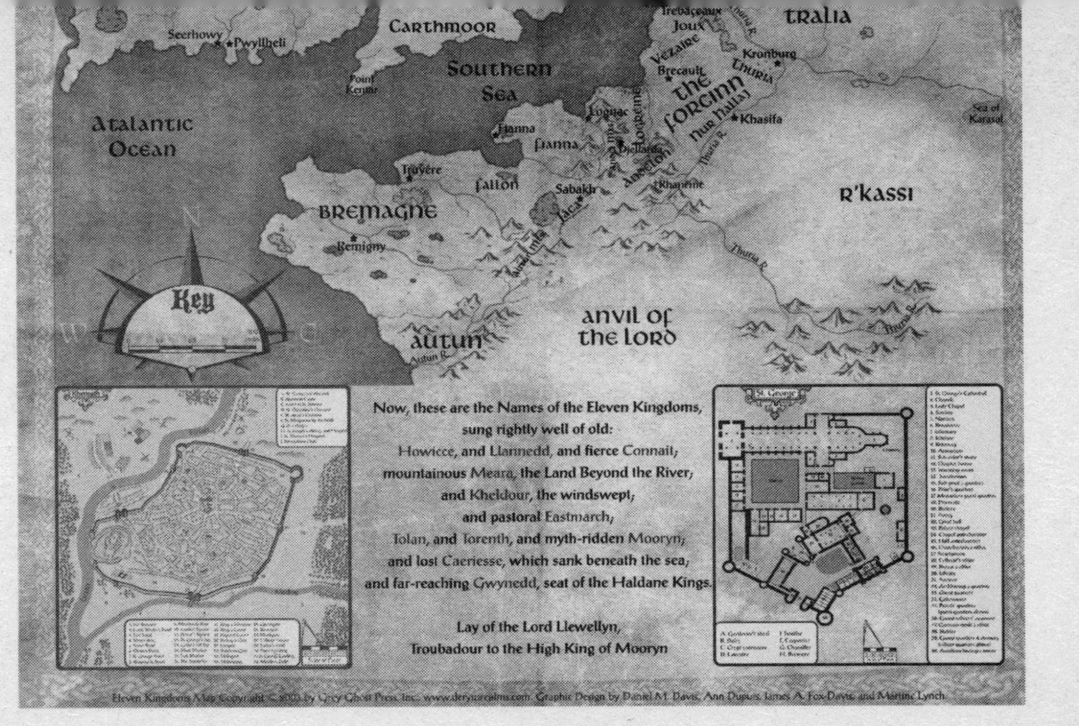
Carthmoor
Seerhowy
Pwyllheli
Southern Sea
Point Kennir
Atalantic Ocean
Tralia
Trebaçeaux
Joux
Vezaire
Brecault
Kronburg
Thuria
The Forcinn
Nur Hallaj
Khasifa
Logiac
Lorreine
Fianna
Djellarda
Andelon
Torvère
Fallon
Sabakh
Rhanvire
Jaca
Bremagne
Remigny
R'Kassi
Sea of Karasal
Thuria R.
Key
N
W
E
Autun
Autun R.
Anvil of the Lord
Now, these are the Names of the Eleven Kingdoms,
sung rightly well of old:
Howicce, and Llannedd, and fierce Connait;
mountainous Meara, the Land Beyond the River;
and Kheldour, the windswept;
and pastoral Eastmarch;
Tolan, and Torenth, and myth-ridden Mooryn;
and lost Caeriesse, which sank beneath the sea;
and far-reaching Gwynedd, seat of the Haldane Kings.
Lay of the Lord Llewellyn,
Troubadour to the High King of Mooryn
St. George

Prologue

"A woman that had for a long time mourned the dead . . ."

—II SAMUEL 14:2

Christmas Eve, 1093

THE fair-haired woman who paused in the doorway to the royal crypt was the Lady Alyce, Deryni heiress to the Duchy of Corwyn and now the wife of Sir Kenneth Morgan, and mother of his son. Fondly she watched as the black-cloaked Queen of Gwynedd touched a wax spill to the torch set in a cresset on a side wall, then used the spill to light a votive candle shielded in red glass.

The child sleeping beneath the stone lid of the sepulcher on which she placed the votive light had been gone more than a year now, but Alyce knew that a day never passed when Richeldis of Gwynedd did not remember this, the second-born of her four sons, and mourn his loss. Blaine Emanuel Haldane had been only nine when he passed into the care of God's holy angels.

Nor did it much matter now just how or why Prince Blaine had met his premature death, though his bravery *had* saved his younger sister from drowning. Gallant though his action had been, the chill he took that day had been the death of him hardly a week later, wheezing for breath and finally succumbing to the illness that gradually filled his lungs with fluid and finally choked out his life. Though the royal physicians had done their best to save him, the boy's condition had been beyond their skill, either to cure him or even much to ease his suffering. Only recently had his mother begun to smile again, and to emerge from the profound depression she had suffered following the young prince's death.

Breathing a heavy sigh, the queen sank to her knees to pray, head bowing over her hands, which were folded on Blaine's tomb. Alyce knelt as well, quietly reaching behind her to pull a basket of greenery closer. Earlier, she and another of the queen's ladies had helped gather cuttings of what sparse winter foliage the royal gardens had to offer, floral tributes intended not just for Prince Blaine but for several other notables buried here in the royal crypt, sleeping with Haldane princes and princesses.

"Please bring the basket, Alyce," the queen said suddenly, getting to her feet and turning.

Rising wordlessly, Alyce brought the basket closer so that Richeldis could select a single white camellia blossom, which she kissed and then laid on her son's tomb beside the votive candle. She then added a sprig of winter holly, rich with berries, and a companion cutting of evergreen, tied with a ribbon of Haldane crimson.

"Sleep gently, my son," the queen murmured, bending briefly to touch her lips to the cool marble.

As she took the basket and moved on to lay tributes at several other Haldane graves, Alyce paid her own respects at another pair of tombs: the Lady Jessamy, wife of Sir Sief MacAthan, and Krispin her son—who also had been the son of the king, though Alyce doubted that Richeldis had ever learned of this. The plan had been that Krispin, heir to the magic of his Deryni mother and the similar magic of the Haldanes, should grow to be a Deryni protector to the king's eldest son and heir, Prince Brion.

But the Deryni were feared in most of Gwynedd, and hated by many, especially Gwynedd's clergy. It had been such fear and hatred that had led to young Krispin's murder, setting at naught all the king's plans. One of those responsible had been a priest, the brother of a bishop, the guilt of all the murderers discovered and revealed by Alyce's own magic. In all, three men had been executed.

Now it was Alyce's son who was being groomed to assume the role meant for the ill-fated Krispin: another child of a Deryni mother. Young Alaric had turned two in September, and Prince Brion was a mature twelve-and-a-half, but already the two were bonding like brothers—and might have been brothers in fact, if the king had had his way.

But in this, at least, Donal Haldane had found himself thwarted before he could even attempt to carry out his intent. Alyce still found herself awed by the loyalty and love that had enabled her husband to forgive the king for what he had tried to do, and to pledge their child to the king's service even before his birth, so that Prince Brion should have his Deryni protector.

Never mind that the two-year-old Alaric would be in no position to do much protecting of anyone for some time. Fortunately, King Donal was yet hale and strong, and might expect to live many more years before his own son came to the throne. In the meantime, God willing, Alaric would be given the time to grow into his responsibilities, and be ready to take them up when the time came.

"So many Haldanes," the queen said softly, intruding on Alyce's reflections as she turned to look at the younger woman. "This is where they all lie, and where I shall lie, one day."

"True enough, madam," Alyce replied lightly, "but, please God, not for many a year."

Behind them, a rustling of fabric reminded Alyce of another waiting just at the doorway to the royal crypt: Zoë Morgan, her husband's eldest daughter, beloved friend from Alyce's schoolgirl days, briefly the wife of her late brother, but still and always her sister of the heart—and now, by dint of marriage with Zoë's father, her stepdaughter as well.

"Alyce, there's a squire clearing his throat at the top of

the stair," Zoë whispered, glancing over her shoulder as she moved nearer.

"He's expected," Alyce whispered back. "He'll be here about the council meeting. Madam," she called, raising her voice slightly, "it's time to go."

"Good heavens, already?" Richeldis turned in surprise, looking younger than her twenty-eight years. "I *will* have time to change, won't I? I can't go to the council looking like a crow, in all this black!"

Smiling, Zoë moved a little nearer, lifting a beckoning arm. "We have time, if you come now, madam. I believe it's Jamyl who's come to remind us. He knows to bring the summons just that bit earlier than he'd need to do."

"Clever Jamyl," Richeldis said with a low chuckle. "He is precisely the kind of squire I like. He must have sisters and lots of other female relatives. Now, if I could only persuade the king to give me earlier reminders when I'm dressing for a state occasion. He does hate it when I'm late."

So saying, she passed a final, wistful caress along the top of her dead son's tomb, then gathered her skirts to pass Alyce and follow Zoë up the stairs, where a mounted escort and a carriage waited at the foot of the cathedral steps to take them back up to the castle.

The doomed man had not gone easily to his fate. Eyewitnesses said he had screamed as they let him fall, scrabbling frantically at the slimy sides of the well-shaft and abrading hands, elbows, and knees nearly to the bone, but finally had drowned. The monks who took charge of his frozen body afterward, giving him decent burial here in the cathedral grounds, had offered what reassurance they could, that the bishop's brother had not suffered long; but raw imaginings of Sepp's final moments were an all-too-regular feature of Oliver's nightmares.

With a shudder and a shake of his head, the bishop turned his face from his brother's grave, swallowing down the sour bile that rose in his throat. Though he very much doubted that Sepp had taken an active part in any murder, it probably *was* true that he had turned a blind eye to the victim's fate—and had Septimus de Nore not been a priest, the sentence meted out to him might have been fitting punishment for one who had countenanced the heartless murder of a child.

But not just any child. The boy had been Deryni—which, so far as Oliver was concerned, all but justified Sepp's actions. Some there were who had come to accept the presence of Deryni in Gwynedd, secretly and not so secretly, allowing them to coexist among decent humans, but Oliver was not one of them. The king, however . . .

Jaws clenching in disapproval, Oliver glanced up at the dark silhouette of Rhemuth Castle looming against the sky beyond the cathedral. Despite civil and canon law that seriously curtailed the rights of Deryni in Gwynedd, Donal Haldane was known to turn a blind eye to the letter of the law when it suited him, and had kept more than one Deryni in his employ and even in his friendship during his long reign. Some even whispered that the dead boy had been Donal's bastard son, gotten on the Deryni wife of one of his former ministers of state who, rather conveniently, had died very soon after the boy's birth. Since both mother and son were now dead as well, it served no useful purpose to dwell on *that*, but it could explain why the king had dealt so severely with those responsible for the boy's death.

Not that many would dispute the sentence meted out to Sepp's two lay accomplices, who probably had been the instigators. The king had ordered them gelded and then hanged, for they had buggered the boy quite viciously before throwing him into the well to drown. And Sepp, because it had been his suggestion thus to dispose of the evidence of the others' crime, had been stripped and flogged for his betrayal of the boy's trust, then flung down the selfsame well as the victim, to share the fate he himself had decreed.

There it might have ended, had Sepp been a layman like the others. But as a priest, Father Septimus de Nore had been entitled to benefit of clergy—which meant that his part in the matter ought to have been heard in the archbishop's court, not the king's—and *that*, Oliver could not forgive. Nor could he forgive the woman who had uncovered his brother's guilt: a Deryni, and therefore to be despised. Though both she and the king had been swiftly and justly declared excommunicate for their part in the trial and execution of a priest by secular authority, both had been reinstated in the good graces of the Church with unseemly haste.

Oliver had witnessed the first such reconciliation—achieved by the threat of Interdict for the entire kingdom, if the king did not capitulate. Oliver had been present on that Maundy night when the king made his formal act of submission before the archbishop: the ritual declaration of contrition and acceptance of the penitential scourging that preceded the lifting of his excommunication. Some variation on this eventual outcome had always been a foregone conclusion, since a king dared not long remain adamant in his defiance of ecclesiastical prerogatives.

Less appropriately, the now-deceased archbishop had also been persuaded to lift the excommunication of the Deryni woman, but a few weeks later—and she had since been wed to one of the king's loyal supporters, and borne him a son.

"Staring at his grave won't bring him back, you know," said a low voice behind Oliver. "You do this every year, my lord."

Grimacing against the rain, Bishop Oliver turned to cast a sour glance at Father Rodder Gillespie, his secretary and general factotum. Cassock-clad and huddled, like the bishop, in a fur-lined cloak with oiled hood and shoulder capelet, the younger man looked as miserable as Oliver felt, bedraggled and chilled to the bone.

"I do it, dear Rodder, because my brother lies still in his grave and unavenged," the bishop said bitterly, "and because those responsible for his death still prosper. The king has many fine, strapping sons, and the woman who denounced my brother will have her son presented at court later today. I was praying for justice."

"And I have been praying for your good health, as you stand in the rain like a child of no good sense!" Rodder retorted, laying a proprietary arm around his superior's shoulders and drawing him toward the open doorway of the passage that led away from the abbey churchyard. "Please, my lord. You must come inside and don dry clothes. The archbishop will be wanting to leave soon for court. He has already been asking for you."

Oliver cast a last, longing glance at his brother's grave, grimly signed himself with the Cross, then let himself be led inside.

Chapter 2

"He shall serve among great men, and appear before princes; he will travel through strange countries; for he hath tried the good and the evil among men."

—ECCLESIASTICUS 39:3

"ALARIC Anthony Morgan, if you don't stop squirming and let Auntie Zoë put your shoes on, I shall tell your father!"

Lady Alyce de Corwyn Morgan turned from her mirror to cast an exasperated glance at her firstborn, both hands occupied with holding hanks of golden hair in place while a maid arranged her coiffure. Auntie Zoë, actually the child's half-sister, did her best to keep a straight face as the wayward toddler glanced guiltily from his mother's face to hers to the offending shoes, lower lip starting to tremble.

"Don't want those!" he declared, hugging two disreputable-looking bits of scuffed suede against the front of a once-clean shirt. "Want *these*!"

"Absolutely not!" Zoë said emphatically, plucking the offending shoes from his grasp and tossing them behind her as she held up a newer green one. "Those are nearly worn through and outgrown—and they'd look utterly shabby with your lovely new tunic," she added, indicating the small black tunic laid out on the chest beside him. Embroidered over the left breast was a green Corwyn gryphon, its details picked out in gold. A border of *fleury-counter-fleury* in metallic gold embellished it at throat, sleeve-edge, and hem.

"No!" said Alaric. "Don't *like* the green ones!"

"Alaric, love," said Zoë, "we don't have time for this today. You know Papa will be very cross if you make him late for court. The green shoes are lovely and soft—"

"No!"

"Here now, what's this about green shoes?" asked a pleasant male voice from the doorway behind them, as Zoë's father—and the boy's—came into the room, accompanied by the youngest of his three daughters, the flaxen-haired Alazais.

Though less colorfully dressed than the women, Sir Kenneth Morgan had also donned formal court attire for the occasion: an ankle-length robe of nubby turquoise wool, its high neck and sleeves lined with silver fox, cinched at the waist with the white belt of his knighthood. Alazais wore a rich brown damask, in contrast to Zoë's gown of heavy rose silk. Alyce, as the heiress of Corwyn, had chosen deep forest green to complement the Furstána emeralds at her throat. All of them sported varying shades of blond hair, though Kenneth's had gone more toward silver than sandy in the past several years.

"He doesn't like the green shoes," Alyce said, half-turning toward the newcomers as she set a narrow silver fillet atop the fine veil her maid had just pinned in place. "He wants to wear those manky old tan ones that even the dogs ignore."

"Does he, indeed?" Kenneth asked, crouching between his son and his eldest daughter and taking up one of the green shoes. "Alaric, is that true? Why, these are very fine shoes. I like them far better than mine."

The boy's rebellion shifted to curiosity, and he leaned forward to peer down at the pointed toe of one turquoise shoe protruding from beneath the hem of his sire's robe.

"I really do prefer yours," Kenneth said, noting the boy's interest. "Not that your shoes would fit me—and even if they did, the color would hardly suit this robe. Frankly, I'd far rather be wearing my comfortable old black ones.

"But sometimes, we have to do what someone else wants. Your mother likes these better, and tells me they are much more suitable for an important court like Twelfth Night. The queen will like them, too—and your mother and Zoë and the other ladies of the court," he added. "Women set great store by such things, you know."

The stream of adult patter utterly charmed away the boy's remaining resistance, so that he made no objection as Kenneth got to his feet and picked him up, holding him close to breathe of the fresh scent of his silver-gilt hair and kiss his cheek. As he braced the boy on his hip, he silently nodded for Zoë to resume shoeing the child.

"My lord, you are entirely too indulgent," Alyce murmured, though she smiled as she said it, and blew him a kiss.

"Well, he *is* my only son," Kenneth replied. "And I'm afraid I indulged my daughters, too," he added, with a fond glance at Zoë and Alazais, both of whom obviously adored both their father and their younger half-brother. "It doesn't seem to have hurt them."

Zoë gave him a smile as she finished fastening the shoes on Alaric's feet, then let her father set him back on the floor so she could pull his new tunic over his head; no one would know that the shirt underneath was less than clean. Then, while she hurriedly ran a comb through his silky hair, Alyce fastened a little fur-lined green cloak around his shoulders, pinning it at the throat with a silver gryphon brooch.

"There, that's perfect. Now you look like a proper little future duke," Alyce said, standing back to inspect him. "Shall we all go down to court?"

THE great hall was filling fast, though the dais at the far end was yet unoccupied, save by pages and squires and other functionaries completing their preparations for court to come. A faint haze of wood smoke hung on the air from the three great fireplaces, leavened by the clean tang of pine resin from the torches along the walls and underlaid by the aroma of damp wool and damp courtiers; for many of those summoned to Twelfth Night Court were obliged to travel from lodgings outside the castle precincts. Sleet and rain were still pummeling the darkened glass of the clerestory windows that overlooked the castle gardens to the left of the hall.

But all within was festive and gay. High above, banners of most of the great families of Gwynedd hung from the hammer-beams and rafters, bright splashes of color against the oak and stone. Behind and above the twin thrones set at the center of the dais, a great tapestry of the royal arms of Gwynedd declared whose hall this was, the Haldane lion gazing over all with regal disdain. The buzz of conversation from the gathering court set the place alive with anticipation.

"Ah, Kenneth, I've finally found you," said a handsome man of about Kenneth's age, who had materialized at his right elbow.

Kenneth turned to regard Sir Jiri Redfearn, like himself, one of the king's most trusted aides. Jiri looked relaxed and unruffled, and gave Alyce and the other two ladies a graceful inclination of his ginger head.

"Jiri. Well met," Kenneth said amiably, acknowledging the other man with a nod.

"The king desires a word before court," Jiri said. "He's in the withdrawing room. Perhaps the ladies would care to warm themselves by one of the fires—except for Lady Alyce and the boy. They're summoned as well."

"Of course," Kenneth replied. "Do you know what this is about?"

"I do, but it isn't for me to say," Jiri answered, though he smiled slightly as he stood aside, indicating that they should precede him. With a glance at his wife, Kenneth took young Alaric's free hand and headed them around the dais to the left, leaving Zoë and her sister to wonder.

Though intended as an informal audience chamber for matters requiring discretion, and a staging area before ceremonies of state, the withdrawing room also functioned as the king's preferred workroom during the winter months—and clearly was serving all three functions today. Two liveried senior squires were putting the final touches to the king's court attire, fussing over the hang of a sweeping sleeve, and documents in varying stages of preparation mostly covered the surface of a table drawn up before the fireplace. A scribe and the king's eldest son were finishing the seals on the documents that required them, the young prince in page's livery.

"Ah, there you are," the king said, turning as Jiri admitted the three and then withdrew.

Donal Haldane had aged but little in the four years since placing the hand of Alyce de Corwyn in that of Sir Kenneth Morgan, bestowing upon him the richest heiress in the kingdom. His carriage was still erect, the clear grey eyes still steady and direct, with just a hint of good humor crinkling their corners, but the once-sable hair now glimmered mostly silver against the collar of his robe of Haldane crimson, and his close-trimmed beard was nearly all gone to grey—though even Kenneth was going grey, and he was twenty years younger.

"You summoned us, Sire?" Kenneth said, neck bending in an easy bow as Alyce dipped in curtsy. At her prompting, little Alaric also produced a fair bow of his own.

Not quite suppressing a smile, Donal nodded and dismissed the squires and scribe with an impatient wave of his hand, though he signed for Prince Brion to carry on with his work. But for the vagaries of fate and happenstance, Alaric Morgan also might have been his son—though perhaps it was as well that Donal Haldane had had no part in the getting of the boy. Fortunately, only he and the boy's parents knew how very nearly it had been otherwise; and the pair's generous spirits and utter loyalty to their king had ensured that the outcome was satisfactory for all concerned. The king now intended to reward that loyalty.

"One of the privileges of wearing a crown is that I am not obliged to explain my actions to my subjects," Donal said, by way of preamble. "But given the extraordinary position in which we all find ourselves, as mentors to a very underage future Duke of Corwyn, I thought it wise to give you advance notice of a decision I intend to announce at court this afternoon. The deed itself is already done; it only wants being made public. Brion, would you please bring me that warrant concerning Lendour?" he added, with a glance at his son and heir.

Quickly, the boy glanced over the rows of documents on the table and extracted one, which he brought immediately to his sire. Donal gave it a perfunctory glance, then extended it toward Kenneth.

"I am today creating you Earl of Lendour for life, *de jure uxoris*," he said, just as Kenneth's hand touched it. "Not only is this fitting reward for your many years of faithful service," he added at the looks of surprise from both Kenneth and Alyce, "but you need sufficient rank to function as regent for a future duke. Besides that, I intend to use you for some important diplomatic work in the next few years, and you'll be more effective as my envoy if you've a rank closer to those with whom you'll be dealing."

"Sire, I—had no idea . . ." Kenneth finally managed to murmur, as Alyce beamed. "But I shall certainly strive to be worthy of the trust you have shown me in this matter."

Donal allowed himself a broad grin. "Rarely have I seen you at a loss for words, Kenneth Morgan," he said. "It also pleases me that, in so honoring you, I also allow dear Alyce to enjoy at least a part of the style to which she would have been entitled, had she been born male. But I would never wish that," he added. "She makes far too charming a woman."

"Sire, you need not flatter *me*," Alyce said happily, slipping an arm around Kenneth's waist. "This is my lord husband's day."

"And yours," Donal corrected. "I would have preferred to make Kenneth duke for life, and you a duchess, but that might be more than my other lords of state could stomach, to set a simple knight so far above them. Even so, there will be jealousy in some circles."

"True enough, Sire," Kenneth agreed, still stunned by the king's generosity.

"This does, of course, put you in the interesting position of being your son's vassal, when Alaric comes of age," the king added with a sly grin, "but you can always resign the title at that time, if you wish—perhaps retire to the country with your lovely wife. By then, you'll be older than I am now, but hopefully your health will still be good."

The last comment seemed casually made, but something in the king's almost-wistful tone caused both Kenneth and Alyce to exchange uneasy glances.

"Sire, is there something we should know?" Kenneth asked cautiously, keeping his voice low.

"Nay, I am well enough," the king replied, though Kenneth thought the denial came all too quickly.

"The announcement will cause comment, of course," the king went on, taking the warrant back from Kenneth and returning it to Brion. "But it is something I have been considering for some time. A few of the council know; most do not. Come the spring, I have it in mind that the three of you should journey to Lendour, by slow stages, to take up your new holding and introduce your eventual successor to his people." He nodded toward the wide-eyed Alaric. "For that matter, perhaps you should travel on to Coroth after that, make a grand circuit of it. The Corwyners should also meet their future duke."

"They should, indeed," Kenneth murmured, with a swift glance at his wife and son. "And is it your intention that we should remain in Lendour?"

"Good Lord, no!" Donal replied. "I need you at my side, just as I'll have you at my side today.

"Now, for some further specifics." The king clasped his hands together and shifted his gaze to Alyce. "You are aware that, once he lived through the dangerous first few years of infancy, I have always intended to acknowledge young Alaric as heir of Lendour and Corwyn. I shall do that today, in the context of knighting the Lendouri candidates. I believe there are two this year?"

"Yes, Sire. Yves de Tremelan and Xander of Torrylin."

"I have heard good report of them," the king replied. "Trained by Sir Jovett Chandos and his father, are they not?"

"They are, Sire," Kenneth confirmed.

"An excellent young man, young Jovett," Donal said

with a nod. "I've been watching his progress. You might keep him in mind as a deputy when you are absent."

He recalled himself and returned to more immediate concerns. "But we were speaking of Lendour's two new knights-to-be. When the first one is called, I shall ask Alyce and Alaric to accompany them forward; Kenneth, you'll already be with me."

"Yes, Sire," both of them murmured.

The growing chatter of children's voices outside the door precluded further serious discussion as, with a smile and a shake of his head, Donal signed for Prince Brion to admit them.

"We'll play the rest as it comes," the king said to Kenneth and Alyce, as the door flew open to an influx of crimson-clad royal children and ladies-in-waiting, followed by the queen. The two princesses, aged eight and four, raced forward to give their sire a hug. Prince Nigel, but a month short of his seventh birthday, held the hand of his younger brother—little Jathan, born but a week after Alaric. A pair of squires preceded the queen, bearing the king's court mantle and the state crown of leaves and crosses intertwined.

"Darling, they're waiting for us," the queen murmured, gathering her train closer to keep it from being trampled by exuberant children. "I do hope you won't be much longer."

She broke into a smile at the sight of Kenneth and his family and, when the couple had made their courtesies to her, came to greet Alyce with a quick hug. She then crouched down and held out her arms to Alaric, who ran willingly to her embrace.

Richeldis of Llannedd had matured gracefully since her arrival at court as a fresh-faced royal bride of not yet fifteen, though frequent pregnancies had thickened her once-slender waist. Like the king, she was gowned in court crimson lined with sable, her dark hair dressed low on her neck and bound across the brow with a simpler version of Donal's state crown. Laughing delightedly, she rose and turned toward the king, one hand caressing young Alaric's silver-gilt hair.

"Donal, would you just look at this little man?" she declared. "What a proper young gentleman he looks today!"

"Aye, he does," the king agreed. With an impatient gesture, he signed for the squires to bring his state robe and crown. "Let's see whether he acts the gentleman at court." He shrugged into the state robe and set the crown on his own head.

"Alyce, I suggest that you take your charming son and join Sir Jovett and the two Lendour lads to be knighted today. Kenneth, you're with me. And we shall hope that today's announcement meets with more favor than the last one I made concerning the two of you."

Chapter 3

"In his days shall the righteous flourish,
and abundance of peace, till the moon be no more."

—PSALM 72:7

RETURNING to the hall, Alaric's hand in hers, Alyce quickly found Zoë and Alazais, who were waiting just beside the nearest of the fireplaces.

"Goodness," Zoë said. "What was *that* all about?"

"Nothing unpleasant," Alyce assured her, though she decided to be vague, to preserve the element of surprise that the king obviously intended. "It's to do with recognizing Alaric as my heir. There's to be some kind of official acknowledgment at court this afternoon.

"And speaking of court," she went on, searching the hall, "we need to find my Lendour men. The king will be knighting two of my squires today, both of them with excellent prospects." She glanced archly at Alazais. "I think we should introduce them to our Zaizie, don't you, Zoë?"

Zoë chuckled softly at that, and Alazais blushed furiously; but one of the reasons Kenneth had brought his youngest daughter to court for the season was to expose her to eligible young men. Geill, the middle daughter, had married the summer before, to a knight in the service of Jared Earl of Kierney, whom both of them now served. Zoë was technically a widow, having been all too briefly married to Alyce's ill-fated brother Ahern, but marriage was once again on her mind.

"I think," said Zoë, "that Zaizie would very much enjoy meeting your incipient knights. I'm sure they are very worthy young men."

"Over there," said Alyce.

Her glance toward the deep window embrasures facing onto the castle gardens turned the gaze of both younger women in that direction, where the king's half-brother, Duke Richard, was assembling the year's crop of boys soon to be made royal pages, all in clean white shirts and scarlet breeches, faces scrubbed and hair mostly tidy. Assisting him were a handful of senior pages to be promoted to squire.

The knights-to-be, about a dozen of them, were gathering farther back with their sponsors, having kept vigil the night before. Each now wore the distinctive garb indicative of the status about to be conferred: the white under-tunic, symbolic of purity; the black over-tunic, as reminder of the grave to which all would eventually succumb; and over all, the crimson mantle, betokening both the royal house to which they owed allegiance and the blood each was prepared to shed in defense of that house.

They all looked much alike, of course, thus uniformly arrayed, so Alyce sought out the red and white of the Lendour banner rather than any individual—and spotted it in one of the niches toward the rear of the hall. Cradling its staff in one green-clad arm was Sir Jovett Chandos, Alyce's childhood friend and a stalwart defender of her rights in Lendour—and also, of late, a young man of particular interest to Zoë Morgan.

"Alyce, there's Jovett!" Zoë breathed.

"Oh, my goodness!" the younger Alazais whispered, eyes wide as saucers as she cast her gaze at the two young candidates standing near Jovett.

Alyce laughed gently, setting her free hand under the younger girl's elbow as she began to press her and Zoë in the direction of the three. Young Alaric looked up at all of them in some bewilderment as he let his mother draw him along.

"I seem to recall a somewhat different opinion two summers ago, when you came with us to Lendour," Alyce teased. " 'Silly boys,' I believe you called them."

"I never!" Alazais began somewhat indignantly. "No, wait . . . Not Yves and Xander?"

"The very same," Alyce replied. "And I'm told that both of them are now become quite excellent swordsmen, well deserving of the accolade. Nor have I heard that either of them is yet spoken for," she added *sotto voce*, with a wink at her youngest stepdaughter.

"Alyce, stop it!" Alazais hissed, blushing prettily.

Jovett had noticed their approach, and immediately called his two charges to attention, for Alyce was Lady of Lendour, even if her sex denied her title to the earldom in her own right. Tall and straight in his court robe of emerald green, with his coppery hair sleeked back in a warrior's knot, it was easy to see how Sir Jovett Chandos had caught Zoë's fancy; and his mind and soul were no less comely than his appearance. As Alyce and her companions drew near, the two incipient knights sank to one knee and bowed their heads, and Jovett dipped the Lendour banner in salute.

"Lady of Lendour!"

"Sir Jovett," Alyce replied, smiling as she caught the billow of red and white silk in one arm and let him take her other hand to salute it with a kiss. He was Deryni like herself, though secretly so, and his unspoken greeting flashed across the bond of their physical contact, even as his fond glance brushed Zoë.

You look well and happy, dear Alyce—and young Alaric has grown.

Sometimes by the day, it seems, came her grateful reply. *Do be certain to admire his shoes,* she added mischievously.

"My lady," he said aloud, bending again in a bow to include all of them. "And can this really be young Master Alaric?" he added, as he righted the Lendour banner. "Why, what handsome shoes you wear today, my lord. Do you think they might fit me?" He drew back the skirt of his long court robe to reveal plain black boots with slightly pointed toes, gold spurs affixed to the heels.

The boy's look of bemusement went briefly calculating, then shifted to pleased recognition. "You're Sir Jovett!" he declared, setting balled fists on both hips. "You have a big spotted horse!"

"Spotted horse?" Alyce murmured, as she and Zoë exchanged puzzled glances.

Feigning wide-eyed surprise, Jovett crouched down to the boy's level, handing off the banner to one of the candidates as he did so.

"Why, I do, indeed, have a spotted horse, young master. And she now has a spotted foal. I'm surprised that you remember."

"I'm not a baby!" Alaric said indignantly. "Mama wouldn't let me ride with you. She said I wasn't big enough."

With a glance up at Alyce and a suppressed smile, Jovett said, "Well, you're much bigger now, so perhaps the next time you're in Cynfyn, your mama *will* let you ride with me. But meanwhile, I should like to present two more of your knights." He straightened and jutted his chin toward the still-kneeling pair. "Or at least they'll *be* knights in a little while."

"Papa told me all about that," Alaric said wisely. "The king hits them three times with his sword an' says, 'You're a knight.' An' they get gold spurs an' a white belt an' a sword, an' then everybody says, 'Hurrah!' "

"Indeed, they do," Jovett agreed, as the boy's mother and his half-sisters did their best not to laugh. (Both candidates had ducked their heads to cover their own grins.) "But he doesn't hit them very hard—and not with the sharp edge. It's done with the flat of the blade, like so."

A dagger suddenly appeared in his right hand from a hidden wrist sheath, and he solemnly reached out to tap Alaric lightly on the right shoulder, the left shoulder, and then on the top of the head. A look of awe came over the boy's face, and he glanced first at his mother, then back at Jovett.

"Am I a knight now?" he whispered.

"No, not yet," Jovett replied with a chuckle, making the

blade disappear again. "It has to be done with a sword; and it takes more than just the sword-touch to make a man a knight. But when you're grown, you *will* be a knight, I promise you. And though I should be delighted to confer that honor when the time comes, I rather think it will be the king who knights you—or maybe Prince Brion."

"But he's only a boy," Alaric said, confused.

"Well, yes, but he's going to be the king someday, just like his father. But before he can knight anyone else, someone older will knight *him*—because only another knight can make a knight."

"Oh," said Alaric. "Could Papa knight me?" he asked, twisting to look up at his mother.

"Well, he *could*, darling," Alyce replied. "He *is* a knight. But someday you'll be a duke, and the king usually likes to knight dukes himself. However, when you *are* grown," she added, at signs of incipient rebellion on the upturned face, "and you're a knight, too, *you* will make knights—because dukes and earls have the right to knight their own men. If you were a knight now, it would be *your* honor to knight Yves and Xander here."

She jutted her chin toward the two candidates still kneeling beyond Jovett, who both saluted the boy with a right fist to the breast—and did their best to restrain grins of honest delight. Alaric gazed at them appraisingly for a long moment, then drew himself to attention and gravely saluted them back.

"Well done!" Jovett declared, chuckling as he clapped the boy on the shoulder in approval. "My lady, he already has command presence."

"Aye, he does," she replied, ruffling the boy's hair fondly. "But now, Alaric, you must give these young gentlemen permission to rise. They've been kneeling quite long enough, though I'm sure they were happy to do so. A nod or a slight bow is sufficient."

Very soberly, the boy made the two candidates a very proper bow, also gesturing with both hands that they should stand. Obediently the pair rose, also bowing to

Alyce and the two women with her. Alazais flushed prettily as Alyce turned to motion her forward.

"My dear, permit me to make these gentlemen known to you: Yves de Tremelan and Xander of Torrylin, soon to be knights of Lendour. Gentlemen, my husband's youngest daughter, Alazais Morgan. And I believe you know his eldest, Lady Zoë."

Amid the murmured exchanges of courtesy, Alyce became aware of a heightened buzz of conversation rippling through the hall and then a gradual quieting. Simultaneously, those milling in the center of the hall began to drift to the sides, clearing a center aisle and also the space directly before the dais. Being already withdrawn into a far window embrasure, Alyce and her Lendour party had only to turn their attention toward the dais where, very shortly, a chamberlain came forth with his staff of office and rapped smartly on the oak floor of the dais.

"My lords and ladies, pray, attend."

The royal family began to enter and assemble in their appointed places, not down the center aisle, because of the inclement weather, but directly from the doorway to the left of the dais, which led to the withdrawing room behind.

First came the younger royal children and their attendants, followed by the queen's ladies and the king's household, including Sir Jiri Redfearn, Kenneth, and several of the king's other ministers of state. As the king and queen appeared, attended by Prince Brion in page's livery, the chamberlain again rapped with his staff of office and announced, "Their Majesties: Donal Blaine Aidan Cinhil Haldane, King of Gwynedd and Lord of the Purple March, and Richeldis his queen, and also His Royal Highness the Prince Brion, Prince of Meara."

The royal couple proceeded to their thrones, but did not yet sit. Prince Brion stood attendance on his mother. The two Archbishops MacCartney followed close behind—Desmond of Rhemuth and William of Valoret, both of them coped and mitred appropriate to the season—and were shown to chairs of state to the right side of the dais.

Before taking their seats, Archbishop William blessed the assembled company, *"In nomine Patris, et Filii, et Spiritus Sancti, Amen."*

Court began with the usual business peculiar to Twelfth Night Courts, with the king receiving a dozen new pages into royal service and promoting several senior pages to squire. Prince Brion was among the latter, having turned twelve the previous June, and proudly knelt before his father with three others to pledge his ongoing fidelity.

After each of the new squires had received a pair of blued-steel spurs and a dagger from the king's own hand, they exchanged their simple pages' tabards for the more elegant scarlet tunics of royal squires, with the king's cipher embroidered on the left breast. Prince Brion was the first of the four to be so invested, and stood thereafter at his father's elbow as duty squire for the remainder of the afternoon. Last of those received as squire that afternoon, separate from the first four, was Jamyl Arilan, nephew of one of Donal's council lords, who previously had trained as page and squire at the court of Illann King of Llannedd, brother to Queen Richeldis.

"Master Jamyl, you are most welcome," Richeldis said to him, as she helped him don the scarlet tunic of a Haldane squire. "My brother speaks highly of you. I wonder that he was willing to give you up."

Jamyl smiled, a poised and confident young man of fifteen, and handsome as his uncle must have been in his youth.

"The king your brother is a man not easily parted from what he wants, my lady, as well you know," Jamyl replied, "but the king your husband can be very persuasive. And I am given to understand that my lord uncle also pled my cause." He nodded to Seisyll Arilan, standing behind and at the king's right hand. "I am honored now to be the second Arilan serving the Crown of Gwynedd."

Richeldis inclined her head in acknowledgment of the gracious reply, and glanced at Seisyll, proudly watching.

"We thank you for your efforts, my Lord Seisyll," she said. "I am certain that this new squire will be an asset to our court."

"That is my fondest wish, Majesty," he replied with a bow.

Next on the agenda was the dubbing of the season's new knights, some come from far afield to receive the accolade from the king's own hand. Most had been in training with Duke Richard, or at least had served as squires at court for several years, and now, having achieved their majority, were deemed ready to assume the duties and privileges of knighthood. All of the candidates had kept their vigil the night before, following a ritual bath and robing.

The court candidates came first, according to the usual custom, with each being brought before the king by his sponsor, there to kneel and be invested with golden spurs. The candidate then received the sword accolade from the king's hand or, in some cases, from the hand of his father or other older male relative who was also a knight, after which the queen girded each new knight with the white belt, symbolic of the purity of his new vocation. After being presented with a goodly sword, the new knight then placed his joined hands between those of the king and pledged his fealty to the Crown of Gwynedd.

Court candidates were somewhat sparse that year, though the half-dozen dubbed were of excellent quality. Jaska Collins and Ulf Carey excelled at horsemanship. The twins Thomas and Geoffrey de Main, whose swordsmanship was equaled by few others of their age, were so different in every other respect that they might not have even been brothers. Trevor Udaut had been the king's personal squire for the past several years, and would remain in royal service. Phares Donovan, the last of them, was a keen archer, especially from horseback.

"Do you like the looks of that one?" Zoë whispered to Alazais, as the queen girded Sir Phares with the white belt. "He's very well connected."

"Zoë, stop it!" Alazais hissed, with a wide-eyed glance over her shoulder at the Lendour candidates.

"Well, he *is* well connected, Zaizie," Alyce agreed, slipping an arm around her youngest stepdaughter's waist. "His father was castellan to the Earl of Marley."

"And it doesn't hurt that he was squire to Prince Brion," Zoë added, "and is utterly devoted to him. Hopefully, he will also prove to be a friend to Alaric," she added more softly.

For answer, Alyce only slipped her arm through Zoë's and briefly laid her head against the shoulder of this, her sister of the heart, grateful that Zoë also would always be a friend to her son. Very shortly, she knew, the king would make public his latest decision regarding all of their fates. Kenneth's appointment as Earl of Lendour would greatly ease her position as well as his, for she would share his rank—and finally have a status at least somewhat commensurate with her station as mother of a future duke.

For a Deryni like herself, of course, it was a double-edged distinction, since it would thrust her into public prominence again, when she had only just begun to live down the notoriety of using her powers to unmask murderers at Twelfth Night four years ago. Already, she had seen the brother of one of the murderers, scowling across the hall at her.

With luck, however, the new rank should help her keep Alaric safe until he was grown and could fulfill the destiny for which he had been born. Toward what else had her life been preparing her, than to support the House of Haldane in whatever way was needful?

Next to be called forward were two candidates from Meara: Alun Melandry, son of the murdered former royal governor of Ratharkin, and Arthen Talbot, youngest son of the present governor. Alun's knighting had a bittersweet quality to it, for he had seen his father put to death at the end of a rope by Mearan rebels when he was too young to do anything to stop it. His reception of the accolade now affirmed his determination to carry on in his father's footsteps, where he would serve among the knights sworn to the service of the present royal governor.

The son of that royal governor, by contrast, was relaxed and almost informal. Presented by his father, Sir Lucien Talbot, young Arthen knelt eagerly before the king, upturned face alight with joy. Behind him, Sir Lucien carried a goodly sword with which his son would be invested, with the straps of a pair of golden spurs looped over the quillons.

"So, Lucien," Donal said with a smile, rising with the Haldane sword cradled in his arm. "How many sons of yours have I knighted now, including young Arthen here? Three? Or is it four?"

"Arthen is the fourth, Sire," Lucien replied, bowing. "You knighted Caspar last Twelfth Night, and Julian the year before. And Joris was first, of course."

"Ah, of course. Well, they all look incredibly like you. I can't keep them straight. The others are not with you today?"

"Alas, no, Sire, but they send loyal greetings and apologies for their absence. I fear that all of them had duties in Meara that precluded their attendance. But they look forward to having their brother join them in service."

"I'm sure they do," the king replied, "though I imagine that the Mearans will hardly be glad to have another Talbot enforcing the king's peace. Sir Alun," he said to the just-knighted Alun Melandry, "perhaps you would be so good as to invest your young comrade-in-arms with his spurs. Lucien, I am also disappointed to see that your lady is not with you this year," the king went on, as the grinning Alun knelt to perform his office.

"As am I, Sire," the Mearan governor replied, "but the reason is a happy one. Our eldest daughter is soon to present us with our first grandchild, so her mother has gone to Laas to be with her for the lying in. When Your Majesty's children are of an age to present you with your own grandchildren, I know you will understand."

"Indeed, indeed," Donal said, chuckling. "When you return home, then, I trust that you will give your goodwife a full accounting of today's honors. And send me word when the child is born." He glanced aside at Sir Jiri Redfearn, standing duty behind the throne. "Jiri, remind me to send an appropriate christening gift."

"Yes, Sire."

As Sir Alun rose, his spurring duties fulfilled, Donal's gaze flicked back to the still-kneeling Arthen.

"So, young Master Talbot. Are you certain you would not prefer to receive the accolade from your father?"

"With all due respect, Sire," Lucien said, before the candidate could answer, "we could have stayed in Ratharkin if my hand were sufficient."

"Arthen?" the king insisted. "Your father is a very honored and puissant knight, else he would not be my governor in Meara."

"Aye, Sire, but you are my king," young Talbot replied. "I have always dreamed of receiving the accolade from your own hand. And I would lief swear you my fealty in person—for the bond between vassal and liege is as hallowed as that of blood."

"Well, I cannot dispute that," the king replied, smiling as he shifted the hilt of the great Haldane sword of state into his right hand and lifted the blade before him. "Arthen Talbot, son of Lucien." The blade flashed downward to lightly touch flat on the young man's right shoulder.

"In the name of the Father, and of the Son," the blade shifted to the left shoulder, "and of the Holy Spirit," the blade lifted to rest on the crown of the young man's bowed head, "be thou a good and faithful knight." Donal lifted the blade to kiss the holy relic enclosed in the pommel, then reversed it to rest the tip on the floor and offered his right hand to the new knight. "Arise, Sir Arthen, and be invested with the other symbols of your new rank."

Only just controlling a grin, Sir Arthen got to his feet, bowing as the queen came to gird him with the white belt of his knighthood, faintly blushing as she buckled it at his waist. Donal handed off the Haldane sword to Kenneth to hold. When the queen was done, Arthen's father presented him with a sword, which he slipped into the hangers at his waist before kneeling again to set his joined hands between those of the king.

"I, Arthen Talbot, Knight, do become your liege man of life and limb and earthly worship; and faith and truth will I bear unto you, to live and to die, against all manner of folk, so help me God."

The king then returned the oath, pledging justice and

protection for the new knight's loyalty, after which the other Mearan knights in the hall gave a whoop of affirmation and surged forward to congratulate their new brother. The brief commotion served to bring young Alaric's attention back to the head of the hall, for he had begun to grow restive at his mother's side as the ceremonies stretched on.

"Pay attention now, darling," she whispered in his ear, as the space before the thrones again cleared and the chamberlain rapped with his staff for attention.

Jovett was lining up the Lendour candidates and bidding their two sponsors to fall into place behind them, each bearing a sheathed sword with spurs looped over the quillons. The newly squired Jamyl Arilan had been drafted to carry the Lendour banner when their turn should come around, and came smartly to attention as the chamberlain cleared his throat.

"Let the candidates from Lendour approach."

At Jovett's nod, Jamyl started forward with the Lendour banner, Jovett following with the two candidates, their sponsors, and several more Lendour retainers. Young Alaric stood on his tiptoes to see them better, only restrained from following by his mother's hands on his shoulders.

"Your Majesty," Jovett said, making a graceful obeisance as his charges did the same and Jamyl dipped the banner, "on behalf of the regency council of Lendour, I beg leave to present two candidates for knighthood: the squires Yves de Tremelan and Xander of Torrylin."

"And I am well pleased to receive them," the king responded, settling back slightly on his throne. "I have heard excellent reports regarding the accomplishments of both Lendour's candidates. However, a striking irregularity makes me loath to confer that honor."

Chapter 4

"He made him lord of his house, and ruler of all his substance."

—PSALM 105:21

FOLLOWING on an instant of shocked silence, a murmur of question and consternation rippled through the hall. Jovett stood stunned, as did Xander; young Yves bore an expression of blank bewilderment, as did both sponsors. Alaric caught the tumult of the various reactions and looked up at his mother for reassurance. Alyce felt the sharp glance of question from her heart-sister, but only slipped her free hand around Zoë's shoulders and slightly shook her head, sending a close-focused thought into her mind, as Deryni sometimes could do with humans.

Don't worry.

Don't worry? Zoë returned, carefully shaping the words in her mind. *Do you know what this is about? Is this why the king summoned you before court?*

Somewhat, Alyce replied. *Just wait and see.*

"Sire, I don't understand," Jovett said uncertainly, as he exchanged glances with his two candidates and their sponsors.

"Allow me to rephrase," the king said. "And please reassure your candidates. This has nothing to do with their suitability for knighthood." He swept his gaze across the waiting courtiers and their ladies, then nodded toward Kenneth. "Sir Kenneth, my sword, if you please—and Lady Alyce, please attend, and bring the boy."

Bracing herself, head held high, Alyce kept her son's hand in hers and led him before the throne, pausing before the first step of the dais to make her reverence. Young Alaric followed his mother's example with a grave, courtly bow that brought a smile to the king's lips. At their approach, Jovett had moved his knighting party to one side, where all of them watched anxiously.

"I see that your young son flourishes, Sir Kenneth," Donal said, settling the Haldane sword in the crook of his arm, its hilt in his left hand. "You have performed your duty well, in providing an heir for Corwyn and Lendour—though methinks it can have been no onerous duty, with so fair a lady at your side." At his nod toward Alyce, a faint snigger rippled through the watching court, but she only inclined her head gracefully at the compliment.

"I am also much pleased with the counsel that you have given with regard to the regency of your wife's lands," the king went on, "which, someday, will be your son's lands. Given his tender age, however, it seems to me that those lands deserve a more tangible symbol of lordship, and sooner rather than later. In addition, as I much desire to continue employing your talents on my own behalf, as I advance in years and my own heir approaches his majority, it seems to me fitting that you possess a more appropriate rank by which you may speak in my name and his, in matters diplomatic."

"Sire, I am yours to command," Kenneth murmured with a taut bow.

"Then I trust you will not object when I tell you that I have this day determined to create you Earl of Lendour for life, by right of your wife." A collective gasp whispered through the hall, but the king only flicked a steely glance out over the assembled court to silence it, and went on.

"Will you, then, accept this honor from my hand, and be my man for Lendour, and continue serving as principal regent of Corwyn?" He smiled and shrugged. "It means that someday, your son will be your feudal superior, when he takes up his ducal coronet—but by then, perhaps you will be ready to retire to some quiet spot with your lovely wife, to enjoy the delights of grandchildren. It is a pleasure I have not yet tasted for myself, but I am assured by my governor in Meara and others who have them that the experience is altogether agreeable."

His droll smile and wink at Sir Lucien and several of his senior council lords who did have grandchildren was answered by gentle chuckles of honest amusement from most in the hall, and defused what might have been an awkward moment regarding Kenneth's good fortune.

"But, enough of this," Donal said, rising. "Kenneth, I'll thank you to kneel." As Kenneth hastily did so, the king shifted the Haldane sword into his right hand and briskly touched it to Kenneth's right shoulder, left shoulder. "I create you Earl of Lendour for life, with all the rights, privileges, and responsibilities that entails. Will you now do homage for your lands?"

"I will, Sire, most gladly," Kenneth replied, lifting his joined hands in an attitude of prayer.

Smiling faintly, the king handed the sword off to Prince Brion and took Kenneth's hands between his own, nodding for him to speak.

"I, Kenneth Kai Morgan, do enter your homage and become your liege man for Lendour, reaffirming the vows I made when your father knighted me. Faith and truth will I bear to you, and to your sons, and to your house, in all things, so help me God."

"And I receive your homage most gladly, Kenneth Morgan Earl of Lendour, and pledge you my loyalty and protection for so long as you keep faith with me."

So saying, the king released Kenneth's hands and dipped into a pocket within his sleeve, producing a gold signet, which he slid onto Kenneth's left forefinger.

"Wear this ring as a seal of fidelity to the oaths you have sworn, and a symbol of your authority," the king said, also receiving from the queen a hammered silver circlet the width of two fingers, set with flat cabochon garnets all around. "And receive this coronet as a mark of my esteem and trust."

He set the coronet on Kenneth's brow, then kissed him on both cheeks and nodded for him to rise.

"That's done, then. You may stand, Earl of Lendour. And for your first official act, if it is your pleasure and that of these young men, I give you leave to bestow the accolade on these, your knights of Lendour."

Kenneth rose uncertainly at the king's gesture, looking both pleased and somewhat taken aback by this further demonstration of royal favor.

"Sire, it is an honor I am right willing to confer in your name, but surely they would prefer to receive it from the hand of their king."

"I should think that, given a choice, they would prefer to receive it from the hand of a loyal and noble knight who has many times saved the life of that king," Donal countered, with a measuring glance at the two kneeling candidates. "And this is fitting, since it is you they should emulate, rather than a warrior no longer in his prime. Sir Jovett, is this acceptable to Lendour's candidates?"

Jovett glanced at the Lendour sponsors, who clearly approved, then made a graceful bow, taking his cue from Alyce's unperturbed expression and the lightning thought she sent his way.

"Sire, it has long been the honor of Lendour's knights to receive the accolade from Lendour's earl, when that has been possible. When young Alaric attains his majority and is himself a knight, such will be his happy duty. But until that day arrives, I can think of few finer exemplars for our young knights than the noble father of their future earl."

"Then, let it be done," the king replied, extending the hilt of the Haldane sword across his forearm to Kenneth. "You may use this."

Kenneth knelt briefly to receive it, reverently touching his lips to the holy relic enclosed in the hilt, then moved beside the throne and turned to face the candidates and assembled court, indicating that Alyce and Alaric should stand to his other side. He occasionally had knighted men in the field before, but the hilt of the Haldane sword in his fist made concrete just how different this was, and would be henceforth. As the first candidate, Yves de Tremelan, came to kneel before him, his older brother following with sword and spurs, Kenneth leaned down to whisper to his son in a sudden flash of inspiration.

"Son, would you like to help Sir Jovett with the spurs?"

The boy grinned delightedly, scurrying to Jovett's side to receive one of the spurs. He watched with grave attentiveness as Jovett affixed the first spur, then knelt to do the same with the second. The straps and buckles were a little stiff, the spurs being new and never worn, but the boy very nearly managed on his own, so that Jovett only had to help him with the final adjustment.

Their whispered consultation brought a smile to the candidate's lips, but he did not speak or turn to look. When the two had finished, the pair of them stood to either side of the candidate and Alaric shyly slipped his hand into Yves's large one as he gazed up expectantly at his father, obviously aware of the solemnity of what was about to occur. Alyce, watching from Kenneth's side, could only barely contain her smile and her pride. Tears were glistening in the candidate's eyes.

"Yves de Tremelan," Kenneth declared, lowering the Haldane blade to touch the young man's right shoulder, "in the name of the Father, and of the Son," the blade arched to the left shoulder, "and of the Holy Spirit," the flat of the blade rested briefly on the bowed head, "be thou a good knight and true." He brought the blade to his lips in salute. "Arise, Sir Yves."

He offered the new knight his hand and raised him up.

"And now, since I am Earl of Lendour by the grace of my lady wife as well as the king's favor, perhaps it would be fitting that you be invested with the further symbols of your rank by the Lady of Lendour—if Her Majesty will allow," he added, with a glance at the queen.

"Most certainly," Richeldis replied, extending the strip of white leather to Alyce, who nodded thanks and moved closer to Yves. Young Alaric stayed beside Jovett, now under Jovett's hands, watching as his mother girded the new-made knight with the white belt.

"Sir Yves, I gird you with this symbol of your unstained honor," Alyce murmured, as she leaned close to pass the belt around his waist. "And I am very happy that you should have received this honor from my own dear husband's hand."

"So am I, my lady," he whispered, hastily knuckling at a tear as she fastened the buckle.

When she had finished, he bowed over her hand and kissed it, then waited as his elder brother brought forth the goodly sword to be presented, laying it into Alyce's hands with a bow. At the king's nod, she gave it into the keeping of Sir Yves, who slipped it into its hangers and then sank to his knees uncertainly between Kenneth and the king, glancing at both of them as he lifted joined hands.

"Sire," he said steadily, "I am now prepared to offer my fealty."

"He is *your* knight, Lord Kenneth," the king said quietly. "It is you who should receive his oath."

"It would be my honor and privilege, Sire," Kenneth murmured. "But is this acceptable to you, Sir Yves? I know that you were expecting to give your oath to the king."

"You are Earl of Lendour, my lord, and I am your knight," Yves said steadily. "I am pleased to give it to *you*."

With an inclination of his head, Kenneth reversed the Haldane sword under the quillons and returned it into the king's keeping, then took Sir Yves's joined hands between his own. The young man met his gaze steadily, his chin lifting as he spoke the ritual words.

"I, Yves de Tremelan, do become your liege man of life and limb and earthly worship. Faith and truth will I bear unto you, to live and to die, against all manner of folk, so help me God."

"And I, for my part, will be a faithful liege to you, Sir Yves de Tremelan," Kenneth answered, "giving justice and protection so long as you keep faith with me. So help me God."

Murmurs of approval surrounded the pair as Kenneth raised up the new knight, accompanied by young Alaric's joyful jumping up and down, quickly curbed by a look from his father. The boy stood with his mother as the knighting process was repeated with Xander in its focus, Alaric again helping with the spurs. He followed happily with his mother when all the Lendour contingent, save Kenneth, retired to the rear of the hall for the next candidates to approach.

"Did I do it right, Mummy?" the boy whispered, when they had gained the relative privacy of the rear door.

"You did it very well, indeed, darling," Alyce replied, with an affectionate ruffling of the silver-blond hair. "I was very, very proud of you."

Chapter 5

"There be spirits that are created for vengeance."

—ECCLESIASTICUS 39:28

SIR Kenneth Morgan's ennobling as Earl of Lendour became the topic of many a conversation in the hours following that year's Twelfth Night Court. Not all of the discussion was favorable.

"My lord, are you ill?" Father Rodder asked in a low voice.

Jarred from his introspection, Bishop Oliver de Nore shook his head. Though normally a witty and articulate table companion, he had been brooding over his trencher through the first several courses, and had already earned puzzled glances from his superiors, the Archbishops Desmond and William, seated a few places up the table on the other side.

"Nay, I am well enough," de Nore allowed. "I was reflecting how well the Deryni witch continues to prosper. Her husband is now Earl of Lendour, and her half-breed son flourishes. It is clear that the king dotes on this cursèd family."

"Sir Kenneth has long been the king's good friend," Father Rodder observed, "and has many times saved the king's life. Surely it is fitting that he should be rewarded for his loyalty and service."

"The service of getting a Deryni brat on that Deryni witch?" de Nore said bitterly. "She denounced my brother, Rodder! Her accusations betrayed him to his death!"

Father Rodder contained a sigh, for he was tiring of this reiteration of old grievances. But since de Nore was his superior, he tempered his reply to diplomatic neutrality.

"I cannot dispute the facts," he agreed quietly. "She did, indeed, have a part in discovering the involvement of Father Septimus in the . . . unfortunate incident. But she is a great heiress, even if she *is* Deryni, with vastly important lands. Surely it is prudent to give those lands into the keeping of a loyal human lord."

"Aye, if it does not corrupt him, to consort with such a sorceress," de Nore conceded, albeit grudgingly. But his eyes narrowed every time his gaze glided in the direction of the pair, noting the eager adulation of the small entourage come from Lendour and Corwyn for the Twelfth Night Court.

ELSEWHERE, somewhat later that night, others more kindly disposed toward Deryni were also assessing the day's events. Lord Seisyll Arilan, senior of King Donal's ministers of state and also senior in an organization embodying everything Bishop Oliver de Nore had come to hate, was contemplating the day's developments as he made his way to the apartment he maintained within the castle precincts—one of the more useful perquisites of his office as a crown counselor. He had left the door locked, but he knew the measure had been little deterrent to the man he sensed waiting behind it.

"I thought I might find you here," Seisyll said in a low voice, when he had closed the door behind him, for he knew the identity of his visitor without having to look.

With a faint smile and the lift of a hand in acknowledgment, Michon de Courcy moved into the light from the fire blazing on the hearth. His collar-length hair was gone grey, the neatly trimmed beard and mustache the same, softening a narrow, aristocratic nose. The cut of his teal-blue robes had been in fashion a decade before. Though quite unalarming in appearance, he was reckoned as one of the most accomplished Deryni of his generation, though he was careful never to reveal this to any of his human associates.

"Sometimes it occurs to me to wonder whether you actually detect me or if we have simply known one another too long," he said easily.

Seisyll allowed himself a low chuckle. "Perhaps a bit of both," he conceded. "I assume you have formed an opinion about the events at today's court."

"If you are referring to Sir Kenneth Morgan's good fortune, I have some thoughts on the matter," he allowed, smiling faintly. "I daresay the Council will also have a few things to say."

"Then, we'd better tell them, so they can say it," Seisyll said archly. "Shall we?" He gestured toward the door to the corridor. "I think most everyone has retired or left by now. I asked Jamyl to make the necessary preparations."

"Damned convenient, having him in the castle now," Michon commented, as he opened the outer door a crack to glance both ways along the corridor, then opened it far enough to slip outside. Seisyll joined him, also scanning with his Deryni senses, then carefully closed the door behind them and locked it. As they headed back the way Seisyll had come, Michon took his arm: two elderly courtiers, apparently the worse for drink, should they encounter anyone.

But they did not. Traversing a succession of shadowed corridors and torch-lit stairways, they finally entered the passageway that led to King Donal's library, though Seisyll led them past that door and on to the next.

A moment they paused there, Michon scanning beyond them while Seisyll probed beyond the door. Then, with a softly indrawn breath, Seisyll set his hand on the latch and gently pushed—at which the door swung soundlessly inward. Faintly smiling, he eased the door wide enough to enter and slipped inside.

The room was dark save for the gentle glow of the fire, with the sound of heavy snoring rumbling in the curtained recesses of a canopied bed. As he cast his senses in that direction, a youthful figure in Haldane squire's livery stepped from the shadows nearer the head of the bed, faint violet briefly flaring around the head of young Jamyl Arilan, who held a forefinger to his lips to caution silence.

Pleased and relieved, Seisyll sent acknowledgment and approval in the direction of his nephew, then leaned back out the door long enough to beckon for Michon, who immediately entered and latched the door behind him. As he did so, Jamyl came to join them.

I'm afraid I denied Lord Harkness the pleasures of his wife's embrace, the younger man sent, *but they'll sleep until morning, and have dreams to compensate. Amazing, the places a squire can go without raising any eyebrows.*

Just so long as they don't stir until we've returned and gotten out of here, Seisyll replied, with a nod toward the bed. *Michon,* he sent to his companion, at the same time extending a beckoning hand.

Together they moved into the center of the room, where a Kheldish carpet concealed the sight but not their awareness of a magical matrix laid out there more than a century before. With the ease of long-accustomed practice, Seisyll moved behind Michon and set his hands on the other man's shoulders, extending his senses even as Michon drew back his shields and accepted control.

A moment Seisyll spared to stabilize the balance between them, then closed his eyes and focused on the pattern of the Transfer Portal beneath their feet, unique to this location, and shifted the energies. The momentary quaver of vertigo was his only sign that anything had changed—except that, when he opened his eyes, they were standing in a niche outside the secret meeting chamber of the Camberian Council, that powerful and clandestine body instituted by St. Camber himself to monitor the magical activities of Deryni and safeguard against abuses of their power.

"I am impressed with young Jamyl's progress," Michon said approvingly, as he deftly reengaged control and shields and glanced over his shoulder at Seisyll, at the same time moving off the Portal. "He seems to have inherited the Arilan talents in full measure. My congratulations."

"Coming from you, I count that as high praise," Seisyll replied, as the two of them headed toward the pair of great bronze doors. "But you must take credit for at least a part of his training. It's a pity that my brother shows so little interest in the subtleties of politics."

"Aye, but at least his sons take after their uncle," Michon noted. "And moving Jamyl to court was a master stroke."

"I am certain he will prove equal to the challenge. Prince Brion is quite taken with him."

"We shall hope that the liking continues once Brion is king," Michon said dryly.

Beyond the great bronze doors, four more individuals were seated around a massive octagonal table crafted of ivory. The amethyst dome that crowned the chamber and arched above their heads looked black at this hour, and seemed to swallow up most of the light from the crystal sphere hanging from the dome's center. Three of the room's four occupants rose as the newcomers entered: Oisín Adair, who bred fine horseflesh when he was not carrying out the Council's directives, and Dominy de Laney, wife and consort of a prince of the Connait, who soon would be stepping down in favor of the fresh-faced younger man coming to his feet at her side. Rhydon Sasillion was still but five-and-twenty, but his potential had marked him out early as a mage of great potential, well worthy of the Council's notice.

Across the table from the three sat Dominy's younger brother, Barrett, blinded as the ransom price for the lives of several dozen Deryni children when but a new-made knight of eighteen, hardly more than a child himself. It was Michon who had taught him how to see again, utilizing his formidable powers in a manner achieved by few of their race. Of late, he had taken up a scholar's life, and tonight wore the emerald robes of a scholar of Nur Sayyid, the great R'Kassan university.

"Greetings to you, Barrett," Michon said, clasping a hand to the blind man's shoulder as he passed to take his own seat. Seisyll made his way to the chair beside Oisín, nearly opposite.

"Khoren will be along shortly," Oisín said, taking his seat again when the two older men had settled. He was wearing fur-lined robes of a deep oxblood hue rather than the worn riding leathers that were his customary attire. "I delivered a new mare to his brother's stud farm a few days ago. He will plead Twelfth Night obligations like yourselves, but I happen to know that he is also much occupied with a rare manuscript that his wife found for him. Were it not for this meeting, I doubt he would surface for days."

The comment produced an appreciative chuckle from both newcomers, for Prince Khoren Vastouni's appetite for obscure arcane knowledge was well known.

"Not another of Kitron's works?" Seisyll asked.

"No, earlier than that," Oisín replied, "though he may have provided some of the marginalia. This one is attributed to a Caeriessan sage known only as Zefiryn, and I am given to understand that Soffrid annotated it. If all of this is true, it is a major find."

The comment elicited sighs of wistful envy, and Michon leaned back in his chair with a feigned look of vexation. "That sounds very like one I've been tracking. Perhaps he will share." He glanced around the table. "What of Vivienne?"

"She sends her regrets," Dominy answered. "This pregnancy is proving difficult."

"I trust she is in no danger," Seisyll said with some concern.

"No, but she has been more comfortable," Dominy replied. "But this will pass. She did send me a somewhat disturbing report concerning recent developments within the royal house of Torenth."

"Is it Prince Nimur again?" Michon muttered, as he took the document she handed him.

"And his brother Torval," Barrett replied. "More to the point, Vivienne has concerns about their maternal aunt, the very troublesome Princess Camille—or Mother Serafina, as she prefers to call herself, these days. We can only give thanks to God that it was Camille's sister, and not Camille herself, who married Torenth, else it would be Camille wearing the consort's crown. As it is, she availed herself of the training to be had at Saint-Sasile and has left her mark on several generations of Furstán nephews and collateral cousins, and not altogether in keeping with the ethical precepts to which we hold."

Seisyll sat back in his chair and folded his arms across his chest, looking irritated. "I am aware of the background. What is it this time?"

"Well," Dominy said primly, "we have known for some time that the Princes Nimur and Torval are regular visitors to Saint-Sasile, where they have formed a particularly close relationship with their aunt. She has other students, of course, but Nimur is regarded as being particularly gifted—and ambitious."

"Yes, yes, this is nothing new," Michon said impatiently. "What has changed?"

"The focus of Prince Nimur's interest," Barrett replied. "Reliable rumor has it that he intends to take up the research that brought Lewys ap Norfal to no good end."

Michon went very still, briefly averting his eyes.

"There is worse, I fear," Dominy said gently, after a slight pause. "Prince Torval also is heavily involved, of course—the two are all but inseparable—and he has far less good sense than his elder brother."

"And why is that worse?" Seisyll asked impatiently.

"Ah," Barrett said. "That, I can tell you. Prince Torval has formed a close friendship with another of Camille's students: a very accomplished and somewhat arrogant Cardosan called Zachris Pomeroy. He, in turn, is foster brother to another of Camille's nephews: Hogan, the posthumous son of her brother Marcus. All the Furstáns are dangerous, of course, but Marcus was also the senior male representative of the Festillic line when he died, inheritor of all the Festillic pretensions to the crown of Gwynedd—which made his son Hogan the Festillic Pretender from birth."

"Not *that* old lost cause?" Michon said impatiently. "Lord, will they never let it go? It is nigh on two hundred years since the Haldanes took it back from Hogan's very distant ancestor Imre, and for very good cause. And how many wars have been fought in an attempt to reassert the Festillic claim? How many lives lost?"

"Far too many," Dominy said flatly. "And everyone here can recite a litany of the fallen, from his or her own family. But the Festils always were a stubborn lot."

"Aye, and they have long memories," Oisín agreed. "They never forget a slight."

"Of course not. They are Furstáns," Seisyll said.

Scowling, Michon passed the report across to him. "Well, this time I fear that the situation may require some direct intervention." He glanced at the doors, then said, "Perhaps Khoren can shed some light on the question. And here he is at last."

Even as he spoke, the doors opened to admit their missing member: Prince Khoren Vastouni, brother of the Sovereign Prince of Andelon. By his formal robes of state, he appeared to have come directly from his brother's Twelfth Night Court, though his disheveled hair suggested that he might have been puzzling over his prized new manuscript. He had left behind his coronet.

"My heartfelt apologies, brethren," he murmured, sweeping into the seat between Dominy and Barrett. "My eldest niece chose tonight to present us with her chosen husband. It would be an understatement to say that my esteemed brother was somewhat taken aback."

A frown creased Dominy's fair brow. "Not Sofiana? Surely she cannot be old enough to marry!"

Khoren simply sighed and raised an eyebrow. "That was certainly her father's impression. But as incredible as it may sound, she will attain her majority on her next birthday, six months hence. I know," he added, lifting both hands in deference to Dominy's scandalized expression. "Fourteen is young to marry, but Sofiana has always known her mind. She avers that she will have none other than Reyhan of Jaca as her consort—and soon. The choice itself hardly comes as any surprise, of course. She and Reyhan have been inseparable since childhood."

"He is of royal blood himself, as I recall," Seisyll murmured. "Some cousin of the Prince of Jaca?"

"Aye, there was a daughter of my grandfather's line who married a grandson of a Prince of Jaca," Khoren replied. "Royal and Deryni blood on both sides, though through the female lines. Still, a suitable match. And they are fond of one another."

"He was an early pupil of the Duc du Joux, was he not?" Barrett asked. "And I seem to recall hearing that he spent a term or two at Nur Sayyid—though that was before I came. Still, his training should match well with Sofiana's."

"There is no doubt of his competence—or hers," Michon said. "I take it that Mikhail gave his consent to the union?"

"Aye, but they must wait for the formal betrothal until July, when she comes of age," Khoren replied. "The marriage will take place at next year's Twelfth Night Court. She seemed happy enough with the arrangement, as did Reyhan."

"I hope, then, that you will be certain she continues her studies during this last year before her marriage," Michon said. "When I had her under my tutelage, she was one of my most promising pupils. I should hate to think that she might fail to reach her full potential because of the distractions of marriage. After all, it is likely that she shall rule Andelon one day."

"She understands that," Khoren replied. "And I have already spoken with her about the importance of completing her training."

"I am happy to hear it," Seisyll said. "And speaking of pupils, Khoren, we were discussing some of the more worrisome pupils of Camille Furstána. Her nephews, in particular, appear to be heading in dangerous directions. And there is another: a Zachris Pomeroy—"

"Zachris Pomeroy is one of the instigators of this folly," Rhydon broke in, speaking for the first time.

Every head turned in his direction.

"You know him?" Seisyll said.

Rhydon inclined his head. "It would be more accurate to say that we are acquainted; I would not regard him as a friend. He holds lands bordering on my father's estate. And as Master Barrett has said, he is foster brother to Prince Hogan, who *is* my friend."

"Ah," said Michon. "And you do not like him, this Zachris Pomeroy."

"Whether or not I *like* him has no bearing on the matter," Rhydon replied. "What they are playing with is dangerous."

"So it is," Michon agreed. "Just how dangerous, you have no idea."

As he glanced away, obviously troubled, Dominy gently laid a hand over one of Rhydon's.

"Rhydon, are you involved in this?" she asked gently.

He shook his head. "I have done only as the Council bade me. Studying with Camille was a way to make the acquaintance of the Torenthi princes."

"Then perhaps you know them well enough to warn them off this folly," Michon said, "and to warn off their friend Pomeroy as well, even if you do not like him. It can only go ill for *any* of them who take up Lewys ap Norfal's line of research."

Rhydon looked doubtful, resentment in the pale grey eyes. "They are neither of them inclined to listen to the opinions of others, my lord," he murmured.

"Well, they would be advised to *start* listening," Khoren muttered. "I cannot speak for the Torenthi princes, but I can tell you that Pomeroy's activities in the Cardosa area have begun to attract unwelcome notice—and from the Church. I will grant you that Cardosa is one of the few places in Gwynedd where Deryni may be relatively open, but that does not give license to abuse one's powers—and Pomeroy, in particular, has been entirely too open, of late. Flagrant, in fact. It can come to no good."

Seisyll snorted derisively and leaned back in his chair. "Camille needs to rein him in hard. She, of all people, is well aware what can happen."

"Aye, she is," Khoren agreed, glancing at the others. "You did know, I trust, that she was present when Lewys ap Norfal's final experiment went awry?"

"Was she?" Dominy murmured, intrigued, as Oisín also

leaned forward expectantly and Rhydon raised an eyebrow in surprise.

"Aye, she was briefly one of his students—and had hoped to be his wife as well."

"Surely you jest!" Barrett repeated, cocking his head intently. "But she was a princess of Torenth before she took the veil."

"And he was of princely blood as well," Michon said impatiently, "of the line of the Dukes du Joux. She was one-and-twenty, and very ambitious. But she lost heart when Lewys died—or at least I hope he died, because any existence he might have retained would have been far worse than any death."

"Did she not also set her cap for you for a time?" Khoren asked gently. "There were rumors for many years afterward. I remember my parents discussing it, when they thought I was asleep."

Michon quirked a mirthless smile. "She . . . made it clear that such a match would be agreeable—though I knew that her real motives lay in her hunger for the powers I might help her unleash." He glanced aside wistfully. "It was shortly after I married that she took the veil and became Sister Serafina."

"And eventually surpassed most of her teachers," Seisyll reminded them, "and became herself a teacher—sometimes of dangerous students."

"Unfortunately, that is true," Michon agreed. "And while it is, indeed, worrying that the heirs of Torenth may be putting themselves at risk, it is perhaps of more concern that this Zachris Pomeroy may be putting ideas into Prince Hogan's head. If Hogan should decide to assert his claim to Gwynedd, slender though that might be, it could be disastrous right now, with Donal no longer fit enough to lead an army and Prince Brion still too young. Best if we can delay *that* folly for at least a decade."

"There *is* Duke Richard," Oisín reminded him.

"Aye," said Seisyll, "he could lead an army. But whether or not he could assume the Haldane powers, I have no idea. Presumably, Donal has made or is making provisions for

Prince Brion to do so, in due course, but the prince is young yet. Best if Prince Hogan can be discouraged indefinitely from exercising his very dubious claim to Gwynedd's crown, and spare Prince Brion the need to meet a magical challenge."

"Then it appears," said Barrett, "that we must take steps to do exactly that. Khoren, might it be feasible for you to approach Camille about our concerns?"

"If you deem it necessary," came Khoren's terse reply. "Geographically, the task logically falls to me. I must warn you, however, that she will see it as meddling. She is not a subject of Gwynedd. Nor are any of her nephews."

"No, but Zachris Pomeroy is," Rhydon muttered.

"True enough," Barrett agreed. "But I doubt Pomeroy knows anything of this Council—unless Camille has told him, of course. But I expect she may consider herself outside our jurisdiction."

"Our jurisdiction is not bound by geography or her pride," Michon said darkly. "Teachers have a moral responsibility to their students. They sometimes forget, in Torenth, that immoderate use of our powers can have serious repercussions. Deryni in Torenth never faced the backlash we endured after the Haldane restoration."

"What are you proposing, then?" Dominy asked Michon, also glancing at the others.

"I would suggest that we authorize Khoren to approach her unofficially, saying that Pomeroy's lack of moderation has come to his attention, and it concerns him—and that it is her responsibility, as Pomeroy's teacher, to rein him in."

"And the matter of her nephews?" Oisín asked.

"He should mention that, too," Michon replied, turning his gaze on Khoren. "You need not elaborate on how you have learned of any of this. Let her worry about that."

"And if she refuses?" Khoren said.

Michon merely folded his hands before him on the ivory table and sat back slightly in his chair, smiling faintly.

"You have a plan," Seisyll said.

Michon inclined his head. "I think we need not go into details just now."

Dominy rolled her eyes. "You do love to be mysterious, don't you, Michon? But God willing, we'll not need your plan. Khoren, are you willing to carry out Michon's recommendations?"

"For all the good it is likely to do," Khoren said darkly, "but I suppose it's worth a try. Meanwhile," he turned his attention to Michon and Seisyll, "I hope you bring us happier news from the court of Gwynedd. Please tell me there were no serious surprises."

Seisyll smiled like a cat with a bowl of cream. "Nothing seriously worrisome. Sir Kenneth Morgan is now Earl of Lendour for life, *de jure uxoris*."

"Is he," Dominy said—a statement, not a question.

"That is a *very* interesting development," said Oisín.

"The appointment *is* a logical extension of Kenneth Morgan's past loyalty to the crown," Seisyll allowed. "And it was actually a very shrewd move on Donal's part, since it puts Kenneth in a stronger position to safeguard Alyce and their son."

Dominy snorted. "You know I have my doubts about the value of a half-breed Deryni," she muttered.

"Well, at least we know he isn't Donal's son," Barrett said reasonably. "And as for being half-breed, he is only two years old. Let's give him time to grow, and see how he develops. At very least, he has loyal parents who will raise him to be loyal—and God knows, Prince Brion will need loyal men around him when he eventually becomes king."

"And Kenneth Morgan is as loyal as they come," Khoren pointed out. "As Earl of Lendour, he will be a strong bulwark to hold that part of Gwynedd against Torenthi incursions."

"So we shall hope," said Seisyll. "For now, however, I think I prefer to keep our focus on the students of Sister Camille Furstána, who are *not* loyal to the crown of Gwynedd, and who may well attempt to overthrow it."

Chapter 6

"Moreover, it is required in stewards,

that a man be found faithful."

—I CORINTHIANS 4:2

As the festivities of Yuletide wound down over the next week or so, winter promised to settle in with a vengeance. The new Earl of Lendour kept Sir Jovett, his two new knights, and the knights' sponsors in Rhemuth for a few days, while he drafted instructions to the regents of which he was now head, then sent them back to Cynfyn to await his arrival in the spring.

Alyce and their son and Zoë settled back into the usual domestic routine for Rhemuth Castle in winter, though the heavy weather curtailed much outdoor activity, and the short daylight hours hampered many indoor pursuits. At least Zoë was there to share the tedium—and Alazais, for a few weeks, though she returned to Morganhall as soon as the weather permitted.

February was grim, and early March little better. The several months after Twelfth Night were always lean, as folk hunkered down to await the spring. Except for a few hours around noontime, close work like reading, writing, and needlework must be done by precious candlelight or rush-light. The children of the court, including young Alaric, chafed at being kept indoors in the inclement weather, and the older ones brooded over their books and ciphering. In the evenings, huddled before fires in the great hall, music and dancing became staples of evening entertainment for the adults and young people, for these were pastimes that could be enjoyed by firelight and torchlight. Many a child was conceived during those long, cold nights when Rhemuth lay wrapped in winter's thrall, though Alyce and Kenneth were not so blessed.

As the winter wore on, the long nights, the forced inactivity, and the monotony of meals eked out from dwindling supplies were beginning to pall on everyone. The fighting men kept up their edge by arms practice in the castle yard or, when the weather turned really foul, by moving their exercise into the great hall. By mid-March, the most hardened warriors were beginning to think even war preferable to the inactivity of the winter.

But spring came at last, along with the celebrations of Easter. Shortly thereafter, as soon as travel conditions would allow it, a delegation from Lendour arrived in Rhemuth to escort their new earl and his family back to Cynfyn, Lendour's capital, where Kenneth Morgan would enter into possession of his lands and present his son and heir to their people. His daughter Zoë traveled with them, as female companion for Alyce and governess for young Alaric, along with two maids and several grooms.

The king had also given Kenneth the service of the newly knighted Sir Trevor Udaut as his aide, for Trevor's father was one of Corwyn's regents. And the two knighted by Kenneth at Twelfth Night had returned with the escort party: Sir Yves de Tremelan and Sir Xander of Torrylin. But by far the most congenial of the fighting men added to the new earl's party was the leader of the Lendour delegation, Sir Jovett Chandos, who managed to spend most of the journey at Zoë's side, and who, on the morning they were to arrive in Cynfyn, finally summoned the courage to approach Kenneth on a very delicate matter.

"My lord, might we ride apart a little?" he murmured,

drawing alongside Kenneth, who was riding with his wife. "There is a matter I would discuss with you in private."

"By all means, go," Alyce said before Kenneth could reply. "I shall ride on ahead with Zoë and the other ladies." *And be gentle with him, darling Kenneth,* she added, only in his mind. *I believe he means to ask for Zoë's hand.*

"We'll catch you up," Kenneth agreed, reining back and indicating that Jovett should fall in beside him. They waited for the rest to pass them by, then followed at the rear of the cavalcade, several horse-lengths behind the last baggage animals.

"So, what's on your mind, Jovett?" Kenneth asked amiably.

The young knight looked distinctly nervous, though his voice was steady as he spoke.

"My lord, I hope that I am in your esteem, and that you have found no fault with my service to Lendour. It has been my honor to serve your lady wife, and I am honored to be now in your service as well."

"And I, to have you in my service," Kenneth replied, restraining a smile as he watched him sidelong.

"Thank you, my lord. I—ah . . ."

"Are you looking for a way to ask me for my daughter's hand?" Kenneth asked gently. "You needn't look so surprised, son—or so apprehensive. Alyce told me you might be asking—and my daughter has made it quite clear to me that she holds you in great affection."

Jovett gaped briefly at this revelation, scarlet briefly washing his cheeks with high color.

"I—am right pleased to hear it, sir," he began. "I had intended to ask for her when we came for Twelfth Night. But when you were named earl . . ."

"Does that change your feelings for her?" Kenneth asked.

"No, sir, not at all!" Jovett blurted, faintly rattled. "But I am only a knight's son, and now she . . ."

"Now, she is the daughter of an earl—an earl who would still be a simple knight, were it not for his wife's rank," Kenneth reminded the younger man. "I know where

I come from, Jovett. I am of no more lofty a family than you are. Do you love her?"

"With all my heart, my lord!" Jovett whispered. "And I promise you that I would do my utmost to make for her a worthy and loving husband."

"Then it's settled," Kenneth replied. "What more could a father ask, than that his children should be happy? Besides that," he added, "such a marriage would bring practical advantages that probably will not have occurred to you." He went on at Jovett's look of question. "I am now Earl of Lendour, Jovett, but I am also in the king's direct service. That means that I needs will be spending much of my time at court with him and Prince Brion. Accordingly, I will need men in Lendour whom I can trust. Who better than the husband of my own beloved daughter?"

Jovett looked dumbfounded for a moment, then shyly averted his gaze. "My lord, I am honored by your confidence in me," he replied, "but I am also young. Surely there are others better qualif—"

"More experienced, perhaps, but few with more promise," Kenneth said firmly. "And inexperience can be remedied. I know you, Jovett. And I know that your father has been serving as one of Lendour's regents for many years—perhaps most of his career. I should like you to serve alongside him, as his deputy and eventual successor. And in my absence, it will be entirely fitting that my son-in-law should begin to speak in my behalf. A strong bond of loyalty already exists between our two families. Joining them by marriage can only strengthen that bond."

"Then—we have your consent, sir?" Jovett managed to murmur.

"Of course you do, with all my blessings!" Kenneth replied. "Now, go to my daughter and tell her your news—though this will set her and my wife all atwitter for the rest of the journey, and then for weeks thereafter. Go, go! 'Tis a woman's prerogative."

With a whoop of sheer delight, Jovett set heels to his mount and galloped up to the head of the column, where Zoë was riding with Alyce and the two maids. Kenneth himself followed at a more sedate pace, finally falling in beside a young knight with little Alaric up on the saddle before him.

"Papa!" said the boy, reaching out one arm toward his sire.

"Hello, son. Trevor, I'll take him with me now," he said to the younger man, reaching across to swing Alaric onto his own mount.

Delighted, the boy settled happily against his father's chest and sat a little prouder. He had even managed to stay clean since setting out that morning. As Kenneth slowly worked them toward the head of the column, the two chatted happily.

The party approached Cynfyn just before dusk, with a glorious scarlet sunset in their wake. Perhaps half an hour before, they had stopped briefly for Alyce to wash her face and hands and tidy her hair before she and Kenneth donned coronets for their entry into the town. Jovett had moved to the head of the column with Sir Xander and Sir Yves, unfurling the Lendour banner before them.

Jovett's father, Sir Pedur Chandos, met them just outside the town gates, along with the seneschal, Sir Deinol Hartmann, half a dozen other mounted knights, and a contingent of the town elders afoot.

"Welcome back to Castle Cynfyn, Lady Alyce," Sir Deinol said, bowing in his saddle. "And welcome to the new Lord of Lendour and his heir." With a nod, he sent forth a page standing at his stirrup, who bore a large ring of keys upon a scarlet cushion. "Sir Kenneth, it is my honor to offer you the keys to His Majesty's castle of Cynfyn."

The page cast a curious look at young Alaric as he came forward and bowed, offering up his charge, and Alaric gazed down with similar interest. But as Kenneth laid a gloved hand on the keys in acceptance, Alaric reached out as one with his sire and firmly grasped the ring, lifting it slightly and looking up at his father in question.

"Thank you, Alaric. And thank you, my lord seneschal," Kenneth replied with a smile, nodding for Alaric to put the keys back. "And my son and I are most pleased to return the keys of Cynfyn into your good keeping. I am even more pleased to present to you your future lord, Alaric Anthony Morgan," he went on, as Alaric dutifully replaced the keys.

The waiting knights saluted with bowed heads and fists to hearts, eyeing both father and son with obvious approval, before Sir Deinol wheeled around to fall in beside Kenneth.

"Cynfyn is ready to receive you, my lord—and my lady. Long have we awaited the return of Lendour's heir."

Their reception into Cynfyn town and then through the gate to the lower ward was enthusiastic, with cheering townsfolk lining the street and casting flowers before them as they rode. Several of the women thrust bunches of posies into Alyce's hands as she and Kenneth passed, and others looped flower garlands around the necks of their horses. One small boy darted out to offer Alaric a crudely carved figure of a horse, which gift elicited a delighted grin and an unprompted thank you.

That night, at the banquet prepared for their welcome, Kenneth and Alyce made more formal presentation of their son to the assembled nobles, then received the renewed fealty of all the Lendour knights who had not sworn before. A little later, Kenneth announced the betrothal of his daughter Zoë to Sir Jovett Chandos, to a roar of approval that fairly shook the rafters of the hall.

"My wife and I thank you for this evidence of your welcome of this match," Kenneth said, when the cheering had died down. "As the father of three daughters, only one of whom is wed, I must confess my delight that a second—and the eldest!—is now to be wed as well. I shall miss her, of course—as shall my wife, for the two are dearest friends as well as being related in . . . complicated ways." He drew both women closer and laid an arm around each one's shoulders, signing for Jovett to join them on Zoë's other side.

"This brings us to a somewhat delicate matter, one that I know will have occurred to at least a few of you. Most of you will be aware that, but for cruel fortune, Zoë would have been your countess, by marriage to my dear wife's late brother Ahern—and in fact, the two exchanged vows as Ahern lay on his deathbed." He paused to draw his daughter closer and gently kiss the top of her head.

"Ahern's untimely death was a tragedy for all of us, but life goes on. I am now your earl; and very happily, my daughter has come to care for your Jovett Chandos, whom she had known for some years as Alyce's childhood friend as well as a young knight of rising prominence here in Lendour—and Jovett, likewise, has given his heart to her. So I count myself fortunate that I shall be acquiring a son known and respected by you all, and who can help to look after Lendour's interests when I must be in Rhemuth with the king.

"Meanwhile, I congratulate Sir Deinol and Sir Pedur and the rest of Lendour's regents here in Cynfyn for training up such a fine cadre of young knights to carry Lendour's interests forward. I am confident that Jovett will continue to be an asset to their numbers—and would, even if he were not to become my son-in-law, for he is a good and honorable man. And when my son is of an age to come into his inheritance—by which time I hope to retire to a quiet life in the country!—I know that he, too, will follow in the footsteps of his illustrious ancestors, and in the traditions that all of you have helped to uphold while you waited for him."

The response of Lendour's nobility, both then and in the days to come, only underlined their approval, both of their new lord and his heir and also of this new alliance with one of Lendour's premier families. Though tradition would have had Zoë marry from her father's manor at Morganhall, among her Morgan kin, it was agreed that the wedding should take place in Cynfyn, among Jovett's people, where Kenneth also was lord, since the pair would make their home there. The date was set for Michaelmas, to be Alaric's third birthday, following the family's visit to Coroth, for Kenneth and Alyce must first present their son to his future Corwyn subjects.

Given this schedule, they lingered hardly a week in

Cynfyn, while Kenneth held the first of his manorial courts and general audiences, met with the regency council to agree upon general strategies for the coming months, and generally acquainted himself with the running of the county, Jovett and Trevor at his side. While they worked, Alyce and Zoë began planning a wedding.

"The castle chapel *is* the logical place to hold it," Alyce said as she closed the chapel door behind them and leaned against it. Beside her, Zoë was carrying a basket of flowers and sweet herbs for the two grave slabs before the altar steps. Alaric had already wandered ahead and was exploring the south wall, where a painted wooden statue of St. Michael gazed down serenely from a wall niche, wings furled around him like a mantle, gauntleted hands at rest on the hilt of a sword worked in gold and silver. The last time the two women had visited Cynfyn, it had been to bury Ahern, and Alaric had not yet been born.

"I had forgotten the stillness and the beauty of this place," Zoë murmured.

"Aye," Alyce replied, "but 'tis a terrible beauty, considering who lies buried here. I would certainly understand if you'd prefer a different venue. Perhaps it isn't the best idea, to begin a new marriage while standing on the grave of one's first husband."

Zoë glanced away briefly, looking wistful, then slipped an arm around Alyce's waist.

"That's long past now," she whispered. "I try not to think about it. I did love him, but he was never really my husband except in name. There wasn't time for more." She brightened and lifted her chin bravely. "I do know that he would have wanted me to be happy."

She picked up a stem of lavender and breathed in its sweet perfume, then shifted her gaze to the grave slabs before the altar. "I try to put it from my mind that he lies in that grave yonder. For me, I shall always remember him as he was on that day he rode off to Meara, eager and excited to finally be doing what he was born to do, when life was simpler for all of us."

"Aye, it was," Alyce murmured. "And if Ahern had

lived, he would now be Duke of Corwyn, with *your* son to succeed him rather than mine—which would be simpler for *me*, I'll grant you—and for Alaric. But then *your* son would be facing what Alaric will face, in times to come."

Zoë glanced at Alaric, who had wandered closer to the end of the chapel, then back at Alyce, a sly smile curving her lips.

"Alyce, if I'm marrying Jovett, my children will *all* be facing what Alaric is facing, won't they? After all, they'll also be half-Deryni."

Chuckling, Alyce only shook her head.

"Be glad that very few people know about Jovett," she replied. "And we must do our utmost to ensure that no one finds out, mustn't we?" She glanced at her son, who now was attempting to climb the altar rail next to the statue of St. Michael. "Alaric, darling, please don't do that!" she called, as she and Zoë started in that direction. "Come and help me and Auntie Zoë with these flowers, would you?"

Stopping in midclimb, the boy obediently swung his leg back down and came to join his mother and sister.

"Mama, can I have a flower for Saint Michael?" he asked.

"Yes, of course you can," she replied, holding the basket down to his level. "What kind do you think he'd like?"

"Maybe a rose," he said, starting to finger through the blooms. "This big red one is—*ow!* It has big, sharp thorns!"

Zoë cocked her head at him and reached for his hand. "Gracious, did you stab yourself?"

Somewhat indignantly, the boy pulled back his hand and sucked briefly at a finger, then reached for the same flower again.

"Alaric, you just saw that that one has thorns," his mother said reasonably. "How about this peony? See what a fluffy head it has?"

"No, want the rose!" the boy said firmly, though his touch was more careful as he picked it up. "Saint Michael likes roses! The thorns are sharp like his sword!"

"I can't argue that," Alyce murmured, as he took off at a run toward the statue of the saint. "Zoë, did we just hear what I think we heard?"

"That he made the connection between the sharpness of swords and of rose thorns?" Zoë answered. "I believe he did. And not yet three."

Alyce only rolled her eyes heavenward as she knelt down beside the graves of her father and brother, taking flowers from the basket. "Dear God, what we both have to look forward to," she murmured, and laid a handful of lavender and rosemary on the grave of Keryell of Lendour. "Here's rosemary for remembrance, Papa," she said. "And roses from your grandson, who already knows about sharp thorns and sharp swords." She sighed as she laid three white roses amid the fragrant herbs. "I wish you could have known him."

As she bowed her head in a brief prayer, Zoë quietly took more flowers from the basket and laid them on Ahern's grave.

"Dear Ahern," she whispered. "Wish me joy, dear heart."

Chapter 7

"Without counsel purposes are disappointed:
but in the multitude of counsellors they are established."

—PROVERBS 15:22

THEY left for Coroth two days later, arriving just before Midsummer. Jovett accompanied them, to continue learning his new duties as Kenneth's official liaison.

A ducal honor guard met them in the long, slanting light of late afternoon as they wound their way down from the foothills above the city, and escorted them into the city through the St. Matthew Gate. From there, growing crowds watched them ride past the cathedral and on up to the castle itself, increasingly enthusiastic as the identity of the party became known.

It had been seven years since Alyce's last visit to Coroth: a time remembered with wistful sadness, since it had been there that she bore her sister's body for burial, laying her to rest among the remains of most of Corwyn's past dukes and ducal wives. Zoë had accompanied her on that journey; Kenneth had been present in the king's party, but with no inkling that he would one day be the father of Corwyn's heir. Now Lendour's banner rode beside that of Corwyn, announcing the arrival both of Lendour's new lord, who was also one of Corwyn's regents, and of Corwyn's young heir. Alaric perched happily on the saddle in front of his father, smiling and waving in response to the crowd.

By the time they rode into the castle yard, most of the regents of Corwyn had gathered on the great hall steps to greet them. Sir James of Tendal, the hereditary chancellor, welcomed them on behalf of his fellow regents and made perfunctory introductions. All of the names were familiar, from years of correspondence with the regents; now faces could be attached to some of those names. The most memorable was Sir Laurenz Udaut, whose resemblance to his son Trevor was unmistakable. It was he who, with his son, conducted the guests to their apartments and offered them refreshment. Since no formal arrangements had been set for the evening of their arrival, the weary newcomers then retired early, to ready themselves for business in the morning.

The next morning was time for Kenneth to make the more formal acquaintance of the regents of Corwyn. A middle-aged courtier identifying himself as Sir Crescence de Naverie conducted Kenneth and his immediate family down to the great hall to break their fast, chatting of inconsequentials to the adults while they ate and watching young Alaric sidelong as the boy tucked into buttered bread smeared with honey, a cold leg of chicken, which he brandished like a club until curbed by a look from his mother, and a cup of small beer. After that, they repaired to the airy tower chamber where the dukes of Corwyn had long carried out the business of the duchy.

Alyce remembered the chamber only vaguely. She had visited Coroth perhaps half a dozen times as a child, and once to bring Marie's body home. Though she had met the Corwyn regents on that occasion, she remembered little of it, for Ahern then had been the heir, and both of them besides had been mourning the death of their sister.

A lighter atmosphere prevailed today as Crescence conducted her and Kenneth to a pair of high-backed chairs set before the round council table. Zoë and Jovett followed with Alaric in tow, shushing him as he tried to swing from their arms. A watchful Trevor Udaut brought up the rear of the little procession.

The council members were already assembled—eight of them—and had risen as Kenneth and Alyce entered. Most of the faces looked vaguely familiar to Alyce, from the brief introductions of the night before, but she could assign names to only a few. At least the bishop was easy to identify by his purple cassock. And Sir Laurenz Udaut nodded and smiled faintly at her look of recognition.

"My lord, my lady . . ." Crescence murmured, inviting the two of them to sit.

Kenneth waited until Alyce had settled into her chair before himself taking his seat to her right, nodding to the council to also be seated. While they did so, Kenneth took Alaric onto his lap, and Zoë, Jovett, and Trevor Udaut grouped themselves behind them.

"My lords," Crescence said again, this time addressing the council as he settled at Kenneth's right, "I present to you Alyce Lady de Corwyn, mother of our future duke, and her husband, Sir Kenneth Morgan, whom the king has created Earl of Lendour for life. Sir Kenneth—or, more properly, *Lord* Kenneth—is now, by these letters patent, premier regent of Corwyn, in right of his son."

Crescence laid a document on the table before them, with the pendant seal of scarlet wax affixed to its bottom, and inclined his head. As it was passed along to the grey-haired man sitting at the opposite side of the table, Crescence said to Kenneth, "My lord, my lady, these are your regents for Corwyn. May I present them to you?"

Kenneth quirked a wry grin that swept the table.

"Thank you, Sir Crescence. And gentlemen, please allow me to point out that I may be the father of your future duke, and one of his regents, but I am only newly become an earl. Until a few weeks ago, I was a simple knight like many of you. Perhaps we would all be more comfortable if you each introduce yourselves, and tell me briefly of your responsibilities. I regret that I cannot yet attach names to all of your faces. We need to remedy that."

A brief murmur of agreement whispered among them, and then the dark-clad man seated to the left of Kenneth and Alyce slightly raised one hand.

"I'll begin, then, my lord. Sir Miles Chopard, secretary to this council."

"Thank you, Sir Miles." Kenneth nodded in acknowledgment, then flicked his gaze expectantly to the man beyond.

"Michael O'Flynn, Earl Derry," the next man said. "Counsel to the duchy. And this is my son Seamus." He indicated a somewhat younger man than Kenneth, seated slightly behind and to his left, with curly brown hair and bright blue eyes.

"My lords," Kenneth replied, inclining his head.

"Síoda Kushannan, Earl of Airnis," said the next man, grey-haired and distinguished looking in the robes of a scholar of Grecotha. "I served Duke Stíofan, your lady wife's grandfather. That was a very long time ago," he added, smiling.

"Then, I shall welcome your experience," Kenneth replied. "And you, my lord?"

The slender, dark-haired man seated beyond Earl Síoda folded his hands with fastidious care, pursing his lips appraisingly.

"Lord Rathold, my lord, counsel to the duchy. And my colleague is the Bishop of Coroth," he added, opening a hand toward the silver-haired cleric at his left elbow.

"Esmé Harris, my lord," the bishop said, inclining his head. "I shall pray that God grants you wisdom in your new estate."

"The bishop speaks for all of us, my lord," said James of Tendal, seated directly across from Kenneth and Alyce. "I am, as you know, the hereditary chancellor. In the absence of a duke, I suppose you might say that I stand in the king's stead in Corwyn. My son Robert serves as my aide, and will eventually succeed me." He nodded toward the younger man at his left elbow, who smiled and inclined his head.

"My lord."

To Sir Robert's left, Trevor's father smiled and shifted in his chair.

"Sir Laurenz Udaut, my lord. Special counsel."

Kenneth nodded and shifted his gaze to the priest seated at Udaut's left. "And you, Father?"

The priest inclined his head. "Tivadan, my lord. Chancellor of the Exchequer."

"A vital function," Kenneth said with a smile. "And you must be . . . ?" he said to the man between Tivadan and Sir Crescence.

"Hamilton, my lord. Seneschal of Coroth Castle. I bid you welcome."

"Well met, Lord Hamilton," Kenneth said. "I look forward to working with all of you."

"And we with you, my lord," said the chancellor. "And we are honored to meet our future duke at last," he added, jutting his chin toward Alaric, who had listened gravely from his seat on his father's lap. "He looks a sturdy lad."

Kenneth smiled faintly. "It is certainly my intention that he should become the man you would wish, eventually to govern Corwyn. I trust that Lord Kushannan will ensure that he learns of his illustrious great-grandsire and other things pertaining to his illustrious ancestry." He glanced at Alyce. "Did you know Duke Stíofan?" he said tentatively.

Alyce smiled and shook her head. "Alas, he died before I was born, my lord. But on many a winter's night my mother told tales of him to me and Ahern and Marie, when we were very small. And Alaric bears his second name, Anthony." She brushed a fond hand against her son's cheek. "Speaking of whom, perhaps Zoë and I should take this young man elsewhere, now that proper introductions have been made, so that you gentlemen can accomplish something useful in what remains of the morning."

As she made to rise, Trevor Udaut pulled back her chair and the other men came to their feet. Kenneth eased Alaric to the floor to put the boy's hand in his mother's.

"Mama!" Alaric whispered, loud enough for all of them to hear. "Do we have to go *now*?"

"I think it's best, darling," she replied, crouching down to his level to look him in the eyes. "Papa and these good gentlemen have work to do. Besides that, I wanted to show you where your Grandmama Stevana played when she was a girl."

The boy's lower lip started to quiver in a pout, but at

Zoë's additional cajoling, he let himself be led from the room.

LATER that evening, as they lay abed, Kenneth acquainted Alyce with the progress of the day's meeting, and pronounced himself well satisfied.

"The king has chosen his Corwyn regents well," he said. "Having met them now, I feel far less daunted than I did before, about having the duchy run from a distance. If you had been allowed to rule in your own right, of course, we'd be here most of the year, which would make things much easier. But given the realities of the situation, I'm quite confident that we can manage."

"Well, there have been regents since my grandfather died, after all," Alyce pointed out, "and that was eight years ago. My father was never Duke of Corwyn; only Earl of Lendour. And sadly, Ahern only ever got to govern Lendour, and then only for a few months." She sighed wistfully. "He would have made a wonderful duke."

"And you would have made a wonderful duchess," Kenneth said, kissing her on the nose. "And you *are* the duchess, in all but name."

She smiled and snuggled closer to his side, taking up the invitation his lips had begun.

BEGINNING the next morning, they settled into what was to become their regular routine for the next few weeks. After breaking their fast in the castle's great hall, where they made a point of chatting with whichever courtiers were present for business later in the morning, Kenneth, his aides, and his future son-in-law adjourned to the council chamber, where they would spend the day hammering out the business of the duchy with its regents. Often Alyce would accompany him, sitting at his side as advisor and sounding board, but on that first day, she and Zoë rode down to the cathedral with Alaric in tow, attended by a maid, Sir Trevor, and Sir Xander of Torrylin, who had accompanied them from Lendour. It was market day, and the cathedral square was crowded with the stalls and goods wagons of local farmers and craftsmen.

"Oh, Alyce, look!" Zoë whispered, as they paused on the cathedral steps while Xander engaged a pair of local men to look after their horses. "Do I see silks on offer over there?" she asked, pointing toward a distant stall where lengths of shimmering silks and damask glistened in the morning sunlight.

"So it would appear," Alyce replied. "I told you that traders from farther east pass regularly through Corwyn's port. After we've been inside, I thought we might try to find some lengths of silk for your wedding gown. Xander," she said a bit louder, "you and Melissa may wait here. Feel free to browse at this edge of the market, if you wish." She did not include Trevor in the order, knowing he would be a discreet shadow for necessary protection.

"Ah, so *that's* why you wanted to come down here so early," Zoë said, as she and Alyce continued up the steps, Alaric between them and Trevor dutifully following. "You'd mentioned eastern silks on the ride from Cynfyn, but I hadn't expected such prompt attention to the mission."

"Well, I can't have you disgracing the family when you walk down the aisle to meet Jovett, can I?" Alyce said brightly. "Whether you're my heart-sister or my daughter, it's my responsibility to make certain you're well turned out. Besides," she added with a sly wink, "you helped me with *my* bridal finery, as I recall."

"True enough," Zoë agreed. "Oh, Alyce." She sighed as they reached the west door and paused to gaze up at the carving above the tympanum, depicting the Last Judgement. "The last time we walked through this door, it was to bury poor Marie. We *have* shared some sad times, haven't we?"

Alyce nodded, remembering the cathedral aisle strewn with the flowers that should have conveyed Marie to her bridal bed, and instead had lined the way to her tomb.

"Aye, both of us," she murmured. The memory of her brother Ahern on that occasion brought unbidden the image of a similar sad journey to bring her brother home to rest at Cynfyn: Ahern, who briefly had also been Zoë's husband.

"But that's all behind us now," Alyce went on brightly, forcing a smile to her lips as they continued into the church. "And we've shared joys as well. God willing, you shall soon be wed to your Jovett. The past is as it is. We must look to the future with hope."

Just inside the doors, they paused to bless themselves with holy water from a stoup carved like a seashell, and Alaric stretched up to gravely dip his fingers in the water and copy what his mother did.

"Mummy," he whispered, tugging urgently at her skirt as they started down the side aisle that led to the crypt entrance. "Does God live here?"

"Yes, He does, darling," Alyce answered distractedly.

"Oh," said Alaric. Then, "God must have lots of houses."

Alyce and Zoë exchanged glances, and Zoë rolled her eyes.

"He's *your* son," Zoë whispered under her breath.

Alyce controlled a smile and hugged Alaric to her side as they continued walking.

"Yes, I suppose He does. God is always with us."

Alaric stopped dead in his tracks and looked up at his mother with wide, apprehensive eyes.

"Is God with us right now?" he whispered.

"Yes . . ."

The boy looked around surreptitiously and took his mother's hand, pressing closer to her leg as he craned at the shadowed side aisles, lit by flickering candlelight.

"Why I don't see anybody?"

"Well, God doesn't have a body like you and me," his mother began.

"No *body*?" Alaric whispered.

"But that doesn't mean He isn't there," Alyce went on. "There are lots of things you can't see, but that doesn't mean they aren't there. Can you see the wind?"

Alaric shook his head.

"But you can see what it does, can't you?"

The boy's brow furrowed as he considered the question.

"I can see things moving," he said tentatively. "I can see the trees . . ."

"Of course you can," she replied. "And would you agree that it's the wind that makes the trees move?"

Slowly he nodded, though he looked dubious. Then: "Mummy, that's silly," he said indignantly. "God isn't made of wind."

So saying, he pulled away from her and ran on ahead to disappear into the open stairwell that led down to the crypt. Following, Alyce and Zoë saw him standing halfway down its length, silver-gilt head thrown back and small fists set stubbornly on his hips as he inspected the stone vaulting above their heads and the sea of tombs beyond. Soon he was wandering among the tombs and craning his neck for a better look at the effigies that crowned some of them. Alyce only exchanged glances with Zoë, rolling her eyes heavenward.

"Well," said Zoë, "you wouldn't have wanted a dull-witted child, would you? And not yet three, either. Good heavens, you don't suppose he'll want to be a priest?"

Alyce chuckled mirthlessly. "My kind can't be priests, remember? Besides, he's going to be a duke."

"Some duke," Zoë replied, smiling, then glanced around, sobering, for they were nearing Marie's tomb, flanked by those of her mother and her grandmother.

"They never put an effigy on it," Alyce murmured, running a hand across the surface of the tomb's alabaster lid, then bending for a closer look at the lettering incised around the base.

"Are you sure this is hers?" Zoë replied, crouching down beside her.

Glancing over her shoulder first, Alyce briefly conjured handfire to light the lettering, confirming that it was, indeed, her sister's tomb, then extinguished the light and rose. At the head of the tomb, a dried floral wreath paid mute tribute to the maid who lay within.

"I wonder who left the flowers," Zoë breathed.

Faintly smiling, Alyce reached out to touch one of the sear blooms.

"It would have been Sé," she said softly.

"How do you know?"

"Father Paschal told me, the last time I saw him. He said that Sé comes every year, around the anniversary of her death, to lay a wreath and spend a night in vigil. He loved her very much. These would be nearly a year old. I wonder if he'll come while we're still here."

"Do you ever hear from him?" Zoë asked.

"Only when there's need," Alyce replied. She rested both hands lightly on the edge of the tomb's alabaster lid. "He seems to show up at important milestones in my life, like my wedding, Alaric's christening." She shook her head gently. "Sometimes I wonder what it would have been like if we had wed—not that I regret any part of my marriage with Kenneth. The king did offer to give him my hand in place of Marie's, after Marie died. But I love him like a brother, Zoë. I never could have married him. Still, we would have been quite a match in power. And now, with his Anviler training . . . The knights at *Incus Domini* are very fortunate to have him."

"Aye, they are," Zoë agreed. Sighing, she reached out to adjust the dried wreath, then bent closer and moved it slightly aside, her breath catching as she ran her fingertips over the simple inscription: *Marie Stephania de Corwyn, 1071–1089.*

"Dear God, it doesn't seem fair, does it?" she asked.

Alyce slipped an arm around Zoë's waist and hugged her briefly. "Life is rarely fair, I'm afraid—though maybe a bit of what we're doing can change that for the future. Besides, sometimes things do happen as they're meant to do. You're happy about marrying Jovett, aren't you?"

"Of course."

"Then, let's see about those silks in the market square, shall we?"

Chapter 8

"There are two ways of teaching and power, one of Light and one of Darkness."

—EPISTLE OF BARNABAS 18:1

THE two women did not find what they sought on that day, but on the next market day, a week hence, they returned to the scene of their earlier searches, this time leaving Alaric in the care of his nurse and a senior squire of whom he was fond. Sir Trevor and a freckled, carrot-topped younger squire named Sylvan accompanied them on this occasion, the latter charged with safeguarding a large empty basket, which they hoped to fill with treasures.

"Zoë, look at this," Alyce said, lifting folds of a fine summer gauze and then measuring off lengths from nose to extended arm. "What do you think? The quality is excellent, and there appears to be enough for a very generous undershift."

Zoë fingered some of the fabric and checked the weave, nodding thoughtfully. "Aye, it could be smocked around the neck with a pale shade to match the over-gown—whatever *that* turns out to be. Or," she added with a grin, "it would make a very fine shirt for Jovett."

"It would, indeed," Alyce agreed. "But will there be time?"

"Beg pardon, my lady," the squire Sylvan said quietly, right at her elbow, "but aren't those royal signals flying from that ship just entering the harbor?"

"What's that?" Alyce said distractedly. As she and Zoë turned to look, Trevor was also gazing in that direction, trying to make out the pennons fluttering from the ship's mast.

"Well spotted, Sylvan," Trevor said, shading his eyes against the summer glare. "It isn't one of the king's own ships, but she's definitely on official business. I wonder what they want."

"Perhaps you'd better find out," Alyce said. "They may simply have dispatches to be delivered—which we can do. Or if they've come to see my husband, they'll need horses to take them up to the castle mount." At Trevor's look of indecision, Alyce sighed and touched his forearm in reassurance. "We'll be *fine* with Master Sylvan to look after us for a few minutes."

"If you're sure . . ." Trevor said doubtfully.

"Trevor, go!" Alyce ordered sternly. "Sylvan is very nearly a knight—and if our arms masters here at Coroth have been doing their job properly, I'm certain he's perfectly capable of guarding two women while they shop for wedding finery."

As Trevor dipped his chin in reluctant agreement and headed off to do her bidding, Alyce gave Sylvan a sidelong look and a wink.

"You *are* capable, aren't you, Sylvan?" she said teasingly.

The squire grinned and blushed and stood a little straighter, bracing his shoulders. "Oh, yes, my lady!"

Alyce gave him a little nod and a smile, slipping her arm through Zoë's. "Excellent. We promise to stay close."

THE pair did stay close to their young guardian, and managed to find and purchase several items of wedding finery by the time Trevor returned, perhaps half an hour later.

"It's Lord Michon, carrying dispatches from the crown

council," he told Alyce, when he had assured himself that she and Zoë had come to no harm. "There's a horsemaster with him called Oisín Adair. Apparently they've been commissioned to look for a suitable horse for Prince Brion's coming of age next summer. They're on their way to visit stud farms in R'Kassi and the Forcinn."

"That's splendid," Zoë said with a smile. "It sounds like Prince Brion finally will acquire the horse of his dreams. Wasn't it Master Oisín who procured those Llanner ponies for the princes, a few years back?"

Trevor inclined his head. "I believe it was, my lady."

"I remember him," Alyce agreed. "He stayed at Rhemuth for several days after delivering the ponies. The queen and her ladies found his company quite amusing. As I recall, one of the junior maids-of-honor was quite taken with him. Will they be staying over?"

Trevor shook his head. "No, my lady. They aren't even coming ashore. Lord Michon said he didn't wish to undermine Lord Kenneth's authority by any appearance that the king is checking on him. I've sent the dispatches up with the captain of the harbor guard. The ship sails with the tide, bound for one of the Tralian ports."

Alyce gave a resigned shrug. "Well, it was very kind of them to serve as couriers. I hope they find a splendid mount for the prince."

THE erstwhile "couriers" did, indeed, sail with the tide, though not immediately to look at horses, for they were under orders from the Camberian Council as well as the King of Gwynedd. Their ship made landfall that evening at the Tralian port of Tortuña, across the straits from the Hort of Orsal's summer residence at Horthánthy. There Oisín secured lodgings for their party at a local inn and, over quite a passable meal in the inn's taproom, gave the four men of their escort detailed instructions regarding the procurement of livery mounts and provisions for the journey inland to R'Kassi.

"I expect that may take you a day or two," Michon added, as Oisín refilled cups all around from a leather jack of ale. "In the meantime, Master Oisín and I have other business in the area, so if you finish before we do, your time is your own until we return. We'll meet here." During the voyage from Coroth, he and Oisín had already contrived to take the men aside individually, so that later, none would be able to summon up any real curiosity over their superiors' "other business."

As for that other business, Michon had already seen to their further travel arrangements. The next day's dawning saw the pair of them boarding a Tralian merchantman bound for the Torenthi port of Furstánan, at the mouth of the River Beldour. It was early afternoon when they caught their first sight of the Abbey of Saint-Sasile, its golden domes and cupolas shimmering in the summer sun.

"A pity we couldn't have arranged to arrive just at dusk," Michon said to Oisín, as their ship glided into the anchorage and they tied up to a buoy. "Have you ever seen the lights of Saint-Sasile?"

Oisín shook his head. "Sadly, no. My foreign trading usually takes me much farther south. I've traveled into Torenth several times, but always by land, and farther upriver."

"Ah, well, then, you may be in for a treat when we leave," Michon said, with a sidelong glance and a grin at his companion. "This is Saturday, yes?"

"You know it is."

"Then, we're in luck. Saint-Sasile is a double abbey, as you may be aware, and all Deryni. To the outside world, their work is perpetual prayer for the salvation of souls, though they also function as an exclusive school for training high-level Deryni. On the eve of every Sabbath and major feast day, the two houses join for Great Vespers and lift souls and voices in prayer—which also raises the shields around the abbey as a visible manifestation of their devotion. It's a sight you'll not soon forget, once you've seen it."

* * *

But first, they must meet with the formidable Mother Serafina, once known as Princess Camille Furstána of Torenth. A pinnace came to take them ashore, landing them on one of the many busy quays bristling into the wide Furstánan estuary. An hour later, they were climbing the last of the wide stone steps that spiraled up to the abbey gate.

The air had been still and close as they came ashore, even oppressive, but it freshened considerably as they made their ascent. Even so, both men were sweating and winded from their exertions by the time they reached the broad esplanade before the gatehouse.

"What if she won't see us?" Oisín muttered, as he and Michon paused to catch their breath and Michon mopped at his brow with a square of fine linen.

"She'll see us," Michon said flatly.

With a show of conviction he was not certain he actually felt, Michon drew another deep breath to fortify himself, stuffed his square of linen into a sleeve, then approached the gatehouse to pull at the chain that would summon a doorkeeper.

Far beyond, they heard the distant jangle of the bell. The heavy gate set into the gatehouse arch was studded with metal bosses the size of a man's fist, each incised with a deep-cut spiral, but it was not only timber and iron that guarded the Abbey of Saint-Sasile. They could feel the tight-leashed power brooding beyond the gate, rich and potent.

After a long moment, one of the metal bosses in the wicket gate irised open to reveal one bright black eye, which darted from one to the other of the men in frank appraisal.

"God give grace, my sons," said a voice of indeterminate gender. "What is it you seek?"

Bowing slightly, right hand to breast, Michon said, "We come seeking audience with the sister and teacher known as Serafina. It is a matter of some urgency."

He felt the feather brush of shields testing at his own, quickly withdrawn, and then the iron boss irised back down with a faint slither of metal leaves closing. A scraping of timber against metal told of a heavy gate bar being shifted, after which the wicket gate swung silently inward. The gatekeeper who stepped from behind the gate wore the stark black robes and ragged beard of Eastern orthodoxy, with his long hair tied back under the cylindrical black hat and veil of a monk.

"There is no urgency within these walls," the man said coolly, his gaze again sweeping the pair of them. "You are not Torenthi, are you."

"With all respect for your office, Reverend Father, that does not change the urgency of our need."

"She does not see foreigners," the monk retorted. "And she is properly addressed as *Mother* Serafina."

Michon bowed again, hand on heart and eyes averted. "I stand corrected, Reverend Father. When last she and I spoke, many years ago, she was still known by another name."

"And yet you knew to find her here," the monk replied. "Surely you must be aware that the woman you knew has been long dead to the world."

"Pray tell her that it is Michon de Courcy who desires audience," Michon said evenly, "and that it would behoove her to hear what I have to say."

The monk's dark eyes narrowed in warning, powerful shields flaring briefly visible around his head like a golden aureole.

"This is not a place in which it would be wise to threaten, outlander."

"Nor would I presume to do so, good Father," Michon said mildly. "But I do feel certain that Mother Serafina *will* wish to see me—if you will be so good as to convey my request to her. Give her this," he added, removing his signet and extending it to the man. At the same time, he let his own shields briefly engulf the ring, to amplify its psychic signature.

The monk hesitated for an instant, his eyes not leaving

Michon's; but then he took the ring and closed it in his hand, stepped back to close the door in their faces. They heard the bar drop, the sound of retreating footsteps, then only the faint murmur of chanting in the distant background. Oisín exhaled a long sigh that he had not realized he had been holding and glanced at Michon.

"So, was that a yes or a no?" he asked softly.

"Oh, most certainly a yes," Michon replied with a tiny smile. "Whether or not the monk recognized my name, he is certainly aware that we are well-shielded Deryni—and if not Torenthi, then we must be that great rarity in Torenth: Deryni from Gwynedd, inquiring at a Torenthi monastery. That alone should ensure that he delivers the message—and *she* will well remember me."

His confidence proved well-founded. Within a quarter hour, they were admitted to the outer precincts of the monastery and given into the charge of two black-clad monks who looked much like the first, one of whom silently handed back Michon's ring and signed that the pair should follow. The men did not offer names, but their shields were seamless and almost undetectable, betokening both discipline and power. Minutes later, the visitors were ushered through the wrought-bronze gate of a tiny courtyard enclosing a miniature garden with a tinkling fountain in the center. Beyond the garden, with its western doorway opening thereon, lay a graceful jewel of a chapel whose golden dome seemed to glow in the afternoon sun.

"You may make your ablutions there, before entering the *hagios*," the taller of the two monks said, with a sparse gesture toward the fountain. "Mother Serafina will join you shortly inside."

Michon inclined his head in agreement, right hand to breast, and received a clipped nod in return. The monks then withdrew and pulled the gate almost closed. As Michon and Oisín moved to the fountain and began to wash hands and faces, Oisín glanced casually in the direction of the gate.

They're still there, you know, he sent, tight-focused.

Of course. And there will be others nearby as well. They are wary of us—but they also know that anyone with a shield like ours is not likely to attempt any kind of psychic mischief here in the monastic precincts, in the midst of all these Deryni. Are you ready?

Oisín merely dried his face and hands on an edge of his cloak and smiled, following as Michon led the way to the chapel door.

Very gently they pushed it open far enough to enter, pausing just inside to probe with Deryni senses and to take it all in. It was dim and much cooler inside the tiny chapel—octagonal in plan, unlike most churches in the West, with a skylight high in the center of the domed ceiling that showed a distant circle of blue sky. Against the eastern wall, a fair-sized icon of the Holy Trinity presided over the sacred space, attended by a painted depiction of Archangel Raphael. A three-branched golden candelabrum burned honey-scented candles at the feet of the icons, the candlelight lending a semblance of life to the painted eyes. To left and right, icons of Auriel and Michael stood guard at their stations north and south, painted larger than a man, each beneath a high, narrow window that admitted air but little light. A votive light of the appropriate color, green or red, burned at each icon's feet. These depictions as well seemed more than mere paintings.

Briefly they turned to survey the wall through which they had entered, where Archangel Gabriel and a heavy icon of the Blessed Virgin presided from the west, the latter encased in gold and jewels except for her face and that of the Holy Child displayed on her lap. A votive in blue glass burned at their feet, like a captive sapphire. On a small table in the center of the chamber, an earthen bowl of sand supported many slender tapers of honey-colored beeswax, their shafts bristling like the spines of some strange sea creature in the bluish light that filtered down from the ceiling shaft.

"What on earth *is* this place?" Oisín whispered close beside Michon's ear. "A chapel or a ritual chamber?"

"Perhaps both," Michon murmured, slightly lifting a hand for silence as he turned his attention to a small door softly opening in the painted wall to the right of the eastern display, which had been invisible when closed. "And perhaps none of this is wholly of this earth."

They almost could not see the two black-clad figures that slipped through the briefly opened doorway, sensed mostly by their movement and the brighter blur of averted faces within the close-shadowed frame of flat-topped caps and waist-length monastic veils fastened close beneath the chin. Neither man stirred as the pair moved before the eastern icons and reverenced them with a deep bow and a sweep of right hands from brow to floor to right shoulder and left.

Turning in their places, the pair then repeated their salute to south, west, and north, finishing in the east once again, after which the taller one retreated to the door by which they had entered and stood with her back against it, hands piously folded beneath her veil and face averted. As the shorter one started to turn toward the visitors, Michon set a hand on Oisín's forearm and sent, *Wait here. Say and do nothing.*

So saying, he moved into the center of the chamber, with the table between him and the woman, and silently inclined his head.

He would not have known her, had he met her outside this place. The Princess Camille Furstána whom he remembered had possessed the charm and vivacity of youth, and a self-assurance that comes of royal blood, but nothing of physical appearance to suggest that maturity might bring anything approaching beauty. The passage of time had not given her that, but age and her vocation had made Mother Serafina a striking woman. Though still slender of form and small in stature, her erect carriage and the flat cap beneath her veil added at least a handspan to her height and gave her a physical authority to match her psychic presence. The eyes, at least by candlelight, were still the same: dark and intense, unwavering in their scrutiny; and the shields behind the eyes were adamantine, as they had been for as long as Michon had known her.

"You indicated that you wished to speak to me on a matter of some urgency," she finally said, her voice low and measured, just as he remembered.

"I did," he said, again inclining his head, "and I do. And I thank you for seeing us."

"It is not usually done," she replied, favoring him with a nod of acknowledgment, "but I was curious to know what would bring you to me after all these years—though I can guess."

"Can you?" he returned, the question also a statement.

She inhaled deeply and let out a quiet sigh, lifting her chin a little defiantly. He could see only her face; the hands were clasped close beneath the veil over her shoulders and upper body.

"Well, I am quite certain that you have not come to ask for training," she said breezily, a faint smile curling the corners of her mouth as she glanced at him sidelong. "But I would venture to guess that you *have* come to ask about the training that I am providing to certain others."

He inclined his head in agreement. "That would be an accurate reading of my intentions," he said neutrally.

Her eyes at once went dark and dangerous. "How dare you!" she breathed, almost inaudibly. "Whom I choose to train, and how, is *my* business, not yours—or the Camberian Council's!"

"In that, you are much mistaken," he replied, in the same low tone. "I trust I need not remind you of what happened to Lewys ap Norfal, when he entertained similarly dangerous notions regarding his powers. Train your nephews, if you must; they are subjects of Torenth, and the concern of her king. If they perish through their folly, that will simply mean somewhat fewer Furstáns to threaten *my* king! But if you persist in training that twit Zachris Pomeroy, he becomes a potential threat to my king—and he is *not* a subject of Torenth!"

She sniffed in derision and lifted her chin defiantly. "What arrogance, to presume that what I teach is folly!"

"Camille, you were there when Lewys failed," he began.

"Camille is dead!" she interjected coldly. "Mother

Serafina has far surpassed the girl who once was. You will address me by my proper name and rank."

"As you wish," he murmured. "But consider this a warning. If one of your students goes astray in Gwynedd, the Council will take a very dim view of your actions. And next time, it may not be an old friend who comes calling."

"We did not part as friends, Michon de Courcy. Do not presume to play on my emotions."

Michon had cocked his head at this declaration, and held up a hand to stay further such revelations.

"How time can alter our memories," he murmured. "But I shall not cause further offense by bringing up bygones. Just remember what I have said."

Her jaw went steely, and her eyes narrowed. "Let the past be past, Michon," she said softly. "Consider that you treat now with a stranger."

"Yes, I can see that," he replied. Clasping his hands behind him, he inclined his head in cool leave-taking. "Should I ask a blessing before I go? I am given to understand that such is expected."

Her lip curled in faint disdain. "I shall pray for you, Michon, as I pray for all who are in need of enlightenment. But I think you would not thank me for what blessing I might give you."

He lifted his chin and braced his shoulders, then gave her another nod, this time in the nature of a dismissal and farewell. "Then it appears there is nothing more to be said. Forgive me for wasting your time."

With that, he turned on his heel and strode briskly toward the outer door, where Oisín quickly opened it for him and followed him outside. Their escort monks were waiting beyond the gate to the little courtyard, and fell in behind them as they retraced their steps to the monastery gatehouse. The sound of the gate closing behind them held a note of finality.

The pair did not speak until they were well down the steps leading back to the harbor. Behind them, in the lowering twilight, a deep-throated bell began summoning the inhabitants of Saint-Sasile for the Great Office of Sabbath Eve.

"Did that go as badly as it sounded?" Oisín finally summoned the courage to ask.

Michon uttered a breathless grunt meant to be an ironic laugh.

"It certainly did not go *well*," he replied.

By the time they reboarded their ship and were under sail, heading back across the straits toward distant Tralia, a ghostly glow had begun to flicker above the spires and domes of Saint-Sasile.

Chapter 9

"Can a maid forget her ornaments, or a bride her attire?"

—JEREMIAH 2:32

THOUGH Michon's visit to Saint-Sasile had been less than satisfactory, his and Oisín's onward journey into R'Kassi yielded far more positive results. In the course of visits to a number of that land's most prominent breeders of fine horseflesh, Oisín identified half a dozen promising two-year-olds of suitable lineage and temperament for Prince Brion's first adult mount. For each of these animals he left sizeable deposits and instructions for their care and training in the coming year, promising to return in the spring to make his final selection.

"In truth, they are all fine animals," he told Michon as they rode back to Tortuña to take ship for their return to Rhemuth. "If all of them develop according to their promise, I shall probably take the lot of them in the spring and keep whatever ones the king does not choose. I have no doubt that I shall find buyers for as many as I care to sell on; and a few may even end up at my own facility at Haut Emeraud."

"I think that neither the king nor Prince Brion will have cause to complain," Michon assured his younger companion.

"The Council, alas, will be less pleased. I wish we could take them better news."

But if the completion of their summer missions had met with mixed results, the same could not be said for that of the new head of Corwyn's regency council. Looking back on that first summer at Coroth, the stay of Lord Kenneth Morgan and his countess at the Corwyn capital could only be counted as a success. Though the Duchy of Corwyn had been formally in abeyance for nearly thirty years, waiting for a male heir to come of age, Malcolm Haldane and then King Donal had chosen well in their selection of a caretaker council to administer these important lands, so vital to the security of Gwynedd's eastern border with Torenth.

Corwyn's origins lay in the turbulent era just before the Festillic Interregnum, when King St. Bearand Haldane was consolidating his kingdom after pushing back the Moorish sea lords. In 826, soon after the overthrow of the Haldane line, the new King Festil of Gwynedd arranged the marriage of his son and heir, Prince Festil Augustus, to the Princess Briona, only child of the last Prince of Mooryn, in the south, thus bringing Mooryn directly under the crown of Gwynedd as its suzerain. Corwyn and Carthmoor, subsidiary princedoms of Mooryn, became semi-autonomous duchies, with Carthmoor settled on Prince Festil and his bride. Corwyn was given to Sieur Dominic du Joux, son and heir of Lord Richard du Joux, who had fought and died for Festil in the conquest of Gwynedd. Dominic's mother had been the Princess Tayce Furstána, a first cousin of King Festil. Hence Dominic was Deryni, like all the Festils, and became Corwyn's first duke.

With the accession of Prince Festil Augustus as Festil II in 839, the Duchy of Carthmoor became an appanage of the Crown of Gwynedd, usually reserved for younger sons or brothers of Gwynedd's kings. Corwyn, however, retained its semi-autonomous status all through the Festillic Interregnum and into the Haldane Restoration, until the reign of King Cluim Haldane, and the repulsion of Duchad Mor's invasion force by Cluim's brother Jashan.

At that time, Jernian of Corwyn, fifth duke and a

comrade-in-arms of the new king, bound himself in personal vassalage to the Crown of Gwynedd. Both he and his son Stíofan had fought for Gwynedd in the Great War of 1025; and Stíofan Anthony, Alyce's grandfather, had ruled Corwyn with justice and compassion for more than forty years: a benevolent and popular ruler in a long line of highly competent dukes. Geography made Corwyn an important buffer with Torenth, and the loyalty of its dukes a vital aspect of Gwynedd's eastern security.

With the loyal Kenneth Morgan now guiding Corwyn's destiny, as caretaker for his young son, Corwyn's regents could finally breathe a collective sigh of relief, knowing their sole custodianship would soon be eased. His visits to Coroth would always be too short for their liking, but they could appreciate the sensitive work that Earl Kenneth sometimes carried out for the king, and the trust placed in him by the Crown, which would also serve Corwyn's interests. This present visit might only last a month, but it was long enough for Kenneth to begin acquiring a more intimate knowledge of the state of the duchy and the men charged with its care; long enough for them to begin knowing him and the child who one day would be their duke.

Alyce, for her part, continued to sit in on meetings of the regency council occasionally, and gave her opinion when asked. But mostly she spent her time reacquainting herself with her ancestral home and showing it off to Zoë and her son.

THEY lingered in Coroth until the end of August—long enough to see the harvest mostly in, and for Kenneth to have established an easy working relationship with the other Corwyn regents. Several times, he went off on patrols along the border with Torenth, taking Jovett and Trevor with him and acquainting himself with the political pulse of the area.

Accompanied by various hosts from the regency council, he also visited most of the major holdings in Corwyn proper. Laurenz Udaut proved particularly helpful and friendly in this regard, as did Earl Derry and his son. Bishop Harris remained aloof, though at least he was not obstructive; but Earl Síoda took very much to heart his promise to begin teaching Alaric about his ducal heritage. Many an afternoon found the pair sitting under a shady tree in the castle gardens, often with one of the stable hounds at their feet, where the old man regaled his young charge with tales of Corwyn's history and its illustrious dukes. By the time the family prepared to head back to Cynfyn for the wedding of Zoë and Sir Jovett Chandos, Kenneth was confident that the duchy was in good hands.

They were to leave for Cynfyn on the first day of September, following a final court and banquet of leave-taking on the afternoon before. At the court preceding that banquet, young Alaric, now hardly a month short of his third birthday, was allowed to sit on the dais on a stool between his parents and personally receive the loyalty of his future subjects. On that day as well, Kenneth knighted several senior Corwyn squires whose attendance at the next Twelfth Night Court would have presented a financial hardship. Alaric wore a miniature coronet provided by Earl Síoda, and a simple tunic displaying the Corwyn arms, and comported himself commendably as future duke, even holding his father's sharp sword between accolades.

One of the new knights, a blond, mop-headed young man by name of Llion Farquahar, had made himself young Alaric's personal favorite by serving as the boy's almost-constant companion through the weeks of their stay, freeing up Alyce's energies to sit in on council meetings or sometimes to ride with Zoë in the surrounding countryside or along the sandy beaches to the west of the harbor. Sometimes this respite simply allowed her and Zoë to stitch quietly on wedding attire with Melissa and other women of the court, without the distraction of a small boy's endless questions and restless poking into *everything*.

Every morning, the squire Llion would take the boy in charge and touch on some facet of his education as Corwyn's future duke, imparting random elements of court etiquette and simple heraldry, even starting him on very basic sword drills, using a dirk for a sword. Even more to Alaric's liking, sometimes Llion would put him up in the saddle of a sedate, retired warhorse and walk beside him for hours.

For him, young Alaric fumbled his father's sword into Sir Xander's hands and darted down from his stool of state to help Jovett buckle on the spurs, and gave Sir Llion an unabashed hug, once the accolade had been bestowed and the white belt girt around his waist by Alyce.

But the lazy days of that summer ended the next day when the party departed for Cynfyn. Zoë and Jovett were charged with excitement about their upcoming nuptials, and Kenneth and Alyce well pleased with the way their time at Coroth had passed; but Alaric wept when forced to say good-bye to his favorite knight, and withdrew into a sulk the farther they got from Coroth. Skirting Tendal lands as they made their way upriver, heading back toward Cynfyn, they stopped the first night at Pladda, a comfortable manor nestled in a curve of the river.

"You know, you *could* ask Sir Llion whether he'd like to join our household," Alyce said to her husband the next morning, when Alaric only picked listlessly at his breakfast, cranky and dispirited. "Alaric doted on him—and more important, he respected him, and minded when Llion told him to do something he really didn't want to do. Also, the time is not that far away when he should begin spending time with other men and boys, rather than with the women. Since he'll need a companion anyway, and someone to be his governor, why not choose one he likes?"

Kenneth nodded. "He seems a bright-enough young man—and I liked what I saw of him on the practice field. We could give him a try, I suppose. If he'd want to live so far from home, that is."

"Dear Kenneth, I think he would welcome the chance," Alyce replied. "His family has a long tradition of service to my house, but I believe they have fallen on hard times in the past generation or so—and he is not the eldest son. He'll inherit nothing. He would benefit greatly from exposure at court, from being a part of *our* court. And you yourself have said that he shows promise."

"Then we shall see if such service is agreeable to him. I'll send Trevor back to fetch him."

"Thank you, darling! I know it will be a good match."

WHETHER or not it was a good match, it certainly improved young Alaric's spirits. They did not tell him why Trevor was being sent back to Coroth; only that he had a mission for Kenneth. But when, two days later, Trevor and Llion joined the column at Dellard's Landing, where they had stopped to water the horses, Alaric's face lit with undisguised joy.

"Sir Llion!" he crowed, pelting across the muddy riverbank to fling his arms around the young man's knees. "Llion, Llion!"

Sir Llion scooped him up in a hug as Kenneth and Alyce approached, grinning as he nodded respect to the pair of them.

"I would kneel, m'lord, m'lady, but I seem to have an armful of ducal heir."

Alyce laughed and set her hand happily on Kenneth's arm. "'Tis quite clear that you are most welcome, Sir Llion. By your presence, may we assume that you are willing to take on this young bundle of exuberance?"

"I am the third of six, my lady, and the youngest is but a few years older than Alaric," Llion replied, smiling. "Our mother died bearing him, so I have always helped with the younger ones. Besides"—he jostled Alaric on his hip—"young Master Alaric and I get on very well, don't we, old chap?"

"Will you take me riding, Llion?" Alaric asked, grinning into the face of his mentor.

"If your parents agree, of course I shall take you riding," Llion replied. "I've even brought your favorite mount." He glanced back at a rawboned chestnut standing hipshot with Trevor and a much finer steed.

"I hope you don't mind, my lord. Having no horse of my own, I took the liberty of seconding old Cockleburr. Lord Hamilton said it would be all right. He isn't much to look at, but he's sound enough for work like this—and I figured he'd be little missed at Coroth. Besides that, your son likes him. Do we camp here for the night, sir, or do we carry on for a while?"

Kenneth smiled and briefly clasped a hand to Llion's shoulder. "We have a few more miles to go, but I see no reason why Alaric shouldn't ride with you and Cockleburr. And we'll see about getting you a better mount at Cynfyn."

"But Papa, I *like* Cockleburr!" Alaric began.

"Which is why he shall become *your* horse, once you've learned to ride him properly," Kenneth replied, watching the boy's eyes light with joy. "But you must do as Sir Llion asks," he added. "I'm putting you in his charge."

"Oh, *yes*, Papa! Thank you, Papa!"

"And I thank you as well, my lord," Llion murmured, gratitude in his eyes as he nodded to Kenneth. "You have given me hope of a real future. I shall do my best to be worthy of your trust."

Kenneth only nodded in turn before following after Alyce, who was already mounting up again with Zoë.

They reached Cynfyn on schedule, pleased to find that all had been made ready in their absence. Zoë's sisters had traveled to Cynfyn for the occasion, the unmarried Alazais with Kenneth's two sisters and Geill with her husband, along with their aunt Nesta McLain, the sister of their departed mother, and, to everyone's surprise, Vera Countess of Kierney, with her young son Duncan, but a few months younger than Alaric.

"I wouldn't have dreamed of missing this," Vera told Alyce and Zoë, the first time they had a moment of privacy, as the two boys played happily with toy knights in the ladies' solar. "Fortunately, Aunt Nesta was determined to come and see Zoë married. We all traveled together from Kierney and Culdi, collecting Morgan aunts and sisters as we came. All of them would have preferred that the wedding be held at Morganhall, of course, but now that Kenneth is an earl, everyone was curious to see the seat of his new estate."

"For all practical purposes," Alyce said, "it's apt to end

up being Zoë and Jovett's new estate, for all the time Kenneth and I will be spending here." She cast out with her mind to be certain they could not be overheard, then leaned closer to the other two women. "What news of the king, Vera?" she asked in a low voice. "And how fares Prince Brion? The letters we've received over the summer only had to do with matters of state."

"Both are well, from what Jared has mentioned," Vera replied. "And the queen writes occasionally. She says that she is much involved with helping the king make plans for Prince Brion's coming-of-age next summer. It's expected that Donal will summon all his lords to attend him and swear fealty to the prince, in support of the succession. Which means that Jared and I shall be traveling to Rhemuth for the affair, along with Kevin and Duncan—unless, of course, I am near another lying-in," she added.

"Is there hope of that?" Alyce asked quietly.

Vera shrugged. "There is always hope—and it would be a happy reason to miss the celebration." She looked away briefly, then smiled. "Did I tell you that Jared is having the most beautiful little chapel built in the garden at Culdi, as a memorial to our dear Alicia?"

"What a wonderful thing to do," Alyce murmured, sorrowing anew over the child Vera had lost earlier in the year. "And Jared is a lovely man, to have thought of it."

"Aye, he is." Vera smiled brightly. "And we *are* trying for another child, believe me."

"And the trying is pleasant enough, I'm sure," Alyce replied with an arched eyebrow. "As our dear Zoë will soon discover."

Zoë blushed furiously, but she was also smiling shyly. "We shall certainly do our best," she said.

To increasing bursts of giggles, their subsequent conversation drifted into ever more explicit discussion of the upcoming nuptials, and what Zoë might expect on her wedding night.

Chapter 10

"Give your daughters to husbands,
that they may bear sons and daughters."

—JEREMIAH 29:6

THE wedding of Lady Zoë Morgan with Sir Jovett Chandos took place the following day at noon in the castle chapel, attended by the two extended families and most of Lendour's regents. Not invited but very welcome nonetheless were two surprise guests from the convent school of Notre Dame de l'Arc-en-Ciel, Our Lady of the Rainbow, where Zoë and Alyce had met. The appearance of Sisters Iris Cerys and Iris Jessilde at the door to the chamber where the bride was dressing produced a squeal of sheer delight from the bride and an astonished smile from Alyce, who had been brushing Zoë's long wheaten hair.

"We've brought a gift for the bride," said Sister Iris Cerys, mischief crinkling at the outer corners of her eyes as she and her companion paused in the doorway, smiling faces framed by the rainbow-embroidered bands edging their pale blue veils. Iris Cerys had shared a room with Alyce for a time, before Zoë, and the slightly older Iris Jessilde had been one of the first to make Alyce and her sister welcome at the convent school. She was also Deryni.

"You lived under the protection of Our Lady of the Rainbow while you studied at Arc-en-Ciel," Sister Iris Jessilde said to Zoë, "so we thought you might wish to be married according to the custom of our house."

With that she produced a fragrant bridal wreath fashioned of roses in all the colors of the rainbow, very like those worn at their old convent school, both by postulants wedding a celestial bridegroom and by former students giving themselves in mortal marriage.

"We wanted to bring you a rainbow canopy as well," Iris Cerys chimed in, "but Reverend Mother said it was too far to bring one all the way to Cynfyn. Since she'd just given us permission to attend, we decided we wouldn't press the issue."

"No, no, this is wonderful!" Zoë assured them, delightedly taking the wreath and inhaling of its perfume. "But how did you even know?"

Iris Jessilde's smile spoke of feigned innocence and a touch of feminine conspiracy. "Dear child, we are not so cut off at Arc-en-Ciel that news does not reach us from the outside world," she said. "Your father wrote to Mother Judiana to inform her of the upcoming marriage of one of our former pupils. When she read the letter out in chapter, it was suggested that at least a few of us ought to travel here to witness it."

"I never thought it would be allowed," Iris Cerys chimed in. "It isn't often that we're given leave to venture outside the abbey walls, but the two of you left quite an impression on our community—especially considering that neither of you ever even considered the religious life. It was a unanimous recommendation. I only wish that all of the sisters could have come along."

"Good heavens, I don't know where I would have put all of them," Alyce said with a laugh. "But I'm very glad you came. Did you only just arrive?"

"No, we stayed two days with a family in the village," said Iris Jessilde. "Lord Kenneth arranged it—and the goodwife has a lovely garden. Hence, the magnificence of your bridal wreath. 'Tis the perfect complement to your gown," she added, smiling as she cast an approving gaze over Zoë's sapphire silk. "But then, blue always did suit you, even if the convent did not."

Zoë returned the smile as she helped Alyce set the wreath on her wheaten hair. "It suited *very* well, while I was there," she said. "And if I had not come to Arc-en-Ciel, I would never have met you and Cerys—and Alyce."

"—who has lent you the wearing of the Furstána emeralds, I see," Iris Cerys said with a sly smile, jutting her chin in the direction of the necklace of blue-green fire at Zoë's throat. "I remember when she wore them for her own marriage."

"*And* her mother's bracelet!" Zoë replied, brandishing the opal and sapphire bangle on one wrist, then hugging Alyce close. "Oh, it's wonderful to have both of you here," she continued, beaming at the pair of them. "Thank you so much for coming!"

A BRIDAL wreath was not the only gift the two sisters of the Rainbow had brought to Zoë Morgan for her wedding day. When the wedding guests had assembled in the little chapel, the pair accompanied the priest to the altar steps, Iris Cerys nodding reassurance to the nervous bridegroom as she and Iris Jessilde spread a small rainbow carpet on the kneeler where Zoë and Jovett would recite their vows. Withdrawing then to the side of the chapel, they sweetly sang the traditional *Ave Vierge Dorée* as Zoë Morgan walked down the aisle with her father. The song brought back fond memories both for her and for Alyce, who followed and stood as witness for the bride.

After the nuptial mass, when bride and groom had made their vows and received the Sacrament, kneeling then on the rainbow carpet for the bridal blessing, Jovett led his bride to the Lady altar, so that the radiant Zoë might offer up her bridal wreath at the feet of the Blessed Virgin—except that, before they turned to leave, Jovett plucked one perfect white rose from the wreath and touched it to his lips.

"This should be Ahern's," he whispered, gazing into her eyes as he gave it into her hands. "Let's lay it on his grave before we leave."

She could not speak to thank him for the gesture, but she managed to nod before they turned to go. Their steps took them back to the altar steps, and the grave slabs at their feet—Ahern and his father, Keryell, both of them Earls of Lendour in turn. There Zoë and Jovett stood a moment with heads bowed in tribute to Zoë's first husband, then bent together to lay the rose on the incised letters of Ahern's name. As they passed on up the aisle and into the little porch of the chapel, they stood aside to let the other guests pass into the yard, and Zoë turned in the circle of Jovett's arm to press her forehead against his.

"You loved him, too, didn't you?" she whispered into his shoulder.

"I did," Jovett replied. "He and Sé were the closest friends of my youth." He sighed gently. "I had hoped Sé might be here, but . . ."

"I know he would wish us joy," she replied, gazing up into his eyes as the guests slipped past them, giving them their moment of privacy. "And thank you for what you did with the rose."

"It seemed right," he replied, tracing the line of her jaw with his fingertips and lifting a strand of wheaten hair. "What went before . . . simply was not meant to be."

"No," she agreed quietly. "But it does no good to grieve over a past that cannot be changed. What matters now is that we have come to love one another."

He answered the sweet and tender kiss she offered with a passion that startled them both. Jovett was grinning sheepishly as they drew apart.

"Dearest wife," he murmured, "I think we had best join our wedding guests, lest we scandalize your late beloved—though I like to think he would approve, given the circumstances."

"I know he would," Zoë agreed, brushing her fingertips tenderly across his lips. Then, with a wistful smile, she touched her fingertips to her own lips and turned to glance back into the chapel where her first love slept, gently blowing him their mutual kiss.

"Good-bye, dearest Ahern. Sleep gently."

Hand in hand, then, the two of them departed the chapel to join their wedding guests.

THE wedding feast was held in the hall of Cynfyn Castle, as festive an affair as had ever occurred within those walls. To honor his daughter and her new husband, Kenneth invited them to preside from the high table, but Jovett insisted that he and his bride could not usurp that honor, and would only *share* it with the castle's rightful lord and lady.

"While I have just become your goodson, my lord, this is still *your* hall. Best if we underline that you shall always take precedence here."

Kenneth was smiling slightly as he nodded. "Well spoken. But you are still the guests of honor here tonight, so you shall sit at my right hand. I trust you'll not object to *that*?"

"I shall try always to carry out your wishes, my lord," Jovett said with a slight bow and a smile—and obediently led his bride in to take their places at the high table, Kenneth and Alyce following in the coronets of their rank.

It was a modest feast by the standards of the court at Rhemuth, but for the bride and groom, it was a taste of the treatment usually accorded only to royalty. After the first course, young Alaric enticed his younger cousin Duncan into several forays underneath the cloths covering the high table, eventually eliciting Kenneth's sharp order for Sir Llion to take both boys in charge and divert them to other pursuits in the garden, so that the adults could enjoy their meal in peace.

Thank you, Alyce mouthed to the young knight, also pointing at her plate. *I'll save you a plate.*

His cheery wave conveyed both understanding and gratitude as he gathered up several more of the younger children and led them out into the castle yard, like a mother hen parading her chicks.

"We shall have to see about finding Llion a wife," Kenneth murmured to Alyce, as he tucked into his meal again. "Such skill with small boys merits a few sons of his own."

"What, and lose his services with our own?" Alyce replied. "He is young yet. There will be plenty of time in a few years—and when our Alaric has gained some maturity."

"You're right," Kenneth agreed. "I had not thought of that. But do keep the prospect in mind."

"I shall indeed."

It was something of an hour later, when the wedding supper was well underway and a troupe of players were offering entertainment, that Kenneth drew his wife's attention to a dark-clad figure standing quietly in the shadows at the far end of the hall.

"Look who has finally made an appearance."

"It's Sé," Alyce murmured, touching a hand to her husband's arm. "He *did* come for Jovett's wedding."

"I told you he would—at least for the feast," Kenneth replied, though he smiled as he said it. "He is a good friend of this family, Alyce."

"He is," she agreed. "Pray, excuse me."

"Of course."

As she started toward him, he moved farther into the shadows just inside the doorway, laying a hand across his heart and inclining his head in wordless greeting as she joined him. He was leaner than when last she had seen him, at her son's christening, shedding weight from a frame already lean and fit, and further refining the high cheekbones, the narrow, aristocratic nose. The close-clipped beard and mustache underlined the new refinement, made him look more lethal. His eyes were still the same startling blue, but with a harder edge.

Only the white belt of his knighthood relieved the stark simplicity of the ankle-length black robe he wore, fastened at the shoulder in the Eastern manner. A few strands of silver threaded the chestnut hair at the temples and in the braid sleeked back and clubbed at the nape of the neck in an intricate warrior's knot.

"Sé," she breathed, only the *shhh* sound really audible.

"My lady." He inclined his head again.

"Kenneth said you would come, but I wasn't sure," she replied. "You have been long silent."

He allowed himself a faint smile, a tendril of his thought caressing her mind in something of the old friendship they had shared since childhood.

"I could not miss Jovett's wedding," he said.

"Were you there, or did you only just arrive?" she asked softly. "I did not see you in the chapel."

Another faint smile curled at the corners of his mouth. "You were otherwise occupied, and I did not mean to be seen. I have learned a great deal since we last met. But did you really think I would not come?"

"No," she replied, affection lighting her eyes. "You have never, ever failed me."

"Nor shall I, while I live," he replied, taking her hands to kiss first one, then the other. As he did so, turning his own hands slightly upward, she caught a glimpse of indigo now marking the insides of his wrists: the thumb-sized crosses denoting a fully vowed Knight of the Anvil.

"You did it," she breathed, holding fast to one of his hands when he would have drawn back, and turning his wrist more toward the light. "So, it's true, what they say about the Anvillers."

He smiled and averted his hands, though he closed her hands in his as he gazed into her eyes.

"And what do they say about the Anvillers?" he murmured.

"That after making final profession, they are marked at wrists, ankles, and side, as a reminder of Christ's holy wounds," she replied.

He inclined his head in agreement. " 'Tis true, though propriety constrains me from showing you the others just now."

"Why, Sir Sé!" she murmured with raised eyebrows, then sobered. "Is it permitted to ask why it is done?"

"You may ask—and I'll even answer," he added, to forestall the beginning of her surprise. "Final vows are solemn, and cannot be rescinded. Nor may we ever deny what we are, if asked. These permanent marks remind us of that." He smiled a mirthless smile. "It keeps us honest."

"More than that, I think," she murmured, smiling a little herself. "The Anvillers are held to be incorruptible. Has it ever happened, that one did not keep faith?"

"Not in living memory."

He glanced around—they seemed to be inside a bubble, for all the attention anyone paid them—then returned his gaze to hers.

"I cannot stay," he murmured. "How is my godson?"

She smiled. "He flourishes, he grows stronger and more clever with each passing day. Would you like to see him?"

"I watched him playing in the garden with the other boys," Sé replied. "That young knight who has charge of him: You have a loyal retainer in that one, Alyce. Cherish him."

She laughed lightly. " 'Twas Alaric himself who chose Llion. The two are devoted to one another. Other than you and Jovett, I cannot think of a better mentor and guardian in these early years."

"In all humility, I shall take that as the compliment I am certain you intended." He lifted one of her hands to kiss it again, then firmly put it from him. "I must go now."

"So soon?" she protested. "Kenneth would love to see you, I'm sure."

He shook his head, faintly amused. "It will be enough for him that *you* saw me. Be well, Alyce, and know that I will always come if you are in need."

With that, he was gone, almost as if he had simply disappeared, though her mind knew that it was but one of the skills he had learned from the Anvillers: the art of stealth. She was smiling faintly as she made her way back to her husband's side and took his hand as she settled beside him.

"Is he well?" Kenneth asked softly, searching her eyes.

"Aye, he is. A most remarkable man is our Sir Sé."

A LITTLE later, when the wedding feast had ended and dusk was settling onto the hills around Cynfyn, the women of the bridal party sang the bride to her bridal chamber, led by Alyce, Vera, and the bride's sisters. The various aunties and the two sisters from Arc-en-Ciel brought up the rear.

Inside, the marriage bed had been readied by Alyce's maids, the bedding made fragrant with herbs, the silken coverlet turned back and the pillows strewn with rose petals. It was the castle's best chamber, lent to the happy couple by Alyce and Kenneth for the wedding night.

When Zoë had been divested of her bridal finery and dressed in a new undershift of fine white linen, her wheaten hair loose on her shoulders, the women tucked her up beneath the canopy embroidered with the arms of Lendour and all of them left her save for Alyce, as the strains of another bridal song drifted gradually closer, sung by male voices as the groom's friends sang him to his bride.

"They're coming," Zoë whispered, eyes wide as she reached out to take Alyce's hand. "Oh, Alyce, I am so happy. Everything has been so beautiful. Thank you so much!"

"'Tis no more than you deserve, sweet sister," Alyce murmured, leaning down to kiss her lightly on the forehead. "Now take your joy of one another, and forget about anything else."

Zoë only nodded, though impulsively she seized Alyce's hand again and briefly drew it nearer to press it to her cheek before releasing it. Alyce, as she withdrew to the door, blew her heart-sister another kiss, then set her hand on the door latch as the song outside finished and there came a soft rap at the door.

Wordlessly she opened it and stepped aside to admit the eager bridegroom, robed in red and accompanied by his father and Kenneth, who led Jovett to the marriage bed and helped him slide beneath the bedclothes beside his waiting bride. Behind them came the priest who had conducted the wedding ceremony, carrying a small silver bowl of water with a sprig of evergreen protruding from its edge. Beyond him, other men of the party stood in the corridor and into the stairwell, softly singing the final refrain of their song.

In the stillness that followed, the priest came into the

room to pronounce a final blessing and sprinkle bed, bride, and groom with holy water. He then withdrew with Kenneth and Sir Pedur as the men and women joined in a third bridal song, this one weaving the harmonies of the surrounding hills and gradually dying away as the singers dispersed.

Sweetly moved, Alyce slipped her hand into Kenneth's as they followed the others back into the hall and Alyce made certain of the accommodations for those staying the night within the castle walls. It seemed to take a very long time. Kenneth, when he had finally seen off the last of his eldest daughter's wedding guests and bidden his other two daughters a fond good night, drew Alyce with him back up the stairs and then—suddenly—into a shadowed alcove, where he enfolded her in a crushing kiss whose heat quickly stirred both of them to passion.

"Wife, I have just one question," he whispered, when they surfaced for air.

"And what question is that?" she managed to breathe. One of his hands was tracing gooseflesh along the base of her throat; the other hand slid down the small of her back to press her closer to his body, where his manhood stirred hard against her thigh.

"Just this," he murmured, nibbling at her earlobe. "Where is *our* chamber, now that you've given our old one to my daughter and her randy new husband?"

She started to giggle at that, but he quickly stifled the sound with his mouth, his kiss leaving her weak-kneed.

"Aye, my lord, don't do that, or we shall never get there!" she gasped.

"D'you think I'd take you right here, under the stair, hmmm?" he purred, not relenting as he nuzzled down the side of her neck and along the curve of her breast.

"Ah, my lord, if it were only that, I should not mind," she assured him breathlessly, "but the gown was expensive, and the floor is none too clean, and—and hard. Not to mention that some of our wedding guests might still be abroad."

"Then, *where is our room?*" he demanded, his embrace beginning to lift her right off her feet. "Show me, or I *will* take you right here!"

Chapter II

"And some there be, which shall have no memorial; who are perished, as though they had never been; and are become as though they had never been born; and their children after them."

—ECCLESIASTICUS 44:9

THE family guests who had come from afar to see Zoë wed lingered at Cynfyn for another fortnight, for they had arranged to travel back as far as Rhemuth with Kenneth and his household and guard escort, since it was very nearly time to return to court for the winter season. Though Earl Jared had remained in Culdi to attend to business, he had sent his own Kierney escort of a dozen knights with his wife and son and his aunt Nesta McLain, who was also Kenneth's sister-in-law. Included in that party were Kenneth's daughter Geill and her young husband, who was one of Jared's knights. Kenneth's two sisters, a single maid, and the two knights of their far more modest household had joined the party when it passed near Morganhall, and were traveling back in the same manner.

His daughter Alazais was to have returned to court with her father and stepmother to stay through Twelfth Night, but in the days since the wedding she had spent a great deal of time with the two sisters from Arc-en-Ciel, who also were to travel as far as Rhemuth with the Earl of Lendour's party. Two days before they were to leave for the capital, she announced that she would prefer to spend the next year studying at the convent school.

"Zoë and Alyce studied there, Papa," she said reasonably. "The finishing would do me good. I did enjoy being at court last season, but it was also . . . a bit intimidating. And I am not at all certain that I am yet ready to wed."

They were seated before the fireplace in the castle's best apartment, reclaimed from Zoë and Jovett after the wedding night. The weather had turned in the past week, and Alyce had mulled wine, anticipating a welcome evening of domestic bliss with her husband, but those plans had been suspended when Kenneth's youngest daughter came knocking at their door. Alaric was long abed in the room he now shared with Sir Llion.

Kenneth passed a cup of mulled wine to Alazais and took a sip of his own.

"You aren't thinking to take the veil, are you?"

"Good heavens, no, Papa! I do intend to marry. At least, I think I do. Just not yet."

"A year at Arc-en-Ciel *would* teach her some useful skills," Alyce pointed out, settling on a stool beside her husband. "It did me no harm, nor Zoë—and 'tis less than a day's ride from Rhemuth, or from Morganhall."

Smiling faintly, Kenneth motioned for Alazais to come and sit on his knee, setting aside his wine to slip an arm around her waist and hug her close.

" 'Tis well that I am no longer obliged to subsist on the income of a simple knight," he murmured, kissing the point of her shoulder. "Thank God that both your sisters are now safely married—and if you go to Arc-en-Ciel for a year, that delays having to provide another dowry right away."

"Papa!"

"But you shall go with my blessing, if that is what you want," he went on, smiling. "I am certain you will enjoy your time spent 'under the rainbow,' and only wish I could accompany you to see you enrolled." He kissed her again, then set her back on her feet. "But the king summons me, so I cannot. Perhaps Alyce would consent to go with you."

He looked at Alyce in question with a raised eyebrow, and she nodded.

"I should be delighted and honored," she said with a smile. "And I should like to take Alaric with me, if I may. I would love for Mother Judiana to meet him; and the sisters and the students will adore him. All of them dote on small children."

"That is easily enough arranged," Kenneth agreed. "Trevor and Llion will accompany you—and Melissa, of course, and a small escort to see all of you safely home. I'll take Xander with me." He picked up his wine again and took a deep draught. "Happily, this visit will be under far less stressful circumstances than applied during your last stay at Arc-en-Ciel—though I certainly cannot fault the arrangements made for our wedding night." His grin had an element of mischief. "It cannot have been the usual done thing for a convent."

"Indeed, not!" Alyce replied, suppressing her own smile. "But I'm certain we shall have a lovely visit—all of us," she added, laying a hand across one of Alazais's. "Your aunts will wish to attend, I expect. And perhaps we can prevail upon Geill and her husband to stop there as well—and Vera and young Duncan, of course, though it remains to be seen whether Arc-en-Ciel can withstand an invasion by *two* small boys."

"I seem to recall that they managed well enough with several young princes, when I came with the king to witness Sister Iris Jessilde's final profession," Kenneth said. "And they were similarly invaded for our wedding."

Alyce rolled her eyes and rose, ready to retire. "They have not reckoned with Alaric Morgan and Duncan McLain," she said archly, "but I'm certain we shall manage." She gave Alazais a fond smile. "You'd best go and tell the sisters that you have your father's permission to go with them, my dear—and inform Geill and Vera of the slight adjustment to our travel plans. If they're to join us, Vera will probably wish to send ahead to Culdi, alerting Jared that they'll be a few days later in arriving home."

* * *

THEIR leave-taking from Zoë and her new husband was tearful on the part of the women, and stoic on Kenneth's part, but the journey itself at least began according to plan. They numbered about thirty in all. Traveling directly westward along the Molling River valley, and taking accommodation along the way, they made excellent progress until they approached the village of Hallowdale, not far from the larger market town of Mollingford. There they stumbled upon the final moments of an incident often rumored to occur, but never witnessed firsthand by any in the company.

Sir Trevor was in the lead, riding beside a squire carrying Kenneth's banner of Lendour. Kenneth himself was farther back along the cavalcade, chatting with Sir Thomas, the senior of the Kierney knights. Xander and another of his own knights rode directly behind Trevor and the banner, with another knight and four men-at-arms interspersed among Jared's knights and the women. Alaric was perched in front of Llion, his preferred place of travel, and Geill's young husband, Sir Walter, had taken up little Duncan in front of him, leaving Alyce to ride with her stepdaughter and Vera, just ahead of Kenneth's aunt, his two sisters, and the two from Arc-en-Ciel, all of whom rode astride. The rest of the knights brought up the rear, with Kenneth among them.

They had seen the first smudges of smoke nearly an hour before they finally came upon its source. Those who bothered to speculate simply assumed that it was someone's house alight, or perhaps stubble being burned off in a distant field. They had seen the latter the afternoon before, all across the fields of a prosperous farm by which they passed.

But this was no burning of fields or a house fire. By the time they rode into the outskirts of Hallowdale, some of the knights shifting forward toward the head of the cavalcade, smoke was billowing upward in a dense black plume, oddly sluggish in the still air. As they approached the town square, a breeze from off the river suddenly gusted back a sickly-sweet whiff of burnt flesh.

In a stomach-churning flash of prescience, Alyce knew what lay in the square ahead, and what had caused her son suddenly to turn his face into Llion's chest with a whimper. It was an impression confirmed all too graphically by her own glimpse of a small crowd ahead, surrounding a blackened stake upthrust in their midst, which still gave off greasy tendrils of smoke. Her horrified glance back at Sister Iris Jessilde made it clear that the Deryni sister had also sensed the horror, and was drawing rein in shock. Simultaneously, Sir Trevor stood in his stirrups and raised a gloved fist in emphatic order to halt.

"What the devil?" Kenneth muttered under his breath, as he kneed his mount out of line and gigged it hard along the procession past Alyce and his son, the Kierney captain right behind him, to pull up sharply next to Trevor and the bannerbearer. Behind him, he could hear growing consternation as the others also began to realize what had happened here at Hallowdale. In the square ahead, several dozen men and women were turning to regard them warily, even defiantly. The smoking stake told its own story.

"Dear, sweet *Jesu*," Kenneth whispered, slowly signing himself with the Cross. And then, turning to the Kierney captain: "Sir Thomas, leave me half your men and turn the column around. Get the women and children out of here. Wait at the outskirts of the town. Trevor, Xander, men of Lendour, you're with me!"

As though the move had been rehearsed, Sir Thomas and half a dozen of the Kierney men turned the column and fell back, bearing the women and children and baggage animals with them as Trevor and Xander formed up the rest behind Kenneth and his Lendouri men-at-arms. As Kenneth pressed his mount forward, his hard gaze searched the upturned faces of the folk who reluctantly parted before him—defiant faces at first, but gradually giving way to his tight-jawed scrutiny, guiltily averting their eyes. Without being told, his knights fanned out behind him to line the eastern edge of the square, halting with hands on swordhilts.

With Trevor at his side and Xander and his banner-bearer following behind him, Kenneth slowly rode all the way around the remains of the pyre, the clip-clop of the horses' steel-shod hooves the only sound save for the faint jingle of harness and the whuffles of the waiting knights' tight-reined steeds. He forced himself to look closely at what was still chained to the stake in the center of the burned-out pyre, and realized that there had been two victims of this town's hatred. One, by its size, could only have been a child.

"Who is in charge here?" he demanded, completing his circuit and turning his horse to confront the villagers, searching the faces that now would not meet his gaze.

"I am the Earl of Lendour. I asked who was in charge," he repeated, his tone sharper now. "By what possible authority has this been done?"

Silence.

"You have usurped the king's High Justice. I want to know by what authority. Speak, or I shall have every man-jack of you flogged until you do—and the women as well, if I do not get an answer! You did not spare *them*"—he jerked a gloved hand toward the evidence before him—"and I shall not spare *you*, if I do not receive an immediate explanation."

"They was Deryni," said a sullen voice from the back of the crowd.

"What?" Kenneth turned his horse in the direction of the voice. "Who spoke?"

"They was Deryni," the voice repeated, as a bandy-legged man with an enormous beard moved clear of the others and gazed up at him defiantly. "And we carried out *God's* justice. The Deryni be an accursed race, an' those transgressed against His law."

He gestured toward the pyre and spat, an eloquent gesture of contempt. Aghast, Kenneth kneed his horse closer to stare down at the man, aware of Trevor half a horse-length behind.

"And who decided that God's law had been transgressed?" he demanded. "Tell me! Who?"

"Th' priests," another man sneered. "Who d'ye think? Th' bishop's preachers come last week, an' told us what to look for. They was Deryni, all right," he said belligerently, jutting his chin in the direction of the stakes.

For a moment Kenneth merely sat there, numb with shock, trying to fathom the kind of hatred that could have made good men commit such evil. The reference to bishops' preachers raised strong suspicions about who might have been behind this latest incident of hatred against Deryni—there had long been rumors that Bishop Oliver de Nore's followers sometimes burned Deryni in the region—but he had never thought to come across an incident firsthand. Being married to a Deryni wife, and one for whom de Nore held a particular hatred, he dared not undertake an immediate investigation of wayward preachers on his own, or challenge their bishop, but he would certainly report this to the king.

"I cannot accept that a loving God had this in mind for even the most notorious sinners," he finally said coldly, sweeping them with his hard gaze.

"The holy Scriptures say that sinners will burn in hell," a new speaker made bold to say.

"Perhaps after the Final Judgement!" Kenneth snapped. "But it was not your place to pronounce that judgement, nor to administer punishment."

"That isn't what the priest said!" another voice shouted.

"What?"

"We knew what to do," the first man sneered. "The woman thought she was better'n us, an' conjured up poisons an' cast spells on innocent folk, an' worked her evil magic so her man could get what was nay his! We dealt wi' him, too." His sly glance over his shoulder drew Kenneth's attention to the body hanging from an upper window of a nearby building, and his jaw dropped.

"And what of the child?" he demanded. *"What of the innocent child?"*

"She were a bad seed! An' how could she be otherwise, with twa sich parents?" one of the women blurted. "Now she canna follow her mam's evil example."

Now well and truly disgusted, Kenneth briefly closed

his eyes, schooling himself to forbearance—for he knew how close he was to snapping—that he must not mete out judgement on his own, in the heat of his anger and outrage, without taking more dispassionate counsel.

"You have done a terrible, wicked thing," he finally said, his voice low and deadly. "All of you will answer to God for it in the Hereafter, and to the king in this life—for be certain that I *shall* report to him what I have seen. In the meantime, you will take what is left of those wretched souls and give them decent burial."

"Respectfully, we will *not*, my lord," said an educated voice he had not heard before, from off to the left.

Kenneth swiveled in his saddle to search out the new speaker: a tall, gangly individual in a mud-colored monk's robe, sharp eyes as black as coal.

"You refuse to do this? You, a cleric? Even the Church does not deny decent burial to Deryni."

"These were not decent Deryni," another man said. "We will not do it."

"And if you force them to do it," said the monk, "they will simply dig up the remains after you have gone, and throw them in the river."

Kenneth was not normally a man to admit defeat, but he knew when he was fighting a battle that could not be won, at least for now.

"Very well," he said quietly. "It seems I cannot keep you from your folly. But know that the matter does not end here. Look to your souls, people of Hallowdale, for your God certainly shall do so. And your king shall certainly know of this as well."

With that, he wheeled his horse around and rode out of that place, Trevor and his escort falling in behind him.

Chapter 12

"There is an evil which I have seen under the sun."

—ECCLESIASTES 10:5

THE rest of their journey was much subdued. The men rode tight-jawed and silent, for what they had seen was a flagrant usurpation of the king's law, whatever personal feelings one might entertain concerning Deryni. For the Lendour men, who served a Deryni lady, the incident hit far too close to home. They gave Hallowdale a wide berth, cutting far to the south, and camped that night in a field, where the reek of burnt flesh did not befoul the air.

No one had much appetite that night. The men muttered among themselves around their campfires, even the most hardened of them shaken by what they had seen. The women had wept most of the way to the campsite, and many cried themselves to sleep that night. Alaric and Duncan were yet too young to understand what had happened, though Alaric had caught some of the emotions; but both were aware of the distress of the adults around them—so much so, that Alyce put both children to sleep in the arms of their knightly protectors, and that night blurred their memories of the experience. But her own memories she could not blur.

The next day was better, but something of the shock lingered as they set out again. Kenneth refused to discuss what had happened, and for a while considered taking Alaric back to Rhemuth with him instead of letting Alyce take him on to Arc-en-Ciel.

"I'm not even certain I should let *you* go, Alyce," he told her, the last night before they were to head in opposite directions, she toward the abbey school with Alazais and the other women and he on to Rhemuth. "And I don't know that I can bear to risk Alaric as well. He is my only son, the son I thought I never should have. If you and he were to meet something like what happened in Hallowdale on the road . . ."

She looked away, troubled. "I didn't tell you, at the time, how very near I came to riding back to join you, after you'd sent the men to take us to safety. But if I had, I honestly do not know what I might have done."

They were in the privacy of a tiny room at an inn on the road approaching Rhemuth from the east, and she opened one hand to a brightly glowing ball of greenish light, which hovered just above her palm. She lifted it slightly and watched it flare higher, to a fiercely burning column of fire that cast a greenish glow on both their faces.

"I was so angry, Kenneth. It would have been so very easy to unleash *this* on those people—and it would have felt *so* good, because they surely deserved to die for what they did, and allowed to be done."

She sighed deeply and closed her eyes, the column of fire dying down to a mere sphere of handfire that she quickly quenched in a closed fist.

"That would have been wrong, of course. It would have made me no better than they, except that I would have had more strength, a power they could not hope to understand or endure. Might does not make right. And it would have reinforced what they say about Deryni in the first place: that we have these terrible powers that we long to unleash against innocent humans—though those certainly were *not* innocent." She shook her head and lowered her fist, made it relax, open and empty, in her lap. "Do you really think that the king will be able to exact justice for the innocents of Hallowdale?"

Kenneth shook his head doubtfully. "I don't know. If the incident was stirred up by itinerant preachers, it would be asking him to take on the religious hierarchy. He did that before for us—for you—and he ended up having to back down. This time—I don't know. But I'm very glad that you didn't do what you wanted to do."

She sighed. "You're right—and I suppose I am glad as well. It only would have made matters worse for my people." She glanced at him sidelong. "I still should like to take Alaric with me to Arc-en-Ciel. It's only less than a day's ride outside Rhemuth; we would join you in three days. You can send as many men with us as you like—and we would have Jared's men as well."

"You would only have them on the way *to* Arc-en-Ciel," Kenneth pointed out sourly. "You'd still have to return to Rhemuth."

"But it's the major route north," Alyce countered, "and it's well traveled at this time of year. I do so want Mother Judiana to meet Alaric. And for Zaizie's sake, I cannot *not* go. She would be so disappointed."

She paused, then laid a hand gently on his wrist. "Darling, if you truly fear for our safety, that close to Rhemuth, you could send more soldiers to meet us at Arc-en-Ciel and escort us back to you. You could even come yourself, after you've reported to the king."

He chuckled aloud at that, aware that he was probably over-reacting, and enfolded her in his arms, pressing his lips to her forehead. But in the end, he agreed to let her go.

He took only Xander with him when they reached the northward road the following day, he to continue south into the city and the women to make their way to Arc-en-Ciel. Alazais wept as she parted from her father, finally understanding the tension under which he and Alyce had lived for all their marriage, and Alyce for most of her life. Alyce rode close beside her, with Llion and Alaric to her other side and Trevor at her back, all of them embedded within the Kierney party. In light of her previous night's conversation with

Kenneth, she found herself worried anew for the safety of her son, and was half surprised that Kenneth had even allowed them to come.

But the spirits of everyone in the party began to lift as they headed north toward Arc-en-Ciel, skirting along the river, spirits cheered by Sisters Iris Cerys and Iris Jessilde, who were determined that Alazais' welcome should not be marred. By the time they caught their first glimpse of the abbey walls, they were riding far less fearfully. Alyce, in particular, put on a cheerful face for the benefit of her youngest stepdaughter.

"It looked very different when my sister and I first came here," she told Alazais, as the rainbow arch of the abbey's gatehouse came into sight. "For one thing, it was winter—and we didn't want to come. Our father had remarried a few weeks before, and our new stepmama did not care for the competition of two nubile stepdaughters. She wasn't particularly happy that our father already had a son and heir, either, but she was certainly determined to remedy *that*, if she could. Meanwhile, the two of *us* were to be packed off to a convent.

"Fortunately, the sisters and the other students immediately made us feel welcome. It was far more of a home than we would have had at our father's court, under Rosmerta's gimlet eye."

Alazais smiled for the first time since Hallowdale. "I remember Zoë's first letters back to Morganhall, after she met you," she said. "I was only seven or eight, but it was clear, even then, that she'd found a kindred spirit. Who would have dreamed where it would all lead?"

"Who, indeed?" Alyce agreed.

The approach to Arc-en-Ciel was much the same as Alyce remembered, other than the time of year. Sisters Iris Cerys and Iris Jessilde and two of Jared's knights had ridden on ahead half an hour before to alert the inhabitants of their approach. The gate beneath the rainbow arch was thrown wide open, and the sister waiting just inside was Iris Rose, a novice when Alyce first had come to Arc-en-Ciel with her sister. Now she wore the rainbow-edged blue veil of a fully vowed sister, and was fairly jumping up and down with excitement as Iris Cerys joined her from within. Iris Jessilde was nowhere to be seen.

"Lady Alyce!" Iris Rose cried. "Welcome back to Arc-en-Ciel! Is it true that you have brought us a new student? Oh, enter in Our Lady's grace!" she added, suddenly remembering the formal words of welcome. "Mother Abbess will be with you shortly."

Alyce smiled as she ducked her head to ride through the abbey gate, Alazais following nervously behind her and Llion following with Alaric, at the beckoning gesture of Iris Cerys. The other women also entered, and Sir Walter with Duncan, but when the rest of the men made as if to stay outside, Iris Rose quickly motioned for them to enter as well.

"Reverend Mother has given her permission," she told Trevor, who clearly was in charge, at least of Alyce and her son. "We shall have to find overnight accommodation in the village for the men, but Sister Iris Jessilde has told us of the trouble you had on the way here, and has given good report of you. Please, please, enter. Your men may wait in the stable yard while we decide what to do."

Alyce, meanwhile, had drawn rein in the center of the courtyard before the chapel doors, where Iris Jessilde was accompanying Mother Iris Judiana down the chapel steps. Llion had dismounted and handed Alaric down to Xander, and came to hand Alyce down as well, going then to assist Alazais from her mount. Alyce took her son's hand in hers and smoothed back the shock of white-blond hair before slipping her other arm through that of her stepdaughter. She was smiling as she led the pair of them before the abbess.

"Dearest daughter. Alyce," said Iris Judiana, opening her arms in welcome. "I see that you have come back to us a mother—and of a lovely boy!" she added, eyeing young Alaric in approval.

"And of a lovely stepdaughter," Alyce replied, as she came forward to kiss the abbess' hand, and then allowed herself to be embraced. "This is Lord Kenneth's daughter Alazais," she said, as Alazais gave a graceful curtsy, "and this is our son, Alaric."

"Both are very welcome," Iris Judiana said warmly. She gave Alazais her hand to kiss, then lightly touched a hand to Alaric's fair head. "Iris Jessilde tells me that Lady Alazais wishes to be enrolled under the rainbow. If she is half the student as you and Lady Zoë, she will be a stunning asset to our student body."

Alazais gave another curtsy, blushing faintly.

"I have also been told of your distressing experience on the road from Cynfyn," Iris Judiana continued on a more sober note. "I shall wish to hear more of it, of course, but perhaps we should first see to the business that brought you here." She turned to Iris Cerys and Iris Jessilde. "Will you see to the robing of our newest student, Sisters? And I believe that Iris Rose has set in train the arrangements for overnight accommodation for your men. The other ladies, of course, will lodge here in the guest quarters. Perhaps Alyce will be so good as to present them to me."

There ensued a flurry of activity in which Alazais was whisked off to robe, Llion was dispatched to coordinate the arrangements for the men, and Alyce presented the ladies of the party.

"Mother, these are some of the remarkable women of my husband's family," Alyce said as the women made their way to the foot of the chapel steps to kiss the abbess' hand in turn. "This is my husband's middle daughter, Geill, and these are his sisters, Delphine Morgan and Lady Claara Winslow, and his first wife's sister, Lady Nesta McLain, who is also sister to the Duke of Cassan—and all of them are aunts to Alazais. And this is Countess Vera McLain, the wife of Lady Nesta's nephew Jared, Duke Andrew's heir—and their son, Duncan. All of them were good enough to travel all the way to Cynfyn for Zoë's wedding, and to interrupt their journey home to share this special day with Alazais—though I must warn you that young Duncan and my Alaric together can be a handful."

"Another handsome boy," Iris Judiana said with a smile, ruffling Duncan's hair. "You are, all of you, most welcome—and the gentlemen are welcome to attend the enrollment ceremony as well, if they wish—especially the two knights charged with the supervision of the children. Sir Llion and Sir Walter, is it?" she asked, glancing to Iris Cerys for confirmation. "Yes. I hope you will not be disappointed if our ceremonial seems a little ragged today. We had little time to prepare, as you know."

"We have all heard tell of the beauty of Notre Dame d'Arc-en-Ciel, Mother Abbess," said Lady Nesta, speaking for all of them. "And we are delighted to be present when Kenneth's dear Alazais is received under the rainbow. I myself studied here, many years ago."

"Did you, indeed?" said Mother Judiana. "We must speak of that later, over supper. But for now, we shall gather in the chapel in an hour's time, after you have been shown to your rooms and given opportunity to freshen yourselves somewhat from your journey."

ALYCE soon discovered that presenting a new student was somewhat different from being one, or from being a student and watching others being received. After briefly repairing to the room assigned for her use—the same one she and Kenneth had shared on their wedding night, four years before, and shared this time with Vera and their respective sons—she left Alaric in Vera's charge and went to the robing room, where Iris Cerys and Iris Jessilde had finished dressing Alazais in the school habit, the same sky-blue as worn by the sisters, but without the wimple and veil. As when Alyce and Marie had been received under the rainbow, what now seemed so long ago, the sisters had braided Alazais's flaxen tresses in the single plait worn by all students of the house and set a wreath of flowers on her head: a quickly woven garland of late summer wildflowers rather than the wreath of roses Zoë had worn to her wedding or the dried winter wreaths Alyce and Marie had worn at their own reception.

"I'm afraid all the roses were too far blown to use," Iris Cerys said, looking up from the rainbow-woven cincture she was tying at Alazais's waist. "But the wildflowers are nearly as pretty."

Iris Jessilde nodded her agreement as she shook out folds

of the blue gown's long skirt. The undergown worn in summer was of white linen rather than the white wool worn in winter. Alazais brushed her fingertips along the fall of pale blue sleeve and looked up shyly at her stepmother.

"How do I look?" she murmured.

"You look beautiful, darling," Alyce said, coming to give her a gentle hug—carefully, lest she crush the floral wreath.

Very soon they were following the two sisters along the cloister walk to the side door of the chapel, under its rainbow-painted arch and into the brilliance of the white marble chapel, where its rose windows cast broad swaths of rainbow-colored light across the interior.

A sweet song of welcome met their arrival—the *Salve Regina*, as Alyce now knew—its subtle harmonies and a breath of incense and honey-sweet beeswax candles enfolding them in peace as they trod the rainbow-striped carpet runner laid along the center aisle. Beyond the choir lay the high altar, ablaze with votive lights shielded with glass in all the colors of the rainbow. Before it, Mother Iris Judiana sat on a backless stool, flanked by two senior sisters.

Passing into the choir, between the ranks of center-facing choir stalls, they came at last to the foot of the altar steps, where Mother Iris Judiana had risen to receive them. She gave a graceful nod in response to the curtsies of the two younger women, then held out her arms in welcome to Alyce, who accepted her brief embrace and then stepped back to present the new arrival, as Lady Jessamy MacAthan had presented her and Marie so long ago.

"Mother Iris Judiana, I have the honor to present my stepdaughter, the Lady Alazais Morgan, youngest daughter of the Earl of Lendour. She has asked that she be received under the rainbow, so that she may learn the gentle arts suitable to her rank. Her father has given his permission and his blessing, as do I."

"I am most pleased to receive her, dear Alyce," Iris Judiana said, as she extended her hands to Alazais. "May she be a credit to this house and may she cleave cheerfully to its discipline. Let her now be enrolled under the favor and protection of Our Lady of the Rainbow, signifying the same by her signature in the great book of our house."

So saying, she gestured toward a small table to the right of the choir, where two of the school's younger girls stood holding a rainbow-striped canopy above an open book. Sister Iris Rose stood behind the table with a quill pen and an inkwell, her brown eyes crinkling with good humor as they approached.

"Be welcome under the rainbow, Alazais," she said, with a curtsy to the pair of them as Alyce led her stepdaughter before the book. The two girls holding the canopy were students, by their dress, with simple rainbow fillets binding plain white veils across their brows.

Smiling, Alyce nodded for Alazais to take the pen, remembering how she had hesitated to sign when first she came, for both she and her sister had feared that they might be coerced into taking unintended religious vows. Iris Rose must have remembered that day, for she smiled at Alyce as Alazais carefully signed her name. When the signing was completed, Iris Rose sanded the signature with pounce to stop it smudging, then carefully turned the signed pages back to where a slip of parchment marked a place much earlier in the volume.

"Here is where your sister signed, when *she* first came to us," she said to Alazais, indicating Zoë's signature. She then turned forward several pages, to another marker. "And here are the names of Alyce and her sister."

Alyce's breath caught as she read the shaky signature: *Marie Stephania de Corwyn,* and she smiled faintly as she let her fingertips trace over the line.

"Ah, dear Zaizie, you know so much more than *we* did, when we first came here," she murmured. "We were afraid we might never be allowed to leave, that we would be forced to take the veil, locked away forever behind cloister walls. How wrong we were. It was probably the best thing that ever happened to us—though your father, I think, was probably the best thing ever to happen to *me*. And Alaric, of course."

With a little sob, Alazais embraced her stepmother in a

fierce gesture of genuine affection, tears in her eyes, then composed herself and stood tall at Alyce's side, nodding to Iris Rose.

"Thank you, Sister," she murmured, as Alyce also murmured her thanks.

Then they were moving back before the altar, the canopy accompanying them, where Mother Iris Judiana bade Alazais to kneel, blessing her with holy water sprinkled from a sprig of fragrant pine, then signaling for two more waiting girls to bring a veil very like those worn by the canopy-bearers.

"Let this daughter be veiled according to the custom of this house," she said, as Alyce removed the wreath of wildflowers and the two veil-bearers set the veil in place, the abbess herself binding it across the brow with the rainbow-plaited fillet.

After that, Mother Iris Judiana raised Alazais to her feet, kissed her on both cheeks, and herself conveyed the new student to the stall that henceforth would be her place in choir. Then, after a few general words of welcome, both to the new girl and the old, she dismissed the community to retire to the refectory, where a simple supper awaited students, sisters, and guests alike.

By then, it was far later than the long summer twilight would have suggested, such that the weary travelers soon retired to the rooms assigned them, and Alazais to meet her new schoolmates and be introduced to the girl chosen to share a room with her during her time at Arc-en-Ciel. All the rest of the Morgan relatives would leave to continue their journeys home the next morning, so Alyce availed herself of one last opportunity to spend some private time with her secret sister.

"This has been a very special time for me, despite what happened at Hallowdale," Alyce murmured, climbing into the bed beside Vera when they had both seen their sons safely asleep at the other end of the room. She glanced around at the room, still light enough to see in the twilight, then snuggled closer to her sister.

"Did you remember that this was my bridal chamber,

when Kenneth and I were wed?" she said with a sly grin in Vera's direction. "This may or may not be the actual marriage bed, but that was a time of happiness that I shall never forget."

Vera smiled and settled the bedclothes closer under her chin, for the temperature was falling, here in the foothills north of Rhemuth. "Marriage does have much to recommend it, doesn't it?" she agreed. "I take it that you are hoping for another child."

Alyce turned onto her back to stare at the ceiling overhead, suddenly sobered. "I think I may have lost one earlier this year, about the time you lost yours."

"What?" Vera sat up to stare at her sister.

"Please don't be angry. I didn't tell you because you were already grieving, and I wasn't entirely certain I had actually conceived. But we mean to make it happen," she said casually, "and the trying *is* agreeable."

"Yes, it is, isn't it?" Vera agreed. Her impish smile reminded Alyce of the delicious late-night conversations that she, Vera, Marie, and Zoë had shared when all of them were unwed maidens, making their first tentative forays into the uncharted waters of their own womanhood. In particular, Alyce found herself remembering Marie—and Sé, who had loved her.

"Did I tell you that Sé made a brief appearance at the wedding?" she asked, turning her head to look at her sister.

"At Zoë's wedding?" Vera looked surprised. "*Did* he? I never saw him. What did he say? How did he look?"

Remembering, Alyce turned her face once again toward the ceiling.

"Leaner than when we last saw him, a bit more careworn. He's taken his final vows with the Anvillers, Vera. He bears the marks. It was a very drastic thing to do, but somehow I think he made the right decision. He was shattered after Marie's death, but now he seems whole again."

Vera went very still, also gazing up at the ceiling. "Then, it appears that he found a genuine vocation," she murmured. "He's a very special man, Alyce. I hope you know that."

"Oh, I do know," she replied. "Even Kenneth recognizes it. If anything were ever to happen to him, I know that Sé would be there if I needed him. And he would be there for Alaric. That knowledge is comforting."

"Indeed." Vera yawned. "Dear me. I suppose we'd better get some sleep. The boys will wake at first light, which comes early. And we must be in the saddle right after morning Mass. Will you go back to Rhemuth tomorrow?"

Alyce shook her head, also yawning. "We shall stay another night, so that I can visit with Mother Judiana. I have much to tell her." She smiled fondly. "She was very like a mother to Marie and me, while we were here. I—need to tell her about what we saw on the road . . . and what I very nearly did."

At Vera's questioning glance in her direction, Alyce took her sister's hand and used the physical link to share her horror and outrage, and how she had longed to lash out with her power and destroy those who had murdered the three hapless Deryni at Hallowdale.

"It would have been very wrong, though," she said, reverting to audible speech. "I could have undone whatever progress our race has made in the past several decades."

"That's very true; you could have," Vera replied briskly. "But you didn't. Granted, you thought about it—but you didn't do it. You needn't ask forgiveness merely for thinking. Mother Judiana surely will tell you that."

Alyce shrugged and allowed herself a faint smile. "I suppose I just want to reassure myself that someone who is genuinely good, who wasn't there, understands my horror."

"Dear Alyce, any sensible person with a jot of compassion in their soul would have been horrified," Vera said sleepily. "It wasn't even human, what those villagers did to those people—whether or not they were Deryni, and whether or not they actually did anything wrong besides *be* Deryni. And I don't think any Deryni could do that to another living creature. We'd hear the anguish in our minds. In time, it would drive us mad. I only hope Kenneth can persuade the king to take action, make a serious inquiry. I certainly intend to tell Jared, when I get back to Culdi."

"Do such things happen in Kierney or Cassan?" Alyce asked.

"Perhaps occasionally," Vera admitted, "though I've never heard of such a case. But Deryni are better tolerated there. Not officially, but the mountain folk are said to have the Second Sight, which may not be all that different from some Deryni powers. Anyway, that seems to make the differences less obvious." Her sigh turned into another yawn. "Your big problem in central Gwynedd is some of those bishops, though. What was the name of that one who gave you so much trouble, just before you married Kenneth?"

"Oliver de Nore," Alyce said coldly. "I heard that he was named Auxiliary Bishop of Nyford over the summer, and it's likely that he'll be given a diocese of his own within the next few years. Both the archbishops like him, as do several of the other diocesan bishops—and that counts for a lot, when it comes time to fill vacancies."

"A pity," Vera said, yawning again. "You'd think they'd see right through him . . . ." She sighed. "But I don't believe we shall resolve this tonight, dear Alyce. I *must* get some sleep. I return to my dear Jared in the morning. Several days from now, at any rate. I do love you, dearest sister."

"And I, you," Alyce murmured, patting her sister's hand, though she did not drift off until long after Vera's breathing had shifted to that of deep slumber.

Chapter 13

"Rejoice not over thy greatest enemy being dead, but remember that we die all."

—ECCLESIASTICUS 8:7

SOME miles south, in the king's private withdrawing room in Rhemuth Castle, the candles burned far later as Kenneth and the king also discussed the very troublesome Bishop Oliver de Nore. Kenneth had briefed the king for several hours immediately after his return, recounting everything he could remember of the encounter at Hallowdale. Sir Xander had also been present for the first part of the briefing, but when he could offer nothing additional, Donal had dismissed him—and then had stormed around the confines of the chamber like a caged lion, swearing fluently and occasionally kicking chair legs or remnants of kindling on the hearth.

"So, will you do something about it?" Kenneth asked, when the king had finally wound down from his initial tirade and asked him to retell the story one more time, to be certain he had all the facts straight.

Donal stiffened, leaning on a windowsill to gaze outside at the lowering twilight, then let out a long breath in a sigh of frustrated defeat.

"There frankly isn't much I *can* do," he admitted reluctantly. "Unfortunately, de Nore is the archbishops' business. He is under their authority, and they are practically a law unto themselves, when it comes to matters of faith."

"Sire—"

"No, listen to me. You saw how they reacted after that whole miserable situation surrounding Krispin's murder. God knows, you and Alyce were a part of it. She was, at any rate. It isn't often that a king has to grovel before a pack of priests, but I groveled. It was the only way to get the Interdict lifted, because I *did* kill one of their own—or rather, I ordered him killed; it's much the same thing, when you're a king. I still was responsible, even if I didn't execute him with my own hand."

"It is part of a king's right and duty to exercise the High Justice, Sire," Kenneth said stiffly. "God's law allows for that. In fact, sometimes God's law *requires* that, if a king is to do his duty to his people. That duty is assumed when the archbishop anoints the new king with holy chrism, confirming his right and duty to rule with justice. And then the king lays his consecrated hand upon the sacred Scriptures and swears an oath to do just that, in justice and honor."

"I know that, dammit!"

"I know that you know it, Sire. I was there when you swore that oath, all those years ago, and I know that you meant and mean to honor it. But those men in Hallowdale—and women, God help them!—took the law into their own hands. They took it upon themselves to act as judge, jury, and executioners, and we shall never know whether their victims really were Deryni, or had really done anything untoward, or had done *anything* besides being in the wrong place at the wrong time. Where is the justice in that, Sire? Where is your duty to protect and defend your people, even against bishops, who are also your subjects?"

THEY were questions with no easy answers, given the circumstances of the incident at Hallowdale. Kenneth's more official report, somewhat cooler for having slept on it, quickly polarized opinions in the crown council, when they learned of it the next day. Especially summoned to the meeting was the Archbishop of Rhemuth, who did not always attend; but when confronted regarding the probable role of one of his bishops, Archbishop William would only defend Oliver de Nore and assert that his brother bishop could not be held responsible for how uneducated peasants interpreted the sermons preached by his circuit priests.

Kenneth, for his part, would not back down from what he had witnessed with his own eyes; and Sir Trevor as well, long in the king's confidence despite his youth, corroborated the accounts of Kenneth and Xander, when he returned to Rhemuth a few days later with Alyce and Alaric and the rest of Kenneth's household.

The matter clearly was not ended. In an effort to clarify exactly what had occurred, and who was responsible, the king did send a commission of inquiry to Hallowdale early in November, but those interviewed stuck doggedly to their assertion that those burned had been discovered to be notorious Deryni, well deserving of their fate, and the villagers had only been following the exhortations of a traveling preacher.

The king had even taken the precaution of sending along Sir Morian du Joux, the Deryni brother of the woman who had borne the ill-fated Krispin. Summoned to the capital from his usual assignment at the court of the royal governor of Meara, and proven loyal through service to the king on numerous occasions in the field of battle, Morian was little known east of Rhemuth, and had been instructed merely to observe the questioning of the villagers of Hallowdale, employing his powers only to detect lies. Kenneth was not permitted to accompany him, for the council thought him too biased, but the king did send Duke Richard, who alone of the commission was aware of Morian's unique talents—and the danger he faced, if the local folk should realize what he was, in that emotionally charged atmosphere.

But Morian was never detected, and the testimonies appeared to have been truthful, as far as they went, given the villagers' rife superstition, misinformation, and lack of sophistication. By all the evidence available, both Richard and Morian concluded that the man and woman executed by the villagers probably had, indeed, been Deryni, even if the exact nature of their alleged crimes could not be determined. (No one would comment on the alleged execution of a child, and Morian had been forbidden to press the issue.) The role of the preacher and even his exact identity remained unclear, and the man had moved on, in any case. Which left the inquiry largely where it had begun.

It was all mostly over by early December. After due reflection on the results of the inquiry, and another meeting with Archbishop William, attended by Duke Richard as well, the king reluctantly was obliged to put the matter aside—though he did promise Kenneth and Alyce privately that if further such incidents came to his attention, he would take a more aggressive stance. It was not what Kenneth had hoped, but he, too, had to put the matter aside, as king and council settled back into the routine of governing through the short days and long nights of winter. The subject of Hallowdale still arose occasionally—though more for the offense against the king's authority than the fate of the victims. But gradually the ministers' energies shifted back to a more comfortable and commonplace succession of advisory meetings with the king, mild court intrigues, and the occasional serious discussion of trade treaties and border disputes. All of this was punctuated by bouts of arms practice moved into the great hall, as the weather worsened, the occasional hunt, and many a less formal discussion before the fires in the great hall, of an evening after dinner. An ongoing topic of happier speculation was the celebration being planned for the following June, to mark Prince Brion's coming of age.

The king's other children were also a focus for Alyce's attention in those months leading into Advent, and especially the ones nearer Alaric's age. After returning from Arc-en-Ciel, Alyce had fallen back into her role as wife and mother, advisor to her husband concerning Lendour and Corwyn—and thereby, advisor to the king regarding these regions—and companion to the queen. She had also obtained permission to enroll Alaric for the schooling given the royal princes and princesses and the children of the queen's other ladies.

Despite all of this, Alyce found those months of waning autumn and early winter bleak and lonely, for Kenneth had been all but obsessed by his quest for justice in Hallowdale. She did receive frequent letters from Zoë, assuring her of her happiness and the fulfillment she felt, working at Jovett's side—and late in November, joyful news of Zoë's first pregnancy—but the letters only made Alyce feel the absence of her heart-sister more keenly, even though she and the queen soon picked up the former intimacy of their friendship and became nearly inseparable. It helped, but she still missed Zoë and the companionship they had shared for so many years—and Vera, whose kinship she must never allow to be discovered. Even Kenneth did not know.

It was as mother to a bright and active young son that she found her greatest fulfillment, as he became less and less her baby and more and more a person. Alaric was quick and facile, a mannerly child, and easily kept up with other boys half again his age. Prince Brion and his brother Nigel were enough older than Alaric that they paid him little mind, save to include him in the teasing they gave their younger brother and their sisters, but Alaric and all the younger children interacted well. He longed to begin his page's training, though he was yet too young for that, but he relished the lessons he shared with the royal princes and the sons of some of the favored courtiers. All the royal children were thriving, with the youngest now three years old—a matter of some concern to the queen, for there had been no royal pregnancy since Jathan.

The prospect of a brother or sister for Alaric was much on his parents' minds as well, as the nights grew longer and the weather worsened, for Alaric had also turned three, a week before Prince Jathan, and Alyce had yet to conceive again. Periodic reports on the progress of Zoë's pregnancy only underlined Alyce's own failure, and she worried that she had, indeed, miscarried earlier in the year; but she suspected that Kenneth's ongoing fervor over the incident at Hallowdale was also taking its toll.

"You must let it go, my darling," she told him one wintry night early in December. "You must accept that there are some things that you simply cannot change, however much your honor cries out for justice. We Deryni have long been aware of this inequity. Come; we shall light a candle for those unfortunate victims, and then let them rest in peace, for they surely are in the bosom of God's love."

He agreed to make the gesture, and went with her hand in hand down drafty and deserted corridors to the chapel royal in fleece-lined slippers and heavy night robes bundled over nightshirts and sleeping shifts, there to light a solitary candle against the darkness and weep together by its light, holding one another against the grief and the fear, for it could have been Alyce burnt at the stake in that distant village, or another like it—or even in the cathedral square of Rhemuth itself, if she were ever discovered in flagrant transgression against the narrow strictures set by the bishops against those of her kind.

Later when they had returned to their chamber, their urgent lovemaking was silent and even violent, as if Kenneth tried, by sheer force of will and flesh, to imbue his wife with something of his fierce protection and strength, though he knew that, if the unthinkable occurred, he might not be able to protect her as he had done before their marriage.

It was a sober winding-down of what had been a year punctuated both by joy and by sorrow. Alyce had hoped that she might have conceived on that night, to cancel out some of the sorrow with hope and new life, but the next weeks of waiting did not prove it so. As Advent counted down to the eve of Christmas, the weather grew increasingly foul, and it became clear that even the rebirth of the Light would be cloaked in gloom.

The king and his family kept the feast of Christmas quietly that year, as befitted the religious aspect of the season, but a ferocious ice storm during the night of Christmas itself curtailed the appearance of the royal family at the cathedral the next morning for the traditional St. Stephen's Day Mass and distribution of royal largesse afterward. It was a far cry from that other St. Stephen's Day when Kenneth Morgan had finally summoned the courage to make his proposal of marriage to Alyce de Corwyn, but the two of them made a virtue of the weather as an excuse to keep mostly to their apartments that day, while Llion amused their son.

On the day following, the Feast of Holy Innocents, the weather improved enough—barely—for the queen and her ladies to venture down to the cathedral at midday with the delayed largesse, for many of the people of the city depended on this bounty from the royal coffers to survive the winter. A resolute Prince Brion assisted his mother and her ladies in distributing the gifts of food and silver pennies from the cathedral steps, well wrapped up against the weather in fur-lined hat and cloak and stout boots, but the younger children they left in the care of those responsible for their supervision when parents could not be around.

For Alaric, that meant stalking the castle halls with the younger princes and several of the junior squires, overseen by Sir Llion. The king had already rescheduled his customary petitioners' court until the morning of Twelfth Night, though he still would hold it on the steps of the cathedral, and had planned a day's hunting while the queen carried out her royal duties; but he and his party returned after only a few hours, wet and half-frozen and without success in the field.

The weather deteriorated steadily in the week leading up to Twelfth Night Court, such that it became clear that many of those normally expected would not be able to complete the winter journey to Rhemuth. On the eve of Epiphany, however, an exhausted and half-frozen rider arrived from Coroth with news that soon would dominate nearly every conversation within the walls of Rhemuth Castle.

"An urgent dispatch from the Corwyn regents, Sire," the messenger blurted out, even as he half-collapsed to one knee before the startled king and extended a sealed dispatch in a gloved hand that shook from cold and fatigue. It was Sir Robert of Tendal, Kenneth realized, as the young man pulled off his fur-lined cap, son of the Chancellor of Corwyn. "The Crown Prince of Torenth is dead!"

"Prince Nimur? He's dead?" Donal repeated, shocked. He and Richard and Kenneth and a few of his other closest advisors had been finalizing the schedule for the next day's court ceremonials around a table set before the fire in the king's withdrawing room, fortified by steaming cups of mulled wine. At Sir Robert's bald announcement, however, every face had turned first toward the gasping newcomer, then toward the king, mouths agape.

"Tell me what you know," Donal ordered, at the same time breaking the seal and unfolding the missive. "Richard, pour him some wine, and someone give him a seat closer to the fire."

Still breathing heavily, numbly fumbling his way to the stool that Jiri Redfearn quickly vacated, Sir Robert peeled off his sodden gloves and gratefully accepted the mulled wine that Duke Richard set between his hands, nodding his thanks as Kenneth removed his own cloak and draped it close around the man's shoulders.

"I know very little beyond what is in the letter, Sire," Sir Robert said, after an audible gulp of the warm wine, as the king scanned the letter. "The Hort of Orsal sent what word we have. His envoy said that rumors had reached the Orsal's court midway through December that the prince was ill. Given the vague nature of the report, and the state of the weather at this time of year, that alone did not seem to justify sending urgent word to Coroth or to you." He paused to fortify himself with another gulp of wine, then set aside the cup and held his shaking hands closer to the fire.

"Then, four days ago, a fast galley arrived in Coroth with word that Prince Nimur had died, just before Christmas, and that Prince Károly had been proclaimed the new heir, to be installed at Torenthály on the first day of the new year."

"Károly?" Lord Seisyll blurted, as Donal gaped in astonishment. "Not Prince Torval?"

Sir Robert shook his head, still collecting himself. "There was no mention of Prince Torval."

"But Károly is the third son. How can that be?" Duke Richard murmured.

"I don't know," Donal replied, numbly handing the missive to his brother. "Something must have happened to Torval as well. There is no mention of him in Sobbon's letter. But as news of Prince Nimur's death spreads, I have no doubt that further details will eventually become available."

"Perhaps from a Torenthi ambassador at tomorrow's court, Sire," Seisyll murmured distantly, though he could guess at the cause of Nimur's death, and thought he might have access to more immediate information that, unfortunately, could not be shared with the king.

Donal sighed, briefly gazing into the fire as if far, far away.

"A chilling thought has come to my mind," he said after a few seconds. "One perhaps not worthy of me, in the face of another father's undoubted grief over the death of his son." At his ministers' looks of question, he went on. "Prince Nimur was in his prime, trained from birth to be a king one day. He would have made *my* heir a formidable adversary. Károly is a decade younger than his brother was, and would never have expected to be the heir. That could make all the difference, when I am gone."

Murmurs of agreement whispered through the room, along with protests that the king's demise was surely far in the future, all subsiding as the king rose.

"We've done enough for tonight," Donal said, heading for the door. "I must think further on this new development. This undoubtedly will unsettle the balance of power in Torenth. Pray God that it delays any realistic plans for making a move against Gwynedd."

THE king's early adjournment of their meeting enabled Seisyll Arilan to begin his own inquiries immediately, regarding the death of Torenth's crown prince. Fortunately,

Michon de Courcy was always resident in Rhemuth at this time of year, because of Twelfth Night Court; and this year, unlike the previous year, Seisyll had been able to arrange for Michon to occupy the guest room next to the king's library, where the castle's Portal lay.

He made his way up to the library corridor and knocked on Michon's door, at the same time probing beyond the door with his mind. Within seconds he heard the latch lift as Michon opened the door and admitted him.

"What's happened?" Michon asked, as he closed the door again, for Seisyll's expression was deathly somber.

"I'll assume you haven't yet heard that Nimur of Torenth is dead—the son, not the father."

"What?" It was not really a question, but Seisyll held out his hand and, when Michon took it, gave the answer his colleague was really seeking, reiterating in an instant the revelations of the meeting he had just left. Michon briefly closed his eyes as he assimilated the information, then shook his head and sighed in resignation.

"He's gone and killed himself attempting forbidden spells," he whispered. "I shall be very surprised if that is not the case. And Torval—something obviously has happened to him as well. Oh, Camille, Camille, what have you wrought?"

He drew himself up with another heavy sigh, then briskly drew Seisyll onto the Portal square in the center of the room, a hand slipping up to clasp the back of Seisyll's neck. Without need for prompting, Seisyll lowered his shields and yielded control, only vaguely aware as the other quickly gathered up the strands of energy surrounding them and reached out for the signature of their destination. Between one heartbeat and the next, they had bridged the two locations and were standing on the Portal square outside the Camberian Council chambers.

"I'll ask you to summon the Council," Michon said, nudging Seisyll in the direction of the great double doors. "It has occurred to me that Rhanamé should know if Prince Nimur really is dead, and perhaps some of the circumstances. I'll return as soon as I can."

Seisyll turned to give a nod of agreement. "Very well. It

is also possible that Khoren knows something, or can quickly find out. I'll ask him, and brief the others while you're gone."

"Excellent." In the next breath, Michon had disappeared—and reappeared standing in the dimness of a trapped Portal at the great university of Rhanamé, on the river that marked the border between Nur Hallaj and the Kingdom of R'Kassi. It was very near where he and Oisín had traveled the previous summer to find a royal mount for Prince Brion, and in fact, both he and Oisín had paid their respects then in the school's great chapel.

The red-robed man seated at the writing desk just opposite the Portal rose as the newcomer appeared on the Portal's base, slowly and deliberately setting aside an elegant swan-feather quill. Michon could feel the faint brush of his shields being subtly probed, but he did not resist, only showing his empty hands to either side and then tracing a pattern known only to initiates of the inner school at Rhanamé.

"Michon de Courcy," he said quietly, identifying himself. "I should like to speak with Master Isaiya, if he is available. It is a matter of some urgency."

With a nod of permission granted, the man beckoned Michon forward, across the Portal boundaries, which Michon could not have passed without leave. It was a more subtle trap than many, that protected the semipublic Portal at Rhanamé, but no less powerful for being less obvious.

Even as Michon complied, a door opened into the room to reveal another red-robed man framed in the doorway, shorter than the first. The man bowed deeply from the waist, hands crossed on his breast, then indicated that Michon should follow.

Michon knew the corridor down which he was led, and followed obediently to a familiar door, where his guide set a splayed hand flat on a symbol in the center of the door, then pushed it open and stood aside. The man inside, who came slowly to his feet, was small and slender, with skin like polished mahogany and white, tightly curled hair cropped close to his head, as was his closely trimmed beard. The eyes were a rich chocolate brown in which Michon knew he could easily sink, looking out at him with the wisdom accumulated in nearly a century of study and contemplation.

"Dear Michon," the man said, holding out both his hands to his visitor, eyes smiling as well as lips. "Allow me to guess the reason for your late-night visit. You have come about Prince Nimur."

Inclining his head both in agreement and respect, Michon came to take the two slender hands in his and kiss them, looking up then into the brown eyes.

"Is it true?" he asked quietly.

"Yes, it is. Please, sit," the man replied, at the same time signing for Michon's guide to leave them.

Michon did as he was told, settling into a high-backed chair with broad arms, similar to the one in which Master Isaiya now resumed his seat, but he knew it was not his place to speak further, until the master proceeded.

"News only reached us yesterday," Isaiya said, "but I suspected that it would soon bring you here as well. I am aware that you were concerned about the direction Prince Nimur's experiments were taking him. I regret I must confirm that your fears for his safety were well-founded."

"May I ask what happened?" Michon asked, when the master did not immediately continue.

"I do not have details of the experiment itself, or what went wrong," the old man replied. "Perhaps we shall never know—nor would wish to—for Prince Torval witnessed it, or perhaps even assisted his brother, and went quite mad. I do not have specific details of that, either, but sufficient to say that the masters in Beldour felt it a serious enough affliction that they barred him from the succession, permanently. The Patriarch came in person to seek our guidance, and reluctantly accepted that this was the wisest course for all concerned."

Michon had visibly recoiled at this revelation, and lifted a hand in apology for his lapse, but Isaiya only nodded his understanding.

"Perhaps you will have heard that the third brother, Károly, now is the Torenthi heir," the master went on. "Quite candidly, I am not certain such will prove beneficial for

Torenth, for Károly has had no preparation for this new role thrust upon him. The next brother, Wencit, perhaps is the more accomplished of the remaining Furstán males, so far as power is concerned, but I have heard misgivings expressed about his scruples. But perhaps Károly will surprise us all, if he has time and the will to augment his training. His father could have another twenty years of vigorous good health. The same probably cannot be said of your king." He cocked his head. "But that is not something he will wish to hear, I think."

Michon had steepled his fingers as Isaiya spoke, elbows braced against the arms of his chair and thumbs resting taut against his breastbone, but now he briefly bowed his head over his joined forefingers, briefly rubbing them against tight-clenched lips.

"The relative ages of both crown princes have been noted already in Rhemuth," he said. "If both their fathers live another twenty years, or even another decade, the two heirs will be somewhat evenly matched. But what concerns me far more at the moment is the incident that claimed Prince Nimur's life. You are aware, I expect, that he was receiving training from Camille Furstána?"

"So I have been told," Isaiya said neutrally.

"What you may *not* have been told is that she has also been training a young Cardosan mage called Zachris Pomeroy."

"I have heard the name," Isaiya allowed.

"He, in turn, has been putting ideas into the head of Prince Hogan."

"Ah, the current Festillic Pretender to the throne of Gwynedd."

"You see the reason for my concern," Michon said.

"I do, indeed. And you intend to do . . . what?"

Michon sighed, wearily lowering his hands to both chair arms. "I haven't yet decided. I very much doubt that Hogan will make any move against Gwynedd while Donal is alive; he is in his vigorous prime, and has only to wait, in hope that Prince Brion will succeed while still a minor. If that occurs, I very much fear the outcome."

"Has Donal made provision for securing his son's magic?" Isaiya asked.

"Unknown," Michon replied. "There was to be a Deryni protector for the prince, who presumably would have been instructed in how to bring him to his father's power at the appointed time; you may have heard how Donal Haldane fathered a son on the daughter of Lewys ap Norfal, intending that the boy should be groomed to serve as Prince Brion's Deryni companion and mentor." At Isaiya's nod, Michon went on.

"Unfortunately for Donal's hopes, the boy was killed a few years ago—a dreadful affair that may have reached your ears, and apparently done, at least in part, because he was known to be Deryni, though no one was aware of his true paternity. I had hoped the mother might be entrusted with the appropriate knowledge, in case her son did not survive to accomplish his mission; but she, too, is dead."

Michon's old teacher was shaking his head, *tsk-tsking* over the waste of it all, but listened attentively as Michon continued.

"There is more. The king is nothing if not audacious. He had planned to attempt getting another such child on the Heiress de Corwyn, who is now the wife of Sir Kenneth Morgan, who last year was created Earl of Lendour for life, *de jure uxoris*. It is not entirely certain how Donal was thwarted in his plan, but Alyce de Corwyn did bear a half-breed son by her husband. Fortunately, Sir Kenneth is an honorable man, and utterly devoted to the king's service."

"And the king?" Isaiya murmured.

"He seems unconcerned," Michon replied. "Despite this alteration of his plan, he dotes on the boy, who is being brought up in the company of the royal princes. But the boy, called Alaric, was only three in September. It will be some time before he is old enough for us to determine how powerful a half-breed Deryni might be, if he can even learn to wield sufficient power to be useful."

"A complex and perplexing situation," Isaiya allowed, himself now gazing at Michon over interlaced fingers. "What do you propose to do?"

"What *can* I do?" Michon replied. "For now, I had simply come to find out more about Prince Nimur's passing—and to throw myself on the mercy of my old master, in hopes that he might have further wisdom to impart."

Isaiya's hands parted in a gesture of helplessness. "I have told you what I know, my son. I was not aware of the involvement of Zachris Pomeroy, or that he was encouraging Prince Hogan—though I shall certainly see what I may learn concerning them."

AFTER leaving Master Isaiya's quarters at Rhanamé, Michon reported back to his colleagues in the Camberian Council, sharing the intelligence he had gleaned. By then, Seisyll Arilan had gathered all five of the others around the eight-sided ivory table, where Prince Khoren Vastouni had only been able to confirm what Seisyll had already learned in the king's presence.

"My informant was present in Hagia Job when Prince Károly was invested as the new heir," he had informed them, "but I learned nothing further of substance. Prince Nimur's burial had been private, several weeks before, and no cause of death was given. Nor was anything said of the reason for Prince Torval's removal from the succession."

But Michon's new information made the reason far clearer.

"Driven mad," Barrett murmured, briefly closing his emerald eyes. "Far better to perish, I think. What he must have seen . . ."

"Best not to speculate," Vivienne said sharply.

Rhydon Sasillion, now fully installed in the chair recently vacated by Dominy de Laney, looked white-faced and stunned, for he had claimed acquaintance with one of the men who presumably had encouraged Prince Nimur to his fatal experiment. Oisín Adair was shaking his head in bewilderment.

"What can we do?" the latter asked, voicing the question in all of their minds.

Seisyll shrugged. "Do what we have always done: watch

and learn, and try to make sense of it all, and perhaps even make a difference in isolated situations. It is far less than we would prefer, but it is better than if we did nothing."

Above their heads, snow was piled thick upon the amethyst dome that normally lit the room, at least in daylight. Michon scowled as he glanced up at it. The chamber was cold and damp in this season.

"Back to Rhemuth, then, for Seisyll and me—though methinks that Twelfth Night Court tomorrow will be much diminished by the inclement weather. At least we need not venture out in it to return."

Khoren gave a nod, rising in his place. "It may well be that some Torenthi ambassador will show up at my brother's court with further news—or in Rhemuth, for yours," he said. "Shall we agree to meet again tomorrow night, as we have tonight?"

With universal agreement, the seven began moving to the doors from the room, and the Portal beyond, that would send them back to their respective homes.

Chapter 14

"As an earring of gold, and an ornament of fine gold."

—PROVERBS 25:12

As expected, remnants of the first great storm of the New Year continued to affect the customary fixtures surrounding Twelfth Night Court. The king's traditional public petitioners' court, already rescheduled from St. Stephen's Day, was moved into the cathedral itself, directly after the Mass of the Epiphany, both of which events were sparsely attended because of the weather.

The business of Twelfth Night Court began several hours late as a result, also notably less attended than usual. The seven-year-old Prince Nigel was among the new pages received that afternoon, afterward standing proudly beside his elder brother in their father's crimson livery, obviously struggling to contain an elated grin. Two older pages were promoted to squire, changing their simple pages' tabards for crimson livery tunics bearing the king's cipher and buckling on the blued-steel spurs that marked this rite of passage.

After that, three senior squires came forward with their sponsors, in turn, to receive the accolade of knighthood. The second of the three was a distant cousin of Michon de

Courcy, sent by his father for the greater prestige that would accrue from being knighted at Twelfth Night Court rather than in a distant baronial court. It was Michon who presented young Estèphe de Courcy, a younger brother carrying the sword and spurs; and it was Michon to whom the king gave the privilege of actually conferring the accolade. As the new Sir Estèphe proudly rose to be girded with the white belt of his knighthood, then knelt again to place his hands between those of the king and offer his fealty, Seisyll Arilan took satisfaction in the knowledge that Estèphe, like Michon and himself, was another secret Deryni, and would be a valuable agent on the western borders of the kingdom.

But no ambassador from Torenth appeared with any further word regarding the hasty shift in the Torenthi succession. Indeed, it would be several weeks before any official notification of Prince Nimur's death reached King Donal's court—and even then, details would be sparse. Various gossip and rumors would drift in sporadically throughout the remainder of the hard winter and early spring, but nothing of substance regarding what had really happened to the eldest Torenthi heir.

The remainder of Twelfth Night Court and the feast that followed passed much as they had the previous year, if on a smaller scale because of the weather, and without the frisson created the previous year by Kenneth Morgan's creation as earl. Afterward, only Michon de Courcy reported briefly to the Camberian Council—but only that there was really nothing to report, save for the expected knighting of his cousin Estèphe.

SOON after Twelfth Night, Kenneth and Alyce returned to Cynfyn with their son and household for the remainder of the winter. There, while Kenneth presided over local courts and consulted with the council that saw to the affairs of Lendour when he was absent, Alyce and Zoë had time and leisure to renew their close friendship and exult together over Zoë's pregnancy. Zoë's husband adored her, and his parents had quite taken her to their hearts, as had the entire court at Cynfyn. The contentment and sense of well-being was palpable, even in the midst of winter, and only increased as Zoë blossomed with the spring.

Later in the spring, Kenneth took Alyce and Alaric with him to Coroth for a few weeks' stay. There, as in Cynfyn, Kenneth attended to his duties as regent, periodically rode out into the surrounding countryside, and continued familiarizing himself with those who looked after the day-to-day running of the duchy. He and Alyce celebrated Easter in Coroth with their young son, who was missing his friends back in Rhemuth, then returned to Cynfyn in time to attend the birth of Zoë's first child, Kenneth's first grandson, christened Kailan Peter Chandos. It was a happy time for all of them; and by late in May, when he and Alyce prepared to return to Rhemuth for the celebrations marking Prince Brion's coming of age at Midsummer, Alyce knew she was finally with child again: a girl, this time, to be born before the turning of the year.

"How *ever* do you know these things?" Kenneth asked with awe, when she had told him her news.

"You aren't disappointed that it isn't another son?" she answered, mischief in her blue eyes.

"Good heavens, no! I adore daughters!"

"Well, you do have a certain amount of experience with daughters," she said coyly. "But you're sure you don't mind?" she pressed. "It will mean a winter confinement—and I certainly shan't be able to accompany you to next year's Twelfth Night Court."

"No, of course you won't," he agreed, thinking aloud. "But you could go to Morganhall for your lying-in. It would be nice if at least one of our children could be born on the Morgan ancestral lands. I'm sure my sisters would be delighted, especially if it meant they might attend the birth of their first niece. I know they would also love the chance to dote on Alaric for the holidays."

"You needn't convince me further," Alyce broke in, laying a forefinger across his lips and smiling. "I cannot think of better midwives to attend me. And I shall do my best to deliver before you must leave for Christmas court."

He grinned and kissed her in answer, then lay back with her nestled in the crook of his arm, curving a hand fondly over her still-flat abdomen.

DESPITE Alyce's protestations that she was only pregnant, not ill, Kenneth insisted that she travel by coach when they left for Rhemuth a few days later. In truth, the conveyance provided far less comfort than if she had made the journey a-horse, but she had Melissa in the coach with her, to keep her company, and Alaric at least started the journey with them.

But he very quickly became bored with this mode of transport, and soon put up such a fuss about being treated like a baby that his father permitted him to ride with Sir Llion for part of each day.

They arrived in the capital early in June of 1095, with but a week remaining before Prince Brion should achieve his fourteenth year and come officially of age. The milestone was mainly one of law, for everyone was well aware that few fourteen-year-olds were ready to assume the full duties of monarchy, but it meant that now, should Donal die untimely, his son and heir would not be required to rule through a regency council.

Such a council was already in place, to be sure, for handling the affairs of the kingdom when the king was occupied elsewhere in his realm. Donal had selected his crown council with care, and had named his brother Richard to preside whenever he was absent—a precedent that young Brion almost certainly would follow, when his father's council eventually became *his* council. It was a reassurance for all concerned, and the prince was as familiar with the council's workings as could be expected of even a precocious fourteen-year-old born and bred to be king.

But along with the public recognitions scheduled to take place with council and court, Donal Haldane intended another, more private recognition to mark his heir's coming of age, to be witnessed by only a select few. The night before the actual birthday festivities, after a private supper with his son, Donal summoned Kenneth and Alyce to join them in his private withdrawing chamber within the royal apartments. Donal himself admitted them.

"Thank you for coming," the king said quietly, standing aside to let them pass and then closing the door behind them. Prince Brion had been sitting at a small supper table lately cleared of the clutter of their meal, and rose as the two came into the room. He looked both eager and faintly apprehensive, perhaps in anticipation of what further the night might bring.

"Sire," Kenneth murmured. "Your Highness."

He cast a puzzled glance at his wife, uncertain why they had been summoned, but Alyce thought she knew, and set a hand on Kenneth's hand in subtle control, her attention focused entirely on the king.

"Sit down, please," the king said, waving them to seats at the little table and himself taking a seat. "I want to explain to all of you what I intend to do tonight. Kenneth, if all goes awry, it may fall upon you to be involved later on, which is why I asked you to be present. Alyce will understand immediately what I am about."

As he spoke, he had been unfastening the wire clasp that held the Eye of Rom in his right earlobe: a great cabochon ruby the size of his little fingertip, set in ruddy gold. This he removed and held before them, gently turning it to and fro so that its heart caught the glow from the candles on the table.

"Only seldom will any of you have seen me without this," he said softly, with a glance at Alyce and Kenneth. "I have told Brion the story of the stone many times as he was growing up, but it will be new to the two of you. According to my family's tradition, it was one of the gifts the Magi gave the Holy Child, after it had fallen from the heavens on the night of His birth. Every Haldane king since Cinhil the Great has worn it—some of them for rather longer than others," he added with a faint attempt at humor. "It is known as the Eye of Rom; I do not know why."

He set it aside and retrieved a small wooden box from the sideboard behind them, then pushed his chair back from the table, at the same time beckoning Brion closer. "Alyce, please bring that cushion for Brion to kneel on. Put it here in front of me."

Both obeyed, Alyce depositing the cushion on the floor at the king's feet and moving to his left. Brion knelt, gazing up trustingly as his father set the box in his hands. Opening the box, Donal plucked out a small, stoppered vial of green glass and a wad of cotton wool, which he passed to Alyce. He then delved into the box again to remove a small, folded packet of crimson wool held by a bright steel pin, its head formed in the shape of a stylized Haldane lion. This he kept in his hand as he leaned past Brion to set the box on the table behind.

"It is not given to any man save the king to actually wear the Eye of Rom," Donal said, pulling the pin from the red wool and handing it to Alyce, who had uncorked the vial and moistened the cotton wool with the pale green liquid it contained. "Nor is the Eye the source of the Haldane power, though it seems to be instrumental in its emergence in due time."

He unfolded the wad of fabric to reveal a small earhoop of twisted gold wire nestled in the folds of crimson wool. Underneath the earring was a small scrap of hard leather, which Donal palmed before setting the nest of crimson wool in Brion's left hand. He then reached behind his son to retrieve the Eye of Rom, turning it in his fingers as he leaned back in his chair. Alyce, meanwhile, was carefully wiping off the pin.

"It is customary that the heir should be introduced to the Eye of Rom on the eve of his coming of age, against the day when he shall bear its burden," Donal continued, setting the Eye in Brion's right hand and closing the prince's over the jewel. "Accordingly, though you will not wear the Eye tonight, I shall prepare you for its future wearing. Until then, you will wear that in its place."

He gestured toward the hoop of twisted gold in its nest of crimson, then glanced at Alyce and carefully received the steel pin back from her. Across the table, Kenneth watched silently, hardly breathing.

"Wipe off his earlobe now," Donal murmured, nodding toward the wad of faintly green-stained cotton wool. "The right one. Then come to his other side and steady his head."

Alyce did as he commanded, again moistening the cotton wool. The green liquid had a pungent, medicinal smell, but she found it not unpleasant. Even so, Brion flinched slightly at its touch, eyes closing briefly.

She wiped the earlobe several times, front and back, then set the wool aside and moved to the prince's other side, took his head between her hands and braced his forehead against her waist. As she did so, his father set the tip of the steel pin against his right earlobe, positioning the scrap of leather behind, and gave a sharp thrust.

Alyce felt Brion tense as the sliver pierced through, but he did not move as Donal twisted the pin slightly to enlarge the wound and then squeezed the earlobe, withdrawing the pin as blood welled from the front wound. He then slid his left hand around the back of Brion's head to brace it and touched Brion's closed right hand in signal for him to open it, picked up the Eye, and touched the stone to the blood trembling, jewellike, on the boy's earlobe.

Brion flinched as the stone touched his blood, breathing in with a hiss and briefly stiffening under his father's hands. In that instant, Alyce, too, felt power stirring, surging between father and son and spilling over slightly against her shields. Even Kenneth appeared to sense that something was happening that he could not see, still seated taut and white-faced at the other side of the little table. But then Brion relaxed again and breathed out a sigh as the king withdrew the stone and set it aside, now marked with his heir's blood—and Brion, too, with its potential.

Wordlessly the king retrieved the hoop of twisted gold and handed it to Alyce, his intention clear. Carefully she took it and wiped it with the cotton wool, again charged from the green vial, careful to clean well around the twisted wires, then handed it to the king and again held Brion's head steady as Donal made ready to insert the hoop of twisted wire through the hole just created.

"This will probably hurt more than the first time," Donal

murmured, positioning the end of the wire and starting to guide it through the raw flesh, twisting as he pushed.

Brion closed his eyes again, jaw tensing as Donal guided the twisted wire through and fastened it, though he did not flinch.

"There, it's done," Donal breathed. "The earlobe may be tender for a few days. Try to keep it clean while it heals, and move the wire back and forth in the wound several times a day."

Relaxing a little, Brion gingerly touched the earring and his ear, a faint smile playing at one corner of his mouth. Then, with an apologetic shrug, he glanced back at the silver goblets discarded on the sideboard and leaned back to retrieve one, holding it nearer the candle and trying to catch a glimpse of his reflection. Donal snorted.

"You look very dashing," he said gruffly. "You're apt to set a fashion trend among the other young men at court."

"To be sure, he shall," Alyce agreed, smiling and casting a glance toward Kenneth, who was quickly recovering his aplomb.

Brion grinned at that, still a boy in that instant. Shortly thereafter, after sharing a celebratory round of excellent Fianna red brought up earlier from the royal cellars, the four participants in the night's work retired to their respective chambers, all of them with much to ponder in the times to come, and a prince with odd dreams to drift through his sleep.

THE next day began with the customary birthday court to mark the prince's natal day, though he had already been awakened early to receive his gift from his parents.

"It's out in the stable yard! Come quick!" his brother Nigel said urgently, shaking him awake before first light. "I *knew* they were going to do it! She's absolutely gorgeous!"

From Nigel's exuberant outburst, Brion knew instantly what his brother was talking about, and threw on the previous day's clothes as quickly as he could, still rubbing sleep from his eyes as he wrenched open the door to his sleeping chamber.

Lord Kenneth Morgan was waiting outside with Nigel, leaning against the wall opposite the door, arms crossed and a sly smile on his handsome face.

"I suspected it wouldn't take much to roust you this morning, Your Highness. Good morning, and congratulations on your natal day. If you'll come with me . . ."

"Is it true?" Brion whispered, wide-eyed, as he followed Kenneth down the corridor toward the stair tower, Nigel eagerly trailing in his wake. "Lord Kenneth, is it true?"

"Is what true, my prince?" Kenneth replied, with an innocent glance over his shoulder. "That today, you are of age? Yes. That last night, your father gave you a tangible token of that coming of age? Yes." Brion's hand flew to his right ear, and he winced as it twinged when his fingers brushed the earring there. "That your birthday present is waiting for you in the stable yard? Yes. That the present is the R'Kassan steed for which you have been longing?" He glanced back again as they reached the head of the stair and grinned. "Yes."

With a burst of delighted laughter, Brion pressed past him and pelted down the turnpike stair, keeping his balance against the newel post to his left, skipping every second step. Nigel followed right behind him, Kenneth bringing up the rear.

Out in the stable yard, his parents and his other brother and sisters were waiting with Sir Seisyll Arilan and several more of the king's ministers, all of them hastily dressed, all of them looking inordinately pleased with themselves. As the two elder princes appeared, Oisín Adair emerged from the opening of the stable arch leading a bloodred R'Kassan mare, whose lead he handed, without ceremony, to Prince Brion.

Chapter 15

"Rejoice, O young man, in thy youth;
and let thy heart cheer thee in the days of thy youth, and
walk in the ways of thine heart, and in the sight of thine eyes."
—ECCLESIASTES 11:9

It was a matter of more than half an hour before Brion could be enticed back inside to prepare for court, for nothing would do but that he should be given a leg up onto the mare's bare back, face creased in a delighted grin, so that Oisín could lead him around the stable yard for a few turns.

The grin lasted well into the morning, when he had bathed and dressed for more formal undertakings. He was still smiling as his parents solemnly led him into the hall where the court of Gwynedd awaited him.

There, after being presented by his father as Gwynedd's lawful heir, now come of age, he was invested with a golden circlet and seated in a chair of state at his father's right hand, no longer relegated to the stool at his father's feet, which hitherto had been his place. From there he received the homage of all the peers of the realm, as his proud parents looked on.

Kenneth and Alyce were among the first to swear, after Duke Richard and the Dukes of Cassan and Claibourne. No one could swear as Duke of Corwyn, since the duchy was awaiting Alaric's majority, but he knelt between his parents in a heraldic tunic quartered of the arms of Corwyn and Lendour, though the Lendour coat was differenced by a label of three points, since he now was the heir rather than abeyant would-be earl. For a while, he was even allowed to remain in the hall, as the less-formal part of the proceedings continued.

"Mummy, is this where Prince Brion gets presents?" he whispered urgently, tugging at Alyce's sleeve.

"Yes, darling, but you must be quiet, or Sir Llion will have to take you outside to play. Can you be very quiet for me?"

The boy agreed, but after the first few presentations, his exuberance and the rising heat in the crowded great hall got the better of him, so that Llion was obliged to escort him outside.

"Llion, was I naughty?" he whispered when they had gained the refuge of the castle gardens beside the hall—where, in truth, most of the other young children of the court had also adjourned, along with a few of the older ones. Seven-year-old Kevin McLain was overseeing several of them, including his half-brother Duncan, Prince Jathan, and the two Haldane princesses.

"No, Master Alaric, you were not naughty," Llion assured him, "but you *were* somewhat noisy. This is Prince Brion's day."

"But I wanted to see his presents . . ."

"You can see them another time, perhaps tomorrow. But look: There is your cousin Duncan over by the fountain, with Princess Silke. It looks like she and Jathan have found something of interest. Shall we go and see what it is?"

Meanwhile, the presentations continued in the great hall: a succession of gifts both great and small to mark Prince Brion's coming of age. First, the ones from foreign dignitaries: a goodly dagger from the King of Howicce and Llannedd, who was the prince's uncle on his mother's side, its blade etched with a line of running Haldane lions with legs and tails intertwined. The King of R'Kassi had sent a silver-mounted and ivory-handled riding crop, along with a fine silver-mounted headstall, to go with the mare purchased from one of his breeders.

From the Prince of Andelon came a new set of steel vambraces engraved with Haldane lions, presented by the prince's younger brother, Prince Khoren. A carved ivory box contained fourteen gold sovereigns, one for each year of Prince Brion's life: this from the King of Bremagne, who had marriageable granddaughters. The diminutive Rather de Corbie, emissary of the Hort of Orsal, had brought a soft leather pouch containing half a dozen fine rubies.

There were also private gifts from friends and members of the court: a new mail hauberk from his uncle Richard, a set of crimson riding leathers from the other squires of the court, a matching hunt cap from the pages.

From Kenneth and his family came a treatise on the bloodlines of the great R'Kassan studs, in which Brion's new mare was prominently listed, and also a history of Rhemuth Castle, lettered by Alyce and illuminated by Zoë during the previous winter. Additionally came silver cups and plates aplenty, and other divers gifts of various kinds.

The unexpected presentation of the forenoon, after nearly all the business of the court had been concluded, was a newly arrived delegation from the King of Torenth, which included one of the Torenthi king's own sons.

"Prince Wencit is *here*?" Donal whispered, when Sir Jiri Redfearn had hurried down the sidelines of the crowded great hall to whisper in the king's ear.

"Aye, and his daughter as well, Sire," Jiri replied. "Probably sent to test whether there might be interest in a royal match, though I expect that would be a dangerous proposition."

Seisyll Arilan had crowded close as Jiri approached, and leaned in to clarify.

"I think it unlikely that such a match would be proposed, given recent relations between the two kingdoms, Sire," he said. "But it would be an expected courtesy for one sovereign to send one of his sons on the occasion of another king's heir coming of age—and Prince Wencit is only third in line to the throne."

"He was bloody well *fifth* in line, six months ago," Donal muttered, "and the new number-two is his brother's son, a five-year-old. Wencit is only two sets of heartbeats away from the throne. He is also said to be one of the most accomplished Deryni of his generation. Who else is with him?"

"The Princess Morag Furstána," Jiri replied. "And one of Nimur's ministers: a Count János Sokrat. I believe you have met him before; probably sent along to keep the young Furstáns in line."

"Very well, announce them when they're ready."

With a brisk nod, Jiri backed off and retreated up the great hall. Donal, with a glance toward Alyce, summoned her a little closer, to stand behind the thrones between him and the queen.

"At least three Deryni, Alyce," he murmured. "Let's keep them honest."

She nodded, then did her best to become all but invisible as a chamberlain's staff rapped three times on the stone floor to call the hall to order.

"Pray attend," came the call, echoing in the hall. "Ambassasdors from the Kingdom of Torenth: Count János Sokrat, accompanying the Prince Wencit and his sister, the Princess Morag Furstána."

A murmur rippled through the hall as the assembly parted to either side of the center aisle. Down this aisle came three black-clad figures, one of them female, attended by a single pair of Torenthi guards carrying a large, soft bundle the size of a small child. The man leading the delegation was tall and straight-backed, clad in a full-sleeved and ankle-length over-robe of black silk damask, open at the front to show a close-collared under-tunic of black silk. The gleam of a curved cavalry blade showed through one of the sides, both of which were slit to the waist for riding. His luxuriant beard was black, though starting to go grey, as was the long hair braided and clubbed in a warrior's knot. The black flat-topped hat set square across his brow added a handspan to his height.

The second man, much younger, was shorter in stature

but similarly clad save for a tawny jewel glittering at the front of his black cap. The jewel gathered russet glints from the man's hair, a rusty red, the sidelocks of which were braided and hung nearly to his shoulders, slashes of russet against the somber black. His sister walked beside him, head held high, gowned in black silks very like the men, but with her face veiled so that only her dark eyes showed beneath a narrow circlet of gold.

The trio strode very nearly to the foot of the dais steps before they halted, never taking their eyes from those of the king. There the leader of the delegation made a deep bow from the waist, right hand flat against his breast. The younger man merely inclined his head, as did his sister, left hand resting easily on the hilt of his sword. The face behind the close-clipped red beard was expressionless, but the pale eyes were cold.

"Donal Haldane King of Gwynedd," the older man said, straightening. "*Nimouros ho Phourstanos Padishah,* King of Torenth and all its provinces, bids me give you greeting on this, the coming of age of your heir, the Prince Brion." His accent was heavy, and Donal had to concentrate to follow him.

"Nimouros sends this greeting as one father to another, in appreciation for the condolences sent by Your Majesty earlier this year when the padishah mourned the death of his own eldest son and heir." He bowed again. "Today, in return, Nimouros offers this gift to *your* heir, the Prince Brion, from the bounty of the lands to the east."

Clapping his hands twice, he turned and the prince and princess moved to either side so that the two soldiers could bring forward their bundle. This they deposited at the foot of the steps before withdrawing to either side. It was János himself who knelt beside the bundle and slowly reached to the curved dagger thrust through his belt, gesturing his free hand toward the bands of twine binding the bundle before slowly drawing the blade to cut the twine.

Several other hands had moved to weapons as the dagger cleared its sheath, but Donal held up a hand to stay untoward aggression as János bent to his task. The two Torenthi soldiers anxiously scanned the assembly, off-hands resting on their sword hilts, though their royal charges looked singularly unconcerned.

"They say in Torenth," said János, as he cut the last binding and began to unfold the heavy bundle, "that the carpets of Lorsöl are crafted under the All-Seeing Eye of God, and that angels assist in their weaving." He gave the bundle a shake to unfurl a cascade of crimsons and black and golds, longer than a man, which shimmered with the sheen of silk as he spread it across the steps. The queen had drawn a tiny gasp as the carpet was revealed, and Prince Brion sat forward in astonishment, but Donal only sat back, smiling, one hand stroking his close-clipped beard.

"It is a princely gift, my lord," the king said, inclining his head.

"It is a gift for a prince," János replied, standing to sweep one hand across the carpet in emphasis and then bowing slightly to Brion. "With care and luck, it will serve Prince Brion and his children and his children's children. I trust that it is acceptable?"

Before Donal could answer, Brion rose and gave the Torenthi envoy a courteous bow. "It is, indeed, a princely gift, my lord, and one that I shall treasure. To receive such a gift is tangible sign that I have, indeed, achieved my majority, for this is no gift for a child. Pray, thank your master for his generosity, and say that I hope it may be a sign of improved relations between our two kingdoms in the future."

János inclined his head. "I shall convey Your Highness' gracious reply." He glanced at Donal. "And now, by your leave, O King, I and my charges shall withdraw, for our mission is completed."

"You have leave, of course, Count János," Donal replied, "but will you not stay with us for a few days, having come all this distance? A tournament is planned for this afternoon and tomorrow, and you are most welcome to join us."

"I thank you, Sire, but we may not tarry," János replied, glancing at Wencit and Morag. "We are still in mourning, as you see, and it would not be seemly. I hope you will understand."

"Of course," Donal replied, inclining his head. "Then I shall give you a royal escort back to Desse and wish you Godspeed, with my thanks.

"And thank God they did not choose to stay," he muttered under his breath when the three had gone and he had retreated to the withdrawing room behind the dais with his brother and his two eldest sons. In an hour, court would reconvene on the tourney field, but Brion and Nigel were eagerly inspecting the sum of Brion's gifts, brought back to the room after court had adjourned.

"But it *is* a fine carpet, Brion," Donal added, watching the boys exclaim over the gifts. "Take care, or your mother will have it in our chambers before you realize."

Brion grinned and ran a hand across the carpet's silken pile. "I suppose I *could* let you borrow it, Sire," he said impishly. "At least for the next four years, I shall be very busy keeping up with Uncle Richard's training regimen, if I hope to be ready for knighthood on time. I doubt I shall be spending much time in my own apartment."

"Probably true enough," Donal agreed, with a wink at his brother Richard. "But you'd best arm for the tournament now. I seem to recall that there is an excellent R'Kassan mare awaiting your foot in the stirrup."

"But I would only ride her for the entry procession," Richard cautioned. "She's a fine animal, but you aren't yet accustomed to one another. Compete on the grey you've been riding of late. Plenty of time for the other."

Brion rolled his eyes, but he knew that Richard was right. "That was what I'd always planned, Uncle. But will you help me arm? I assume that I do have your leave to wear the new hauberk and vambraces, since I've been party to their fitting?"

"If you wish," Richard agreed. "Just remember that they are somewhat heavier than what you've been wearing. In this heat, you'll feel every bit of the extra weight."

"I hadn't thought of that," Brion replied, obviously taking his uncle's caution to heart. "All the leather straps will be stiffer, too; not as agile. Maybe I'll just wear them for the opening parade, and switch back to my familiar harness when it's time to compete."

"A wise decision," Richard said with a nod. "In time, you'll wear the new armor as easily as you wear your skin—and you'll have several more sets before you're fully grown. But it's important to choose your equipment for the conditions. Today, I think you want agility."

"You're right, of course," Brion replied. "Nigel, would you like to squire for me this afternoon?" he asked, with a glance at his younger brother. "The first thing I'll need is some help getting these things back to my apartment."

The eager Prince Nigel beamed at being asked, and proudly scooped up the vambraces and several other items to lead the way from the room.

THE afternoon's tournament was something short, as tournaments went, and quite warm, but all were able to compete who wished to do so, especially the younger men. Prince Brion himself opened the tourney, riding onto the field in his new hauberk and vambraces and mounted on the bloodred mare. Later he and his father presided at the tourney, where Brion was permitted to award most of the prizes. Several prizes he himself competed for and won, much to his delight and the proud witnessing of his parents and uncle.

Alaric and the other younger children at court were also allowed to attend, though they spent more time running and playing with one other than actually watching. Sir Llion and Sir Xander had offered to supervise them, but several of the senior squires took over that duty late in the afternoon so that Llion and Xander themselves could compete. For these contests, the children formed an impromptu cheering section for Llion, who was a favorite of all the children, and were well rewarded for their loyalty when Llion took a prize while riding at the quintain.

But the younger children were banished to the nursery when it came time for the banquet that followed. Alaric was happy enough with that arrangement, being hot and tired and dusty, and was quite content to be bathed and tucked up in bed by Melissa after eating with the other young children.

For the adults, that evening saw a lavish feast of many removes, at which Prince Brion sat in a place of honor between his parents and was served by Prince Nigel and then by the king's counselors of state. More impromptu gifts followed during the course of the meal, which was also interspersed with divers entertainments. In the intervals suitable for dancing, the prince also acquitted himself well, soon losing his self-consciousness and partnering several of the younger ladies of the court with ease and grace.

"He is becoming a fine man," Kenneth murmured to Alyce as they watched the prince dancing with a daughter of the Earl of Marley.

Alyce nodded, smiling slightly. "Aye, and he will turn many a head before he weds—and not a few, even afterward."

"Pray God, he'll prove to have his father's discretion," Kenneth replied. "It must be a fearful thing, to be a king."

Later, when Kenneth and Alyce retired to their room, Alyce broached a delicate subject with her husband.

"Darling, I need to ask you about something," she said by way of preamble, as she brushed out her hair. "You may have noticed that I spent much of the afternoon chatting with Vera. We were lamenting the heat, and she pointed out that summer in Culdi is far milder than here in the capital or even at Morganhall. She has invited me to accompany her and Jared when they head back in a few days, to stay through the summer—maybe even until the baby arrives. It would be a change for Alaric as well; you know how he adores the company of his McLain cousins."

From the bed, Kenneth leaned back on his elbows and gazed fondly at his wife, somewhat taken aback by the prospect. With the summer shaping up to be a warm one, he had already decided that his wife and son should retreat to cooler climes to await the birth of the child Alyce was carrying, but he had thought to send her to his own keep at

Morganhall, with his sisters, hardly a day's ride north of the city.

"We had already discussed sending you and Alaric to Morganhall," he said. " 'Tis far closer to court."

"True enough," Alyce agreed, "but even if I stayed with you in Rhemuth, I doubt I should see much of you, given that summer is the season when the king most needs you at his side. And so far as my health is concerned, surely the distance matters little enough in these early months. Granted, I should miss what moments we might, in fact, be able to squeeze from the king's demands, but at least it would be cooler in Culdi." She lifted the mass of her golden hair up off her neck and tossed it over one shoulder, letting out a sigh of relief.

Kenneth pulled a sour face, but it was also one of resignation, for he knew she was right.

"Carrying a child must be difficult enough, without doing it in the heat," he said. "I shall speak to Jared in the morning."

Chapter 16

"There were two women, the daughters of one mother."

—EZEKIEL 23:2

IN the end, Lord Kenneth Morgan decided to accompany his wife and son northward to see them safely settled for the summer. Traveling in the combined entourage of the Duke of Cassan, the Earl of Kierney, and their respective households, the journey was pleasant enough, though a sultry stillness had settled along the river, only easing as they started their ascent into the foothills above Culdi.

There Kenneth saw them ensconced at Earl Jared's country house above the town, and left Sir Llion as governor for his young son, along with two men at arms. Entrusting wife and son and their modest household to the protection of Earl Jared, he then headed back to the capital and a busy summer of service to the king.

For young Alaric, the lazy summer days flew by in the company of his McLain cousins: Duncan, who was his own age, and the somewhat older Kevin, who was the heir. For Alyce, the ensuing weeks were to be among the most idyllic she had spent since her time at Arc-en-Ciel, made all the sweeter for the company of the sister whom she had not known until adulthood. In addition, the seclusion away from court enabled the two women to share some of their Deryni training, for the pair had been exposed to very different teachers.

The latter part of that summer also marked the beginning of Prince Brion's official life, as he embarked with his uncle, Duke Richard, and a small entourage on an extended progress into some of the outlying areas of the kingdom he would one day inherit. He rode the bloodred mare, whom he had named Sevalla, reveling in the harmony of horse and rider that was building between them—and marveled at her easy gaits and intelligence and amiable disposition.

Riding northward first, along the River Eirian, the royal party stopped briefly at Culdi, to call on the Earl and Countess of Kierney and the Countess of Lendour, then ventured westward into restless Meara, where they were the guests of Lord Lucien Talbot, the royal governor at Ratharkin. There, attended by Duke Richard, Prince Brion sat in court for several days beside the governor and heard cases brought before the local assize. Over dinner on the evening before they were to depart, the governor offered his assessment of the prince's performance.

"Frankly, Your Highness, I was more than pleased," Lord Lucien allowed. "You obviously have paid attention to your tutors, and have learned from the fine examples set by your father and your uncle." His gaze flicked to Richard in honest admiration. "I do not say this merely to flatter, sir. Your royal nephew bears the Haldane sense of justice in full measure."

Richard inclined his head in acknowledgment, smiling faintly. "Thank you, Lucien. It is always heartening to have one's own opinion confirmed by an unbiased source."

"But do the Mearans agree?" Brion said impatiently. "One day I shall have to govern these people, Lord Lucien. And Uncle, you are all but *obliged* to tell me I am doing well, because you are my teacher."

His smile broadening, Richard leaned closer to lightly punch the prince in the left bicep. "It is precisely because I *am* your teacher that I must be honest in my assessment,

Nephew. But granted that you still have much to learn—as have we all—your instincts are sound, and you have a good heart. Your father may be justly proud, and *I* am proud. I think you will make a more than passable king."

"From you, Uncle, that is high praise, indeed," Brion replied with a grin.

ANOTHER week they stayed in Ratharkin, making short excursions into the surrounding countryside to meet a few of the local folk and assess the local temper, then headed northeastward. They stopped the first night out at Oisín Adair's stud farm of Haut Emeraud, where Brion inspected some of the other horses in Oisín's distinguished string of breeding stock, and thanked Oisín again for finding the incomparable Sevalla.

Following the river seaward through the earldoms of Trurill and Transha, the prince and his uncle paid courtesy calls at both courts, then continued across the lush plains of the Purple March and thence northward into the mountainous lands of old Kheldour, where they spent several weeks in the company of Ewan Duke of Claibourne, come into his title earlier in the year.

"I cannot tell you how honored I am, my lords, to have two Haldane princes at my table," the duke said, after the final day's successful hunting. Three deerhounds lay at their master's feet, but they were dining on wild boar tonight, not venison, brought down by Duke Richard's spear in the culmination of a most satisfactory chase. Earlier in the evening, Duke Ewan's duchess had joined them briefly so that their six-year-old heir, Lord Graham, could bid the company good night, but now only the three men remained, two princes and a duke, savoring the last of the meal and a fine flask of Bremagni wine.

"It has been an instructive visit," Richard replied, lifting his cup in salute, "and we thank you for your hospitality."

* * *

THE remainder of Kenneth's summer was likewise well occupied with important work. In the several months after Prince Brion's coming of age, the Earl of Lendour undertook several embassies for the king, traveling to Joux, Vezaire, and twice to the Hort of Orsal's summer residence at Horthánthy, across the straits from Coroth, where he also met with Corwyn's fellow regents. Interspersed amid trade negotiations with the nearest of the Forcinn states, he had hoped he might learn more about the death of Prince Nimur of Torenth and, more important, gain some indication of the sort of man Brion eventually would have to face in Prince Károly, the new Torenthi heir; but even the Orsal's agents could tell him little regarding the change of succession, or Károly the man.

In all, it could be counted as a successful season's work, though he had managed only two short side trips to Culdi to visit his family. Toward the end of September, therefore, having reported to the king on his latest mission, he requested and obtained leave to make a more extended visit, for the end of the month would see Alaric's fourth birthday.

"Did you bring me a present, Papa?" the boy asked, tugging at his father's boot as Kenneth dismounted.

"Oh, I think I *might* have a present for you," Kenneth replied. He swept the boy into a hug, returning the enthusiastic kiss that Alaric planted on his cheek, then set him down to take Alyce into his arms.

"Mmmm," he said, when he had kissed her soundly. "And here is my dearest wife, and our daughter as well," he added with a smile, splaying the fingers of one hand over her rounded belly and then bending to kiss the bulge. "Are both of you well, darling?"

"We are well, indeed, now that you are here," she replied. "Are you permitted to stay for a while?"

"Not as long as I would like," he said, bending to scoop up Alaric again and brace him on his hip, "but longer than before. But I could hardly miss being here to celebrate the natal day of our little man." He gently tousled Alaric's white-blond head. "Has he been behaving in my absence?"

"He has, indeed," Alyce replied, "though he and Duncan together do lead poor Llion a merry chase, and sometimes they lure Kevin into trouble as well."

"They shall be leaders among men!" Kenneth declared, giving his son another hug. "And Llion is pleased with his progress?"

She glanced back to where the young knight was bantering with Trevor Udaut, who had accompanied Kenneth and was holding their two horses, one with a large wicker pannier strapped to its saddle's cantle.

"I believe you can go ahead with your plans," she said, smiling.

"Excellent."

THE next day was Alaric's birthday. It began like most days, with Melissa helping him to dress while they chattered about what the day might bring. As a special treat, he was allowed to go downstairs with his parents to eat in the great hall with the adults—a privilege not often granted, though he managed to acquit himself with grace and good manners. Porridge was easy enough to master, and ended up mostly in his stomach, sparing his clean tunic. The honey drizzled on his chunk of fresh bread proved somewhat more challenging, but he managed to confine the few wayward smears to his face and hands, which his father helped him wash off when he was finished.

"That was very nicely done," Kenneth told him as he set aside the damp cloth he had used for the deed. "You're becoming quite the young man."

Alaric merely gazed up at him hopefully, well aware what day it was, and that gifts were customary on one's birthday.

"Now," said Kenneth, setting his balled fists on his hips in a pose that reminded Alyce where their son had learned that same posture. "You asked yesterday about a present."

The boy's eyes lit, and he grinned as he glanced at his mother.

"Well, you'd better go out to the stables and speak to

Llion," Kenneth told him. "I think he got little sleep last night, looking after it for you."

The boy took off at a dead run, Kenneth and Alyce following more sedately, so that by the time they reached the stable yard, Alaric was staggering from the stable arch with a long-eared brindle puppy clasped under its front legs, the hind legs and tail dangling nearly to the ground.

"Papa, he's wonderful! Thank you!" the boy cried.

"I'm glad you like him," Kenneth replied, coming to catch up the animal's hind end. "But you must support his weight, if you're going to pick him up. It makes him feel more secure. Better yet, let's put him down on the ground."

Watching earnestly, young Alaric released his end of the dog as his father set the back legs on the ground. The puppy immediately squirmed around to start licking his face, staggering with the ferocity of his tail-wagging as the boy hugged him close.

"He likes me!" Alaric laughed, face scrunched up against the puppy's kisses. "What's his name, Papa?"

"Well, he hasn't got one just yet," Kenneth replied, "so I reckon you'll have to give him one." He smiled. "You should also know that Prince Brion picked him out especially for you. The mother is one of the prince's own favorite hounds, and he thought you would like a royal dog. He should be quite a hunter when he's grown—and he'll get quite large. Prince Nigel has one of his littermates."

Alaric's face had been creasing in an even bigger grin as the puppy's lineage was unfolded, and he suddenly plopped down in the dust of the stable yard as the puppy tried to climb into his lap, tail still wagging furiously as it continued licking his face.

"I got a royal dog!" he crowed. "Oh, thank you, thank you, Papa!"

Chuckling, Kenneth took Alyce's arm and walked her on toward the castle gardens, where they whiled the morning away in sweet conversation and gentle dalliance before Kenneth took off with Jared and the other men for an afternoon's hunting.

* * *

THAT night, after they had dined at Earl Jared's table and Kenneth had shared the news of court with Jared and Vera and the others privileged to dine at the high table, Alyce and Kenneth retired to the chamber she had called home for the past three months. Alaric was tucked up in his bed in the adjoining room, the puppy curled up in the hollow of his arm, and Llion slept in the room just beyond. The castle was settling into stillness for the night, though red still streaked the summer sky in the west. A gentle rain had begun to fall with the lowering darkness.

"I *have* missed you," Kenneth murmured, watching her in the mirror as she brushed out her hair. "That, alone, is reason enough to bring me here. But there is another reason for my visit at this time—in addition to Alaric's birthday. I've come to relay a message from the king."

She stiffened slightly, then laid down her brush to turn and look directly at him.

"What message?"

"He asks that you—Name Alaric." He shrugged as she cocked her head to stare at him more sharply. "He said that you'd understand what that meant."

She sighed and nodded a little distractedly. "Oh, I do. It's . . . a preparation for the time when Donal must set his Haldane imprint in place, so that Alaric will be able to act for Prince Brion when Donal is gone."

"By your reaction, I take it that this is something outside the normal," Kenneth said quietly, "even magical. Is there danger?"

She shook her head. "No danger. It simply isn't often done for so young a child."

"I see."

She sighed and considered, then came to sit beside him on the bed. "I shall need your help."

"You know I will do anything you ask," he replied, taking one of her hands to kiss its palm.

Laughing gently, she leaned closer to kiss him on the

mouth. "Darling Kenneth, what would I do without you? May I read exactly what the king told you?"

"You mean, read my mind?"

"Yes."

He inclined his head in agreement. "Do what is needful."

Smiling, she slid her hands to either side of his face, thumbs resting lightly on his temples.

"Close your eyes and relax, dearest Kenneth," she murmured.

THE next morning was spent in domestic activities, Kenneth retiring to the stable yard with Llion and Jared and several of the other knights while Alyce occupied herself in the solar, settling before her loom and humming an ancient tune as her fingers slipped an ivory shuttle back and forth among the threads of warp and weft. In the garden below, she could hear children's voices, shrill and excited: Alaric playing with his two McLain cousins.

She glanced outside and smiled at the sight, savoring the late summer air with its scent of sunlight on grass, clean earth, and recent rain. Alaric had found the damp flowerbeds and the pond and was rapidly initiating the slightly younger Duncan into the joyous mysteries of mud. The seven-year-old Kevin was doing his best to remain aloof and clean, as befitted the ducal heir to Cassan, playing quietly with his toy knights on a patch of stone paving beside a more formal fountain, but it was apparent that his interest in the younger boys' mud was fast becoming more than academic.

No matter. The late-morning sun was warm after the chill of the previous night's rain. Melissa, Alyce's maid, and Bairbre, the maid who looked after Duncan and Kevin, would be less than pleased at having to bathe three squirming boys this evening, but it was the first real rain of the autumn; the summer had been dry. Not for months had the weather permitted such boyish pursuits. Alyce laughed aloud when she saw that Kevin had finally succumbed to temptation and was making mud moats and mottes and castles with as much gusto as either of the younger boys.

She heard a rustle behind her and turned to see Vera entering the room with Bairbre, her riding habit of earlier in the day exchanged for a gown of honey-brown the exact shade of her hair, which gave her grey-green eyes a tinge of the sea. While it was well-known that the two countesses were related by marriage, only the two of them knew that they were, in fact, twins, cunningly separated at birth by their Deryni parents so that the second-born Vera might be brought up secretly in a human family, without the Deryni stigma that had been Alyce's lot for all her life.

Now Vera was Countess of Kierney, by marriage to the widower Jared McLain, whose first countess had died giving him his eldest son and heir, who was playing in the castle yard with Alaric and Duncan. Not even Earl Jared knew that his second wife was full sister to Alyce de Corwyn, one of the last of the High Deryni heiresses.

"I wish you could have ridden with us, earlier," Vera said, coming to embrace her. "I doubt your daughter would have approved, however." She smiled as she glanced down at Alyce's rounded belly, then nodded dismissal to her maid. "Thank you, Bairbre. You may go now."

As they drew apart, both of them laughing companionably, Alyce took one of Vera's hands and led her closer to the window.

"Vera, you really must look at this," she said, her casual tone for the benefit of the retiring maid as she directed her sister's gaze toward the garden below. "I fear that my son has been an exceedingly poor influence on yours. Our maids will be appalled when they learn how dirty three noble children have managed to get in less than half an hour."

Vera laughed and moved back into the room to perch on a stool where she could survey her sister's weaving. Alyce had been working on the background of a hunting scene showing Castle Culdi high on its hill, with a band of horsemen galloping across the fields in the foreground, bright banners flying. Somehow, she had managed to convey a sense of foggy mystery, as though the riders floated across an early-morning meadow. Vera ran an appreciative finger across the tightly woven threads as Alyce sat down beside her.

"How *ever* do you manage to get this effect?"

Alyce gave a mirthful chuckle and took up her shuttle again.

"We had a Kheldish weaver at my father's court when Marie and I were young," she replied. "He was old and sick, even when we first met him, but he still could weave. Father had him tutor us. It seemed a safe enough skill to teach Deryni children."

Vera glanced at the door, which the maid had closed behind her, then passed a hand between them and the door. The spell was not a potent one, but it would muffle their words beyond discernment by any unseen listener. Like Alyce, she had learned early to guard her secrets as though her life depended on it.

"Was the man Deryni?" she asked in a low voice.

Alyce shrugged. "I don't know. He never said, and I was too young to know to ask. But I realize now that much of what he taught me was the ancient cording lore. Of course, he couched it only in terms of the physical manipulations involved." She smiled as she slipped back across the years in memory. "Our governess, poor, dull lady, thought it but an advanced weaving technique. She had no patience with learning it herself. Had she but known . . ."

"Praise God she did not!" Vera snorted. "But, could a human even learn the lore behind the cording?"

"I don't know that, either. It was only after he was long dead that I began to understand what he had taught me—and poor Marie never did manage to learn it. Now she is gone, and I dare not use it myself except to enhance my wifely pastimes, as you see here." She indicated the tapestry with a sweep of her hand. "I sometimes wonder why we are given such training, if we may never use it."

She fell silent at that, and Vera did not speak. In that instant they had passed from idle reminiscence to consideration of one of the greatest enigmas of their lives. After a moment, Alyce glanced at the doorway again, then scooted her stool closer to Vera's with a rasp of wood against stone.

"I've had a message from the king," she said.

Vera looked at her sharply, apprehension stiffening her fair features.

"Oh?"

"'Tis nothing ill," Alyce assured her, "other than the timing, perhaps. Sooner than I had hoped, but—" She kept her eyes on her weaving as she took up her shuttle again and continued.

"Before Alaric was born, Kenneth and I . . . made an agreement with the king that our son should serve his son. It was an easy enough promise then, and even while he was still an infant.

"But when we brought him to court for Prince Brion's coming of age this summer, the king informed us that he wishes Alaric to come to court as page to Prince Brion as soon as he reaches his tenth birthday—sooner, if anything should happen to me or to Kenneth."

"Page to the prince!" Vera relaxed visibly and nodded. "But, that's welcome news—or, do you fear his reasons, that he simply wants Alaric nearby, where he can be watched more closely? After all, 'tis no secret what he is."

Alyce shook her head again. "No, it is not that." She drew a deep breath and let it out in an effort to relax, carefully setting aside her shuttle. "Vera, he intends that Alaric should be . . . bound to Prince Brion's service by magic, not just as page and future squire and knight, but to assist when the time comes for Brion to assume his father's full power."

"He would trust a Deryni with this?" Vera breathed.

"It is only a Deryni who *can* do this," Alyce said softly. "It is what Alaric was born to do." She did not add that the king very nearly had been the boy's father. "Kenneth and I agreed to this, soon after I discovered I was with child. The time now has come to begin his preparation."

Wide-eyed, Vera sat back and merely gazed at her twin, trying to take it all in, too stunned for speech. Then she came to slide her arms around her sister's shoulders and they simply held one another, clinging together in fear and futile comfort.

A little later, when their fears had been somewhat

assuaged by creature comfort in one another's company, they drew apart to dry their eyes and sniffle forlornly and force reason to prevail once again over human doubts and worries. Alyce swallowed with difficulty and drew herself up straighter, still clinging to her sister's hand, and forced a tight, desperate smile.

"Foolish women, we, to weep when there is a chance to give our sons a better life. We are of the High Deryni born. We were bred to better things."

Vera nodded: a curt, constrained dip of her chin, trying to match her sister's bravery. "You speak truly. Has . . . has the king yet told you what must be done?"

"Aye, some. He commands that first of all Alaric must be Named, according to the ancient traditions of our people—though how he has learned of this custom, I know not."

"Is it wise to Name so young a child as Alaric?" Vera asked. "He is only just four. By tradition, he should have near twice the years."

"The essential element is that he understands the difference between right and wrong—not his years," Alyce replied. "What concerns me most is that he not be frightened at his first encounter with serious magic. The ritual is not dangerous, as you know, but it could be very alien to a four-year-old, even one as precocious as my Alaric."

After a few seconds, Vera said, "Suppose I were to Name Duncan at the same time. Would that help?"

Alyce snorted softly. "Did I not just hear you say that even Alaric is young for this, and that a child should have twice the years before he is Named?"

"Well, I cannot let you do this alone," Vera said reasonably. "Or Alaric. At least if the boys are together, they will have one another to make it seem less strange."

Hardly daring to believe it, Alyce gently laid a hand on her sister's shoulder.

"I prayed that you would say that," she whispered. "Would you really agree to do this for us?"

"How could I *not*?" Vera replied.

Alyce smiled and shook her head slowly. "How I do love you, dear sister."

"And I, you."

"Enough to do this thing tonight?"

"*Tonight?* So soon?"

Alyce nodded and took a deep breath. "I know it isn't much time, but who knows what the future may bring? I could die in childbirth—and the king is not young. But now, tonight, you and I are both here, and the boys are here, and—please say you'll do it, Vera."

Vera sighed wearily, suddenly looking far older than her twenty-five years, then nodded.

"Tonight. So be it."

FOR their working place, Alyce chose the tiny Lady chapel that Earl Jared had caused to be built the previous summer, in the heart of the castle gardens. It was there that he and Vera had finally laid their stillborn daughter to rest, at the feet of the chapel's statue of the Blessed Virgin; and it was there that Alyce had already spent many hours pondering her situation and what they must do.

Later that afternoon, while the maids tackled the task of scrubbing the mud off two exuberant boys—Kevin declared himself grown enough to take his own bath—the two mothers brought baskets of "sewing" into the shade of the garden, there to disappear for a time into the chapel's cool recesses and make their preparations. Kenneth and Jared had gone out with a hunting party around noon, and returned early in the evening.

After they all had supped, Alyce drew her husband aside and told him privily what he must know of the evening's plans. Alaric had been long ago tucked up in bed and was sleeping peacefully. Sir Llion did not question that the puppy had been relegated to his room for the night, and would ask no questions in the morning.

"I never guessed that Vera is your sister," Kenneth said to her in a low voice, as they gazed down at their sleeping son. "Does Jared know?"

Alyce shook her head. "Nay, and he must *not* know," she replied. "Not because he might think the lesser of Vera, or of Duncan—he is a good man—but because all of them will be safer that way. Right now, you are one of only three people who know the truth—and Vera and I are the other two." She closed her eyes briefly. "Actually, I lied; there may be four. I'm sure you remember Father Paschal, who was my family's household chaplain. He knows, or knew. But I am not certain he is even still alive . . . though I hope I would have heard, if he had passed on."

Kenneth glanced away briefly, pondering what she had said, then took both her hands and grazed her knuckles with his lips before raising his gaze to hers again.

"I remember Paschal, of course. Is he . . . one of you?"

She nodded.

"But—"

"I know," she whispered. "And I know that we are supposedly barred from the priesthood. But Paschal is Bremagni-born, and R'Kassan-trained. Matters in the East are not the same as here." She shrugged. "But I have not heard from him in some time. He is quite elderly by now, if he still lives."

"And he knows about Vera," Kenneth said.

"Yes." She leaned her cheek against his hand and closed her eyes, shivering, and he briefly stroked her hair. Then:

"Dearest Alyce," he murmured. "I think I understand some of what you are doing, and a little of the why. Both would be dangerous, if found out. But if one does not know, one cannot betray that knowledge, even under coercion. Can you . . . block me so that I may not speak of this? Please. Do this for all of us," he added, when her expression mirrored her reluctance.

"Very well," she whispered. "Afterward. But for tonight, I need your active support—your protection. And I need your senses unclouded. Will you help me?"

"You know that I will, dearest heart," he replied, turning her hands to kiss both palms.

Chapter 17

"And thou shalt be called by a new name, which the mouth of the Lord shall name."

—ISAIAH 62:2

JUST past midnight, they and Vera and two small, sleepy boys made their way quietly down to the garden and its mortuary chapel, the two boys bundled in fur-lined capes against the late-night chill. The mothers led their sons; Kenneth brought up the rear, a sword at his hip. Jared had taken himself off to bed soon after supper, declaring himself bone-weary from the day's hunting, though the opinion had been reinforced by his wife's deft suggestions. The rest of the castle slept.

The two women had oiled the hinges of the chapel door that afternoon, so their entry was silent save for their whispered admonitions to the children to be quiet in God's house. As they led the boys inside, the women's long, hooded cloaks swept in a flurry of leaves that scattered and then settled as Kenneth followed inside and closed the chapel door behind them. The silence, after the latch clicked into place, was profound.

Wordlessly Kenneth took up a guardian position with his back against the door, his dark green cloak almost invisible in the moon-dappled shadows. He had unsheathed his sword at Alyce's gesture, resting its point on the stone between his feet, his bare hands curved over the quillons, eyes downcast. Though he seemed distant, almost unaware of the presence of Vera and the sleepy Duncan, Alyce knew that his seeming detachment masked an acute awareness, if not an understanding, of what he was being called upon to perform. Young Alaric clung to his mother's hand and watched all with wide-eyed curiosity, not understanding why his father stood so still and solemn and did not smile at him.

They had entered from the south. The Lady chapel was small and square, little larger than an ordinary room, its ceiling spanned by plastered ribs that framed painted frescoes of the night sky. To their right, a Presence lamp washed ruby over the carved ivory intricacies of the altar and its delicate reredos. In the far northwest corner, angled to oversee the entire chamber, a painted statue of the Virgin stood vigil over a second candle flame shielded in glass of the color of a summer sky. Beneath the flagstones at the Virgin's feet lay the mortal remains of Vera and Jared's stillborn daughter, reinterred there only weeks before.

Moonlight filtered dimly through the stained glass of the east window as the two women led their sons into the center of the chamber. A small, square table lay in readiness there, its surface covered by pristine white linen that touched the polished marble floor all around, low enough that the children could see its surface. Upon this table four unlit candles in silver holders were set in a line.

A sheathed sword lay on the floor in front of the table, half hidden by the folds of the tablecloth, its cairngorm pommel glowing in the lamplight like a watchful eye. Other necessities had been placed beneath the table, where the children could not see them.

"Alaric, we must give reverence to God," Alyce prompted in a low voice, suiting her own actions to her words as she made a deep curtsy toward the altar and the Presence symbolized by the vigil lamp.

The child Alaric carefully pushed back the hood of his cape and bowed his golden head, stubby legs bending in solemn imitation of adult genuflection. Beside him, his aunt and his cousin also made their obeisances, young Duncan sleepy-eyed but attentive as he held his mother's hand and watched her for further instruction.

With a smile, Vera led both boys behind the table, the three of them kneeling in a line with Vera in the center. As she folded her hands, the boys did the same, watching with fascination as Alyce knelt beside them and extended her palms over the center two candles.

"Blessed art Thou, O Lord our God, King of all creation, Who hast sanctified us by Thy commandments and hast commanded us to kindle this light."

At a slight movement of her hands, fire flared beneath them so that she had to draw them a little apart, to keep from being burned. She heard Alaric's sharp intake of breath at the creation of fire, and Vera's hushed *"Shh!"* as she closed her eyes and continued the invocation.

"Blessed art Thou Who hast kept us alive and sustained us and brought us to this place," she murmured. "May we be consecrated, O God, by the light of Thy countenance, shining upon us in blessing and bringing us peace. Amen."

"Amen," Vera repeated, the boys adding their own tremulous echo to hers.

Next Alyce took up the two remaining unlit candles and handed one to each of the children, gently guiding her son's hand to light his from one on the table. Alaric scrambled to his feet and watched the flame in awe as his mother released his hand, for he had never been allowed to hold a lighted candle by himself before. Beside them, Duncan was grinning widely as he, too, held his first lighted candle. Alyce smiled as she took each boy's free hand and led them back a few paces behind the table.

"Now, come and sit here, on either side of me," she whispered, crouching down as they settled cross-legged on the floor and listened eagerly. "Put your candles on the floor in front of you and pay close attention. We are about to do some very grown-up things, which most children do not get to see until they are much older than you are. This is a very special privilege."

"We be good, Auntie Alyce," young Duncan piped.

"I know you will, darling. Now, watch what your mama does. She's taken one of the first candles that I lit. Alaric, watch your auntie Vera. Someday, when you are grown, you may have to do what she is doing, all by yourself.

"Now, did you notice the four candles around the room?" Alyce gestured toward the larger, fatter candles set on the floor at the four quarters of the room and caught the movement of both young heads nodding.

"Good. Now, watch as she lights them, starting with the one in front of the altar," she instructed. "Those are called Ward candles. To ward means to guard or protect. The Ward candles guard the four quarters, and each of them is named for one of the archangels. Can either of you tell me who is the archangel of the east?"

Both young pairs of eyes turned toward the altar, where Vera was kneeling to touch a lighted taper to the first Ward candle, which was set on the floor before it. Alaric glanced up at his mother tentatively.

"It's . . . Raphael?" he said a little uncertainly.

"It is, indeed. The Archangel Raphael is the Healer, the guardian of the element of air. Duncan, do you know who is the archangel of the south?"

Duncan looked to the right, where his mother had just lit the second candle, not seeming to see Kenneth, standing against the door.

"That's Michael," he said confidently. "He has a big, fiery sword."

Alyce nodded her approval. "That's absolutely correct. St. Michael is the leader of all the hosts of heaven, and he represents the element of fire, in the south. Alaric, who is the archangel of the west?"

Vera was lighting the candle behind them now, and Alaric twisted around to look at her before returning his attention to his mother.

"The archangel of the west is Gabriel, who-did-bring-glad-tidings-to-our-blessed-Lady," he rattled off proudly, a rote answer that he obviously had memorized from some catechism. Alyce suspected that Father Anselm, the chaplain at Rhemuth Castle, might have had a hand in that.

"Very good," she murmured, allowing herself a reassuring smile. "And what element does Gabriel command, do you know?"

Alaric considered the question briefly, then pronounced wisely, "Water."

"Correct!" Alyce smiled as she smoothed his white-gold hair. "Saint Gabriel rules the element of water. Now, Duncan, the last one is yours. See, your mother lights the candle in the north. Do you know whose candle it is? This one is a little harder."

She almost had to laugh at the intensity of Duncan's expression as he searched for the answer.

"He's the archangel for earth," he said after a studied pause. "And his name is . . . his name is . . . I forget! It's too hard!"

"Never mind, darling. You got it partly right. He *is* the archangel of the earth, and his name is Uriel. Say 'Uriel,' both of you."

"Ur-i-el," the boys repeated obediently.

"Good. Now, see, Duncan, your mother has lit Uriel's candle, and now she comes back around to the east, because the east is the source of light, where the sun comes up. When setting Wards, we always start and finish in the east, to do honor to the Light of God. Will you remember that for me?"

Both boys nodded solemnly as Vera returned to the table and knelt to set down her candle with its mate. They watched with fascination as she took a charcoal brazier from under the table and set it between the two candles, brought out a small dish of incense with a spoon of carved horn.

She held her hands over the charcoal for only a few seconds before it began to smolder, to the boys' chortling delight. She gave them a stern glance, which at least produced silence, then spooned a few grains of incense onto the glowing charcoal and raised the censer a little toward the altar, inclining her head slightly in homage.

"Stetit Angelus justa aram temple," she murmured, continuing the phrase as she set the censer down long enough to get to her feet.

"Mummy, what she said?" Alaric demanded in a loud whisper, tugging impatiently at his mother's sleeve.

"Shhh. Those are ancient words of blessing, darling," Alyce explained. "She said, 'An angel came and stood before the altar of the temple, having a golden censer in his hand . . . ' "

As the fragrant smoke spiraled upward, dispersing in the draft from a partially opened window, Vera picked up the brazier and carried it toward the eastern quarter again, again speaking in Latin.

"Ab illo benedicaris, in cujus honore cremaberis, Amen."

" 'Be thou blessed by Him in Whose honor thou shalt be burned,' " Alyce translated for her two rapt listeners. "Now, watch what happens as she walks around us to visit the other quarters. She's tracing out a circle to protect us. It's possible that you may see something in the smoke she leaves in her path. Tell me if you notice anything strange."

As Vera traced the circle with incense, Alyce could feel and see the next layer of energy being built around them. A glance at the two children confirmed that they, too, were aware that something was happening. By the time Vera had returned to the center of the circle to cense the three of them, Alaric was craning his neck to look at the candle-marked boundaries, squinting as if trying to focus on something that was not quite clear to his untrained eyes.

"What did Auntie Vera do, Mummy?" he whispered, tugging at her sleeve again and looking again at the candles. "Something funny. I see it, but I don't. It's all fuzzy."

"Shhh, just watch," Alyce murmured, resting her hands on both the boys' shoulders.

The incense was back on the table, and now Vera moved around the circle again, this time sprinkling the perimeter with water from a small earthen bowl. When she had completed her third circuit, the haze of the protective circle was unmistakable. Alaric's cherubic face was wreathed in smiles, and Duncan's a study in delight as he pointed out the golden glow to his cousin. As Vera came to kneel before them with her bowl of water, Alyce caught their gaze and laid a finger across her lips for silence.

The two watched intently as first Alyce and then Vera dipped two fingers in the water and blessed themselves. But this, at least, they understood, for they had done it many times before. Very solemnly, for children so young, each of the boys followed suit, neither of them spilling even a drop in their determination to do things correctly. Both of them watched expectantly as Vera set the water bowl on the little table and changed places with Alyce.

Alyce could feel the boys' eyes following her as she went to the other side of the table and unsheathed the sword, heard their little gasps of wondering as she lifted it point-upward before her and moved toward the eastern Ward. With both hands wrapped around the hilt to steady the weight of the weapon, she brought the hilt to eye-level and closed her eyes, breathing a silent invocation from a bygone time, whose precise sense was no longer accessible to conscious thought. The crimson light of the vigil lamp and the warmer fire of the eastern candle burnished her face to richest gold, save where the shadow of the quillons fell across her forehead.

She extended the sword in salute then, the hood slipping from her pale hair as she threw back her head and gazed for an instant along the length of shining blade, her eyes momentarily dazzled by a light brighter than mere reflected fire, which rippled along the polished metal.

Then she was lowering the tip of the sword to touch the floor, turning to the right to trace the circle of protection a third and final time. Golden light followed her blade where the sword passed, merging and growing with the earlier glow to rise in an increasing wall that curved inward far above their heads.

She could not see anything besides the light as she walked, though she could feel Vera's sustaining strength adding to her own and knew that the boys were watching with awe. As she completed the circuit, she felt the shielding canopy of the circle close above their heads with a satisfyingly hollow surge of energy, a golden hemisphere of light that obscured what lay outside.

She saluted the east again, then brought the blade to

ground and laid it on the floor at the foot of the eastern candle. She could feel the prickling, tingling sensation of the circle's protection surrounding them all as she returned to her son's side and crouched down beside him, disarming his apprehension with a smile. Vera had already drawn Duncan away from his cousin, the pair of them standing closer beside the table, and was speaking with him quietly.

"Alaric, my love," Alyce murmured to her son, lightly touching his forearm with one hand. "Did you like what Mummy did?"

Alaric rolled his eyes upward to study the canopy of light again, then pursed his lips speculatively, nodding. "Mummy made light," he said in a whisper. "How you did that, Mummy?"

"One day you shall learn, my love. Just now, though, Mummy has to help Aunt Vera for a little while. Will you do something for me while I'm busy?"

At his nodded assent, she tucked the fur-lined cape more closely around his baby legs and moved his almost-forgotten candle a little closer to his crossed feet. Alaric was already intrigued, watching everything she did with great interest.

"I'd like you to watch this candle for me," she said.

His eyes darted obediently to the flame, and Alyce brushed his forehead with her hand, watched the grey eyes go glassy, the long-lashed eyelids droop in trance.

"That's right. Now sleep a little while, my love. Go to sleep."

Another touch, a passing of her hand downward, and the grey eyes closed, the white-gold head nodding against the chest. Alyce touched her lips lightly to her son's forehead and sealed his sleep, then returned to where Vera was kneeling beside the standing Duncan, one hand steadying the candle he held in his two chubby ones.

"Very good," Vera was saying, as Alyce came to kneel on Duncan's other side. "Now, I want to ask you another question. Can you tell me the difference between right and wrong?"

Duncan nodded confidently, the light of his candle reflecting twin stars in the enlarged pupils of his baby eyes.

"You can? Well, then, will you tell me about something that's wrong?" Vera encouraged.

Again, Duncan nodded. "It's wrong to break promises, and—and to hurt people and animals, and make them cry. I don't like to hurt things, Mummy."

"I know you don't, darling," Vera said, giving the boy a quick hug. "And as you grow up, I want you always to remember that. Will you do that for me?"

"Yes, Mummy."

"Thank you! Now, because I love you very, very much, I am going to give you a very special present. It's another name, besides the ones you already have: a special name, a magical name, a name for you to use when you're being very, very good, and you're not to tell anyone else what it is. Would you like that?"

"Can't tell anybody?" Duncan asked, cocking his head to one side in puzzlement. "Not even Papa an' Kevin an' Alaric?"

"Well, perhaps Alaric, someday, but not even Papa and Kevin. This is a very special, secret name, all your own, because one day, when you are a big, grown man like Papa, you will be very strong, and you will have great power to help people or to hurt them. You must promise that you will only help them. Will you promise me that, my love?"

Duncan's eye had lit with wonder at the story his mother told him of someday, when he was grown up, and he nodded earnestly. Alyce was certain he was seeing his father and other great knights in his young mind, and wished there were some way that she and Vera could impart to both the boys just what their heritage actually meant.

But not yet. Such knowledge was too dangerous to entrust to such young children—especially Duncan, whose Deryni heritage was yet unknown beyond those present in the room. God willing, she and Vera would have many years to train both Alaric and Duncan in the ways that they should go; but if not, then what happened here tonight must be so binding that, even later, their sons would be able to piece together the path they should walk.

Smiling reassurance, Alyce took Duncan's candle and set it on the table, then laid one hand on the boy's shoulder as Vera reached under the tablecloth to withdraw a quill and ink, a slip of parchment, a small earthen bowl, never before used. She watched as her sister put the quill in Duncan's baby hand and dipped the ink and guided it to trace out the letters of the name they had chosen for him.

"Your special name shall be *Phelim*," Vera said softly, finishing the round stroke of the *P* and then moving on to the *H*. "*Phelim* is a name that means a good person, someone who tries always to do the right thing."

Together, their hands traced the *E*, the *L*, moved on to the *I*.

"Sometimes it may be hard to live up to that name," Vera went on, as they finished the final stroke of the *M*, "but I know you'll try ever so hard, won't you?"

Duncan frowned at an ink blot on one of his fingers and nodded distractedly as his mother laid down the pen and put the slip of paper into the earthen bowl.

"There's my brave, clever boy. And you must always try to be brave for good things."

"I be brave for you, Mummy," Duncan said gravely. "I always protect you."

"I'm sure you will, my darling."

Vera took the dagger that Alyce passed her from under the table and wiped the blade on an edge of her cloak.

"And Mummy must be brave, too. Mummy must prick her finger, and then Phelim must prick his. Will that be all right?"

As Duncan watched wide-eyed, soft lips agape, Vera touched the point of the dagger to her right index finger and pressed until it drew blood. One drop she allowed to fall on the parchment beside her son's new name, before briefly sucking the wound clean. Then, as she held the dagger for Duncan, Alyce let her hand slip from Duncan's shoulder to the back of his neck, extending control and blocking pain as the little boy fearlessly put his own finger against the dagger point and pressed.

He drew back a little as the skin was punctured, but more from surprise than any real discomfort or fear. He watched almost clinically as his mother squeezed a drop of his young blood onto the parchment beside her own.

Then, as the boy sucked on his wounded finger and watched her absorbedly, Vera opened a locket around her neck and withdrew a coiled hair—Jared's—which she laid on the parchment and anchored with a drop of wax from Duncan's candle.

"Now, as this parchment burns," she said, putting the candle in Duncan's hand and guiding him to set the parchment alight, "remember that this is a secret name, which you must tell no one. Because if a bad person knows your secret name, it can make him strong, and he might be able to hurt you."

She watched Duncan watch the smoldering flame until it had died away and there was only a residue of ash in the bottom of the earthen dish. Then she pressed her thumb to the ashes and traced a smudged cross on her son's brow, the while murmuring the words of a blessing. Eyes closing at her touch, Duncan breathed out with a little sigh as his mother's mind caressed his. Then Vera laid both her hands on his brown hair, her own eyes closing in trance.

Alyce watched for several seconds, briefly adding her own strength to the patterning being done, then withdrew unobtrusively and got to her feet. Moving to where the sword lay at the foot of the eastern Ward, she lifted it and saluted the east, then touched the point to the floor at the left of the eastern Ward and swept it up and back down in a tall, narrow arc, opening a doorway to the altar steps.

She knelt, her hands on the quillons of the sword, as Vera led the dreamy-eyed Duncan to the threshold with his candle and waited. Fearlessly he passed through the doorway, leaving the circle, and mounted the three shallow steps alone, there to stand on tiptoes while he set his candle on the altar. When he was satisfied with its placement, his head bobbed in a bow and then he rushed back through the doorway and into his mother's embrace. Vera hugged him close, murmuring words of endearment and stroking his hair to lull him into slumber as she gathered him into her arms, giving Alyce a relieved smile, for Duncan's part in the ceremony now was complete.

But as Alyce rose and moved to seal the gateway again, she started and then froze as a shadow moved in the chapel doorway, obscured by the haze of the protective circle. She had warned Kenneth not to interfere, to admit no one, but now a slit of dappled moonlight was widening behind him, outlining the silhouette of a second hooded figure in the doorway.

"Kenneth?" she called softly, instinctively raising the sword across the gateway in a guard position and preparing to close it instantly, if needed.

Kenneth did not reply, only stepping aside with bowed head while the second shadow, cloaked and hooded in black, slipped past him and moved westward along the periphery of the circle, still unrecognizable in the shimmer of the golden light. Black-gloved hands pushed back the fur-lined hood as the intruder passed the northern Ward.

"No, it isn't Kenneth," said a frighteningly familiar voice, low but unmistakable. "There is no need to fear. Do not close your circle."

Chapter 18

"And as a mother shall she meet him."

—ECCLESIASTICUS 15:2

ALYCE gasped as the king came into full view between the northern and eastern Wards, still moving toward her and the open gate.

"Sire!"

In her hands, the sword seemed suddenly to turn to lead, its tip weaving and slowly sinking until it touched the floor. Beside her, Vera drew the sleeping Duncan close against her breast and stared at the king in speechless fear. It had been daunting enough that Kenneth now knew her true identity—and that of her son. For the king to know as well . . . Granted, tonight's working was being done at the king's behest, but neither of the sisters had anticipated that Donal might come in person, or that Vera's participation with Duncan now placed both of them in danger of exposure.

"My apologies if I have given you cause for alarm," Donal said, bowing slightly to Alyce as he unbuckled his sword and wrapped its belt around the scabbard. "I thought you might expect me. Lady Vera, please be assured that your secret is safe with me."

Before either of them could speak, he had turned to

make a spare but dignified obeisance toward the altar, also laying his sword along the angle of the altar's lowest step. Then he was filling the light-limned gateway with his presence, his grey eyes locked with Alyce's as he laid his hand over hers on the sword hilt.

Numbly she relinquished the weapon, driven back a step by the intensity of his gaze. As Donal took her place at the threshold, he turned his attention to Vera, giving a formal bow over the quillons of the sword that, in his hands, seemed almost toylike.

"My lady, I must ask you to retire. I shall assist my lady Alyce in what further must be done. Take your son and go to bed, and speak of this to no one."

Vera did not tarry. With an anxious glance at her sister and a quick curtsy to the king, she swept Duncan onto her hip and slipped through the gateway and away, not daring to look back. When she had gone, when Kenneth had closed the door behind her and again set his back against it, looking like a stranger, Donal drew the tip of the sword slowly across the open threshold of the circle, left to right.

Golden light flared in the sword's track, sealing the breach in the glowing canopy, briefly gilding his face as he bent to lay the sword across the threshold. Heart still pounding, though she had not moved, Alyce retreated another step as he turned the intensity of his gaze upon her again, driven back by his sheer magnetism.

Though no longer young, Donal Haldane was still a man to be reckoned with—potent, dangerous—even if he had not been a Haldane, and king. This night he wore a plain black cloak and austere riding leathers of no particular distinction, and the sword he had laid at the altar step was plain; but his bearing would have proclaimed him a man of means and authority even if his attire did not. Only the fine ruby affixed in his right earlobe gave further hint of his true station. Protector he had always been, and occasionally mentor. She could not help wondering why he had come.

He smiled then and released her eyes, turning his attention to the removal of his worn leather gloves. Suddenly she found that she could speak again.

"I truly did not expect you here tonight, Sire," she said softly. "It did not occur to me that you would wish to assist me in this matter."

"Did it not?" He raised one eyebrow in slight amusement as he slipped his gloves under his belt. "Nonetheless, I *am* here, and alone save for the three of us, and dare not tarry too long before my guard escort discovers I am not at Castle Rundel, an hour's ride from here, and fears for my safety. Will you prepare me, please? I would not profane your circle further by my untimely entrance."

Surprised, she managed a nod and drew the hood of her cloak back onto her pale hair, took his hand, and led him into the center of the circle, where he crouched by the table on one knee. After renewing the incense, Alyce censed him with the sweet smoke, offered him the holy water so that he might dip his fingers into it and bless himself.

He closed his eyes and remained motionless for several minutes after that, head bowed, his breathing light and barely audible, and she wondered again how he knew what must be done, how he had learned of this most ancient of Deryni traditions, when he was not himself Deryni. She watched him sidelong as she quietly exchanged Duncan's ash-smudged bowl for a new one and brought out a fresh slip of parchment. She glanced briefly at Kenneth, once again a silent shadow in the doorway.

As for Alaric, he had not stirred, through all the interruption of the king's arrival. He still sat huddled in his tiny cape, eyes closed in deep Deryni trancing. His candle flame gilded his face and washed the white-gold hair with yet more gold, playing light and shadow on the soft contours of his features. She started to go to him, but her movement triggered Donal's awareness and he came to his feet, laying a restraining hand on her wrist.

"Nay, I shall bring him," the king said softly. "There is a bond between us. He will come to me."

Numb, her senses whirling, Alyce watched him go to her sleeping son, remembering how very nearly he had also been Donal's child instead of Kenneth's. Roused by the king's soft word and touch, the boy put his small hand into the king's larger one, smiling, and scrambled to his feet, picking up his candle and walking with Donal to the table where his mother waited anxiously.

Pushing back her apprehensions, Alyce knelt down beside her son so that they were at the same level, smiling to reassure him as her eyes searched his wide grey ones with love.

"Hello, my darling," she murmured, watching his face light at the sound of her voice. "Did you have a little nap?"

"Oh, no, Mummy, I wasn't asleep," the boy replied, shaking his head with the gravity of an adult. "I watched the candle, just like you said. I watched and watched."

With a smile, she took the candle from him and set it on the table, then hugged him close for just a moment before withdrawing to look at him again, her hands enfolding his lightly between them.

"Darling, Mummy wants to ask you a few questions. It will be like school, when Father Anselm teaches you about the saints. Would that be all right?"

The boy nodded solemnly, and Alyce echoed his nod. Suddenly it was very important that he answer well, as much for the man who stood behind him as for her own reassurance. Alaric was only just four, so she knew she was asking a great deal, but Duncan, who was even younger, had answered well enough. . . .

"Alaric," she began, "I know that Father Anselm has talked to you about the difference between right and wrong."

Alaric nodded solemnly.

"Do you think you can tell me about something that's wrong? Can you give me an example?"

The boy cocked his head thoughtfully, then looked at her with all the wisdom of his four years.

"Do you mean just naughty, like when I kick Cousin Kevin, or really bad?"

Alyce had to concentrate to keep from smiling at the sagacity of that answer. She need not have worried about her son's understanding.

"Something really bad, I think. Tell me about something that is really wrong."

"Oh. Well, killing people, or hurting them on purpose. Taking things that don't belong to you."

"I see. And what do you think about people who do those things?"

A stormy look came across the boy's face. "They shouldn't do them, Mummy! God doesn't like it! The king doesn't like it, either!"

"The king?" Alyce resisted the urge to look up at Donal, still standing motionless behind the boy, and wondered whether Alaric was aware of what he had just said. "What do you know about the king, my love?"

"Well, he works for God," the boy said in a matter-of-fact tone. "Papa told me. He says that we should love the king, almost as much as we love God, and we should keep our promises to him, and we should try to help him do good things."

Alyce heard Donal make a small, strangled sound somewhere between a cough and a smothered chuckle, but she dared not look up to see which it was. God knew, she had not coached the boy in his answers, and certainly had not expected that the king might be present to hear them, but she thanked whatever lucky providence had made Kenneth spend time regaling the boy with tales of kingly attributes.

As much to cover her relief as anything else, she hugged Alaric close once again, at last chancing a look up at the silent king. Donal's grey eyes were glittering with mirth, his lips pursed in the only expression he could manage without breaking out into a very unkingly grin.

"Yes, we *should* help the king," she whispered, stroking her son's golden head and brushing his hair with a kiss. "You've answered very well. In fact, you've answered so well that Mummy is going to give you a special prize. Would you like that?"

"A prize?" he replied, as she reached her arms around him and picked up the quill, putting it in his hand and guiding it to the inkwell.

Donal also knelt beside them, one hand resting lightly on the boy's shoulder, though Alaric seemed not to be aware of that fact.

"I am going to give you a new name, a secret name," Alyce said, as she guided his hand in a first vertical stroke. "It will be a special name, a name of power, for when you are a grown man, and it will be—"

"His name shall be *Airleas*, which means a pledge," Donal interrupted softly, his free hand touching Alyce's just as she was starting to form another letter besides an *A*.

In an instant of bewilderment, Alyce felt her hand moving into the second stroke of the *A* as if that were the letter she had intended all along, her voice picking up where it had left off, only with Donal's words.

"Your name shall be *Airleas*, which means a pledge." Her hand, with the boy's enfolded in it, finished the *A* and swept into the *I*, the *R*. "A pledge is a promise. So this name means that you are to keep your promise to do good things and to help the king."

The *L* and the *E* flowed off her quill and swept on into the second *A*, the final *S*.

"Airleas," she said again, as she laid the quill across the back of the table and wondered what had become of the name she had chosen. "Air-le-us. Say it for me."

"Air-le-us," the boy parroted.

"Which means?"

"A promise."

"That's exactly right. A promise or a pledge. *Airleas*."

She picked up the parchment and blew on the ink to finish drying it, then laid it in the little earthen bowl. Almost, she could not remember that there had ever been another name besides Airleas. She wondered, as the last memory of that other name faded, just what the king had done to her, and why—though she could not bring herself to resent it. Already, Donal's hand had closed around the hilt of the little dagger, now held it braced against the snowy table covering. The blade flashed candlelight once in Alaric's eyes, catching and holding his fascinated attention.

Alyce drew a deep breath, suspecting that Donal had done that intentionally, not feeling further words necessary. Almost absently, she pressed her forefinger to the dagger's point until it drew blood, let a drop fall on the parchment they had just inscribed.

Alaric watched the process gravely, not hesitating when Donal turned the blade slightly toward him. He pushed his smaller fingertip onto the point without flinching, gave no sign of pain or fear as the blood welled. Without prompting, he himself touched the first glistening droplet to the parchment before popping his wounded finger into his mouth.

As Vera had done, Alyce then produced one of Kenneth's hairs to seal the naming, affixing it to the parchment with wax from Alaric's candle. But when she would have passed the candle to Alaric for him to light the parchment, Donal stayed her hand, rising to peer back in Kenneth's direction and lift a hand in summons.

"Kenneth, join us, please," he said softly. "Leave your sword, and come 'round the way I came."

Dutifully Kenneth leaned his sword against the door frame and began circling to the left to flank the circle, keeping a wary eye on the golden shimmer at his right shoulder. As he came, Donal moved to the east and picked up the sword laid across the threshold, saluted the east, cut a new gate before the altar. He lifted the blade in challenge just as Kenneth came into the gateway, bringing him to an abrupt halt with steel against his breastbone and empty hands half lifting, their gaze locking along the length of shining steel.

"Know that no deception is possible within this circle," the king said quietly, then lifted his blade in permission and salute, reversed it to shift to his other hand, grasping it under the quillons. "Now enter in peace."

Visibly bracing himself, Kenneth took the hand that Donal extended and passed through the gateway, waiting as the king resealed the gate and laid the sword across the threshold. Alyce had been watching all of it, and beckoned for her husband to join her on Alaric's right as the king sank down on the left.

"You have seen how the children were sealed to their Naming," Donal said quietly to Kenneth, taking up the dagger. "For a simple Naming, your hair was sufficient to link you to your son, but the work eventually required of Alaric will be anything but simple, and it may be that he will need your assistance. Such assistance requires a bond of blood—but only a drop," he added with a faint smile, handing the dagger to Kenneth. "I would have you in my service long after tonight."

At his nod of reassurance—and Alyce's—Kenneth briskly nicked a fingertip with the blade and smudged his blood on the parchment beside hers and Alaric's. But when he handed the dagger back to Donal, offering it hilt-first, the king turned its point against his own thumb, not flinching as the blade bit and royal blood welled around it, dripping onto the parchment. When he had set aside the blade, briefly sucking at his wound, he took Alaric's two hands in his and fixed him with his grey Haldane gaze.

"Alaric Anthony Morgan, *Airleas*, be thou *my* son as well as theirs," Donal whispered, gazing deeply into the boy's eyes, "and be the pledge for Haldane blood, now until forever. . . And say *Amen*."

The boy's mouth moved obediently in the response, but his voice was only a whisper, his eyes wide as saucers. Smiling, the king kissed him gently on the forehead, then glanced at Alyce and nodded slightly.

Numbly, as though she watched through another's eyes, she saw herself putting her son's candle in his hand, heard herself telling him to light the parchment. As the parchment flared hot and bright, burning with the faint aroma of singed blood, the boy watched in fascination, pupils black as ink. Kenneth had subsided back on his hunkers, eyes closed and head bowed, hands resting easily on his thighs with fingers splayed, now oblivious to what was taking place.

When the parchment had burned to ash, Alyce dipped her thumb in the residue and traced the cross on her son's brow as she sealed his name by word and thought. Then the king was laying his hands on either side of Alaric's head and delving deep, crowding her out to watch helplessly as he set his will upon the young mind.

When he had finished, he allowed Alyce to enfold the

boy in her arms again, himself rising to go to the edge of the circle where the sword lay across the threshold. Kenneth had lifted his head as the king rose, aware once again, and watched him cut the doorway to the east and gesture for Alyce to proceed.

Not speaking, Alyce put her son's candle in his hand and led him to the threshold, gently nudging him to go through. The boy went fearlessly up the three steps to place his candle beside that of his younger cousin. When he had returned to his mother's arms, a pleased grin on his face, he melted into her embrace and laid his head on her shoulder, asleep in one softly exhaled breath.

Wordless with wonder, Alyce sank into a sitting position with her son cradled in her lap, taking comfort in the circle of Kenneth's arm, watching as the king laid the sword across the open doorway and came to crouch before them. She could not bring herself to question what he had done, or even to offer comment. She knew only that what had occurred had felt right, if unexpected, and that he was fully her match in all that they had done together that night.

"I will come again when he is older, to complete the binding," the king said quietly. "It is not necessary for you to understand all aspects of what has occurred tonight; only that I have done what I felt necessary. He will have suffered no harm.

"Of course, you will speak of this to no one," he went on, eyeing both of them. "Not even to one another—nor, Alyce, to your sister."

She nodded, not daring to speak, as he glanced back at the sword across the gateway, then returned his piercing gaze to her and Kenneth and the child sleeping on her shoulder, while getting slowly to his feet.

"Guard him well, my faithful friends," he said in a low voice. "And know that you have a king's gratitude for your love and loyal service."

For a moment, as he stood there silhouetted against the candles at the altar, it was as though he drew their glow around him like a mantle, enveloping the four of them. But then the grey eyes shuttered, and the moment was past. With a slight bow, he turned and moved back to the eastern quarter to pick up the sword.

SHE little remembered closing the circle, or putting the sleeping Alaric to bed, or returning to her chamber with Kenneth, just as she was unable, the next morning, to recall many details of the night's work. She knew that the king had come into the chapel, that the two of them had Named Alaric by a name she had not chosen—and her beloved Kenneth had played an unexpected part. But the whole affair had taken on a dreamy, unreal quality that increased with each passing day—and Kenneth, for his part, said nothing.

It was not for want of wondering. Kenneth remembered that night, perhaps more clearly than Alyce, though he understood far less. When, a few days later, a courier arrived with a summons back to Rhemuth and duty, he brought the order to Alyce, where she was dozing in the dappled shade of the garden, near to the little chapel. Alaric was down for a nap, as were Duncan and Kevin, and Vera had gone hunting with her husband and several of their retainers and their wives.

"Unwelcome news, I'm afraid," he said without preamble, showing her the document with the king's seal as he came to kiss her on the forehead. "I'm commanded back to court. Not merely summoned, mind you, but 'commanded.' He's given no specific reason, but it can't be trivial. He knows I had hoped to stay longer, perhaps even through the New Year. But it may be some weeks before I can return. And if the weather is bad . . ."

She did her best to hide her disappointment as she took the missive from him and quickly scanned it, but Kenneth knew. But he did not anticipate her next words.

"Perhaps I should go back to Morganhall for my lying-in, then," she said matter-of-factly, looking up at him from under long lashes. "The summer heat is past, and 'tis far closer to Rhemuth—and much less apt to be snowed in.

And I should very much like to have you at my side when our daughter is born."

"And I should like to be there," Kenneth replied. "Do you think that Vera would come there to be with you?"

"I don't see why not," she answered. " 'Twould be easier for her and Jared, as well, especially if Jared is also called to court—which could well happen, since you have been called. They would like another baby, you know—and that's rather difficult if they hardly see one another."

"There is that," Kenneth agreed. "But Culdi is larger, and far more comfortable."

"But not as close to Rhemuth, and you," Alyce countered. "Morganhall will be fine. And your sisters will be thrilled to have a new baby to coo over."

He inclined his head in agreement. "I'll not argue that."

"Then, it's settled," she said.

KENNETH dared not delay to travel with them, for the king seemed to require his presence urgently—and, in fact, *had* summoned Jared as well, by means of another courier who arrived later that evening.

"You have no idea what this is about?" Jared asked him, handing him his own summons.

Kenneth shook his head. "None whatsoever. But Alyce had already asked whether Vera and your boys might accompany them to Morganhall. There's room—just. And it's far closer. You could see your wife more often," he added with a sly grin. "I know you'd like another bairn."

Jared's smile spoke volumes. "I'll not deny that," he said, "though it isn't for want of trying."

"Well, you can try more often, if your wife is at Morganhall," Kenneth retorted. "Shall I write to my sisters, and tell them the ladies are coming?"

"Do," Jared agreed. "Better yet, we can stop there on our way back to Rhemuth and tell them in person. The women can follow by easier stages. And I'll have extra provisions sent as well. They'll have more mouths to feed."

Kenneth inclined his head in thanks. "My sisters will be grateful."

HE and Jared left the next morning, charging Trevor and Llion with the task of moving their wives and sons by slow stages. On reflection, Jared offered the use of his coach—which Kenneth gladly accepted. It was a ponderous thing, but easier and safer than travel by litter, with Alyce now seven months gone.

"And Lady Alyce is not to travel by any other means save the coach, no matter how she might protest," Kenneth told the two knights, "with plenty of pillows and featherbeds to cushion her."

"Kenneth, I am not *ill*!" Alyce protested. "I am simply pregnant."

"Yes, and you are carrying a precious burden: our daughter," Kenneth replied coolly, though he smiled as he said it, a hand lightly skimming her abdomen. "Trevor, you have your orders."

"Aye, m'lord," Trevor said with a grin.

Alyce made a moue at her husband, but then she twined her arms around his neck and drew him down for a kiss before heading off to begin packing for the journey.

THE distaff-halves of the two families were resettled at Morganhall by the middle of October, much to the delight of Kenneth's two sisters—and with the approval of Alaric, Duncan, and Kevin as well, for there were other children to play with, and more hounds to induct Alaric's new puppy into the canine mysteries. Claara, the younger of the sisters, had been widowed young, and had a daughter and granddaughter staying with her until the spring. Little Clarice was nearly four, slightly younger than Alaric, and as full of mischief as any child Alyce had ever seen.

By contrast, Kenneth's other sister, Delphine, the elder of the pair, had never married, but she adored her nieces and nephews, and was delighted to have the extra company through the end of the year, especially with the promise of additional provisions to feed them all. It was Delphine who ran the Morganhall estate on her brother's behalf—and usually turned a profit.

She was also, it soon emerged, an accomplished poet, and soon had enlisted Alyce's services in copying out a small collection of her poems as a Christmas gift for her brother. The familiar work set Alyce to remembering the days she and Zoë had spent together in the scriptorium at Arc-en-Ciel, and the illuminated book the two of them later had crafted for the king for another Christmas, now several years past.

She wrote to Zoë shortly after her arrival at Morganhall, informing her of the move down from Culdi and her scrivening project, and inquiring after Zoë's new pregnancy, for her heart-sister was due to deliver early in the new year.

"I wish Zoë could be with us," she said wistfully to Vera, as the two of them sat in a sheltered patch of sunshine in a corner of the stable yard and watched their sons romping with the new puppy. Farther off, Llion groomed Cockleburr and prepared for a ride. "Perhaps next summer I shall take Alaric to Cynfyn for a few months; you could join us, if Jared agreed. Little Kailan will be walking by then. And maybe he'll have a baby brother."

Vera smiled and nodded, basking in the sunshine and inhaling deeply of the musky stable-scent and the tang of autumn leaves burning in the nearby garden.

"It might be possible," she replied. "It would certainly be pleasant. Maybe I will . . ."

In that moment, as the two sisters sat in the autumn sun and dreamed of the future, all things seemed possible.

Chapter 19

"Whom, being his firstborn, he nourisheth with discipline, and giving him the light of his love doth not forsake him."

—ECCLESIASTICUS 17:18

THE work on Delphine Morgan's manuscript occupied much of Alyce's time in the weeks that followed, as her pregnancy advanced and sitting became preferable to more strenuous exertion. She was obliged to hastily put the manuscript aside, however, when her husband paid her a surprise visit late in October.

"I think our daughter may arrive early," she told him, later that night, as she lay contentedly in the curve of his arm after a day spent watching him interact with their son. "She is certainly very active. Here, feel." She took his hand and placed it on her abdomen so he could feel the baby moving.

"Maybe you miscalculated," Kenneth said, though a delighted grin creased his face at this tangible evidence of the new life his wife was carrying.

"It's possible. I had thought she might be born around Christmas, but now . . ."

"So long as she and you are healthy," Kenneth said happily. "And I *will* try to be here for the birth. Incidentally, I had a letter from Jovett last week, tucked in with more official correspondence from Cynfyn. He tells me that both

Kailan and Zoë are getting bigger by the day, and *she* says she thinks the new baby is determined to kick out her ribs. They both seem certain that it will be another boy. Could they really know that?"

Alyce shrugged, smiling. "*I* knew; but Zoë isn't Deryni. Heaven knows whether Jovett has the skill. Men usually don't, since they don't bear. Now, if *Sé* were to put his mind to it . . ."

"Is that an Anviller talent? Determining the sex of babies?" Kenneth asked, grinning.

"I doubt it," Alyce replied, "though they are very talented. I don't suppose you've heard from him?"

Kenneth shook his head. "I had thought he might make an appearance in June, for Prince Brion's coming of age. It's the sort of thing that his order tends to keep track of. But I suppose he was otherwise occupied."

"And Brion—is he still on his progress?" she asked.

"Aye, but they should be heading south any time now. The weather will turn very soon. The last I heard, they were up in Claibourne."

"Duke Ewan probably has him out hunting," she replied, snuggling closer to his side. "He'll probably catch his death of cold. The queen told me once that Haldane males are about the most stubborn men in all of creation, and she long ago despaired of making them dress sensibly or come indoors when the weather is foul!"

"They do love their hunting," Kenneth agreed. "In Brion's case, though, I can hardly blame him. Duke Richard's last letter said that the new mare is absolutely sensational in the hunting field. Brion couldn't be more pleased. It seems that Oisín Adair's reputation is well deserved."

"So it seems," Alyce agreed, shifting to ease her back. "In the spring, after I'm more of a size to consider getting on a horse again, perhaps you might have him look for a nice Llanner mare for me. And it won't be long before Alaric will need a proper pony: something gentle and reliable. There's only so much he can do with Cockleburr, though Llion swears that horse treats the boy like he was made of glass."

"I'll mention your concerns to Master Oisín the next time I see him," Kenneth agreed. "And I think I'll see about getting Llion a better mount as well. I should've done it months ago. Cockleburr really is about ready for honorable retirement."

"So long as you keep him around for Alaric's sake," Alyce replied. "He's still worth his keep—a fine old beast for a beginning rider."

"I promise you he shall have a place with us for the rest of his life," Kenneth agreed sleepily.

KENNETH stayed only two days before returning to the capital, for he had no leave to remain longer. A letter from Zoë arrived two days after his departure, though it mostly confirmed news that Kenneth had already shared with Alyce. It did, however, include a quick sketch of an emaciated lion chewing on the tail of a very fat squirrel, alluding to the teasing artistic assessments the two of them had made regarding one another's work during the many hours they had shared in the scriptorium at Arc-en-Ciel.

Alyce wrote back that very day, reporting her progress on Delphine Morgan's scrivening project—nearly complete—and adding her own, less competent drawing of a very fat lion with several squirrels' tails in its teeth.

I wish you were here, she added in a postscript. *We could compare fat bellies, and our babies could have kicking contests to see which one bruises its mother's innards the most! Your A.*

The weather turned the next day, but Alyce sent the letter off by courier nonetheless. With luck, Zoë would have it by mid-November. Another day saw Delphine's project completed.

"And in good time," she told her husband's sister by the fire that night, as she watched Delphine turn the pages and admire the fine calligraphy and embellished capitals. "I shan't be comfortable bent over a writing desk again until after this baby is born!"

"This is beautiful, Alyce," Delphine murmured. "Thank you so much. I know Kenneth will be pleased."

It was early in November, only a few days later, when late-night visitors clattered into the yard at Morganhall, unannounced and unexpected. The night was brittle with cold, and Alyce had been reading by the fire in her bedchamber, drowsing over a difficult passage in the writings of Pharaïlde ní Padramos—a gift from her husband on his last visit. She looked up at an urgent knock on her door, somewhat startled when Sir Llion then slipped inside without waiting for permission.

"Llion?" she said somewhat reproachfully, drawing a fur-lined robe more closely around her shoulders, for she was in her night shift.

"Riders in the yard, my lady," he murmured breathlessly, his eyes wide and awed. "It's Lord Kenneth, with three others. I—I think one of them may be the king!"

At once Alyce put aside her manuscript and rose, one hand drawing the outer robe more protectively over her pregnant belly as she slid her feet into fleece-lined slippers. Her hair was braided for the night, its heavy plait spilling over one shoulder.

"Something has happened," she murmured, half to herself. "Go attend them. I'll be down directly."

The young knight dipped his chin in agreement and withdrew, but before Alyce could do more than slip her arms into the sleeve-slits of the outer robe, her mind racing over conjectures about the reason for another royal visit, the door opened again.

She turned to see Kenneth framed in the oak-limned doorway, still cloaked and booted and spurred, a fur-lined cap in his gloved hands. His handsome face was taut, devoid of expression.

"The king is here," he said, closing the door behind him. "I've left him in my writing room. He's . . . not well, Alyce. There's been a tragic accident at Rhemuth. Prince Jathan is dead."

"Jathan?" She sank back onto her chair. "Dear God, he can't be. What happened?"

Shaking his head, looking near to collapse himself, Kenneth braced one arm along the mantel, fingering the cap in his other hand.

"He had begged for a pony for his birthday, but Donal said he was too young." He sighed heavily, closing his eyes, not wanting to remember.

"But Jathan was headstrong, as you know. A week ago, he went into the stables before dawn. He saddled the pony that used to be Brion's—God knows how!—and took him out into one of the paddocks alone."

"But that pony was steady," Alyce murmured, stunned, "and Jathan is—was—a good rider . . ."

"Aye, he was—for a four-year-old," Kenneth agreed. "But horses are horses, and odd things can spook them at odd times and for odd causes. No one saw it happen." He drew himself up and made himself continue.

"A little later, when the grooms began their morning duties, one of them noticed the stall door open, and no pony. More annoyed than worried, he went looking for it." He shook his head wearily.

"He soon spotted it grazing on the far side of the paddock, but something looked . . . wrong. When he went to investigate, he found the saddle slipped under the pony's belly and—and Jathan . . . with his foot caught in the off stirrup."

A sob caught in Alyce's throat as she closed her eyes, shaking her head. "Dear God," she whispered.

"He . . . must have been dragged for some distance," Kenneth went on reluctantly. "And kicked . . . several times. He was still alive when they found him, but he—died in the queen's arms a short time later. The entire court is stunned." He shook his head again.

"They buried Jathan two days ago, beside Prince Blaine. Brion is still on progress in the north, and has not yet been located. Donal is distraught. I think his heart is broken. But he insisted on coming here tonight. I believe he means to finish what he started at Culdi."

"Dear, merciful Lady, I cannot imagine what he is suffering," Alyce murmured through her tears. "To lose a second child so quickly—it is hardly three years since Blaine . . . And Jathan was so young, nearly the same age as Alaric."

Kenneth gave a stiff nod, acutely aware of the precariousness of life.

"It's Alaric he's come to see," he said quietly. "But he's asked to see you first. I told him I'd send you."

"Will you not come with me?"

Kenneth's footsteps were as gentle as his voice and his touch as he came and took her hands in his, kissed the palms tenderly. "Not this time, my dear. Go to him. I'll wait by Alaric's door."

Wordlessly she nodded and squeezed his hand, letting him help her drape an additional shawl over her fur-lined over-robe but keeping her face averted so he would not see her tears. But by the time she had descended the tower stair and crossed the rush-strewn great hall, her eyes were dry and she had composed herself to meet the man who waited.

She rapped lightly on the door to the writing room and entered without waiting for a response, securing the latch before she turned to look for him. She could see an unfamiliar hat hooked over one of the finials of Kenneth's favorite chair, which was angled to face the blazing fireplace. She stifled a quick gasp of shock as he stood and turned to face her, leaning heavily on a walking staff.

Even prepared to see him grief-stricken and distraught, she had not expected this. The puissant king who had come to them only weeks before, still powerful and strong, had been replaced by a haggard shadow of that man. His black riding leathers hung loosely on his stooped frame, a heavy dagger on his belt pulling almost painfully at his shrunken waist. His hair and beard had gone nearly all to grey, as had his complexion, and his face was lined by creases and wrinkles that had been mere hints of laughter before.

His eyes had changed the least: still grey and clear, but more world-weary now, with a starker shadow of grief in their depths. His hands were white-knuckled on the carved staff he had used to get to his feet, but he managed a reassuring smile as he extended one hand for hers and merely clasped it tightly.

"So, we are quite the pair," the king said softly. "I, pining for yet another lost son, and you, blossoming with the promise of new life yet to be born."

She attempted a brief, wan smile, but could not gainsay his observation.

"Sire, I am so sorry to hear of your loss," she murmured.

"Aye. Three sons have I lost now." He released her hand and sank back into his chair, looking, if possible, even more ashen. "This string of sorrows underlines my mortality, and makes it all the more urgent that you and I complete our final work. Where is the boy?"

"He is sleeping just now," she replied, a little stunned at his urgency. "Kenneth and I will bring him in a few minutes. I—Sire, you do not look well. Forgive me for saying so, but you make me fear that your need for him might come sooner than either of us had hoped. Is there something I should know?"

He looked away, not answering, then leaned his staff in the crook of his arm and beckoned her closer, again taking one of her hands as she knelt beside the chair. His eyes sought hers urgently as he searched for his next words.

"Alyce, can you forgive me for what I've done to you and Kenneth and the boy? God help me, if I could have seen some other way, I would have taken it—I tried to—but even I have not been wholly free of choice. I suppose it comes with the crown. Perhaps our children will be more fortunate."

She glanced at their clasped hands, sharing his sorrow.

"I did not think the King of Gwynedd subject to *any* other's choices."

"He is," Donal whispered, his eyes closing briefly, as if in pain. "God help him, he is."

"And what of Prince Brion," she said softly, unsettled a little by his distress. "Is he ready for what is to come? Will he be able to stand in your place when—when you are gone?"

"As well as any king of tender years, and better than most. But that is why I have come to you tonight, Alyce: to make provisions against that day."

"God grant that it may be long in coming, then," she murmured. "Alaric is so young. Surely there were others of Deryni blood who could have served you just as well, who have the years already to work the Haldane magic for your heir."

"There *was* another, as you know," Donal said softly, barely breathing the words. "By now, he would have been very nearly old enough—but he died."

"I do know, Sire," she whispered, declining to mention the murdered Krispin's name. "But . . . could you not enlist the services of some other Deryni?" she ventured, after a beat. "Sir Morian, perhaps. He is said to have served you well in Meara—or so I had heard. Kenneth has told me of his usefulness."

"Not for this," the king murmured.

Trembling, he pulled her hand closer to clasp it between both of his and press it to his heart, gazing beyond her into a realm where reality was different and children were not called to do an adult's work. Rarely had she felt so at peace and so protected, though reason told her that the feeling was illusory.

They remained that way for several seconds before he eased his caress of her hand to stare down at her again. His eyes held her immobile as she gazed up at him, her heart pounding as though it might burst from her breast, and she could not seem to move, knew herself to be completely at his will.

But then he blinked and shook his head ever so slightly, leaned down instead to kiss her hand. She felt a constriction rising in her throat as he released her and turned his face away, but she forced herself to push it down as she also pushed herself ponderously to her feet. When he did not speak for several seconds, she cleared her throat expectantly.

"Shall I bring him now, Sire?" she asked softly.

"Please do."

She heard him settling back into the chair as she fled the room.

KENNETH was waiting for her at the top of the landing as he had promised, compassion in the sea-grey eyes as he slipped an arm around her thickened waist and accompanied her into their son's room, where she summoned handfire to light their way. Alaric stirred in his sleep as they approached his cot, smiling a little as he dreamed. His fine golden hair was tousled and a little damp where it curled against his neck, his face angelic in slumber. Alyce bent and kissed his cheek tenderly, then took a candlestick from beside his bed and passed a hand over the wick, flaring it to life even as she quenched her handfire.

The boy stirred again and opened his eyes as she gazed down at him, Kenneth at her side. He looked a little bewildered, and started to make a little whimpering noise, but Alyce held one finger to her lips and shook her head as her husband pulled back the blankets and gathered him up with a reassuring hug. At that, Alaric yawned sleepily and ground a chubby fist against his eyes, one arm going around Kenneth's neck as he was carried from the nursery in his nightshirt, bare legs dangling. Alyce did not take her eyes from him as she picked up one of the blankets and followed with the candle to light their way.

In the writing room, the king was still seated before the fire, his carved staff cradled in the crook of his arm. He smiled faintly and gave a nod of approval as Kenneth set the boy on his feet to face him. Alaric seemed bewildered at first, and looked questioningly to his mother as she locked the door and made a slight curtsy before taking a place at the king's right.

"Good evening, Alaric," the king said.

At the boy's look of uncertainty, Kenneth crouched down beside his son, one arm around him in reassurance.

"Alaric, you remember the king," he prompted, directing the boy's attention to the seated man. "What duty do you owe to His Majesty?"

At once the boy drew himself to attention and made the king a grave and correct bow as he had been taught. In return, the king gave him a reassuring smile and held out his right hand, silver flashing at his wrist as he turned his palm up. Alaric smiled, too, as he laid his small hand in the king's great, scarred one in perfect trust, grey eyes searching grey.

"Come and sit beside me, boy. I want to show you something," Donal said, patting the chair and then helping Alaric scramble to a seat half in his lap and half supported by the carved chair arms.

The boy squirmed a little as he settled into the circle of the king's arms, for the royal lap was bony, and the royal belt bristled with adult accoutrements of infinite interest to a small child. He started to touch one careful, stubby finger to the great jewel in the hilt of the king's dagger, but Alyce reached out and touched his forehead lightly, extending control. He subsided at once, settling back in the royal embrace to turn awed, attentive eyes on the king.

Smiling, Donal reached around the boy and removed a wide silver bracelet-cuff from underneath his right sleeve. A handspan wide, its only adornment besides the mirror-polish of the metal itself was an angular, stylized pattern of running lions, their legs and tails intertwined. Donal breathed several times upon the silver, then buffed it against the fur lining of his leather cloak. As he displayed it then between the thumbs and fingertips of both hands, Alaric within the circle of his arms, the polished metal flashed firelight into the boy's fascinated eyes.

"Alaric, this is a very special bracelet," Donal said. "I doubt you'll ever see another like it."

Curious, the boy craned his neck for a better look as the king turned the bracelet to show him the three runes engraved inside. Alyce could see him trying to make sense of the symbols, and sensed his frustration as he discovered that they were not the letters that his mother and Father Anselm had taught him. Abruptly she realized that Donal had sensed it, too; knew his faint amusement as he caught her eyes in a piercing glance for just an instant before laying a fingernail under the first sigil.

"One," the king murmured.

Alaric went briefly rigid, eyelids fluttering, before his eyes rolled upward and he slid into profound slumber, slumping bonelessly against the king's chest. Kenneth, who had withdrawn to watch from nearer the fireplace, gasped and took an involuntary step closer, but faltered when Alyce shook her head and half raised a hand to stop him. As he paused, caught between concern and indecision, Donal laid his open hand across the boy's closed eyes and murmured a few words, which even Alyce could not hear. Power glittered in the fog-grey eyes then, as he looked up and ensnared Kenneth's attention in an irresistible binding.

"Kenneth, you look like you could use a rest," he said softly. "Have a seat."

Instantly obedient, Kenneth backed up a step and sank down on a small stool near the hearth, completely focused on the king's every flicker of movement. Watching him, Alyce thought she knew now how Donal had gotten past her husband that night of Alaric's Naming.

"Now have a little sleep," the king went on, not bothering to watch further as Kenneth's eyes closed and his chin sank to his chest.

Swallowing, Alyce returned her attention to Donal and heavily lowered herself to her knees, beside his chair. She felt his eyes upon her as she tucked the blanket she had brought around her son, expecting only to lend assistance in establishing the necessary link with her son. But at once she sensed the king's mind reaching out to hers as well, probing, insinuating itself into her consciousness and beyond.

Compliant, adapting, she let herself relax into that profound trance state he required for what must be done, letting him guide in setting the compulsions that must wait and germinate in Alaric's young mind, until it should become time for Brion to come into the full knowledge of his father's vast powers—and time for Alaric to facilitate that coming.

And there was more that she had not expected, for

Donal next turned the rapier force of his will upon *her*, laying one of his hands over one of hers and drawing her deeper into trance. Already poised at the edge of consciousness, she suddenly knew herself to be yet another tool in Donal's wielding. As he drew her into a deeper reservoir of power than she had ever sensed was possible, she lost consciousness of anything at all . . .

Some little while later she became aware that her knees were numb from kneeling, that her head throbbed from her exertions, that Donal had withdrawn from their contact, finishing whatever it was he had set out to do. She opened her eyes to see him replacing the silver bracelet on his wrist, watched him press a brief, fervent kiss to Alaric's temple where the pulse throbbed.

"I have taken the liberty of setting a second set of instructions—in you," he said quietly, glancing at her sidelong. "If Alaric is still young when I die, you will have the ability and knowledge to help Brion to his Haldane powers—though, once I set the block, you'll remember none of this unless there is a need. I hope you do not think too ill of me."

"You have empowered *me* with the Haldane triggers?" she breathed, wide-eyed.

"You yourself said it, my dear," he replied, smiling faintly. "It will be several years before Alaric is old enough to do what is needful. In the meantime, my son may need a Deryni to assist him: one whom I may trust implicitly. I have delegated that function to you. God willing, you shall never be called upon to exercise it."

The revelation left her feeling numb and almost violated as Donal turned the focus of his attention away from her. As he gestured vaguely toward her nodding husband, Kenneth stirred and yawned and came to, blinking in the firelight.

The royal hand was on her arm then, helping her to her feet. Memory of the specifics of their working fled even as she rose. Still a little disoriented, she half-sat on one arm of Donal's chair, easing the small of her back with both hands as the king shifted her sleeping son to wrap the blanket more closely around him and raised his eyes to Kenneth's.

"You may take the boy back to bed now," he rasped in a voice that reflected all the weariness and grief of the past week. "All has been done that is needful. He will sleep until morning, after what we have just done. And while I shall not require you to forget what you may have seen and heard tonight, you will not speak of it, save to Alyce. Go now."

Kenneth nodded and got stiffly to his feet, his age, too, showing in his movements. Tenderly he gathered his sleeping son into his arms, pausing so that Alyce could brush her lips against the boy's forehead as she, too, rose.

Then he was gone, and the boy with him. As the door closed, Donal sighed and also got to his feet, leaning heavily on his staff as his eyes sought hers.

"I do not know when we shall see one another again," he said softly. "All has been done as it must be. Brion is already prepared, and now Alaric, and both will be ready when it comes time for them to work together. Nor will either of them be haunted by any knowledge of their roles until that time comes." He paused for just an instant, cocking his head. "Have you any regrets?"

She returned his gaze, finally without apprehension, and found that, indeed, she had none.

"No, Sire. No regrets. Duty is not always easy to bear, but I think we were both obliged to accept, a long time ago, that we must make the best of what our circumstances have decreed. I am honored to have been of service to you and your son."

"Alyce, the honor is all mine, for you have served my son in ways you could never have dreamed," he answered, moving closer to awkwardly take her in his arms.

He pressed his lips to her forehead in something like a kiss, then buried his face in her hair and inhaled of its perfume, simply holding her close for several seconds. She could feel his heart beating, where her cheek pressed close against his chest, and for just an instant it seemed that she had always belonged there, safe in the circle of his arms.

Then he was pulling back with a gasp, the grey eyes haunted by a pain that had nothing to do with his grief over his lost son or the ache of his weary body. Hardly daring to keep looking at her, he brushed her jawline with his fingertips as if to memorize its curve for all eternity. Then he tore his eyes away and thrust her from him, turning to lurch painfully from the room, leaving her trembling beside her husband's chair with a hand pressed to her throat to still the sob that threatened to undo them both. She did not try to stop him, and he did not look back.

Chapter 20

"He shall not depart out of darkness; the flame shall dry up his branches, and by the breath of his mouth shall he go away."

—JOB 15:30

KENNETH was given little opportunity to speak to his wife afterward, for the king insisted on returning immediately to Rhemuth. Donal had left his queen alone with her grief, and Prince Brion might return home at any time.

The weather worsened as they rode south. The first snow of the season caught them on a deserted stretch of road still several hours' ride from Rhemuth: icy rain, at first, which quickly changed to sleet and then to slushy snow.

They took shelter when it became clear that this was no passing shower or even a fast-moving storm, huddling under the canopy of ancient and venerable trees ranged around a roadside shrine to some obscure saint; but by then, they were soaked to the skin. Kenneth and one of the guards who had accompanied them managed to start a fire, which gave at least a little respite from the numbing cold that settled in the predawn hours; but Donal insisted on resuming their journey at first light, in what now had turned to honest snow.

"He'll catch his death of cold," the guard officer grumbled

under his breath, as they checked girths and prepared to mount up again. "Sire, will you not at least tarry long enough to dry out?"

"I cannot longer leave the queen alone in her grief," Donal said stubbornly, leading his mount from under the trees, irritation edging his voice. "Kenneth, tell this man that I know what I am doing."

Forcing a wry semblance of a smile, Kenneth said, "Leonard, he *does* know what he's doing. After all, he is the king."

Chuckling despite himself, Donal accepted a leg up from Kenneth and settled in his saddle as the others mounted as well.

"Yes, I am," he agreed. "And now the king wishes to go home, with all speed." He sighed and glanced aside at Kenneth as they prepared to move out. "But with Jathan's laughter gone," he murmured, so that even Kenneth could barely hear, "it will never be the same."

They rode into Rhemuth at mid-morning, shivering in the hard frost that remained in the wake of the previous night's snow. The snow itself had mostly disappeared under the early morning sun, but that only left their footing muddy and sometimes precarious.

They stopped at the cathedral on the way into the city, where Donal slipped in by a side door and made his way down into the crypt, Kenneth accompanying him. The noonday Mass was in progress, the sound of the sung responses drifting on the chill air along with the scent of incense and the more pungent smell of dampness as they descended the stair.

Cap in hand, Kenneth waited in the doorway of the royal vault with his head bowed as the king entered and shuffled heavily to the yet uninscribed slab that marked Prince Jathan's final resting place. Fragrant boughs of evergreen lay atop the slab, along with a battered toy rabbit made from rough-woven linen and stuffed with wool. The coffin that lay beneath the slab had been pitifully small, like so many other Haldane coffins interred in the cathedral crypt, for childhood illness and mishap took their toll among royal children as well as those not so nobly born. Near a dozen Haldane children of this generation lay there, not only the three now lost by Queen Richeldis but the many stillborn and short-lived infants born to Donal's first queen, Dulchesse: pitiful evidence of her dogged but ineffectual attempts to breed a Haldane heir. Dulchesse herself also lay there, as well as the tragic Krispin MacAthan.

Awareness of all these dead Haldanes drifted across Kenneth's recollections as he watched the king drop heavily to both knees beside the grave of his latest Haldane bereavement and lay his splayed hands upon the blank slab, head bowed. After a moment, the king's hand moved to clasp the stuffed rabbit toy and clutch it to his bosom, shoulders heaving with silent weeping. Having lost children of his own, Kenneth tried not to think about what Donal must be enduring as he mourned this newest loss, and tried especially not to think of the danger into which he had just allowed his own son to be placed, in service of the king kneeling before him.

Only after several minutes did the king lift his head and cross himself, heaving himself painfully to his feet. Kenneth was there to assist him when he faltered, setting an arm under the king's elbow to steady him as he straightened and replaced the stuffed toy amid the evergreen boughs.

"Kenneth, I've lost another of my boys," the king said in a strangled little voice, shaking his head as if denying might reverse the tragedy. "I pray that God will take no more from me. Was it because of Krispin, do you think? Is He punishing me for my infidelity?"

"Sire, I am not your confessor," Kenneth said gently.

"Nay, nay, I know that," the king replied. He briefly bowed his head into a hand covering his eyes, taking another deep breath to steady himself.

"Forgive me," he murmured after a moment, lifting his head and squaring his shoulders. "We must return to the castle. Brion may have returned by now." He shook his head. "He will be horrified to learn that his own pony was his brother's death."

"He cannot be blamed for that, Sire," Kenneth replied. "Brion will know that."

"Aye, in his mind," Donal agreed. "But his heart will say otherwise. If I die untimely, Kenneth, you must be a true friend to my son. You must make certain that all my sacrifices have not been in vain."

"I shall do what I can to serve him, Sire, as shall my son. You have my word on it."

BUT Brion had not returned, nor had any of the king's outriders been able to locate him precisely.

"We presume that he is still somewhere in Kheldour," Tiarnán MacRae told the king, reporting when Donal had summoned him to the withdrawing chamber at the head of the great hall. "He left the Duke of Claibourne a week ago. If he headed directly home, he may be in the Rhendall Mountains, caught by early storms."

Donal, huddled before the fire with blankets around his shoulders and hot bricks under his feet, shook his head and took another gulp of mulled wine, listening despondently while Tiarnán and Jiri organized additional parties to go in search of the missing royal heir. Upon his initial return from his clandestine visit to Morganhall with Kenneth, wet and cold from a night on the road, Richeldis had tried to persuade her husband to take a hot bath and retire to his bed, but the king had stubbornly refused, only conceding to change into dry clothes.

Prince Brion did return, the very next morning, though the king was dozing by the fire when the prince's party rode into the castle yard in the middle of another snow shower. No one dared to tell Brion the terrible news as he and his uncle raced through the great hall and into the king's withdrawing chamber, Kenneth and Tiarnán right behind them. Their brisk, breathless announcement concerning a skirmish in Eastmarch, delivered to a just-awakened king, caused Donal to order fresh horses saddled immediately, his harness brought, and a troop called out to accompany him.

"Donal, it isn't necessary," Duke Richard assured him, countering the command with a gesture. He was nearly as excited as his nephew. "Brion handled the situation like a seasoned campaigner. Granted, he had some guidance from his old uncle, but he would have done just as well if I hadn't been there."

"Is that true?" Donal asked his son, somewhat taken aback.

Prince Brion grinned, eyes briefly averting in honest modesty as he cast off his damp cloak and flounced onto a stool closer to the fire. Four months in the saddle with his uncle and sampling the fare at some of the finest tables in Gwynedd had sparked an adolescent growth spurt, putting muscle and inches on the gawky fourteen-year-old who had ridden out of Rhemuth in July. The jacket of the crimson riding leathers donned new at his coming of age a month before his departure now strained across the shoulders and fell open down the front, also gone short at the wrists; the leggings he wore were obviously borrowed, for they did not match. Even his face had lost much of its boyish contour, the refinement only enhanced by the fact that he had not cut his hair during his absence, and now wore it tied back at the nape.

"They were only some rabble, Sire: minor vassals of the Earl of Eastmarch." His voice had broken, too, and it was a young man who now spoke, no longer a boy. "But you'll want to keep an eye on that area in the future. It appears that Rorik of Eastmarch may be getting ideas above his station."

"Some of his men were occupying lands in the Arranal valley that rightly belong to Marley," Richard explained, also sitting. "When we showed the royal colors, they pulled back quickly enough. After that, Brion decided that we ought to pay a quick call on Earl Rorik, so he could remind Rorik in person that aggression against his neighbors would not be tolerated. I do believe that Messire of Eastmarch got the message." He glanced sidelong at his royal nephew and smiled. "Your son and heir did well, Donal."

Donal had begun to smile as the story unfolded, and started to give Brion a pleased dunt on the bicep. But then he remembered the more terrible news weighing on his soul, only temporarily put aside in the relief that his eldest son was safely returned; for Brion clearly did not yet know of his younger brother's tragic death. As the king looked briefly away, grief stilling his expression, Kenneth quietly sent Tiarnán on his way and closed the door, himself remaining just inside the door and doing his best to become invisible. Brion's face fell.

"Sire, is it not what you would have wished?" the prince asked hesitantly.

Stifling a sob, Donal beckoned for his heir to come and sit beside him. Richard went very still.

"Donal, what's wrong?" the royal duke said, for he had finally noticed that Donal, Kenneth, and all the court they had seen were in mourning.

"There was . . . an accident while you were away," Donal said haltingly. "Brion, your brother Jathan . . ."

"What's happened?" Brion demanded, his face going ashen.

"He's dead," the king said baldly, flinching as Brion recoiled at the news. "He—"

"What happened?" Brion repeated, steel in his voice. "Whoever did this, I'll kill him!"

"Then kill your accursed pony!" Donal blurted. "For the wretched beast was your brother's death!"

"Donal, *no*!" Richard breathed, horrified, as Brion simply stared at his father, aghast.

Trembling, Donal closed his eyes, not wanting to remember but haunted by the image of the bloodied Jathan, lying motionless in his mother's arms . . . and slipping away. And there had been nothing anyone could do.

"You know how he loved that pony, how he *coveted* that pony," he whispered.

"I was going to give it to him at Twelfth Night," Brion

managed to choke out, voice cracking, as tears runneled down his cheeks. "And I was going to teach him how to ride it. How did he—?"

Shaking his head, Donal reached to take his son's hand and forced himself to recall the terrible details.

"He went out to the stables early, before the grooms were even up," he said woodenly. "Somehow he managed to saddle the pony, but he didn't get the girth tight enough. He led it out to the paddock and got on . . . and somehow he ended up with his foot caught in the off stirrup, and the saddle under the pony's belly, and—and—" He shook his head, tears streaming down his face. "He died in your mother's arms."

Brion wept then, sliding to his knees at his father's feet to lay his head in Donal's lap and sob, no longer a confident prince flushed with the success of his first adult mission but a grieving boy who had lost a brother. Richard, too, was dashing at tears with the back of a hand, for Prince Jathan had been a beloved nephew. Kenneth, silent witness from his post against the closed door, could only pray that the three princes would soon find the strength and comfort to deal with their grief. It was several minutes before Brion regained enough composure to get shakily to his feet, sniffling and wiping at the tears on his cheeks with both hands as he drew himself erect.

"I—I should like to see my brother," he said to his father.

Donal shook his head numbly. "You cannot, son. We buried him six days ago."

"You *buried* him?" Brion repeated, blank incomprehension in his eyes.

Donal looked away. "I sent outriders to look for you as soon as it happened," he replied, his voice a little strangled, "but I could not ask your mother to delay overlong. As it was, we waited several days." He swallowed noisily. "He lies beside your brother Blaine."

Brion slowly nodded. "Then I shall go to him," he said quietly. "But first, I must go to my mother. Sir Kenneth, may I ask you to accompany me?"

Kenneth straightened from his post against the door and bent his head in agreement. "I am yours to command, my prince."

Brion only just recalled his manners enough to give his father a perfunctory bow before fleeing through the door that Kenneth hastily opened. When they had gone, Richard poured a cup of mulled wine for himself and another for his brother, setting the warm cup in the king's hand.

"Should I go with them?" he asked. "After he has seen the queen, of course."

Donal shook his head wearily. "Kenneth is good with helping men deal with their grief. And you have left me with little doubt but that Brion is a man now."

"Still," Richard breathed, "it is hard to lose a brother."

Donal shrugged, sipping at his wine. "No harder, surely, than to lose a son."

"I wouldn't know, on either count," Richard said. "I do know that I shall lose *you* some day—if you don't lose me first! But as for sons . . . Well, let us just say that I should probably find a wife before I worry about *that*."

Donal leaned back in his chair and drank again, somewhat recovering what composure he still could summon and smiling faintly. "I have given you little time to think of that, have I? I'm sorry. I truly do recommend it, Richard—and fatherhood."

Richard also smiled, lifting his cup in salute, relieved that his brother's melancholy seemed to be lifting, if only momentarily. "I shall take you at your word on both counts. You may certainly be proud of *your* son. He truly did handle the situation in Eastmarch with a wisdom far beyond his years."

"I am very glad to hear you say that," Donal replied. "And I'm sure the men will be very glad that they don't have to go out in this weather. I must confess that *I* wasn't all that keen, though I would have done it. If we are very, very fortunate, I think we can breathe a sigh of relief now, and mostly relax until the spring, when time will have eased our grief."

* * *

It was a noble aspiration, but one fated not to be obtainable. After a somewhat subdued supper with his brother and his queen, and indulgence in the hot bath Richeldis had recommended earlier, the king retired with sufficient determination to tackle several pieces of important correspondence before making his way to the queen's bed, where he managed to exercise his conjugal duties with considerable vigor. Afterward, both he and Richeldis attributed his heated state to the ardor of their coupling, meant to exorcise some of their grief of the past week.

But it became clear, the next morning, that the heat of the night before was more than passion. He awoke feverish and achy, with a scratchy throat and the beginnings of a runny nose, all of which got worse as the day progressed, though he insisted on keeping to his usual schedule.

"You've taken a chill, Sire," Kenneth said reproachfully. "You should wrap up in bed and stay warm."

"A king has no time for that!" the king declared, though the declaration would have carried more weight, had he not been obliged to wipe at his nose and running eyes with a soggy square of linen.

"Donal, don't be a dolt!" Richeldis told him later that afternoon, noting his peaked appearance when they returned to the withdrawing room from hearing the younger children recite their catechism for Father Anselm. Brion and Richard were seated at the work table nearer the fire, taking turns dictating a report to a scribe concerning their actions in Eastmarch, and Kenneth was bent over several maps with Tiarnán and Jiri Redfearn.

"Donal!" the queen repeated, tugging at his arm. "You've overdone, and not taken proper care of yourself, and now you've caught a cold. You're going to be miserable, whatever you do."

She slid her arms around his neck, leaning closer to whisper as she nuzzled near the Eye of Rom glittering in his right earlobe. "Darling, why don't you come to bed with me?" she whispered. "Good gracious, you're burning up! But no matter; we could try to sweat it out, the way we did last night, mmm?"

He snorted, both pleased and scandalized that she would speak of it, but also mindful that they were not alone.

"Perhaps I *should* retire early," he said casually. "Our son seems to have handled things well enough without my presence."

"Sire, shall I send for your physician?" Tiarnán asked.

"No doctors," Donal said gruffly. "I'll take supper in my lady's chamber, and make an early night of it."

But though the king did preside briefly at the high table in the great hall that evening—an informal meal always set out for those resident in the castle—he only picked at his food. Richeldis did her best to tempt him—with the promise of further romantic dalliance as well as delicacies sent up from the kitchen, once they retired, though both had lost their appeal as he crawled, shivering, into the queen's bed and curled up beside her.

His condition worsened during the night, and had become full-blown misery by morning. Delegating the day's appointments to Prince Brion and his brother Richard, the king stayed abed and slept for most of the day, wheezing when he was asleep and wheezing, sneezing, and coughing when awake. That evening he did allow the royal physician to examine him, but Master Cillian could only recommend a light diet and plenty of fluids, and herbal remedies to hopefully lower his fever and ease his aching joints.

All of which was of little avail, for his condition declined with each passing day, as increasing congestion impaired his breathing and fever fuddled his mind. His wife rarely left his side in the next week, and Prince Brion likewise spent hours in waiting, lest his father rally enough to summon him. Kenneth, for his part, fretted for the king's health not only for the sake of Donal himself, and the welfare of the kingdom, but also for the impact this illness might have on Alaric, if the king should fail to recover.

After the first few days, the priests began a campaign of prayers for the king's recovery, while the king's council uneasily saw to the business of running the kingdom with Duke Richard at the helm and Prince Brion at his right hand. At least in public, no one dared to speculate on how things might change under the direction of a new king only just come of age.

THE king lingered hardly a fortnight, drifting in and out of consciousness but never really lucid enough to convey proper instructions to his heir. He slipped away in the early morning hours of the fourteenth of November, cradled in the arms of his beloved queen and surrounded by his two surviving sons, his half-brother, and most of the members of the royal council, with two archbishops praying for the repose of his soul.

"He's gone," the royal physician murmured, when a final breath rattled from Donal's lips and no more followed. As he leaned closer to confirm, then gently closed the king's eyes, Richeldis gave a tiny sob, turning her head away. Duke Richard drew himself to attention and made a final bow to his dead brother, then a deeper one to his nephew, who was now become Gwynedd's sovereign lord at fourteen years of age.

"The king is dead," Richard said steadily. "Long live the king!"

Looking dazed, the new king bent to kiss his sire's hand a final time, then slipped the Haldane Ring of Fire from a slack finger, though he did not put it on, only closed it in his fist, which he then brought to his chest in salute, head bowed.

The eight-year-old Prince Nigel, now become heir presumptive until his brother should produce an heir, came next to pay his respects, urged forward by Kenneth, tears trickling down his cheeks as he bent to kiss his father's cheek. His two sisters had said good-bye a few hours before and been taken to their rooms, though it was doubtful whether they slept. The two archbishops, after approaching to bow deeply to the silent figure in the queen's arms, then withdrew a short distance and knelt in prayer, beginning the traditional litany for the dead.

"Requiem aeternam dona ei, Domine . . . Et lux perpetua luceat ei.

"Tibi, Domine, commendamus animam famuli tui Donal . . ." O Lord, we commend to Thee the soul of Thy servant Donal, that, having departed from this world, he may live with Thee . . .

Chapter 21

"He left behind him an avenger against his enemies,
and one that shall require kindness to his friends."

—ECCLESIASTICUS 30:6

FEW in Rhemuth Castle slept much in what remained of that night, as scribes began to prepare the letters announcing the king's death and the crown council began drafting preliminary plans for the late king's state funeral. The archbishops, retiring to the cathedral, set in motion a succession of Masses for the departed king's soul and began their own discussions regarding the new king's coronation. Given the difficulties of winter travel, it was suggested that the ceremony should coincide with Twelfth Night Court, hardly six weeks away, when most of those required at a coronation would already have made plans to journey to Rhemuth. King and council concurred.

That day, while a sleep-deprived new king let himself be swept along with the endless minutiae of taking up the reins of government, deftly guided by Duke Richard, the late king's body was prepared for burial and laid out in state in the chapel royal, where a rota of Haldane lancers was organized to provide a continuous guard of honor, augmented by additions of knights and other notables.

Meanwhile, the royal apartments were cleared of the late

king's personal belongings, the dowager queen moved to the quarters traditionally reserved for royal widows, adjacent to the royal gardens, and the few personal items belonging to Prince Brion moved into his new lodgings. It was Lord Kenneth Morgan who, that first evening after Donal's passing, returned to the late king's apartments privily to deliver certain Haldane regalia into the new king's keeping.

"Lord Kenneth," Prince Brion said dully, himself answering Kenneth's tentative rap on his door. The jet-black of his hair and the black of his mourning attire made his pale face appear to hang in midair against the semi-darkness in the chamber beyond.

Kenneth glanced past Brion into the obviously empty reception chamber, then nodded to the boy. Brion had allowed his mother to appropriate the Lorsöli carpet he had received in June, so there was little yet in place to mark the space as his own.

"May I come in, my Liege?" he said quietly.

Not speaking, Brion inclined his head and stepped aside to admit the older man.

"I've brought several special bequests from your father," Kenneth said, when the king had closed the door. "They probably would have come to you in time, but he wanted to be certain that you understood the importance of these particular items." He produced a cloth-wrapped bundle from underneath his cloak, about the size of a man's two fists. "Shall I show you?"

Somewhat taken aback, Brion gestured vaguely toward a small table set before the fire, flanked by two straight-backed chairs with arms. The movement caught firelight in the stones of his father's ring.

"Please," he murmured, as he moved toward the table, himself settling onto one of the chairs.

"Thank you, Sire." Kenneth set his bundle on the table and took the other chair, then reached into the pouch at his waist to produce a much smaller lump of folded fabric.

"I think this may be the more important of the two items," Kenneth said, unwrapping the lump to disclose the Eye of Rom, glowing like a burning coal in its cocoon of scarlet velvet. "I don't think I ever saw your father without it, in all the years I served him." He gestured toward the more modest hoop of braided gold wire still affixed in Brion's right earlobe. "Shall I help you change over?"

Brion's hand had gone to his ear as Kenneth spoke, and he nodded somewhat dazedly, reaching out with his other hand to not quite touch the Eye of Rom as the older man rose to come to his other side.

"Thank you," the young king whispered, as Kenneth bent to the task of opening the hoop. "It did occur to me, right after he died, that the Eye of Rom now belonged to me. But I thought it might have seemed . . . well, ghoulish, to just take it from him right then—far different from merely putting on his ring."

"No, you did the right thing," Kenneth said quietly. He removed the hoop and put it in Brion's hand, then took the Eye of Rom from its nest of velvet and carefully threaded its wire through the royal earlobe. Brion closed his eyes as the deed was done, biting at his lip as Kenneth closed the fastening.

"There, that's better," Kenneth said. So saying, he returned to his chair to begin unwrapping the larger bundle, containing his smile as the young king exhaled a deep breath and dared to look at him again, gingerly touching his right ear.

"Should I . . . feel different?" he asked softly.

"I don't know," Kenneth replied truthfully. "It's my understanding that my wife will be able to clarify many of the questions I'm sure you must have." He folded back the last layer of fabric in the larger bundle to reveal a wide silver cuff-bracelet engraved with a pattern of running lions with their legs and tails interlaced. "When you speak to her, you'll want to have this with you. And that Haldane cloak clasp that your father always wore."

Brion nodded, picking up the bracelet to finger it thoughtfully. He was already wearing the cloak clasp, though it was half-hidden in the folds of his fur-lined black cloak. He brushed it with his fingertips, then looked up at Kenneth again.

"They have something to do with my father's Haldane powers, don't they?" he said softly.

Kenneth averted his gaze, for he had been forbidden to speak of the matter—in fact, was not *able* to speak of it.

"I cannot answer that, Sire," he whispered. "Please do not ask me, for both our sakes."

Brion looked questioningly at him, head cocked in consideration. When Kenneth offered nothing more, the king shrugged and leaned back in his chair.

"Very well. I'll accept that for now." He turned the bracelet in his hands again, then clasped it to his right wrist and sighed. "I can hardly believe that he is gone," he mused aloud, glancing at the dancing flames in the fireplace, then at Kenneth. "Somehow, I never imagined that it would really happen. You *will* stay by me, won't you, Sir Kenneth?"

"You have my word, Sire. I shall never abandon you."

"Thank you."

Brion drew another deep, steadying breath, then let it out explosively and sat forward, looking uncomfortable.

"They've taken him to the chapel royal to lie in state until the funeral," he said then, not meeting Kenneth's gaze. "Will you . . . come with me to pay my respects—now, when there are only the guards and maybe a few family members?"

"Of course, my prince," Kenneth replied.

THEY had known there would be a guard of honor, partly drawn from the late king's most faithful retainers, but they had not reckoned on the monks, come up from the cathedral to pray for the king's peaceful repose. Brion stiffened in the doorway of the chapel with Kenneth at his elbow, taking the measure of what lay at the other end of the chapel's center aisle besides his father's body.

The four guards, all battle-arrayed, stood motionless at the corners of the black-draped catafalque on which King Donal lay, their eyes averted, gloved hands resting on the quillons of their naked swords. The body itself was a blur of Haldane crimson, which immediately caught the eye, but even Kenneth could sense the appraising gaze of the monks turning toward them from the shadows beyond the bier, where a dozen of them, white-robed and hooded, knelt with prayer beads dangling from their clasped hands, their prayers a soft murmur that set the chapel a-hum.

Six tall funeral candlesticks also guarded the bier, three to each side, the only light in the chapel save for the Presence lamp above the tabernacle and the bank of blue votive candles before the statue of the Virgin. By that bluish light, the white-robed monks looked decidedly sinister, disapproving.

"Why did *they* have to be here?" the young king muttered under his breath, so that only Kenneth could hear.

"Surely you cannot have thought that they would *not* be here, my prince," Kenneth replied. "The archbishop will have sent them, as a mark of respect."

Scowling, the new king lingered a moment longer just inside the west door, steeling himself. Then he pushed back the hood of his cloak and walked briskly down the center aisle, Kenneth like a shadow at his heels.

The guards remained motionless as Brion approached the bier; the monks ducked their heads over their prayer beads. Kenneth hung back a little as the new king paused to bow to the altar and then moved closer to stand to the right of his father's bier and bow again, this time to the dead king.

They had laid Donal out in a crimson mantle of state and an under-robe of white damask, reminiscent of what he had worn for his coronation, more than twenty years before, with the crown of Gwynedd on his brow and the Haldane sword laid atop his body, the hands clasped over the hilt. For the first time in many years, Kenneth thought, he looked at peace.

Much moved, he inclined his head in respect, then blessed himself and breathed a prayer for the king's soul. After a moment, Brion bent to gently kiss his father's cheek, then turned away, grief in his eyes as he rejoined Kenneth and they headed back up the aisle.

* * *

WORD of the king's death took three days to reach Alyce at Morganhall, for another early winter storm had swept in from the north the day before, burying the hills in heavy, sticky snow. The courier who brought Kenneth's letter was exhausted and half frozen, soaked to the skin, and could barely speak at first, as he allowed himself to be led to the warmth of the great fireplace in the hall. There, while he waited to put the letter directly into Alyce's hands, he let himself be wrapped in several dry blankets and plied with hot mulled ale while he gasped out the first grim news through chattering teeth.

The servant who came to fetch Alyce was Master Leopold, steward of the manor. He found her in the solar, where she had been reclining by its fire beside Vera and Kenneth's two sisters, who were mending linens. Alaric and Duncan were playing with toy knights and blocks on the hearth, and Kevin was reading in the stronger light from a neaby window. All four women looked up as he entered, instantly sobered by his expression.

"Beg pardon, my ladies, but a courier has just arrived from Rhemuth."

"In *this* weather?" Claara started to protest, looking scandalized.

"I fear he's brought ill news," Leopold went on, cutting across her as he locked his gaze on his master's wife. "The king has died, my lady. Sir Jaska Collins is waiting in the hall with a letter from Lord Kenneth. He says he has orders to deliver it only into your hands."

Alyce had gone very still at the news, and she carefully eased herself to a sitting position as Vera set aside her stitching; her sisters-in-law gasped and then began whispering urgently to one another.

"You should have brought him straight up," Alyce said numbly. "I'll go to him at once. Did he say when it happened, or how?"

The steward shook his head. "Unknown, my lady. He's

half-frozen and exhausted, so I've left him by the fire to thaw out."

Nodding, Alyce eased herself to her feet and pulled a shawl more closely around her shoulders. Now in the final weeks of her pregnancy, she moved ponderously toward the door, then let the steward precede her slowly down the stairs to the great hall. Sir Llion was conversing animatedly with the newcomer, who rose at once as Alyce entered, clasping his blankets around him with one hand and favoring her with a quick bow as he produced a sealed square of folded parchment.

"Thank you for coming, Sir Jaska," she murmured, taking the letter as Sir Llion pulled another chair closer to the fire and held it while she sat. "I trust that you are thawing somewhat."

"Aye, m'lady. I am sorry to be the bearer of such ill news."

"When and how did it happen?" she replied, not taking her eyes from him as she broke the letter's seal.

"Three days past," Sir Jaska replied, sitting again at her gesture. "Apparently he took a chill about a fortnight ago, and never really managed to shake it off. They say it went to his lungs, but I think his heart was broken."

The remark about taking a chill made her wonder whether Donal's secret journey to Morganhall had led to his death, but it was also a reminder of the sons the king had lost, and the eldest, now become king, whom he had hoped to keep safe at whatever cost.

"Aye, Prince Jathan's death will not have been easy to endure," she said vaguely. As she began to skim the letter for more details, she found herself thinking of Donal's other sons who had died untimely. She was heartened to learn that Kenneth had already ensured that Prince Brion took possession of the items she would need to seal his Haldane powers—for it was certain that, now, it would be she and not her young son who must catalyze what Donal had set in motion for his heir.

"Do you know what arrangements have been made?" she asked, when she had finished reading.

Sir Jaska shook his head. "Not when I left, my lady. What with the weather, I doubt they'll try to delay the funeral until word can get out. I doubt many could get there much before Twelfth Night. But I'd guess that this means they'll plan for a Twelfth Night coronation, since so many already plan to attend that court. That's only six weeks away, but it's always best to crown a young king as soon as possible—just so that no one gets ideas about taking advantage of his youth."

She had reached much the same conclusion regarding the coronation, and for some of the same reasons, but she reckoned that few would try to take advantage of Brion Haldane once he *was* crowned. And cupping a hand over her pregnant belly, she thought she should be safely delivered and able to travel by then.

"You're probably right," she said, glancing at the letter again. "Much as I should like to offer my condolences to Prince Brion in person, that obviously isn't possible until this baby has arrived. It will be for my husband to represent the family for now. And by Twelfth Night, I'll be able to bring Alaric as well, to swear fealty with his father." She sighed.

"Make certain you get a couple of good meals and a night's sleep, Sir Jaska," she told the courier. "I'll wish to send a reply, but it can wait until morning. For now," she glanced at the steward, "Leopold, please ask Father Swithun to attend me. We must ask him to say a Mass for the king—both our departed liege and the one who now is."

Chapter 22

"And she being with child cried, travailing in birth, and pained to be delivered."

—REVELATIONS 12:2

THE next days stretched into a week, the week into a fortnight, and more. Daily Alyce sought the signs that might herald her lying-in, but to little avail. Ten days after Kenneth's first letter, a second arrived, with a sketchy account of King Donal's state funeral and confirming Twelfth Night as the date for King Brion's coronation. A week into December, after several more rounds of letters, Kenneth himself arrived from Rhemuth, with greetings from the new king and permission—within reason—to remain at Morganhall until Alyce gave birth.

"You must be very near to term," Kenneth observed, dismissing Xander to visit with Vera and Llion and the boys while he and Alyce settled by the fire with a jug of mulled ale. He had left Trevor in Rhemuth with the king.

"I certainly hope so!" Alyce retorted. "How is the king?"

"As nervous as a cat in a room full of hounds—though he has Duke Richard to look after him, and Jamyl Arilan has taken on squiring for him," Kenneth said. "For *my* part, I had very nearly reached the end of my tether in Rhemuth, what with crotchety crown counselors and irritable bishops.

Brion will be the third Haldane king I have served, but I don't remember this much contention when old King Malcolm died and Donal was crowned." He sipped from his cup, then lifted it slightly in concession.

"Of course, Donal was a grown man then, in his forties, and I was a green young knight, and still learning my trade. I don't suppose this current batch of bureaucrats is any better or any worse. At least Brion should be safe enough in Rhemuth, until we can get him crowned. I'm just weary."

"My poor darling," Alyce murmured, coming to stand behind his chair and knead at his taut shoulders.

A little later, when they had supped with the household, and tucked up Alaric, and retired to the privacy of their bed, Kenneth at last dared to reveal something of what had gone on privately concerning the new king.

"I'm not certain how much he's aware of, regarding whatever it was that Donal did to prepare *him*," Kenneth told her in private, as they lay curled together in sleepy contentment. "I did what I was ordered to do, but I have no idea why; and I certainly couldn't tell him what I didn't know." He cocked his head at her in the light of the candle burning beside the bed. "It isn't at all usual, to confide any of this to a human, is it?"

She smiled dreamily, as baffled as he.

"Dearest heart, I have no idea what is usual, especially when it concerns Haldanes," she replied. "None of this was supposed to happen the way it is now unfolding. Krispin should not have died, Donal should have lived many more years, and we should never have been involved in any of this."

"But we are," Kenneth said. Sighing, he splayed a hand across her belly, smiling as he felt the baby kick. "We're going to have another warrior," he said, grinning. "Or a warrior-princess," he amended. "Have you any idea when he or she will arrive?"

"*She* will arrive when she's good and ready," Alyce retorted, smiling smugly, for she had already been able to touch the tiny mind with hers. "I had thought to name her Bronwyn Rhetice. Do you approve?"

"Aye, a noble name for a noble lass," he agreed. "There was a Bronwyn among her Morgan ancestors, sister to Charlan Kai, who was the faithful companion of King Javan, and died at his side."

"And there was a Rhetice who was wife to Corwyn's second duke," said Alyce. "That's why I chose those names. Our little lady will have a high heritage to live up to."

"I am certain she shall rise to the challenge," Kenneth said languidly, laying his head on her breast as one hand slid along the bulge of her belly to stroke the softness of her thighs. "And I think we should do our best to encourage her arrival as soon as possible, don't you?" he whispered, as his caresses began to send delicious shivers through her belly.

HER contractions began early the next morning, sending a tizzy through all of Morganhall as Kenneth's sisters sent for the midwife and began organizing the birthing chamber, and Vera hovered anxiously. The midwife came, but judged that her services would not be needed until much later in the day, possibly even well into the night.

In fact, she was unneeded even then, for Alyce's labor slowed dramatically, not resuming until well into the next day. When it did resume, her pains were long and hard. Vera and the two Morgan sisters stayed with her every minute, seeing to her every need, though they asked Kenneth to leave before the actual birth. By the time Alyce delivered, it was early on the morning of the twelfth of December, and she had lost a good deal of blood.

But the predicted girl-child was strong, with a lusty set of lungs, and soon was nursing vigorously. Kenneth inspected the new arrival soon after the women had cleaned up mother and child, and pronounced his daughter perfect in every way. Later in the afternoon, after Alyce had napped, Kenneth brought in their son to see his new sister. The boy approached in wonder, eyes wide with curiosity, tiptoeing to the side of the bed where his mother cradled the new babe in her arms.

"Is that my sister?" he whispered.

Smiling, Alyce tilted the babe so that he could see, and Kenneth lifted him higher, to sit on the edge of the great bed.

"Alaric, this is your sister, Bronwyn," he said.

"She's so little," the boy breathed. "If I touch her, will she wake up?"

"I don't think so," Alyce replied. "She's had a very hard birthday. Just be very gentle."

As she nodded encouragement, Alaric reached out a tentative finger to stroke the baby's downy head.

"She's got soft hair," he said, grinning.

"She has hair just like you had, when *you* were a wee baby," Alyce replied.

"Can I hold her?" came the next question.

"Well . . ." Alyce began.

"Oh, I think we can arrange that," Kenneth said, glancing at Alyce's maid as he helped the boy down to the floor. "Melissa, could you bring some pillows over here?" he asked, pulling a heavy chair with arms closer to the bed.

Lifting Alaric up to sit on it, he then arranged several pillows on his lap. The boy craned his neck to watch as his father gathered up the swaddled infant and brought her over to the chair, carefully setting her in her big brother's arms, resting on the pillows, and knelt down beside them.

"Papa, she's so little," the boy breathed, his eyes wide as he glanced up at his father. As he gently touched one of the little hands, the baby's fingers closed around one of his, producing an excited grin.

"I think she likes me!" he whispered.

"She's your sister," Kenneth replied, smiling. "And because you're the big brother, you must always take care of her, and keep her safe."

"I will, Papa, I will!" Alaric said. "When will she get bigger?"

"Every day," Kenneth answered. "And you must help Mama and Melissa take care of her, so that she'll grow strong and healthy. You'll do that won't you?"

The boy's grinning nod left no doubt that he was more than willing to assume his fraternal responsibilities.

* * *

Two more days Kenneth remained at Morganhall, before making a quick trip to Rhemuth to check on the king and report the birth. Though he returned in time to celebrate Bronwyn's first Christmas, he found his wife less recovered from her confinement than he had hoped.

"I'm fine," she insisted, as she met him in the hall, though her color was poor, and she had engaged a wet nurse from the village.

"*Is* she fine?" Kenneth asked his sisters later in the afternoon, when Alyce had retired for a nap.

Delphine, solid and dependable and slightly older than he, drew him closer to the fire, where Claara was playing with one of her grandchildren. Vera had stayed to read in the chamber where Alyce slept, and Llion had taken Alaric and Duncan outside for a run-around in the garden with Alaric's hound-puppy.

"I don't know," Delphine said in a low voice, drawing Kenneth to a seat a little apart from her sister. "Claara says it is nothing, but I am frankly worried. I fear it may be the milk fever, though she denies she has any of the symptoms. She did lose a lot of blood. She does not rest enough. She pushes herself too fast, but she is determined that she must be strong enough to travel to the coronation. Can you not make her see some sense?"

Kenneth sighed, leaning his forearms on his thighs to interlace his fingers.

"She can be a very stubborn woman, Delphine," he said. "And seeing the new king crowned is very important to her." *And to him,* he added in his own mind. "But there is time yet."

But time was running out for Alyce de Corwyn Morgan. She had been feverish for the first Mass of Christmas, which she insisted on attending, and was worse the following day. She spent most of St. Stephen's Day in bed even as she directed the packing of her gowns for the trip to Rhemuth and the coronation. By Childermas, two days later, even she was forced to admit that her illness was serious.

And Kenneth, himself poised to head back to the capital, was torn between loyalty to his new young king and devotion to his wife.

"You will *not* be able to go with me to the coronation," he told her sternly, when Claara had gone out of the sickroom to fetch clean compresses. "You must rest, regain your strength."

"But Prince Brion needs me," she whispered desperately, clinging to his hand.

"No, your *children* need you!" came Kenneth's retort. "*I* need you!"

"He needs his powers awakened," she choked out, tears streaming down her face. "Without them, he is likely to perish the first time some Torenthi interloper faces him down in a magical challenge. What if that Torenthi prince and princess show up at his crowning?"

"Darling, they won't," he began.

"No, listen to me! Alaric was to have been the instrument of that awakening, but he is too young by many years. Donal knew that. It means that *I* must do it, though it cost me my life."

"No! That is too high a price to pay!" Kenneth blurted, seizing her hand and pressing it to his lips.

"It is the price I agreed to pay," Alyce countered. "Kenneth, I gave my word!"

"But you are ill," he protested. "It can wait until you are well. Surely he will be safe at his own coronation. He will be surrounded by guards."

"Would he be safe from someone like *me*?" she demanded, flaring her shields around her head in an emerald aura; and then, at his tight-lipped resistance, raising her free hand in a fist that opened to release a column of green flame that gushed briefly upward, so powerful that it left a scorch-mark on the ceiling.

He flinched from it, turning his face away until it had subsided, then dared to look at her again.

"I do not know," he admitted. "But there has been no challenge by Deryni in many years. Surely he can be protected for another week or two, until you are well."

"Then, perhaps you could bring him to me," she said quietly, exhausted by her exertion. "It would ease my mind. If I need not expend the energy to go to him, perhaps I can marshal it to do what must be done *here*."

"No," Kenneth said flatly. "I will not leave you. And he would not come merely on my written word. Not so close to his coronation. He is of age, Alyce, but he is still a boy; and I left him in the care of Duke Richard and the crown council. *They* would not let him come."

"Then I must go to him as planned," she said, "and pray that God will give me the strength to carry out what I have promised."

Kenneth summoned up a deep sigh, shaking his head, but it was more in resignation than any further attempt at fruitless resistance. If anyone knew the cost of duty, it was he.

"Very well. I shall go. I cannot fight you indefinitely."

"Thank you," she mouthed, drawing his hand nearer to kiss it. "I promise that I shall rest while you are gone."

"See that you do!" he said sternly, though he managed a faint smile as he bent to kiss her burning forehead.

He started forward, Brion starting to follow like the dutiful squire he pretended to be, but Delphine put out an arm to stop him.

"You won't be needed in my lady's chamber, sir squire," she said somewhat imperiously. "The kitchen lies down a level, through that arch. Go warm yourself by the fire, and ask Cook to give you something to eat."

"No, I need him with me," Kenneth retorted, reaching back to seize Brion's shoulder and urge him along, before the king could think of a suitable response that would also preserve his anonymity. "He has a message from the king, which hopefully will cheer my dear wife."

"Oh. Very well, then."

Somehow Kenneth managed to keep his expression neutral as he drew the king with him up the turnpike stair. Brion easily stayed in character as a squire, for until a few weeks before, he had served ably as a squire in his father's service—and would retain that rank until he earned the accolade of knighthood at age eighteen, even though he now was king. As they reached the level of the upper solar and moved along a narrow corridor toward the principal sleeping chamber, Kenneth glanced at the king appraisingly.

"I don't know how much you caught of what my sister told me," he said softly, "but the outlook apparently is not good. I have no idea whether this has been a wasted trip."

"I understand," Brion said, inclining his head. "What I don't understand is why she insisted she had to see me before the coronation, when her health is in jeopardy."

Kenneth sighed, pausing before a tiny window just outside a heavy oak door. "Brion, I don't know how much your father told you about your Haldane inheritance, and I am not personally involved in securing that for you. But I do know what was done in my presence, to make the appropriate preparations, and I have an inkling what further must be done—though I am not able to speak of that, even to you. I . . . can't even tell you why I am not able to speak of it." He allowed himself another heavy sigh to brace himself. "I just pray to God that she knows what she's doing."

With that, he knocked lightly on the door and entered.

Inside, his sister Claara was bent over Alyce's supine form, wringing out a wet cloth over a ceramic basin.

"How is she?" he asked, coming to the opposite side of the bed to take one of his wife's slack hands in his. Brion prudently remained by the door, trying to be unobtrusive, waiting until Kenneth should dismiss his sister and leave them in privacy.

"Oh, Kenneth, Kenneth," his younger sister murmured, gently shaking her head as she reapplied the wet cloth to Alyce's forehead. "I'm so glad you got here in time. She's burning up with fever."

"I can feel it," Kenneth replied, touching the back of his hand to her forehead, then bringing the hand he held to his lips. "Claara, I need a few minutes alone with her. Could you please leave us for a little while?"

"Of course," Claara said quietly. "Perhaps your squire would like something to eat. Lads that age usually do."

"He'll wait," Kenneth said curtly, though Brion was already shaking his head. "He's brought a message from the king. Come over here, lad. And Claara, why don't you have something to eat yourself? I'll keep watch."

Not speaking, Claara inclined her head and slipped past Brion, who closed the door behind her.

"Latch it," Kenneth said quietly, "then come over here."

Silently Brion obeyed, coming to stand at the other side of the great bed, opposite Kenneth. Alyce's eyelids had fluttered open during their converse, and she managed a weak smile for her husband, but then she turned her burning gaze on the new king.

"Brion!" she whispered. "Thank God! And thank you for coming, Sire." She paused to swallow. "Needless to say, I should rather have been able to come to you."

"And I, my lady, for it would have meant that you were not ill."

Alyce smiled again, briefly closing her eyes. "Courtly like your father. And like your father, you must have the means to defend yourself." She looked up at him again. "Did you bring the Haldane brooch, and the silver bracelet he gave you?"

Eager now, Brion pushed back his right sleeve to show her the wide bracelet cuff, engraved with a pattern of running lions. "I pinned the brooch inside my cloak," he added. "It wouldn't have done for anyone to have seen it and recognized me."

"Please let me hold the bracelet," she whispered, holding out her free hand, "and come around to sit here beside me."

Without demur, the king removed the bracelet and put it in her hand, then came around to sit on the stool Kenneth had pushed closer with one booted toe.

"Help me sit," she murmured to Kenneth, who eased her more upright and inserted several pillows at her back to support her. After a moment to compose herself, she turned the bracelet to gaze at the three runes engraved inside, then set her forefinger over the first one and whispered, *"One!"*

The word triggered an immediate reaction. As she gasped, her eyelids flickering, her entire body went rigid for a long moment. Then she exhaled in a long-drawn sigh and relaxed. With a second breath she opened her eyes, very calm now, but Kenneth could see the rapid pulse in her throat, and the quickening of her breath.

"Dear God, I had not known what would be required," she whispered, very deliberately setting the bracelet aside. "So much to do, so little time. My prince, it may be that I shall not be able to complete the entire sequence just now. I may not have the strength. But some, at least, I think I can awaken in you. Please give me your hands," she invited, offering the king her palms.

Without hesitation, the king leaned forward to set his hands on hers, though the heat of her flesh caused his glance to dart downward in alarm.

"Pay no mind to that," she ordered, as she closed her thumbs over the backs of his hands. "Steady him, Kenneth," she said to her husband.

Deftly, Kenneth moved behind the king's stool to set his hands on the royal shoulders, bracing Brion's back against his chest. Alyce closed her eyes, her lips moving slightly.

Though Kenneth could sense nothing of what then began to pass between her and the king, he felt Brion's long, shuddering gasp just before his body stiffened and the raven head snapped back against his shoulder.

He could not guess what the effort was costing his wife, but it was hard enough on the king. For a long moment Brion ceased breathing altogether, balanced on a long-drawn breath—long enough for Kenneth to begin worrying.

But then, with a gentle sigh, the tension drained from Brion's body and he began breathing again: great, gasping gulps that gradually eased as the process slackened off, though he remained a dead weight in Kenneth's arms.

A gasp from Alyce shifted his focus back to her as she, too, stirred, head moving groggily from side to side as she opened her eyes.

"God help me, I can do no more," she whispered, tears brimming as she weakly lifted one trembling hand first to her own forehead, then to Brion's. "Go now, my prince, and rest beside the fire."

Vague awareness flickered in his eyes as he opened them, but he rose like a sleepwalker and did as she commanded, staggering a little to sink down on the hearthrug and cradle his head on one arm. As soon as he had settled, Kenneth sat on the bed beside his wife and gathered her into his arms, briefly bending to touch a kiss to her fevered brow.

"Too late," she murmured, her voice thin and thready. "I only had strength to complete some of the work. I have awakened the Truth-Reading talent, which will stand him in good stead as king . . . and I sensed a stirring of shields—I know not how much they would withstand. But more, I cannot. So tired . . ."

"No more now, my love," he whispered. "Rest. Regain your strength. There will be time and strength enough to complete your work later, when you are well."

"Would that it were so. . . ." Her reply was all but inaudible. "But I am spent. That work now will fall to Alaric, when he is grown. In the meantime . . . you must guide our new king as best you can, and guard our son so that he may fulfill what has been ordained. Promise me . . ."

"No! *You* will recover to finish the work!"

"I cannot," she replied, weakly shaking her head. "Promise me!"

"I—I promise," Kenneth breathed, tears blurring his vision.

"I will haunt you, if you keep not your promise," she said with a faint smile. "One thing more: I wish to be buried at Culdi, in the chapel that Earl Jared built for his stillborn daughter."

"At Culdi?" Kenneth blurted. "Why at Culdi? Shall you not lie here, with my Morgan ancestors? Or at Cynfyn or Coroth, with yours?"

Alyce briefly closed her eyes, a faint smile curving at her lips. "Culdi once belonged to St. Camber, my love—if anyone should ask why. And I *will* lie with Corwyn-kin. Little Alicia McLain would have been my niece. Remember that Vera is my twin."

He shook his head, looking troubled. "I had put it from my mind."

"And you must *keep* it from your mind," she replied. "No one must ever know, for her children must be protected. But because of this kinship, I wish you to foster our children with her and Jared when they are older, for you will be much at court with the king. You are cousin-kin to Jared through several branches of your family, so no one will think it odd. In time, as our children grow to maturity, it is my hope that Vera will be able to teach them something of their Deryni heritage. Would that I could be here to see those years . . ."

"You *will* be!" Kenneth whispered emphatically, wishing that words could make it so.

She shook her head weakly, fatigue and fever drawing her toward eternal sleep.

"Bring me my children, dearest husband. I would bid them good-bye. . . ."

"Alyce . . . !"

But she drifted into unconsciousness then, so Kenneth took advantage of it to fetch the children, as she had requested. Bidding Melissa to bring the infant Bronwyn, he went himself to wake his sleeping son. Llion roused as he entered the room, sleepless anyway, for concern about Alyce, but Kenneth raised a staying hand as he went to Alaric's bedside.

The boy stirred reluctantly, the grey gaze hazy with sleep, but Kenneth wrapped him in a sleeping fur and hoisted him onto his hip, carrying him back into the room where Alyce lay, leaving Llion stationed outside the door. Sitting carefully beside her, he let Alaric down onto the bed, bare legs dangling over the edge. Melissa had laid the sleeping Bronwyn on the other side, in the crook of her mother's arm, and was wringing out a fresh compress over a basin of water.

"She still burns with fever, my lord," the maid whispered, as she wiped Alyce's brow, unable to look at him.

Biting at his lip, Kenneth waved her back and took one of his wife's slack hands in his to gently chafe it.

"Darling Alyce, your children are here," he murmured. "You wanted to see them . . ."

After a moment, her eyelids flickered and her eyes opened, though they were fever-bright and not focusing well. Her drifting gaze found her son's, and she mouthed a kiss in his direction before turning her head to press her lips to the top of her daughter's downy head.

"God's angels guard you, dearest daughter," she whispered. "I wish we had been given the time to know one another better."

The infant stirred, the blue eyes briefly opening to meet her mother's in a salute of soul meeting soul; then she snuggled closer and went back to sleep with a sigh. Eyes bright with tears, Alyce pressed another kiss to Bronwyn's soft cheek, then glanced beyond to Melissa, who was waiting anxiously.

"Please take her back to her cot, dear Melissa, and bless you, for your love. Care for her when I am gone."

Silently weeping, Melissa ducked her head in agreement and came to gather the infant into her arms, then ducked to kiss Alyce's free hand before turning to flee the room. Young Alaric watched her go, confusion in the grey eyes, then turned back to his mother in concern.

"Mama, why is Melissa so sad?" he asked.

Alyce briefly closed her eyes, tears brimming among her lashes, then took his hand in hers and drew him closer as Kenneth fought to hold back his own tears.

"She's sad because I have to go away, my darling," she told him honestly. "I don't want to go, but I must."

He cocked his head at her, a pout pushing at his rosy lips. "Did the king say you have to go?" he demanded.

"No, no, darling. He would never do that. I wanted to *help* the king—and I *have* helped him, as best I can. I want you to promise me that you will help him, too—all the days of your life. Will you do that for me?"

Without hesitation, the boy lifted his chin and nodded bravely, tracing a cross on his chest with one small forefinger.

"Cross my heart an' hope to die, Mama!"

"No, cross your heart and *live*, my love!" she corrected, gazing into his eyes and again making that soul-connection. "Grow up to be a wonderful, strong, courageous man like your papa! Now, come and give your mama a big hug and a kiss."

He crawled closer to fling himself down beside her with his arms around her neck and his face nestled against her shoulder, starting to cry. She held him close for several seconds, memorizing the feel and the smell of him for all eternity, then passed her hand across his brow and took him into trance.

Kenneth bowed his head, unable to watch—and incapable of comprehending whatever it was that passed between mother and son as her life waned—but he looked up again as Alaric stirred, to sit up and then bend down to kiss her cheek a final time, his tears in check.

"I be good, Mummy," he whispered.

"I know you will, my darling, my *Airleas*," she murmured, blinking back her own tears. "Go with Papa now."

She closed her eyes then. It took all of Kenneth's strength of will to lift their son down to the floor and lead him to the door, where Llion was waiting outside to take him back to his room.

"Is she—?" Llion began softly.

Kenneth shook his head. "Please take the boy back to bed now, Llion, and stay with him through the night. I'll remain here until . . ."

With that, he ducked his head, unable to speak more of it, and put his son's hand into the young knight's larger one, firmly pressing the pair of them out into the corridor and closing the door behind them. Returning to his wife's side, he retrieved the king's silver bracelet and went to the fire to slip it back on the royal wrist, also tucking a fur-lined cloak around his sleeping sovereign. Brion's own cloak had fallen open so that the Lion brooch was exposed, so he unpinned it and put it in the king's hand, closing the slack fingers around it.

Then he returned to his wife's side to keep vigil until the end, carefully lying down beside her to slide an arm beneath her shoulders and cradle her to his breast, lips pressed tenderly against her feverish temple. Sometime during what remained of the night, he drifted into sleep, and she, into eternity.

Chapter 24

"She hath given up the ghost; her sun is gone down while it was yet day."

—JEREMIAH 15:9

SIR Kenneth Morgan awoke shortly before dawn to find his wife cold and still beside him. The last candle had guttered out and the fire had gone to smoldering ashes, providing only a faint glow against the chamber's gloom.

He lay there until dawn began to stain the sky beyond the chamber's arched window, holding her lifeless body close, gently stroking her golden hair, allowing himself the rare indulgence of tears. But as the house began to stir, he collected himself and gently rose, splashed water on his face, went briefly to his sisters' rooms and to Vera's, to inform them of her passing. On his way back, he summoned Melissa to begin doing what was needful for his wife's body. After that, he roused the sleeping king to impromptu squiring duties, both of them retreating to his writing room, where Kenneth set about making arrangements for her funeral.

"I have several letters to write, and I need to get you back to Rhemuth as quickly as possible," Kenneth said, pulling out pen, ink, and parchment, all business now. "I'm thinking to send you back with Llion. I hate to take him away from Alaric at a time like this, but he's the only one I can trust to be discreet about the fact that you've been here. Do you remember much of what went on last night?"

Brion shook his head as Kenneth sat down at his writing desk and set pen to parchment. "Very little. And when we first arrived, I kept wondering when someone was going to recognize me."

"You are fortunate that, outside court, most people have little idea what you look like—yet—and most squires look greatly alike. That will change once you're crowned, of course. Meanwhile, rejoice in your freedom."

"I had already noticed the difference, back at Rhemuth." Brion paused a beat before continuing, sinking down on a stool not far from Kenneth. "This is a terrible time to ask this, Sir Kenneth, but will you stay beside me, be my guide?"

"Always, my prince," Kenneth said softly, setting down his quill.

A WHILE later, Sir Llion came with a servant bearing a breakfast tray, and with questions regarding the arrangements.

"Llion," Kenneth said, setting the tray aside and dismissing the servant. "Just the man I wanted to see. I'll need you to accompany this squire back to Rhemuth with as little fuss as possible, and no questions asked."

Llion glanced at the "squire" in Haldane livery, then looked again more closely, his eyes widening.

"I am who you think I am," Brion said, smiling faintly as he stood a little straighter and shook hands with a dazed Sir Llion. "But Sir Kenneth says I may trust you. And I'd rather the rest of the household didn't know I've been here. I needed to see Lady Alyce before she died, and it never would have happened if I'd had to go through formal channels. Will you keep my secret?"

"Of course, my Liege," Llion murmured. "Ah—aren't you being crowned in less than a week?"

"All the more reason to get him back to Rhemuth," Kenneth answered, handing Llion a letter he had penned to

Trevor, informing him of Alyce's passing. "And can you find him something besides Haldane livery to wear? There will be heavy traffic on the roads to Rhemuth, as people begin arriving for the coronation, and I'd rather no one took too close a look at him."

"I get to wear a *disguise*?" Brion asked, a pleased twinkle in his eyes.

Llion snorted, unable to contain an answering smile. "Sire, you will be following a long tradition of kings who go among their people incognito." He glanced at Kenneth. "Will Morgan livery do, my lord? I should be able to locate something that will suit."

"My king, wearing *my* livery . . ." Kenneth rolled his eyes. "See to it, then. And Llion—"

"My lord?"

"Please tell Lady Vera and my sisters I'll be down directly. And ask Father Swithun to attend me, if you will." He sighed. "We have sad duties to perform today. Sad duties for all of us."

SIR Llion left with the king within the hour. Kenneth, for his part, had the household assemble at noon in the hall, where the priest led them in prayers for their departed lady. Alaric was taken to play with Duncan, Kevin, and the steward's son, who was a year older. Afterward, Kenneth announced that his wife's requiem would be celebrated the following morning at the local church outside the manor walls, where she would be interred with generations of Morgan ancestors and wives. He did not add that later, when suitable arrangements could be made in Culdi, her body would be moved from Morganhall.

A little later, Kenneth retrieved his son and took him up on the roofwalks of the house, well-bundled against the cold, where they could see for miles. There they inspected the roof slates and lead gutters, chatting of commonplace things while Alaric stooped from time to time to prod at the remains of a pigeon's nest or occasionally retrieve a feather or bit of speckled shell. The boy seemed oblivious to what had occurred only hours before, and studiously avoided mentioning his mother.

They supped together and paid a visit to the infant Bronwyn before Kenneth tucked his son into bed for the night and retired to write more letters, the ones he had been avoiding. The one to Zoë was the most difficult: his beloved Zoë, soon to give birth to her own second child, who would be devastated to learn of the passing of her heart-sister. The one to Mother Judiana, at Arc-en-Ciel, was little easier—and he had no idea where to write to Sé Trelawney, though perhaps Jovett would know. Jovett, at least, would be at the coming coronation, and might even be in Rhemuth already.

Later that evening, in the castle's tiny oratory, Kenneth kept a solitary vigil beside his wife's body, recalling her grace and strength and the lives she had touched. Nearby lay the volume of Delphine's poetry that she had penned for him for Christmas. His sisters and Vera had paid their respects and retired.

He had debated whether to bring Alaric down to see her, but decided it was better that the boy remember his mother the way she had been, alive and vital and loving. Time enough, tomorrow, to endure the reality of her absence; for now, Kenneth could still pretend, for a little while, that she only slept, and would soon awaken. He had not yet decided whether a four-year-old should be expected to attend a funeral. Before leaving the nursery he left instructions with Xander that, when Llion returned, he was to be sent to the oratory immediately.

It was toward midnight when Llion at last made an appearance. Kenneth was sitting on a straight-backed chair beside his wife's open coffin, wrapped in furs against the cold and trying not to fall asleep. Vera and Melissa had braided her golden hair like a coronet across the crown of her head and dressed her in a clean white shift, laying her in a mantle of Corwyn green that lined the coffin and spilled over its edges.

It had been Xander's idea to drape the banners of Corwyn and Lendour across the lower half of the coffin, covering her from waist to toes. Earlier, Kenneth had folded back the veil of fine white linen covering her face, so that he could sear her image into his memory before they closed the coffin in the morning. This soon after her death, and by the flickering light of the watch candles set at the corners of the bier, he could, indeed, imagine that she only slept, that soon the rosy lips would part and the eyes would open to gaze lovingly into his, like a window into heaven.

"My lord?" Llion's voice intruded softly on his grief, and Kenneth looked up with a start to see not only Llion but his wide-eyed son, one small hand closed in the young knight's larger one, the other hand dangling an unidentifiable stuffed animal by its tail.

"I hadn't thought to bring him down here, my lord," Llion apologized, "but he insisted on seeing his mother. Xander said you'd asked for me."

Sitting up straighter, Kenneth held out his arms to his son, who ran to embrace him like a limpet, burying his face in his sire's shoulder. The boy was shaking as Kenneth held him tight and stroked the white-gold hair, and the face the boy finally lifted to his father was tear-stained, the lower lip aquiver.

"Here, now, what's this?" Kenneth whispered, wiping away some of the tears with his thumb and gazing into the boy's eyes. "Where is my brave knight?"

For answer, Alaric took a quick glance over his shoulder at his mother in her coffin, then hid his face against the stuffed toy in his arms, smothering a sniffle. With curious detachment, Kenneth thought the animal might be a cat. It had droopy lengths of black wool trailing from the end opposite the tail, where whiskers might be.

For a long moment he merely continued to caress the boy, holding him close for comfort, until finally he glanced back to where Llion waited anxiously, and nodded dismissal. After a few more minutes, he gently kissed his son's cheek and again drew back far enough to look him in the eyes.

"You must be very, very sad," he said quietly. "I know *I'm* sad."

Alaric sniffled, scrubbing at his eyes with one balled fist, then sniffled again and gathered his toy animal to his chest, not looking up.

"Papa," he said tremulously, after a moment, "why did Mama have to go away?"

"I don't know, son. She got very sick—too sick for anyone to help her. But she didn't want to go. She didn't want to leave us. She loved us very, very much."

The boy turned to look over his shoulder at his mother again, then squirmed to be put down on the floor beside the coffin, resting one hand tentatively on the green silk spilling from inside. After a few seconds, Kenneth slipped to one knee beside him, embracing him in the circle of one arm.

"I loved her so much," the boy said tremulously, gazing at the still form. "Can I kiss her good-bye?"

"You already did that, son," Kenneth said gently. "Maybe you don't need to do it again."

"But I want to!" the boy replied, lifting his chin defiantly.

"All right, then," Kenneth agreed. "We'll both kiss her good-bye. All right?"

Nodding, Alaric said, "You first."

"Very well."

Shifting closer toward the head of the coffin, Kenneth half-rose to lean over it and press a kiss to her forehead, then crouched back down and glanced down at his son. Alaric had edged closer, but then he thrust his stuffed toy into his father's hands with a whispered, "Hold this," and began digging in the little pouch at his waist.

Wisely saying nothing, Kenneth watched as the boy produced what appeared to be two pigeon feathers from the depths of the pouch, each about as long as one of Kenneth's fingers. Inspecting them gravely, Alaric smoothed one where it had gotten rumpled in the pouch, glanced at the coffin, then tipped his face up toward his father.

"Can you lift me up, Papa?" he said.

"Better yet, suppose I make a step for you?" Kenneth replied, setting aside the toy and shifting onto one knee, so that the other made a step on which the boy could climb up.

Looking intent, Alaric clambered up the step thus offered, braced by his father's arm around his waist, and set both hands on the sides of the coffin, a feather in each hand, gazing at the occupant for a long moment.

Then he leaned down carefully to kiss the cold forehead, wrinkling his nose at the faint odor of death. But before straightening, he reached into the coffin to slip a feather behind each of his mother's shoulders. He was nodding slightly as he leaned back into his father's embrace, obviously satisfied with what he had done, though Kenneth had no idea why he had done it.

"Alaric," he said softly, after a few heartbeats, "why did you do that?"

Calmly, the boy stuck out his arm to retrieve his stuffed toy from his father, and hugged it to his chest.

"Father Swithun said she's with the angels now, Papa," he said with utter conviction. "So she'll need wings."

"Oh," Kenneth breathed. "Yes, she will."

"And I think I'll give her Lady Whiskers to keep her company," the boy added, leaning forward to tuck his toy beside her. "That way, she'll remember me."

"That's . . . a very good thing to do," Kenneth agreed, choking back fresh tears. "But I'm sure she will always remember you. And *we* shall remember *her*."

He settled back onto his chair at that, gathering his son into his arms to cradle him against his heart. Soon both of them drifted into sleep for what remained of the night, until two carpenters from the stable yard came to close the coffin.

IT began to snow later that morning, the last of 1095: a hushed and pristine backdrop for the modest funeral procession that began to form up in the yard at Morganhall, just as a solitary bell began to toll in the church without the manor walls. They were family, mostly, who gathered to walk behind the coffin of the fair Alyce de Corwyn Morgan, for in the dead of winter, and with the new king's coronation only days away, it was impossible to gather any others who might have wished to be there, had the times been otherwise, or to delay the burial until they could attend.

Kenneth had asked six of his household knights to bear his wife's coffin, Llion and Xander among them; but as they hoisted it onto their shoulders and began their slow march down to the church, following the processional cross and the priest with his two acolytes and the banners of Corwyn and Lendour, it struck him that one of the black-cloaked knights looked very like Sir Sé Trelawney.

All the way to the church, Kenneth tried to get a better look at the man without being obvious, Alaric's hand in his—for the boy had insisted on attending. Vera and her Kevin followed directly behind, along with Delphine, Claara, Melissa, and several other members of the immediate Morganhall household; Duncan had been left with the kitchen servants while they did the day's baking, being deemed too young to attend. Under the circumstances, Kenneth was well content to keep it very much a family affair.

And an affair for family it surely was, he realized, as he watched the knights carefully deposit his wife's coffin on the black-draped catafalque before the altar, for one of the black-clad men *was* Sé, who very much had been a part of Alyce's family, friend of her childhood—though God alone knew how he had learned of Alyce's passing, or had managed to get there in time for the funeral.

But when the six men bowed to the altar and then began melting back to take places in the congregation, the man Kenneth had been watching turned and looked him directly in the eyes, setting right hand to breast and inclining his head in graceful acknowledgment before easing back with the others to disappear in the sea of black-clad mourners.

Kenneth was never able to spot him again, though he watched for him all through the Requiem that followed; and it was another knight who took his place when it came time to carry Alyce's coffin down into the crypt. But he found himself taking comfort in the belief that Sé Trelawney had, indeed, been there, as he had promised he would always be there for Alyce and for their son.

Later, after her coffin had been laid beside those of his Morgan kin, who were also kin to their son, all of the family mourners—though Sé was not among them—returned to Morganhall, where Kenneth made it known that he intended more formal memorial Masses to be celebrated in his wife's memory in the spring or summer at Cynfyn and Coroth, befitting her status as Countess of Lendour and Lady of Corwyn. It was not the time to mention that her body would eventually find a different resting place, per her own wishes. For the nonce, at least, there was a new king to be crowned in less than a week: a task to which all the household's energies now must turn, and as would have been her wish.

Given the stress of the previous several days, most of the family elected to retire early that night, though Kenneth spent an hour with Xander and Llion organizing what must be taken with them back to Rhemuth in the morning. Kenneth, especially, desperately needed sleep before heading back to Rhemuth the next day, as did Llion, each of whom had already completed a round trip to the capital in the past two days to fetch and return the king.

It was Xander who roused them the next morning at first light, which came late at midwinter. Alaric had slept in his father's bed that night, and tumbled awake with energy abounding at the prospect of the journey back to Rhemuth with his father. Kenneth was not sure the boy understood about the importance of the coming coronation, but the trip itself held appeal for a four-year-old. Xander took over the responsibility of getting him fed and bathed, so that Kenneth and Llion could concentrate on finishing the packing of the few items they would need for the journey.

After washing and dressing in the plain black he had worn the day before, Kenneth stumbled into his son's room, where both Xander and Llion now were attempting to finish dressing the boys.

"I'm wondering whether it's necessary to put so young a child into mourning for the coronation," Kenneth said, as Xander tugged an over-tunic of heavy green wool over the boy's usual winter garb of white shirt and black leggings. "I didn't yesterday, because it's hard enough for a lad to lose his mother at his age. On the other hand, I think it's particularly important to have him at my side when I swear fealty. It will underline his status as the future Duke of Corwyn, despite his Deryni blood."

Llion glanced at the new heraldic over-tunic spread on the bed behind him, ready to pack; Alaric had outgrown the quartered tunic he'd only just worn in June for Prince Brion's coming of age. Though Melissa had spent hours sewing a narrow border of Lendour red and white along the edges of the garment, the Corwyn device itself was almost sober enough to pass for mourning. The fine black wool of the field was relieved only by its heraldically improbable green Corwyn gryphon, picked out in gold, and the brighter relief of Kenneth's gold double tressure *fleury-counter-fleury* now surrounding the beast, from his Morgan line.

"The new tunic is already mostly black, my lord," Llion pointed out, as he bent to do up the buckles of the boy's boots. "I might suggest removing the Lendour border, except that it's important to make that reminder as well, both that he is your son and that he is heir to both honors. A pity he's outgrown the old quartered tunic, though the Lendour red and white would have been a bit garish for mourning."

Kenneth nodded soberly. "We'll leave it as it is, then," he said. "Go ahead and pack it. My mourning will have to be sufficient for both of us."

Chapter 25

"For a bishop must be blameless, as the steward of God."

—TITUS 1:7

THEY departed for Rhemuth a little later under clearing skies, though the cold was still bitter, chilling to the bone. Kenneth's sisters and Vera had come to see them off, all three of the women teary-eyed, for it was unlikely that Kenneth would visit Morganhall again soon. Vera, however, was to leave for Rhemuth the following day with her own escort, for she and her sons were expected to rejoin Jared for the coronation.

Alaric rode with his father, surrounded by his strong arms and warm cloak, with Xander and Llion flanking them, ahead of a further escort of four liveried Lendouri lancers. A pair of squires followed with two pack animals on leads—modest enough train for an earl in mourning and an underage duke, but they turned heads as they passed lesser folk.

The two lead lancers carried the cased banners of Lendour and Corwyn, black crepe spilling from the heads of the staves. All of the escort party wore wide mourning sashes from right shoulder to left hip, slashing the bright red and white of Lendour with black. Kenneth himself rode all in black, with Alaric's dark green all but invisible inside his father's cloak.

They passed a night at Arc-en-Ciel, where his letter had arrived the day before and the sisters gave them refuge and serenity. Mother Judiana gave them her blessing after the sisters' Requiem Mass for Alyce the next morning, before they continued on their way. The river road grew more crowded as they headed south, and by noon of the second day the bright sun had begun to turn the snow to muddy slush, further churned by the passage of many hooves and feet and wagons.

Lord Kenneth Morgan's somber party came within sight of the city walls midway through the afternoon. They stopped at the barge station at King's Landing to water the horses and uncase the banners. It was then, as they mounted up for the final stage of the journey into Rhemuth, that they caught the first faint sound of a great bell tolling in the city.

Kenneth exchanged glances with Llion and Xander, but neither ventured comment. Given the major deaths of the past two months, first Prince Jathan and Donal and then Alyce, no one was prepared for another—and the tolling bell might merely mark the passing of some prosperous citizen of Rhemuth being buried from the cathedral. But as they drew nearer the river gate, other bells joined in, all tolling the passing of a soul.

They gained no further clue as they rode through the gate and clip-clopped up the stone-lined thoroughfare toward the cathedral. But as they entered the cathedral square, Kenneth spied a flurry of activity before the cathedral steps, where several black-robed clerics were handing out dispatches to half a dozen mounted couriers in the archbishop's livery, ready to depart.

With a glance and a nod, Kenneth sent Xander across to investigate while the rest of them continued to pick their way along the crowded perimeter of the cathedral square. A few minutes later, Xander rejoined them, shaking his head in disbelief.

"It's very nearly as bad as it looks, my lord," he said to

Kenneth, as he drew his mount head-to-tail with Kenneth's, and stirrup-to-stirrup. "They say the Archbishop of Valoret took a very bad fall coming into the city this morning, up at Bishop's Gate—horse slipped on ice and went down. Apparently the good archbishop bashed out his brains on an abutment that had the audacity to be where he landed; died almost instantly. They're saying that the coronation will have to be postponed until a successor can be elected. That could take weeks or it could take months."

Kenneth shook his head, greatly troubled. "We did not need this, with a new king only barely come of age," he murmured. "He is still king, of course, but 'tis always better if a young one is crowned quickly." He quirked a sour smile at Xander and Llion. "Still, I cannot say that I shall greatly miss my lord of Valoret."

"They could replace him with someone worse," Llion pointed out.

"Aye, and I can think of several," Kenneth agreed, "though this is neither the time nor the place to speculate on that." He sighed and signed for Llion to move closer.

"Take charge of the boy," he said, as he lifted Alaric across to the young knight's saddlebow. "Xander, you're with me. Postponing the coronation is going to set many cats among many pigeons. Prince Brion will need our support. Llion, we'll meet up with you later at the castle. Meanwhile, you're in charge."

With just the two of them, it was much easier for Kenneth and his aide to make their way up the rest of the hill to the castle yard, where Duke Richard's squires and pages had their hands full dealing with the influx of new arrivals and their mounts. As Kenneth and Xander dismounted, a senior squire came running up to take their horses: young Jamyl Arilan.

"The king has been asking for you, my lord," Jamyl said, catching the eye of another squire and beckoning him closer. "And I was so sorry to hear of your loss. The Lady Alyce was a beautiful and gracious lady."

"Thank you, Jamyl. She was, indeed." Kenneth scanned the yard as he rescued his saddlebags from the cantle and handed them across to Xander. "We heard the news about Archbishop William—and believe me, the ecclesiastical vultures have already begun gathering. Have you any feel for the implications?"

As the nephew of one of the king's senior crown counselors, and only a year from knighthood, it was just possible that Jamyl might have overheard something useful, but he shook his head.

"This is the sort of thing that cannot be anticipated, my lord. But if you're asking my opinion, I would say that they'll not want to go forward with the coronation until a new primus can be elected. Crowning the king is one of the most jealously guarded prerogatives of Valoret's archbishop."

"I suppose it's too early to speculate on who that new primus might be," Kenneth said, looking around the yard at the other new arrivals. "Where is His Majesty now?"

"He's conferring with some of his advisors, my lord," Jamyl replied. "I believe my uncle may be among them. Shall I take you to him? They're in the winter withdrawing room."

"I know the way, Jamyl. Thank you. But if you could keep an eye out for Sir Llion Farquahar, I'd appreciate it. Do you know him by sight?"

"Aye, my lord."

"Good. He has charge of my son, along with a small escort of my Lendour lancers. I hope that accommodation can be arranged."

Jamyl nodded. "Sir Trevor has already arranged lodgings for your immediate party, my lord. I'll see what I can do about the lancers."

"Thank you."

With a final nod, Kenneth headed up the great hall steps, Xander at his heels. Trevor met them just inside, where Kenneth received his aide's condolences and left Xander, continuing on toward the dais at the far end. Dodging the servants who were setting up the trestle tables for supper in the hall, he headed directly to the king's private withdrawing room behind the dais, where he found Brion,

Queen Richeldis, and a handful of senior advisors seated around the writing table near the fire: Duke Richard at the king's right hand, Earl Jared, Jamyl's uncle Seisyll Arilan, and Archbishop Desmond of Rhemuth, brother of the deceased William.

The king immediately came to his feet as Kenneth entered—an instinctive gesture of respect belatedly mirrored by the other men, with varying degrees of sincerity. The queen did not rise, but her nod of sympathy was clear, for she and Kenneth's wife had been close; and Earl Jared, though he did not know the full extent of the kinship between his own wife and Kenneth's deceased one, at least was aware that the two women had been close friends. Duke Richard had always been a friend of Kenneth and an admirer of his wife, Seisyll Arilan more coolly so. Archbishop Desmond, by contrast, seemed reluctant and even resentful at the peer pressure that obliged him to rise, for he did not like Kenneth Morgan, who had married a Deryni and given her a son.

"Lord Kenneth," the king said, indicating a place on Richard's other side and sitting again, looking vaguely uneasy. "All of us were stunned to hear of your wife's untimely passing. Thank you for coming to us at such a difficult time."

The hidden message was clear: that Brion was distancing himself from any speculation regarding too close a recent intimacy with the Morgan family. Most certainly, he would not disclose anything of his midnight visit to Morganhall.

"Thank you, Sire. I am Gwynedd's to command," Kenneth replied, with a respectful neck bow. "I served your father, and I hope to serve you as well."

"If you serve me half as well as you served him, my lord, then I shall be well served, indeed," Brion said, the grey eyes speaking of his complete awareness that some of that service could never be revealed. "Please, join us."

Again he indicated the chair beside Richard, which Kenneth this time took, bowing to the queen before sitting.

"Welcome, dear Lord Kenneth," the queen said quietly.

"May we take it that you have heard about the archbishop's untimely passing?"

Kenneth inclined his head. "I have, my lady. A most astonishing accident. My lord Desmond, you have my condolences."

Archbishop Desmond gave a curt nod, but only what civility required.

"We were discussing alternative plans for the coronation," Duke Richard said, as all of them settled. "His Grace of Rhemuth informs us that he is not prepared to proceed until a new primate can be elected. I hasten to point out that riders are being dispatched as quickly as the letters of summons can be written, to convene the curia at Valoret for an election."

"Yes, we saw some of them leaving as we rode through the cathedral square," Kenneth said.

"Fortunately, many of the bishops have already arrived here or are on their way," Seisyll pointed out for Kenneth's benefit. "They'll be redirected to Valoret for the election—which should expedite the process. In the meantime, we have agreed that Twelfth Night Court should proceed as planned—except, of course, that our new king will not yet have been crowned."

"That will not affect most of the customary business of the court," Duke Richard said. "Other than creating knights, which he may not do until he himself is knighted, even an uncrowned king reigns, if he be of age—which, happily, our Brion is." He smiled briefly at his royal nephew. "I have no doubt that he will perform admirably."

"Aye, he has been well prepared," Queen Richeldis said softly, eyes downcast.

The grief in her tone, and in the very set of her shoulders, put an awkward silence on the room, and elicited a sympathetic glance from Richard, still dealing with his own grief over the loss of a beloved brother.

"Richeldis," he ventured, "every king knows that this sort of thing might happen, and makes the necessary preparations. Donal was not remiss in that regard. There will be a period of transition, certainly; and both Brion and

Nigel will continue their training, as their father would have wished; and we shall advise him as best we can." He cast his gaze around the table and managed a pained smile.

"As for the rest of us, I think it will become increasingly clear, as our new king grows into his maturity, that a new generation will be taking its place upon the stage—and it is only right that a young king should have young knights to attend him, and young advisors." He glanced at Kenneth. "I fear that even you and I are getting a bit long in the tooth to qualify as 'young'."

Kenneth smiled in agreement, thinking of the young knights in his own service and the fierce loyalty they owed to him and to Gwynedd.

"I'll not argue *that*, Your Highness. Serving Donal was a privilege and an honor, but even he was a demanding taskmaster. I shall have a much harder time keeping up with a younger king." He smiled at Brion, then glanced at Seisyll. "Your nephew will be part of that generation, my lord. I spoke with him briefly when we arrived. He seems a fine young man."

Seisyll inclined his head. "His teachers at Tre-Arilan seem to think so, as did Her Majesty's brother. But I am glad that he serves Gwynedd now—as your Alaric shall serve, in a few years. Time, indeed, to make way for the next generation."

Before Kenneth could think how to respond, Archbishop Desmond cleared his throat.

"Sire, I should be about my duties," he said gruffly. "I must accompany my brother's body back to Valoret for burial, and then I must convene the synod to elect his successor."

"Yes, of course," Brion murmured. "Go, by all means."

"With one proviso, please, before you do," Duke Richard noted quietly. "We shall need a bishop present at Twelfth Night Court, to witness the oaths—not just of the new squires and pages, but such others of His Majesty's new vassals who have traveled from far away, and who may not have the luxury of remaining at court until a new primate can be elected and installed. With an uncrowned king on the throne, believe me, it is best to let them affirm their fealty now, while we have them here in Rhemuth."

"Certainly," Archbishop Desmond agreed. "I shall delegate someone to that duty." He rose, bowing slightly to Brion and to the queen. "If I may retire, then, Sire?"

THAT night, the late Archbishop of Valoret lay in state in Rhemuth Cathedral while those bishops currently in the city for the now-delayed coronation kept watch by turns. At noon the following day, Archbishop Desmond celebrated a Requiem Mass for his departed brother, assisted by his brother bishops, after which many of the citizens of Rhemuth filed past his bier to pay their respects. The new king was prominently in attendance, accompanied by most of the key members of his court.

Afterward, as the king and his party were preparing to depart, one of the bishops detached himself from the cluster of the others and approached the king. He was a burly bear of a man, younger than most of his brethren, with bushy brows and more the demeanor of a fighting man than a man of the cloth. On him, the episcopal purple looked vaguely out of place, as did the well-manicured hand he pressed to his pectoral cross as he bowed to the king.

"Your pardon if I intrude, Sire," he said smoothly. "My name is Patrick Corrigan. Archbishop Desmond has asked that I attend you at Twelfth Night Court tomorrow."

King Brion stiffened slightly, but he inclined his head in a gracious enough acknowledgment.

"Thank you, my lord. Your presence will be most welcome."

"Thank *you*, Sire. May I expect that you and the court will first be attending Mass here in the cathedral, as is customary?"

Brion inclined his head.

"Then I shall return to the castle with you afterward," Corrigan said. "Until then, Sire, by your leave . . ."

With that, he bowed again and withdrew to return to his fellow bishops, who were taking up stations to keep watch while the townspeople continued filing past the dead archbishop to pay their respects.

"I could have wished for some other bishop," Duke Richard murmured, though he kept his voice low so that only Brion and Kenneth could hear.

Kenneth looked at him sharply. "You have something against him?"

Richard shrugged. "He is young yet in his office, and has yet to show what he will become as he settles into his authority." He glanced at Kenneth, then back at the retreating bishop. "You would do well to keep a wary eye on him, my friend. He is a friend of Bishop de Nore."

"And an enemy of Deryni?" Kenneth guessed.

"Aye."

"Then, I shall, indeed, be wary, my lord. Thank you for the warning."

KENNETH kept that warning in mind throughout that evening and into the next day. Alaric and Sir Llion had remained at the castle while the royal party went down to the cathedral for the archbishop's Requiem Mass, and Kenneth took the young knight aside when he returned.

"I would guess that there's no immediate danger," he told Llion, when he had drawn him to a place of privacy atop one of the castle ramparts. "There is no reason that anyone should take any kind of direct action against my son, at his tender age, but odd things can happen to Deryni." He then told him, in brief, of the fate of young Krispin MacAthan, five years before.

"I had heard rumors of it some months later, back in Coroth," Llion said, when Kenneth had finished. "I was only a very junior squire, but all the boys were talking about it." He shook his head. "We were all appalled that a priest could be involved in such a deed—and a bishop's brother, at that."

"Well, Oliver de Nore has not forgiven my wife's part in uncovering the guilty parties," Kenneth replied. "And if it had been up to our remaining archbishop, I might never have been allowed to wed my fair Alyce." He sighed. "The old king took our side to resolve the issue, but only by humbling himself before the bishops. I have done my best to remain out of their sight since then."

"I shall do my best to keep Alaric out of their sight as well," Llion said with a tiny smile.

"I know you will, Llion, and I appreciate your loyalty," Kenneth replied.

Chapter 26

"Do nothing without advice;
and when thou hast once done, repent not."
—ECCLESIASTICUS 32:19

ARCHBISHOP William's funeral cortege left Rhemuth early the following morning, after a simple celebration of the first Mass of the Epiphany. Later that morning, the king and his court rode down to the cathedral for more solemn observances, at which Bishop Corrigan presided, then processed back to the castle for Twelfth Night Court, under sunny skies.

It was a less festive occasion than it should have been, for custom required that the court remain in mourning until a new king was crowned. Accordingly, King Brion wore deepest black in memory of his late father, though the fabrics were sumptuous, and a prince's coronet crowned his sable head. He also wore the other accoutrements of his Haldane heritage: the royal brooch with its Haldane Lion clasping his mantle, the Ring of Fire, and the Eye of Rom glowing in his right ear.

But the Haldane sword was not yet his to wield. His uncle, Duke Richard, had charge of that, and would later use it to give the accolade to several young candidates for knighthood.

First, however, there were official greetings to be delivered from neighboring rulers already present for the now-delayed coronation, presentations to be made, petitions to be offered up. Fortunately, there were no Torenthi princes to send shivers up the spines of Kenneth Morgan or Seisyll Arilan or Michon de Courcy, though Count János Sokrat did make an appearance on behalf of the King of Torenth to express his condolences over the passing of the late king.

To all of these, King Brion responded graciously and competently, much as his father might have done. Watching from his place near the throne, Kenneth could see much of the old king in him, and knew that Donal Blaine Haldane had trained his heir well. Occasionally Brion would glance aside at one or another of his advisors for guidance or confirmation, but for the most part he moved the business of the court along smoothly, and seemed to enjoy himself.

He definitely enjoyed the next item on the agenda, once the foreign ambassadors had been received: the investiture of the new crop of royal pages, come to be sworn in and receive their crimson tabards from the hands of the king. The promotion of several senior pages to squire also brought a smile to the new king's lips, though he was technically still a squire himself; and Prince Nigel, serving their mother as duty page for the Twelfth Night Court, watched the proceedings with wistful longing, for it would be several years before he was old enough to join them.

Only two knights were made that day: young Arran MacEwan, a distant cousin of the Duke of Claibourne, and Ewan de Traherne Earl of Rhendall, whose family obligations had delayed the original plans for his knighting, several years before. For both of them, King Brion conducted the ceremony of knighthood without deviation from what had always been done, save that it was Duke Richard's hand wielding the Haldane sword, with Brion's hand atop it. But both new knights then swore fealty with their hands between those of the king, to the evident satisfaction of all concerned.

Following this routine business, the rest of the court

progressed mostly according to expectation. Given the delay anticipated before the new king could be properly crowned, those peers present were summoned forward to renew their fealty to the Crown of Gwynedd. Kenneth had already given the new king a fealty unsuspected by any of the others present, and had renewed his oath as an officer of state with the other members of the crown council, shortly after Brion's accession; but when the earls were called, he went forward with his son at his side, to kneel and set his hands between those of the king.

No words accompanied the renewal of these oaths, for none were needed; but before Kenneth could rise, Brion smiled and briefly laid a hand on young Alaric's head as if in blessing, and leaned forward to murmur words intended only for Kenneth's ears.

"I look forward to the day when the heir of Corwyn, my father's *Airleas*, may take his place among my other peers," he said quietly, before letting his hand slip softly from the silver-gilt head.

Kenneth doubted that the king's words meant much to the four-year-old Alaric, but Kenneth found himself greatly moved as he rose and the two of them made way for the next earl and then the barons. Leading his son back to their place among his Lendour knights, he put the boy in Sir Llion's charge, then returned to stand with the king's advisors beside the throne.

There followed a further succession of the king's subjects, seemingly endless, coming to pay their respects or offer gestures of loyalty. Later on came more official greetings from neighboring lands, with emissaries and ambassadors offering the felicitations of their masters and presenting gifts.

One of those present who did *not* go forward was a man from distant Cardosa, who had no business before the throne of Gwynedd. But his presence was noted by at least one of the crown advisors standing at the king's side, and another man amid the throng gathered in the great hall, who had affirmed a baron's oath of fealty earlier in the afternoon. Both men were members of the Camberian Council.

"What was *he* doing in Rhemuth, and at the king's court?" Michon muttered to Seisyll Arilan, as the two of them withdrew into one of the window embrasures during a lull in the banqueting that followed.

"You saw him, too, then?" Seisyll replied, with an automatic glance out across the crowded hall. "I was fairly certain I'd caught just a glimpse of him, as the peers were coming forward to swear, but then I couldn't find him again, and I thought I'd been mistaken. Are you certain?"

Michon folded his arms across his chest and turned to gaze out the window to the dark garden beyond, though in fact he was studying the crowd behind them, reflected in the black of the window glass.

"Oh, he was here, all right," he said, "hardly an arm's length away—and he saw that I had recognized him. But then people moved between us, quite possibly at his instigation, and I lost him. But it was definitely Zachris Pomeroy."

"The devil take him!" Seisyll said under his breath. "What do you suppose he was up to? Spying for Prince Hogan? Surely you don't think he came here to kill the king."

"Not this time, or not yet," Michon murmured, with a glance toward the dais, where the king sat at the high table between his mother and his brother Nigel, all of whom were laughing at the antics of a jongleur's sleight-of-hand, as was Duke Richard, seated on the queen's other side. "I've already told your nephew to stay close; and he knows what Pomeroy looks like. Sir Kenneth is also nearby, as always, though he doesn't know about this specific threat—and I don't know of a way to warn him without revealing ourselves."

He nodded toward the left side of the dais, where Jamyl Arilan was carefully topping up Bishop Corrigan's wine from a pewter ewer, a towel over one shoulder of his Haldane squire's livery, though his gaze roved continually, always returning to the king. Farther along the table, Sir Kenneth was chatting companionably with Sir Trevor Udaut, though he, too, turned his glance often in the king's direction.

"I still don't like it," Seisyll muttered. "What can we do?"

"We tell the Council, once the king has retired for the night," Michon said, "and meanwhile, we keep a sharp eye. And I would say that we bring Jamyl with us later, except that I'll feel more certain of the king's safety if we leave him here while we're away. We can brief him afterward."

OTHERS voiced similar concerns much later that night, in the Camberian Council's secret meeting chamber.

"The gall of the man!" said Vivienne de Jordanet. "Rhydon, did you know he was planning this?"

Rhydon Sasillion, the youngest of their number, sat back in his chair with a tiny sigh.

"If I had known, I would have told you," he said patiently. "Please remember that I am not an intimate of Zachris Pomeroy; I *cannot* be and still keep my oaths to the Council. Nor am I any longer a student of Camille Furstána—again, because I cannot be. I am good at what I do, brethren, else you would not have invited me to join your number, but I am not good enough to hide such shields as I possess from the likes of her. I do still have a casual relationship with Pomeroy, but I have given him to understand that I have not the nerve to become involved in his political ambitions."

Across the table, Michon lifted a hand in acceptance of Rhydon's declaration. "Peace, Rhydon. We are well aware of what a difficult position we have asked you to function in. What is *your* assessment of the reason for Pomeroy's appearance at the king's first Twelfth Night Court?"

Rhydon inclined his head in appreciation of Michon's gesture of conciliation. "He is ambitious, as we all know. His support for Prince Hogan grows with each passing week, for he knows that a Festillic return to power would mean titles and lands as his reward, if he assists it.

"Having said that," he went on, "I would guess that tonight's excursion into forbidden waters was intended simply to observe the new Haldane king and ascertain his weaknesses—besides his obvious youth. After all, Pomeroy made no hostile move toward the king."

"Not directly, no," Seisyll muttered, "or not that we

know of. But we have no way to know whether he perhaps subverted some of those around the king, laying his web of treachery in preparation for more serious assaults."

"Well, whatever the cost, we must at least get the boy safely crowned," Michon said, "and try to learn what part of the Haldane legacy he may have at his beckoning. Rhydon, can we rely on you to track down Pomeroy, to monitor his movements? For if he comes near the king again, I *will* have his life!"

Rhydon nodded. "I have three or four men I can call upon, who know him by sight and are also reliable and discreet."

"Deryni?" Oisín asked.

"Of course," Rhydon replied, "though I would hope not to compromise them. We are, all of us in the eastern borders, wary of what is happening, in general, to those of our blood."

"As are we, farther west," Oisín agreed. "I shall certainly put out the word in my area, though I doubt Pomeroy has business that would bring him there."

"He had no business in Rhemuth," Barrett said darkly, "yet he chose to go there."

"And it cannot be for any good purpose," Vivienne agreed.

"It seems to me," said Khoren, speaking for the first time, "that it might behoove us to neutralize this particular threat before it can become more focused."

"I tend to agree," Vivienne said. "Even his continued existence represents a grave danger to the king."

"If you are saying what I think I am hearing," Barrett said softly, "that is a cold assessment."

"Cold or not, let me make it perfectly clear, then," Vivienne replied. "If he is found again in the king's vicinity, I say take him out—before it is too late!"

IT was Rhydon who was designated to spearhead the effort, for his prior acquaintance with the renegade Deyrni was most likely to give him access. They had reckoned it most probable that Pomeroy would make his move at the coronation, at the earliest, the exact date of which now depended upon the election of a new Archbishop of Valoret. Even then, he might not show—it was possible that his intentions had been misinterpreted—but they could not take that chance.

Accordingly, while Rhydon went on the hunt, confident that he could carry out his mission—or at least set it up—those members of the Council also having legitimate reason to stay close to the king's household did so, in those days and weeks following Twelfth Night Court. Rhydon, in particular, made certain to keep in touch with his Deryni contacts at the borders; but of Zachris Pomeroy there was no sign for many weeks.

Meanwhile, the Gwynedd Curia ground through their deliberations regarding who should succeed to the See of Valoret. Competition was spirited, for the office carried considerable secular power in addition to being the highest ecclesiastical office in the land. Archbishop Desmond presided over the deliberations, being senior in rank, though he could not have been said to be neutral in his outlook. Other serious candidates for the office were several, and evaluated as much by their hard line against Deryni as their spiritual soundness and administrative ability. Of the fifteen bishops attending, perhaps three could be considered as serious contenders.

At the top of the list was Desmond MacCartney himself, Archbishop of Rhemuth for the past four years and its auxiliary bishop for several years before that. O'Beirne of Dhassa might have been a good choice, but at sixty-five and in failing health, he was perhaps too old. Paul Tollendal, the energetic Bishop of Marbury, seemed a far better choice, at fifty-two, with a solid reputation as a bulwark against Deryni incursions from the east, and already fifteen years' experience in his episcopate.

Also in the running, at least on paper, was Cosmo Murray, the aged Bishop of Nyford, whose adamant stance against Deryni was echoed in his far younger auxiliary, Oliver de Nore. But at seventy-four, Murray was adjudged too old, and de Nore too young at forty-five.

Sadly, the assessment regarding Murray proved correct before the synod even settled down to serious deliberations, for the old man passed away during one of the sessions, simply nodding off and falling off his bench.

Bishop Murray's death occasioned a recess of several days to see to his funeral obsequies, after which Oliver de Nore was confirmed to the See of Nyford by acclamation before leaving for Nyford to bury his predecessor, which really could not be delayed. It also took de Nore out of the running for the slot in Valoret, having just been elected to Nyford—an event that gave several royal observers cause for relief.

The deliberations ground on, with balloting finally narrowing to two candidates: Paul Tollendal and Desmond MacCartney. In the end, perhaps it was Archbishop Desmond's relatively shorter tenure in Rhemuth that became the deciding factor for many of the delegates—hardly ten years a bishop, against Tollendal's fifteen. On the second day of March, in the year 1096, the Curia of Gwynedd elected Bishop Paul Tollendal of Marbury to be Archbishop of Valoret and Primate of All Gwynedd. For his successor in Marbury, the curia chose the itinerant Bishop Fisken Cromarty.

Word was sent to Rhemuth at once by fast courier, that Archbishop Paul's elevation and enthronement would take place in Valoret's All Saints' Cathedral in five days' time, to allow clergy from the surrounding areas to attend. The curia and archbishop-elect also recommended that the king's coronation date be set for the twenty-fourth of March. On hearing this news, the new king announced his intention to ride at once for Valoret to see the new archbishop installed. It was not a popular decision.

"I like it not, Sire," said Seisyll Arilan, speaking in council the morning the news arrived. "Your coronation is but three weeks away, and if you go to Valoret first, that will leave hardly a fortnight for final preparations when you return."

Brion rolled his eyes like the teenaged boy he still was, even though a king, and schooled his response to the tone and words he knew a king must use.

"My lord, we have been preparing for nearly three months now, and we have been cooped up for all the winter long. I need to get out among my people, as my father was wont to do; and I may be saddled with this new archbishop for many years, for good or ill. Best if we start off on the right foot, whereby I pay my respects to him as a dutiful son of the Church and then he pays his respects to me as his new king. I should prefer to begin that process *before* he comes to Rhemuth to crown me. I want it clear from the beginning just where we stand."

Duke Richard raised an appraising eyebrow, seeing much of the young king's father in him. "If that is what you intend, Sire"—the preamble left no doubt that he accepted the boy's authority—"then we must make certain that you remain safe for your journey. I would advise taking troops with you to Valoret—perhaps a score, in addition to a modest household." He held up a hand to stave off the objection about to leave Seisyll's lips. "Any more would make it impossible to travel quickly, and would take more time to organize than is possible, with the coronation but a few weeks away. Less might be foolish, from the standpoint of safety."

Brion glanced in question at Kenneth, who inclined his head in agreement.

"It seems a reasonable plan to me, my prince. But if you plan to do it, best we ride straight through, and leave this very afternoon, before word can get out of your plans. That will also lessen the possibility of ambush along the way."

"Surely you don't fear *that*?" Queen Richeldis said, wide-eyed at what had already been said—and not said.

Kenneth shrugged. "He is yet an uncrowned king, my lady. And if aught should happen to him, his heir is only nine. I think I understand why he wishes to do this thing—and I cannot fault his reasons, having myself suffered the less-than-welcome attention of bishops in the past—but there *is* a danger. That is a part of the lot of kings, but at least we can minimize it, if His Majesty agrees."

"His Majesty certainly agrees!" Brion retorted. "The sooner we leave, the better! I've been waiting for weeks! It's time to start acting like the king you all believe me to be."

"And he is, indeed, acting like a king," Richard said mildly, though he was smiling as he rose. "I advise you all to travel light," he continued. "Kenneth, if you'll help my eager nephew to pack what he'll need, I shall see to the lancer escort. Tiarnán and Jiri, you'll accompany us."

"Take my nephew as well, Your Highness, to see to the king's squiring," Seisyll quickly interjected.

Richard inclined his head in agreement. "I will welcome an Arilan on this venture—and I know that you yourself do not relish the idea of a two-day dash upriver in the spring snows."

"No, those days are behind me, I fear," Seisyll replied, smiling. "Besides, Her Majesty may have need of my counsel in your absence."

LATER that night, when the royal troop had ridden out, Seisyll Arilan assembled the Camberian Council in their domed meeting place.

"I should prefer that he weren't going," he told the six others seated around the octagonal table, "but his reasons are sound. And while Paul Tollendal would not have been my first choice as archbishop, I can think of several worse."

Michon de Courcy snorted and leaned back in his high-backed chair. "So can I," he replied, "and one of them is now become Bishop of Nyford. Someone really must do something about that man."

"You cannot just assassinate a bishop!" Vivienne retorted. "That would be sacrilege."

"And so is regicide," Barrett countered.

"So far as I know," Oisín Adair drawled, "it isn't bishops who might be trying to assassinate the king."

Rhydon sat forward impatiently. "No, it's Zachris Pomeroy and his associates, and there is no 'might' about it. I am confident that is what he intends to do, and this is exactly the sort of opportunity he'll have been waiting for." At the others' looks of question, he went on.

"Surely you don't think he would show up at the coronation, not knowing whether Brion Haldane has his father's powers. Besides, he isn't after Brion for his own cause; he wants to put the Festillic Pretender on the throne—and Prince Hogan certainly isn't yet ready to face down a fully-functional Haldane king."

"He has told you this?" Vivienne asked, aghast.

"Not in so many words, no," Rhydon replied. "But killing Brion now, before he has settled into his kingship, would certainly make it easier for the future. The heir is underage; and *his* heir is Duke Richard Haldane, a childless bachelor. It would take only a few deaths to leave Gwynedd without a clear heir, open for a king of the old Festillic line to take back the throne."

Michon chuckled, then lifted a hand, half in apology. "You have spent too much time with Camille Furstána and her nephews, Rhydon. You make this sound almost a good thing, though I know you do not mean that." He drew a deep breath and settled slightly forward, fingers interlaced before him.

"The question is, will Zachris Pomeroy take advantage of the king's presence to make his move in Valoret?" he went on. "It is, after all, closer to the border, and closer to Cardosa, where Pomeroy has been building his power base for Hogan and the other Furstáns. We can take no overt action, of course—nothing that would reveal our existence to the human population—but it seems to me a wise thing for several of us to make ourselves present at the cathedral, especially at the time of the archbishop's enthronement. For if I were Zachris Pomeroy, that is when and where I would strike, heedless of the fact that to do so would be to desecrate holy ground. I do not think that would much matter to such as he."

Silence greeted this declaration, but it was of the thoughtful sort rather than born out of any disagreement. After a moment, Seisyll gave a heavy sigh.

"I made certain that Jamyl was included in the king's party," he said quietly, "just in case Pomeroy should get wind of the king's visit to Valoret and try to apprehend him there. If he does, we may rely on Jamyl to do what is necessary from within, though we shall have to be careful to ensure that he is not discovered as Deryni. I do not know the king's status, regarding the Haldane powers, but I have hope that at least some of them have been awakened. It is little known, but he made a secret visit to the Lady Alyce de Corwyn as she lay dying. Given her involvement with the late king, it is possible that she was able to help Prince Brion."

"You have a plan?" Oisín asked quietly.

Michon nodded. "I do."

Chapter 27

"For they intended evil against thee: they imagined a mischievous device, which they were not able to perform."

—PSALM 21:11

THEY had reckoned that for the next day or two, at least until the king arrived in Valoret, he would be in no particular danger, since he was on the move and no one knew he was coming. That gave the Camberian Council time to organize their strategy, for Rhydon to assemble his operatives, and for Seisyll to contact his nephew, already on the road with the king, concerning Zachris Pomeroy. Jamyl dared not pass on the warning to anyone in the royal party, lest he be obliged to reveal his source—and himself as Deryni—but he assured his uncle that he would maintain particular vigilance, and would somehow make contact with Rhydon once they arrived in Valoret.

Which occurred just at dusk on the afternoon before Paul Tollendal was to be installed as Archbishop and Primate. The arrival of twenty Haldane lancers in the cathedral's stable yard, and with the king among them, provoked a flurry of initial alarm followed by consternation, as men in black habits and then a few in episcopal purple poked their heads from the chapter house doorway and then began spilling onto its steps, for no one had reckoned that the king might venture out of Rhemuth before his coronation, and certainly not as far north as Valoret.

"Sire, this is a pleasant surprise. You are most welcome!" said a young bishop Brion did not recognize, though Kenneth did: Faxon Howard, one of the itinerant bishops, and kin to Vera Countess of Kierney. Unlike the others coming warily onto the chapter house steps as the king and his immediate party dismounted, Bishop Faxon looked genuinely pleased.

Brion acknowledged the bishop's greeting with a neutral nod, but made no move to approach, allowing his companions to close ranks around him—Richard and Tiarnán and Jiri Redfearn, and Kenneth at his back—as more bishops emerged from the arched doorway, finally some that he knew by sight. First came Esmé Harris, the Bishop of Coroth, followed by Archbishop Desmond and Patrick Corrigan, who had rejoined his brother bishops immediately after Twelfth Night to assist in the deliberations. None of them looked particularly pleased to see Kenneth Morgan in the king's party.

"Reverend Father," the king said, nodding again. Though the stark black he wore was as much for anonymity of travel as for mourning for his late father, it lent him a gravity that belied his youth and stature; his companions stood nearly a head taller than he. Behind him and spilling back through the stable gate, the yard was awash with the Haldane crimson of the lancers' pennons.

"Your Majesty, we were not expecting you," Archbishop Desmond said baldly. "Ah—should you not be preparing for your coronation?"

The king's gaze flicked over the other clerics massing all around the archbishop. The resentment of some of them was only thinly veiled.

"I have had some weeks to prepare, my lord," he replied. "And it seemed to me right that I pay my respects to our new Primate as he is enthroned—as he shall do for me in another few weeks' time. I fear I do not know Bishop Tollendal by sight. Perhaps someone would be so good as to present him to me."

Accompanied by a flurry of furtive whispering, the mass of purple-clad clerics parted raggedly, allowing a slight, stoop-shouldered figure with a shock of faded ginger hair to pass among them, eyes humbly averted and hands clasped decorously at the waist of his faded purple cassock. Pausing abreast of Archbishop Desmond, he briefly lifted his gaze to the king's, inclined his head in respect, then glanced expectantly at Desmond, who drew himself up with an air of resignation.

"Brion Haldane King of Gwynedd, I have the honor to present the Most Reverend Paul Tollendal, lately Bishop of Marbury and now become Archbishop-Elect of Valoret and Primate of All Gwynedd. My Lord Archbishop, His Majesty the King."

Handing off his reins to Kenneth, Brion started forward, removing his leather cap as he came. The discreet coronet embroidered around the crown and nearly hidden by the upturned brim was the only mark of his rank—that, and the Eye of Rom in his right earlobe. The archbishop-elect, for his part, came slowly down the steps to meet him, hesitantly extending his right hand when they met at the bottom, where the king briefly bent to kiss the episcopal ring. With the archbishop standing on the bottom step as the king straightened at ground level, Kenneth noted that it made the two nearly the same height.

"Please allow me to extend felicitations on your election, Holy Father," Brion said, again inclining his head. "I shall pray that our future dealings may be amicable and harmonious."

Bishop Paul bowed in turn. "Thank you, Sire. It is always a blessing when leaders may work together toward the common good. And may I say that you honor us with your presence? I did not expect it, this close to your own coronation."

Brion smiled faintly, his gaze flicking briefly over the other bishops and their scowls. "So it would seem. But I am a very young king, my lord, and I fear that I have not yet gained the patience or perhaps the wisdom to sit by idly, when there is so much to learn. I trust that my presence will not inconvenience you overmuch. My men will look after me. Please do not feel that you must dwell on extra ceremony on my account, for I am sure I shall have my fill of it back in Rhemuth, when you come to crown me king."

The new archbishop smiled at that: an expression of genuine amusement that surprised the king, for no one had reckoned that Paul Tollendal might possess a sense of humor. Some of the king's party were smiling faintly as well, though Kenneth, at least, was well aware of the reputation of the man about to become the highest ecclesiastical authority in the land.

"I shall take you at your word, Sire," the new archbishop went on, inclining his head as he beckoned aside for a man in abbot's robes. "And I hope you will take no offense that we can offer you only such humble accommodation as the cathedral's guesthouse can provide; the castle has not had royal visitors in some time, and it will not be possible to make it ready on such short notice. I fear that your lancers will be obliged to make do in the stable loft, if you wish to keep them near you."

"That will be sufficient, my lord," Duke Richard said, speaking for the first time, and signing for the captain of lancers to dismount and draw nearer. "The men are well accustomed to billeting in the field, so a stable loft will seem to them great luxury. And the rest of us are most grateful for whatever arrangements you are able to make on such short notice."

"Then, may I invite you into the refectory, Sire, Highness?" their host replied, extending a hand in the direction of the cloister arch. "It will be warmer there, and I am certain that we can offer at least some token of suitable hospitality after your long ride. For some hours, our deliberations have been distracted by the aroma of fresh-baked bread and mulling wine. Clearly, your arrival is meant to encourage us to succumb to temptation. Please, come, and we shall get to know one another better."

THE enthronement of Paul Tollendal as Archbishop of Valoret and Primate of All Gwynedd was to take place at noon the following day, at the city's All Saints' Cathedral. That evening, the man at the focus of the planned ceremony hosted the king and his uncle for a modest private supper in his new apartments, accompanied by congenial if guarded conversation regarding past differences between Crown and Church, and how such might be avoided during the tenures of the new king and archbishop. The rest of the king's immediate party supped with the cathedral chapter, and the lancers with the officers of the archbishop's household guards.

Afterward, Kenneth and Sir Tiarnán spent an hour with the captain of lancers and the captain of the archbishop's household guard, familiarizing themselves with the interior of the cathedral and discussing possible security issues for the morrow, for Brion was still an uncrowned king, protected neither by the mystique accorded an anointed sovereign, as God's representative within his kingdom, nor by the fullness of his Haldane legacy, abbreviated by Alyce's untimely death. Awareness of the latter part of this vulnerability had made Kenneth doubly uneasy about making the journey to Valoret, but Brion had been insistent.

Meanwhile, with the king's men thus occupied, the king's squire found his opportunity to make contact with Rhydon, who had arranged to meet Jamyl in the cathedral's sacristy. The vast building was mostly deserted at that hour, with physical preparations already completed for the morrow's ceremonials. Jamyl could hear the distant voices of Kenneth and the others walking the galleries high above the clerestory aisles, but nothing moved in the nave below, where the only illumination besides the votive lights in the various side chapels came from a few torches left burning for the inspection party. Above, he could see more torches moving along the galleries, which would keep him aware of their whereabouts.

The sacristy door was standing slightly ajar as Jamyl approached it, gliding from shadow to shadow. He paused just outside for a moment, briefly rehearsing his cover story, should there prove to be anyone inside besides his expected contact; he dared not risk a psychic probe, since their adversary was another Deryni. Then, with a softly indrawn breath, he gently pushed the door open far enough to slip inside and softly close it. He was startled, nonetheless, to find Rhydon all at once standing in the center of the chamber, pushing back the cowl of a monk's robes and laying one finger across his lips to caution silence.

A second gesture seemed to lower a veil around them, deadening the distant sounds of the voices far outside. Another beckoned for Jamyl to approach, as Rhydon moved toward the center of the chamber to bend and grasp a corner of the fine Kheldish carpet covering the floor before the altar, walking it back to expose the tessellated floor beneath. In its center, barely visible by the light of the altar's Presence lamp, Jamyl could just make out a vaguely circular design.

"Come closer," Rhydon whispered, crouching down on his hunkers beside it. "You need to know about this."

At once Jamyl did as he was bidden, for the faint tingling just discernible at his feet told of a Portal matrix embedded in the mosaic design. At the other's gesture of invitation, he shifted onto his knees to lay both hands flat on the center of the tiled motif, closing his eyes to extend his senses, grasping the psychic prickle of the Portal's unique energy signature and setting its pattern deep in memory. As he looked up with a nod, dusting his hands against his thighs, Rhydon smiled faintly and got to his feet, Jamyl also rising so that the two of them could turn the carpet back over the Portal seal. With a glance at the door, Rhydon drew his younger companion back into the shadows nearer the vesting altar.

"Take special care tomorrow," Rhydon murmured, "and stay close to the king, if you can." His voice was hardly more than a whisper of breath against Jamyl's ear. "I've seen no further sign of Zachris, but I know that he is about. I did see one of his henchmen here at Mass this morning, which is very out of character for men of his ilk. It could well be a prelude for Zachris to make an appearance tomorrow, possibly by means of this very Portal. He certainly would know about it; there are Portals at many of the cathedrals, from the old days. I'll have a man stationed nearby, but if you can keep the king away from this end of the church, that would probably be wise."

Jamyl nodded. "I understand. Sir Kenneth is already planning to bring him and Duke Richard in by a side door," he said. "They'll be sitting in the choir, close against the choir screen—not visible from the nave. You really think that Zachris Pomeroy would come *here*?"

Rhydon's lips tightened. "What better place and opportunity, to strike a blow for Prince Hogan's cause? Killing the king before he can be crowned would throw the kingdom into turmoil, and give Hogan a unique opportunity to seize the crown before the succession can be resolved."

"But—Prince Nigel is the heir, and Richard after him," Jamyl began.

"Nigel is nine years old. Nor is it at all certain that he could wield the Haldane power, even were he grown to manhood. Richard fares no better in that regard—nor Brion himself, for that matter. Whatever preparations Donal was able to make, he did not expect to die with his heir still so young; and he had not reckoned on Alyce de Corwyn dying at the same time. God alone knows whether her son will be able to function, when he is old enough."

Jamyl closed his eyes briefly, in vain attempt to shut out even the thought of the struggle that could follow.

"Go and get some sleep now," Rhydon ordered. "I was able to arrange for your brother to be included in the choir coming down from Arx Fidei tomorrow. I have it in mind that he should complain of feeling ill, just before things begin, and be sent to sit in the sacristy while he recovers."

"To guard the Portal?" Jamyl only barely managed to keep his voice to a whisper. "Rhydon, he's only twelve years old—and if there's trouble, it could cost him his chance at the priesthood."

"If there's trouble, and Zachris has free access to this Portal," Rhydon replied, "it could cost the king his life."

Jamyl swallowed hard, unwilling to consider either outcome, flinching as Rhydon laid a hand on his shoulder in commiseration.

"Perhaps I should not have reminded you that the stakes were so high," Rhydon offered, faintly apologetic. "But be of good cheer. With any luck at all, we shall see no sign of Zachris Pomeroy or his minions, and everything will go smoothly."

ALL through the following morning, that seemed to be the case. Final preparations began just after Matins, with the principals assembling in the chapter house an hour before noon to robe and receive their final instructions. Meanwhile, the supporting clergy began gathering outside with all the trappings of the Church's highest ceremonial: the monks in their habits and church capes, the clergy in cassocks and white surplices, and the bishops wearing sumptuous copes and miters behind the grand processional cross, with acolytes bearing the matching candlesticks—the set said to have been given by the great King Bearand Haldane, encased in sheets of beaten gold and studded with rubies and pearls; the golden thuribles and aspergilla, the great Gospel Book with its jeweled cover depicting serried ranks of the blessèd who gave their patronage to All Saints' Cathedral, the bright silken banners of the various saints associated with Valoret and with Gwynedd.

It was a bright, sunny day, if still bitter cold, so the various masters of ceremony were able to line up the processions of choir and cathedral chapter and supporting bishops in the cathedral square instead of in the smaller cloister garth within the abbey walls. The fine weather had also encouraged a good turnout from the local townsfolk, eager to see their new archbishop enthroned, for whom the spectacle of the cathedral at work provided periodic and welcome diversion from their workaday lives. Well before the noon Angelus, people began converging on the cathedral square from all directions, gawking at the processions lining up outside as they shuffled inside to jostle for the best vantage points.

The king and his uncle came over from the abbey guesthouse only minutes before the ceremony was to begin, both still dressed in mourning for the late king, slipping in through a side door to take their places in the choir; with luck, they would be taken for minor clergy, amid so much other black, as would Tiarnán and Jiri, who attended them, along with Jamyl Arilan.

Kenneth had seen to the placing of the lancers earlier in the morning, all of them with black monks' robes over their mail and leather. A few would be stationed in the king's vicinity; more were in the body of the cathedral itself, several more in the narrow walks above the clerestory aisles, these armed with short recurve bows underneath their robes. For himself, Kenneth had declined the invitation to sit with the royal party, choosing instead to roam at large in the galleries above, where he might be more quickly aware of any threat to the king.

But nothing untoward occurred during the service itself. On the last stroke of the Angelus bell, when all the principals had taken their places, the various processions of choir and clergy began entering the cathedral, ecclesiastical impedimenta aglitter, to the accompaniment of chanted hymns and psalms and the sweet aroma of incense.

In due time, in the course of a Solemn High Mass, Paul Tollendal was acclaimed and enthroned as Archbishop of Valoret and Primate of All Gwynedd, with all the bishops present swearing him obedience. The new archbishop then presided for the remainder of the Mass, himself coming down from the altar to offer the sacred Bread to the king and his party; Archbishop Desmond followed with the Cup. The action immediately focused attention on the recipients thereof, prompting a whisper of speculation throughout the nave as to who they might be. Though somewhat vexed that their identities had been compromised, Duke Richard kept the king and his party in their places as the final prayers were said, the dismissal given, the last Gospel sung.

Afterward, as the various processions and choirs retired and the cathedral began to empty, the new archbishop paused on the cathedral steps to give his blessing to the cheering crowd. The king and his party lingered near the sanctuary to meet a few of the lesser participants whose efforts normally went unrecognized. In the aftermath of a religious ceremony, the risk seemed slight. Brion found that he enjoyed meeting his subjects, who warmed immediately to the gracious and personable youth who had become their king. As the royal party began moving toward the nave, Duke Richard dispatched Jamyl into the galleries to fetch Kenneth down, for they were expected back in the refectory momentarily for a meal with the new archbishop and his clergy.

"You can also tell him to stand down the lancers," Richard told him. "I'm sure they're ready for a hot meal."

Crossing into the north transept, where he had last caught sight of Kenneth lurking in the gallery above, Jamyl took a shortcut he had learned the night before, worming his way up one of the intramural turnpike stairs, then sidling along a narrow passage that a full-grown man would have found difficult to navigate, especially if he were armed; but Jamyl bore only a dagger on his belt. As he came out on one of the clerestory walks, he spotted Kenneth not far ahead and hailed him.

Kenneth had already anticipated the order to dismiss the lancers, so Jamyl joined him as they headed back toward the semicircular walkway that skirted the apse, still high above the cathedral floor, intending to pick up men as they went. Jamyl was in the lead, and it was he who literally stumbled over the first sign that all was not as placid as it seemed: the dead body of one of Brion's lancer archers.

"Dear God, he is *here!"* he breathed, one hand flying to the hilt of his squire's dagger even as he recovered his footing and crouched lower, his other hand briefly brushing the dead man's forehead, probing with his powers as his eyes scanned frantically ahead and all around. Behind him, Kenneth's sharp exclamation of query focused the imperative to take immediate action. But though he was still weeks shy of his sixteenth birthday, Jamyl Arilan rose to the challenge, making the split-second decision of a man

and a Deryni, to take a massive gamble with Lord Kenneth Morgan and compel his cooperation by the force of his will, because there was no time to ask permission.

Kenneth!

Jamyl's mental shout had its intended effect. Kenneth, in the process of crouching and craning to peer past Jamyl, immediately looked at Jamyl instead—and was brought up short by the squire's sharp, blue-violet gaze. He overbalanced and sat down hard, hitting the back of his head against the side of the wall. The pain was sufficient to distract him just enough that he did not think to avoid the hand that darted out to grasp the side of his neck. Nor was he able to evade the accompanying probe that surged across the link of flesh to thrust into his mind.

For Kenneth, whose previous experience of Deryni powers had been limited to the tender ministrations of his wife, and a few very specific and largely superficial interactions with the late king, Jamyl's touch was surgical and not altogether gentle, clashing against primitive shields that Kenneth had not known he possessed, and which Jamyl certainly had not expected.

Nor had he expected that Kenneth would be able to resist at all, though he knew that, if he chose, he could simply rip through the human lord's puny defenses and do what he liked. But that stark realization brought Jamyl immediately to his senses, for mind-ripping the loyal Kenneth Morgan, betraying his trust, was unthinkable.

At once he moderated his probe, though still he pressed for compliance, this time calming and reassuring, at once explaining and begging forgiveness, all in an instant.

Do not resist me, I beg of you! This is part of a plot to kill the king, Jamyl sent, *the work of a man called Zachris Pomeroy.* He sent the image of a dark-haired man with dark eyes into Kenneth's mind. *He serves the cause of Prince Hogan, the Festillic Pretender!* He shifted to verbal speech as it became clear that he was causing hurt to the one man whose assistance he most needed at this moment.

"Please! I do not mean to hurt you, but hear me out!" he gasped. "*You must help me!* He has come to kill the king if he can, but I may not tell you how I know this! I am loyal, I swear to you! Trust me! Help me! Even now, the king may be in mortal danger!"

KENNETH staggered as Jamyl released him, breath rasping ragged in his throat, but it never occurred to him to refuse what the young Deryni begged, implored—for Deryni, Jamyl surely was, and no less bound to the king's service than Kenneth himself. Of that, he was certain! Had he taken time to analyze, stark reason would have shrieked that it was folly to accept such revelation and direction at face-value, forced upon him by a Deryni, but his heart sensed that Jamyl Arilan was true, and that the king's life might very well depend upon their swift action.

Scrambling to his feet, eyes anxiously searching the shadows ahead—and already refining Jamyl's plan—Kenneth gestured urgently for Jamyl to go back the way they had come, himself snatching up the bow and an arrow from the dead lancer's hands and taking off in the direction he and Jamyl had been headed. He fumbled to nock the arrow by feel as he ran, for Jamyl had given him the face of the man he was now seeking—a man who would surely kill the king if he could—and he knew he would have but an instant to act, if he found him.

He nearly ran full-tilt into the next pair, sheltering in the shadow of a galleried walkway at the angle of the transept crossing. They were Brion's own lancers, but they had arrows nocked to bowstrings as they peered down dispassionately at the king and Duke Richard, who were deep in conversation with Bishop Faxon Howard, paying no mind as they strolled into the transept crossing far below.

One of the men was already in mid-draw; Kenneth stopped him with an arrow in his heart, before he could let fly, then launched himself at the other man, wildly flailing with the bow before him, shouldering him hard enough to send him over the low parapet that ran along the clerestory walk. Oddly, the man let out nary a sound as he fell to his death, only narrowly missing a startled monk, whose tray of empty cruets clattered to the floor with a discordant crash of chiming metal and shattering glass as he stumbled backward in alarm and looked up.

"What the devil?" Richard cried out, instinctively yanking Brion back from the crumpled form as he and the king also looked up.

Discarding his now-useless bow, Kenneth peered over the parapet only long enough to be certain that neither prince had been hit, then gestured urgently for them to be away.

"There's treachery afoot! Some of our men are compromised! Get him to safety!"

He did not wait to see what they did; only pelted onward to the end of the gallery—he could see no one there—then tried to squeeze through the narrow doorway of a tight turnpike stair that spiraled downward within one of the columns that supported the transept crossing. He had to detach his sheathed sword from its hangers and hug it close along his body to get through, and it hampered him on the way down, but he knew he had to get to the king, to protect him from his own men as well as Zachris Pomeroy; for the Deryni assassin had managed to infiltrate the cathedral, probably inserting some of his own men into the ranks of Brion's lancers, and he was able to seize men's minds, was subverting more of the lancers, one by one. Any one of them could be potential regicides.

Emerging to sounds of a vigorous scuffle at the bottom of the stair, he found Richard grappling with another of the lancers, who was struggling violently to wrench free—almost certainly, another of Pomeroy's unwilling conquests, for Kenneth knew the man to be loyal.

Brion and Bishop Faxon had also thrown themselves into the fracas and were attempting to assist Richard by tackling the man's flailing legs—and getting kicked for their trouble. Beyond, more lancers were approaching at a run from all parts of the cathedral, with Tiarnán and Jiri among them. But given what Kenneth had seen above and here, he realized he could not be sure of any of them.

"Richard!" he shouted, as he ran toward them. "Either

knock him out or kill him!" At the same time, he interposed himself between them and the oncoming lancers, flinging aside the scabbard from his sword and adopting a posture of challenge as he thrust his free hand upward in an emphatic order to halt.

"All of you, *hold*!" he ordered. "Drop your weapons! Don't ask why, just do it! *Now!*"

If they defied him for whatever reason, he knew he could not stop all of them, for there must be close to a dozen, but he took the chance that most of them probably had *not* been compromised.

"I said, put down your swords. Do it!" he repeated, gesturing with his sword and starting to back off just a little, edging closer to the king.

Behind him, amid the garbled sounds of muffled grunts and heavy breathing and harness clanging against the floor, he heard a smothered gurgle, abruptly choked off, and Richard's satisfied *humpf* as he dealt with their would-be assailant. In front of Kenneth, Jiri and Tiarnán had laid down their weapons immediately, and now were making gestures urging the wary and bewildered lancers to do the same.

Which they began to do, starting to lay down swords and bows . . . except for one man far at the back, with a monk's robe over his livery, who was edging away from the others—and then made an abrupt bolt for freedom.

"Stop that man!" Kenneth shouted, pointing with his sword as he took up pursuit, plunging into the midst of the confused lancers and trying not to skewer anyone as he bulled his way through. Their sheer mass slowed him down, even though they were trying to get out of his way.

Breaking free, he pounded down the nave after his quarry, shoving aside flustered clergy and lingering townsfolk, jumping over fallen ones or dodging to avoid tripping over them, caroming off pillars as he tried to keep his quarry in sight.

Far at the west end, a group of monks saw him coming, alarmed by the shouts echoing from that end of the cathedral, and pointed urgently toward the baptistry chapel in the northwest corner, very near the door to the sacristy, where two black-clad figures were circling and feinting in a deadly dance that suddenly exploded into a knife-fight, quick and violent and bloody. Nearby lay the crumpled forms of several more black-clad bodies. Kenneth had nearly reached the struggling pair when another black-robed man burst from the sacristy doorway, sword in hand, and launched himself at Kenneth.

They met in a clash of ringing steel and grunted exclamations that sent frightened onlookers scurrying for cover in archways and behind pillars. After an initial flurry of heated attacks and parries, Kenneth's attacker disengaged, backing off briefly in more calculating assessment.

Again they engaged, feinting, testing, neither doing any damage—until Kenneth's attacker suddenly launched another flurry of furious attack. After half a dozen ringing exchanges, blade slithered along blade until the two swords locked at the cross-guards, the two men eye-to-eye, each straining to shift the balance. Kenneth attempted to disengage, but his opponent would not be budged, his cold gaze catching Kenneth's in what immediately became an attempt to seize his will. He was Deryni, Kenneth realized, and moreover, almost certainly the man of whom Jamyl had warned him.

Wrenching away his glance, Kenneth finally managed to disengage, worried now, sword sweeping before him in guard as he circled a few steps, looking for an opening. He probably had the edge in experience and even skill, but his opponent was at least a decade younger. From far at the other end of the nave, he could hear urgent shouting, and the sound of running footsteps, and prayed that more of his opponent's associates had not launched a separate attack on the king.

They closed again, with Kenneth well aware that this time the stakes were even higher than his own possible loss of life. After another flurry of exchanges, they locked blades again, but Kenneth kept his gaze averted and spun out from under the other's blade, ending crouched in a guard position a dozen paces away, breathing hard. The running footsteps were closer now—whether friend or foe, Kenneth knew not.

But there would be no renewal of *this* battle—at least not with swords. Though Kenneth's opponent again raised his blade, a look of calculated loathing in the dark eyes, this time he stretched forth his sword-arm to sight along his blade, a sneering smile twitching at the corners of his mouth. Then, though the sword tip sank slowly toward the floor, the man's other hand lifted in a fist that, as the fingers opened, brought forth a spitting ball of orange fire.

As the man's arm cocked back to throw, all Kenneth could think to do—and it was his body that reacted instinctively, not his brain—was to flatten himself to the floor, at the same time rolling as far aside as he could, even as lightning arced from the man's hand. The lightning seared past where Kenneth's torso had been, narrowly missing a ribbed column and taking a smoking gouge of masonry out of the wall beyond.

He recoiled from the sight, and saw, to his horror, that Duke Richard and the king had very nearly reached what was about to become a deadly killing zone, and that his Deryni attacker now was turning his blade toward the king, fire again in his other hand, a look of triumph in his eyes as he again cocked his arm to launch another magical strike.

"Nooooooo!" Kenneth screamed.

In that same instant, his eye caught motion high in the clerestory above him: a black-clad and hooded archer looking down, drawing a little recurve bow to full-nock, the barbed arrowhead lowering to bear directly at him.

Except that, when the gloved hand let fly, the arrow thudded into the throat of Kenneth's attacker, who clawed at his throat with a strangled gurgle—and enveloped his own head in flames, slain by his own magic. Kenneth's gasp was lost in the shouts of nearby witnesses and the sound of footsteps approaching, as he twisted to look back up to the clerestory.

For an instant Kenneth did not move; nor did the man above, who paused with hand to ear and bow-arm still extended, face obscured by his hood.

But then the bow-arm slowly lowered, the other hand pushing back the hood from bright blue eyes and chestnut hair sleeked back in a braided warrior's knot. Looking grimly satisfied, Kenneth's savior inclined his head in a graceful bow, then jutted his chin beyond Kenneth, where Jamyl's desperate knife-fight had shifted onto the floor. The hand that the man raised in salute and leave-taking, just before he stepped back from the gallery's parapet, was marked at the wrist with a tattooed cross.

Chapter 28

"Then they brought out the king's son, and put upon him the crown."

—II CHRONICLES 23:11

EVEN as his unexpected rescuer's identity registered, Kenneth was squirming upright, sword somehow still miraculously in his hand, searching wildly for the king and Duke Richard. He spotted them farther back in the nave, where they had followed Kenneth's example by throwing themselves to the floor at the threat of magic, and were picking themselves up. Bishop Faxon and several monks helping them to their feet, all solicitous. Relief washed over him in a wave, but it was not complete. The direct and immediate threat to the king might be neutralized, but Jamyl—

Fearing the worst, he staggered in the direction he had last seen the squire, but Jamyl's fight was over, his body all but hidden beneath that of his much larger opponent. There was blood on the floor around the pair: a great deal of it.

Heartsick, Kenneth started to reach for the body on top, to drag it clear, then jerked back as the man moved. To his relief, the vague movement proved to come not from the larger man, but from Jamyl himself, trying to squirm out from under.

"*Jesu*, he's heavy!" Jamyl's head emerged from under the dead-weight of the other man, profound relief in his eyes as he saw Kenneth cautiously stretching out his sword to prod the body on top.

"He's also quite dead, m'lord. Can you help me get him off?"

At once Kenneth laid aside his sword and scrambled closer to grab a handful of the dead man's clothing and heave him clear of Jamyl, who was breathing raggedly and covered with blood.

"Christ, he *is* heavy!"

"He felt like a horse on my chest," Jamyl gasped, struggling to sit up. "He's wearing a breast and back, and steel vambraces—which didn't leave me much in the way of targets."

Together they heaved the dead man onto his back, where the cause of his death became immediately evident. The hilt of a Haldane squire's dagger was protruding from under the man's chin, its blade driven up through the jaw and into the brain. The man appeared to be the one Kenneth had chased down the nave and lost.

"Well, at least *you* got him," Kenneth muttered. "He got away from *me*."

Behind him, the sound of running footsteps told of further company about to arrive, and monks were beginning to creep from their hiding places and venture closer, now that the danger appeared to be past. Meanwhile, Kenneth was making his own assessment of Jamyl's condition, prodding tentatively at a great bloody rent in the younger man's sleeve.

"Is any of that blood his, or is it mostly yours?" As he said it, he glanced up at the gallery behind them, but he could see no sign of Sé Trelawney. If others had seen him, it was likely they had taken him for one of the lancer archers.

Jamyl winced as he made his own inspection of his wounded arm, grimacing as his hand came away red.

"Mmm, mostly mine, I'm afraid, though some of it probably comes from that fellow."

He nodded toward the nearest of the other men sprawled in the vicinity, who wore a cowled monk's robe like the others. The man appeared to be breathing, but his face was covered with blood from a deep cut that sliced from the bridge of his nose downward past the right-hand corner of his mouth.

"Another nasty friend, eh?" Kenneth retorted, tight-jawed, as he reached for his sword.

But Jamyl grabbed urgently at Kenneth's hand with his bloodied one and shook his head, the blue-violet eyes engaging Kenneth's as they had up in the gallery—though this time, no compulsion accompanied the intensity of his gaze.

"He is not one of them, my lord," Jamyl said very deliberately. "He is . . . an associate."

"An associate?" Kenneth repeated. "What kind of—"

"Not now, my lord!" Jamyl whispered, casting an anxious glance beyond Kenneth, for Richard and the king were nearly upon them, both with swords in their fists, and Bishop Faxon Howard not far behind.

Do not betray me! came Jamyl's further plea, as he collapsed back, moaning, though his double-squeeze of Kenneth's hand told Kenneth that the moan was more for effect than an indication of real discomfort.

"Jamyl!" Brion cried, sheathing his sword as he pressed between the gathering monks to approach. Richard was heading on to check the other body, its features charred beyond recognition and an arrow through its throat. "Is he all right? And who the devil is that?" he added, pointing at the dead man with a Haldane squire's dagger protruding from underneath his chin.

"I don't know, Sire," Jamyl said baldly before Kenneth could answer. "He was attacking one of the monks as I came down from the galleries," he added, jutting his chin in the direction of his wounded "associate." "When I tried to intervene, he attacked *me*."

"See to both of them," Bishop Faxon ordered, beckoning toward some of the other clergy personnel hovering nearby. "And see whether any of the others are alive."

"It looks like one of our archers got this one," Richard said, prodding the other dead man with a toe. "Sweet *Jesu*, how did he get so burned? Look at his hand and face!"

"He was Deryni, my lord!" said one of the monks, who came scurrying from behind a nearby column. "Look!" He pointed toward the damaged wall, with its singed and pocked mortar. "Praise God, that your man was able to stop him!"

Later inquiry among the remaining Haldane lancers never revealed just who had shot the arrow that stopped the man, and none of the archbishop's guards ever admitted to it. Nor did Kenneth enlighten them. But he knew beyond any doubt that he, and quite possibly the king, owed their lives to the timely intervention of Sir Sé Trelawney.

Later that evening, with Jamyl patched up and mobile, if looking a bit peaked, Kenneth Morgan was obliged to give a fuller reckoning to the king and his uncle regarding what had happened that day in the cathedral. Sitting after supper with Brion and Duke Richard—but not the new archbishop or any of his associates—Kenneth chose his words carefully, very aware of the need to protect the secret identity of his erstwhile ally, who was excused from serving table on account of his injury, but installed nonetheless in a chair by the fire, his injured arm supported in a sling to ease his wound. He had long before decided that he would not mention Sé. He did not know what connection there might be between the Anviller knight and the squire sitting across the table from them, but he knew he must protect both of them, if at all possible.

"There is really very little to tell, beyond what you already know," Kenneth said, topping up Duke Richard's cup and then his own when Brion passed a hand over his own cup and shook his head. Jamyl was still nursing his initial cup, along with his wounded arm, and likewise declined.

"I met up with Jamyl after you sent me to stand-down the archers, up in the clerestory galleries, and we found Milo Guthrie dead." That much was true. "I sent Jamyl across to the other side while I took Milo's bow and continued forward—and saw the two men drawing down on the two of you. So I shot the first one and rushed the second; I'd only the one arrow, but I'd known I'd only have time for one shot, if there was more treachery."

He paused to take a swallow of wine, carefully choosing the next part of his story. Knowing that Alyce had at least begun awakening Brion's ability to Truth-Read, he knew he dared not lie outright, but he could be economical with his details. Everything had happened very quickly.

"After that, it was a matter of getting downstairs to you as quickly as I could. As I threaded my way down that ridiculous internal turnpike stair at the transept, afraid that I was going to get stuck, it occurred to me that only a Deryni could have subverted any of our men in the space of only a few hours—and that maybe he'd gotten to more than just the two I'd killed. That's why I ordered the ones on the ground to drop their weapons. When the one in the back broke and ran, I figured he had to be our infiltrator."

"And Jamyl had gotten down by then," Brion said eagerly, still smiling at the image Kenneth had conjured of getting stuck in the turnpike stair, "so he was able to corner him there by the baptistery chapel." He flashed his squire a pleased grin, eliciting a raised cup and a wan, answering smile.

"He very nearly crushed me to death, Sire," Jamyl allowed, seizing on the opportunity to embroider on the humor Brion was finding in the story. The king *was* only fourteen and a bit, after all. "He was wearing mail and a breast and back under those monk's robes. The only place I could get at him was above the neck—though that certainly sufficed."

Brion shivered deliciously, though Richard looked thoughtful—and *he* was the one to be convinced, Kenneth realized, though the prince's next comment suggested that he was not questioning the story.

"I didn't teach you that," Richard muttered, "though it's a good move. It would certainly stop a man quickly. Did you learn that in King Illann's service?"

Jamyl only shrugged and lifted his cup to the royal duke in salute, then drank again, hoping the assumption would suffice.

"Humph," was all Richard said, though his tone was thoughtful and not at all suspicious. "I wonder if we'll ever know who he was—or the other one, who was tossing lightning at us. The armor is Torenthi; at least the breast and back are. Very fine workmanship—and the other man's sword is worth a small fortune. *Someone* is going to miss them. . . ."

"Aye, and they'll have friends," Kenneth said. "I'm sure

the word will get out. Whoever they were, they were enemies of Gwynedd."

"Aye, *that's* a certainty!" Richard retorted.

But Kenneth knew precisely who one of the dead men was, and by whom he had been sent, thanks to Jamyl—whose Deryni identity had been a *complete* surprise.

As for any connection between Jamyl and Sé Trelawney, other than their shared Deryni heritage . . . Kenneth took a long pull at his wine, well aware that Deryni were very good at keeping secrets.

THEY had considered leaving Jamyl behind for a day to rest with the monks, but he woke the next morning declaring that he was fit enough to travel. During the night, while checking on his wounded "associate"—who would always bear the scar of the day's misadventure—he had also learned of another body found in the cathedral sacristy, armored like the man he had killed, and with not a mark upon him. Hearing that, he asked about the boy chorister who had taken ill before the ceremony; but the monks assured him that the boy had rejoined his choir immediately after Mass, long before trouble erupted. Jamyl suspected that the story's full telling might only be revealed when he had talked to his brother, but he kept his suspicions to himself as he retired at last to his bed and a restless night's sleep.

Thus reassured, he was, indeed, fit to travel the next day—and he was fit enough for other things as well. Before leaving for Rhemuth, Kenneth and Richard took the opportunity to interview all the remaining lancers, lest some remained under the influence of the mysterious attacker Jamyl had slain; but there were none. It was Jamyl who brought the men, one by one, into the room set aside for that purpose in the abbot's apartments; but even the brief transit down the corridor to get there was sufficient for him to satisfy himself that no one else had been tainted.

Kenneth quietly accepted Jamyl's subtle assistance, and managed to convey the impression to Brion and Richard that his confidence in the questioning was due entirely to the interrogation skills of Richard and himself.

Despite Jamyl's protestations that he was fit, they spent three days traveling back to Rhemuth instead of two, though that still would leave them with nearly a fortnight before the coronation. They had sent a pair of lancers on ahead to advise the queen and crown council of their imminent arrival.

All of the royal household were there on the great hall steps to greet them as they rode into the castle yard, the queen coming right down onto the muddy forecourt to grasp at her son's stirrup, clinging to him as he swung down to embrace her. Prince Nigel and the king's two sisters were also waiting to greet them, and Brion spared each of them a hug and a few words of cheer before mounting the great hall steps to receive the welcomes and good wishes of his ministers of state.

Seeing Seisyll Arilan there among them, nodding greeting to his nephew as they all dismounted, reminded Kenneth that Seisyll, too, must be Deryni like his nephew, though he found himself taking comfort in the realization that at least one more Deryni secretly served the House of Haldane. He did not know whether Jamyl would tell his uncle of confiding in Kenneth Morgan—he hoped not. The elder Arilan had always made Kenneth vaguely uneasy, though he had chalked it up to personality differences; now he knew the real reason. But he also knew that he would do his utmost to protect both these courageous Deryni who were pledged, like him, to protect the king and the royal house of Gwynedd.

But there was one person missing from the welcome home, whose well-being now became Kenneth's focused concern. The first thing he did, when he had seen his horse looked after and taken his leave of the king and Duke Richard, was to seek out his son.

Hurrying inside, he made his way down the great hall to the stairwell that led up to the apartment he had been assigned before the present mission. Sir Llion was waiting for him just at the entrance to that stairwell, with a small, towheaded boy in his charge. Young Alaric gave a squeal of joy as he saw his father, breaking away from Llion's grasp to come racing across the stone flags as his father knelt on one knee to receive him.

"Papa! You're back!" the boy cried, flinging himself into his sire's embrace to shower him with kisses. "Papa, Papa!"

"I take it that you missed me," Kenneth replied, hugging the boy in return and glancing up as Llion sauntered nearer, smiling faintly. "Will Sir Llion tell me that you've been good?"

"Of course I have!" Alaric replied indignantly. "I promised Mama. And I can write all my letters now; Llion helped me practice. I can even read—well, some," he added, at Llion's look askance.

"Well, then, you shall have to show me," Kenneth said, standing with the boy in his arms to exchange a handclasp with Llion.

As the two adults climbed the wide turnpike stair, Alaric riding happily in his father's embrace, Llion gave a sketchy report of his young charge's activities in Kenneth's absence, and Kenneth, in turn, gave the young knight a bare-bones account of what had transpired when the new archbishop was enthroned.

"We got at least two of the instigators," Kenneth told Llion, "but it was a near-run thing. We have Master Jamyl's clearheadedness partially to thank for it." He did not add that, without Jamyl's assistance, both the king and his royal uncle might have returned from Valoret as the subjects of a funeral cortege, and that the nine-year-old Prince Nigel might now be King of Gwynedd.

The next days seemed to evaporate with little to show for them, as preparations for the coronation of Brion Haldane shifted into their final phases. A week before the scheduled coronation day, foreign emissaries and nobles from the outlying regions began to arrive, again swelling the city's guest accommodations to near-capacity.

Visitors staying in the castle dined in the great hall every night, though the fare was far simpler than what would be provided on coronation day. Most evenings, the young king made a point of joining his guests, at least for a little while, always attended by Jamyl and with at least one crown counselor at his back. Usually, it was Kenneth.

Through all these days and nights, Kenneth often pondered the whys and wherefores by which both his and the king's lives had been saved by the presence of an elusive Knight of the Anvil, who had been the childhood friend of Alyce de Corwyn Morgan, and who once had been a knight of Lendour.

It came as little surprise to Kenneth, then, that Sé Trelawney was present on coronation day as well, as the new archbishop crowned Brion Donal Cinhil Urien Haldane King of Gwynedd. Kenneth never saw him in the lead-up to the ceremony; but as Brion swore his coronation oath, right hand set upon Holy Writ, Sé was there in the background, the hood of his black mantle pushed back, standing with arms folded across the breast of his long black robe, just above the white slash of his knight's belt.

He was there—though no one else seemed to be aware of it—when Brion knelt beneath a golden canopy to receive the marks of holy chrism on head and breast and hands, sealing him to the service of his kingdom.

And he was there when Archbishop Paul lifted Gwynedd's great state crown of leaves and crosses intertwined and spoke the ancient words of king-making over Brion's bowed head:

"Bless, we beseech Thee, O Lord, this crown, and so sanctify Thy servant Brion, upon whose head Thou dost place it as a sign of royal majesty . . ."

Kenneth was certain he saw Sé standing just behind the other bishops, hands upraised in benison, with the tattooed crosses dark against his inner wrists, and he seemed to hear other words inside his head.

In the name of Holy Camber, be king for all thy people of Gwynedd, human and Deryni, and reign in wisdom for all thy days . . .

And finally, Sé was there to offer up his fealty with the other Lendour knights, kneeling to place his joined hands briefly between Brion's. Kenneth could not hear what passed between then, but Brion told him later that evening, as Kenneth led the happily exhausted king to the royal apartments to help him disrobe as he prepared for bed.

"Did you see that Anviller who came up with the other knights to pledge fealty, Kenneth? He told me he had been a close friend of Lady Alcye. He showed me the tattoos on his wrists, and said that he could not give me the same fealty that the other knights gave, because he now served a different Lord, but he said that if it were within his power, he would always be there when I had need.

"He told me that he was Deryni, and that his powers were mine to command, if ever I should need his services—within the limits of his vows to his order, of course. And he told me that he would look after you and your son as well: that both of you were pledged to my service in a very special way, and that one day, your Alaric should be my Deryni protector, and awaken the full measure of my father's Haldane legacy." Brion paused slightly in his disrobing.

"I remember that something happened in that regard when you brought me for that last visit to your wife's bedside. He knew about that, and he said that she had awakened a part of that legacy as her last act of service and duty to the Haldane line. . . ."

"He told you all of that, my prince, in the time it took to set his hands between yours?" Kenneth asked, when the king had wound down and was gazing distantly at the fire on the other side of the room. He did not doubt that Sé had conveyed all of this to the king—and in the blink of an eye—but he wondered whether Brion grasped the full significance of the gift he had been given.

"He did, Kenneth," the king replied, an odd expression coming across his face as he thought about what he had actually said. "I know he did; it's all very clear. But I cannot, for the life of me, explain how he must have done it."

"I expect it will come to you in time, my prince," Kenneth said gently. He smiled as he watched the king yawn hugely and crawl beneath the coverlet of the great, canopied state bed. "I have no doubt now that a good many things will come to you in time."

Afterward, when he had drawn the bed curtains, extinguished most of the candles, and left instructions with Jamyl, who would sleep in the adjoining room, Kenneth let himself out and returned to his own quarters, where his precious son slept. Sir Llion lay on a pallet at the foot of the boy's cot, also sound asleep.

Moving quietly, so as not to wake either one of them, Kenneth slipped his sword from its hangers and laid it on his own bed, then eased closer to Alaric's bedside to gaze down at his sleeping son, the future hope of the Haldanes, and perhaps of the Deryni race.

"Laddie, laddie, what have we done to you?" he whispered softly, crouching down beside the bed. For he was coming to realize that the recent attempt on the king's life was likely to deepen the danger facing his son in the years ahead: a son who now had no Deryni mother to protect him. When word got out that the king's would-be assassin had been Deryni, public outrage would only reinforce the already widespread belief that Deryni were dangerous, their very existence a threat to Gwynedd's crown and to all honest folk. And if the Zachris Pomeroy affair were not enough, one had but to recall the incident at Hallowdale and too many others like it, which were becoming all too frequent—and not even Donal Haldane had felt competent to address *that* growing threat.

Would Brion Haldane be able to do any better? A new king only just of age, and without the maturity or experience of his late father?

And Alaric was a decade younger than the king, his Deryni heritage widely known—and already entrenched in the royal household and in the new king's affections. As he grew into maturity, there would always be those who feared him, who mistrusted him, who would have no compunctions about trying to take his life, even as they had taken the life of young Krispin MacAthan.

It was a dangerous time to be Deryni—or to be the father of a Deryni. Without doubt, the next few years would present many challenges, as Kenneth strove to protect his son and still serve the king to whom both of them had pledged their ongoing loyalty only hours before.

Fortunately, it appeared that unexpected and powerful allies did exist, as both Jamyl and Sé had proven at Valoret, to protect not only the king but also those who served him; for Kenneth himself might have perished at Valoret, had it not been for the pair. (He did not know whether the two had worked in tandem, or whether the intervention of both at once had been a coincidence; that bore further reflection, and careful observation.) Might there be others as well, looking out for the king, for Kenneth—and for Kenneth's son?

Briefly closing his eyes, Kenneth Morgan made a prayer in his heart, that God and all His angels might keep the boy safe in their care. He imagined, too, that his dear Alyce might now be numbered among those who watched over the innocent, given angel wings by the farewell of a small boy who had tucked feathers into his mother's coffin to speed her on her way. A tear runneled down his cheek, but he knuckled it away before bending to press a gentle kiss to his son's brow.

"You shall serve a great king, my son," he whispered, as he got quietly to his feet. "Not right away—but one day. And there will be men to help you, as you grow into your manhood and your destiny."

Turning away, he moved quietly to the window and drew back the edge of the curtain to glance into the courtyard below, where moonlight gilded the cobblestones and little moved.

"But for now," he murmured under his breath, "I pray that you may be given the time simply to be a boy."

Off to the east, silver limned the horizon with the promise of dawn. It would be Brion Haldane's first full day as the now-crowned King of Gwynedd.

APPENDIX I

Index of Characters

*indicates a deceased character, or one only mentioned indirectly

*AHERN JERNIAN DE CORWYN, LORD—deceased Earl of Lendour and Heir of Corwyn, Deryni; brother of Alyce de Corwyn and briefly the husband of Zoë Morgan.

AIRLEAS—magical name given by King Donal to the boy Alaric Morgan.

ALARIC ANTHONY MORGAN, MASTER—three-year-old son of Alyce de Corwyn Morgan and Sir Kenneth Kai Morgan; half Deryni.

ALAZAIS MORGAN—youngest daughter of Sir Kenneth Morgan.

*ALICIA MCLAIN, LADY—stillborn daughter of Jared and Vera McLain.

ALUN MELANDRY, SIR—a new-made Mearan knight, son of the murdered former royal governor of Ratharkin.

ALYCE JAVANA DE CORWYN MORGAN, LADY—Heiress of Corwyn and Lendour, Deryni wife of Sir Kenneth Morgan and mother of Alaric and Bronwyn.

ANDREW MCLAIN, DUKE—Duke of Cassan, father of Jared.

ANSELM, FATHER—a chaplain at Rhemuth Castle.

ARRAN MACEWAN, SIR—a new-made knight of Claibourne.

ARTHEN TALBOT, SIR—newly knighted youngest son of Sir Lucien Talbot, royal governor of Ratharkin.

AURIEL, ARCHANGEL—Torenthi name for Uriel.

BAIRBRE—maid to Vera Countess of Kierney, who also looks after Duncan and Kevin McLain.

BARRETT DE LANEY—blind member of the Camberian Council; brother of Dominy de Laney.

*BEARAND HALDANE, KING SAINT—pre-Interregnum Haldane king who pushed back the Moorish sea lords and consolidated Gwynedd.

*BLAINE EMANUEL RICHARD CINHIL HALDANE, PRINCE—second son of Donal King of Gwynedd, 1083–1092.

BRION DONAL CINHIL URIEN HALDANE, PRINCE—firstborn son and heir of King Donal; later, King of Gwynedd.

*BRIONA, PRINCESS—only child of the last Prince of Mooryn, wife of Prince Festil Augustus.

*BRONWYN MORGAN—a sister of Charlan Kai Morgan, who died in the service of King Javan Haldane.

BRONWYN RHETICE MORGAN, LADY—infant daughter of Alyce and Kenneth Morgan, younger sister of Alaric.

CAMILLE FURSTÁNA, PRINCESS—daughter of Prince Zimri Furstán and Chriselle, a Festillic heiress; aunt of Prince Hogan Furstán; now known as Mother Serafina, a nun at Saint-Sasile, an all-Deryni monastic establishment at Furstánan, in Torenth.

CASPAR TALBOT, SIR—third son of Sir Lucien Talbot, brother of Sir Arthen Talbot.

*CHARLAN MORGAN, SIR—distant cousin of Sir Kenneth Morgan, loyal knight in the service of King Javan Haldane, with whom he died in battle.

CILLIAN, MASTER—a royal physician at Rhemuth Castle.

CLAARA MORGAN WINSLOW, LADY—widowed younger sister of Sir Kenneth Morgan.

CLARICE—a granddaughter of Claara, and grand-niece of Sir Kenneth Morgan.

*CLUIM HALDANE, KING—great-grandfather of King Donal.

COCKLEBURR—a retired warhorse selected by Sir Llion as a first training mount for Alaric Morgan.

COSMO MURRAY, BISHOP—Bishop of Nyford; dies during the synod convened to elect a successor to Archbishop William MacCartney in 1096.

CRESCENCE DE NAVERIE, SIR—special counsel to the Regents of Corwyn.

DEINOL HARTMANN, SIR—seneschal at Castle Cynfyn.

DELPHINE MORGAN—unmarried older sister of Sir Kenneth Morgan, chatelaine of Morganhall in his absence; an accomplished poet.

DESMOND MACCARTNEY, ARCHBISHOP—Archbishop of Rhemuth, brother of Archbishop William.

*DOMINIC DU JOUX, SIEUR—son of Richard du Joux, a follower of Prince Festil of Torenth, and Princess Tayce Furstána, a first cousin of the new Festillic king; first Duke of Corwyn.

Dominy de Laney—sister of Barrett, member of the Camberian Council.

Donal Blaine Aidan Cinhil Haldane, King—King of Gwynedd, Prince of Meara, and Lord of the Purple March.

*Duchad Mor—Torenthi Deryni general who unsuccessfully attempted to invade Gwynedd in 985 on behalf of the Festillic Pretender of the day.

*Dulchesse, Queen—childless first queen of Donal Haldane.

Duncan Howard McLain, Master—son of Jared Earl of Kierney and Vera, Alyce's twin sister; cousin of Alaric.

*Elaine MacInnis, Lady—first wife of Jared Earl of Kierney, and mother of Kevin McLain; died in childbirth.

Esmé Harris, Bishop—Bishop of Coroth, and member of Corwyn's council of regents.

Estèphe de Courcy, Sir—a young cousin of Michon de Courcy.

Ewan de Traherne, Sir—Earl of Rhendall, a new-made knight.

Ewan MacEwan, Duke—Duke of Claibourne.

Faxon Howard, Bishop—an itinerant bishop, kin to Vera Howard McLain.

*Festil, King—first of the Interregnum kings of Gwynedd, a younger son of the King of Torenth.

*Festil Augustus, Prince—son of Festil, later Festil II.

Fisken Cromarty, Bishop—itinerant bishop elected Bishop of Marbury in 1096, in succession to Paul Tollendal.

GABRIEL, ARCHANGEL—guardian of the element of water.

GEILL MORGAN, LADY—middle daughter of Sir Kenneth Morgan, married to Sir Walter, a young knight of Kierney.

GEOFFREY DE MAIN, SIR—a new-made knight, non-identical twin to Thomas.

GRAHAM MACEWAN, LORD—six-year-old heir of Ewan Duke of Claibourne.

HAMILTON, LORD—seneschal of Coroth Castle.

HARKNESS, LORD—visiting lord put to sleep by Jamyl Arilan.

HOGAN FURSTÁN, PRINCE—Festillic Pretender to the throne of Gwynedd, posthumous son of Prince Marcus, nephew of Princess Camille/Sister Serafina, and Jonelle Heiress of Gwernach, by which right he was sometimes known in later life as Hogan Gwernach.

HORT OF ORSAL—ruler of the Principality of Tralia, premier of the Forcinn Buffer States.

ILLANN, KING—King of Howicce and, after the death of his mother, Queen Gwenaël, King of Llannedd; brother of Queen Richeldis and uncle of Brion and Nigel.

*IMRE FURSTÁN OF FESTIL—last Interregnum King of Gwynedd.

IRIS CERYS, SISTER—a professed nun at Arc-en-Ciel, formerly Cerys Devane, former roommate to Alyce de Corwyn.

IRIS JESSILDE, SISTER—second daughter of Jessamy MacAthan, a professed nun at Arc-en-Ciel.

IRIS JUDIANA, MOTHER—Superior at Arc-en-Ciel; daughter of a Bremagni duke, educated at Rhanamé.

IRIS ROSE, SISTER—a professed nun at Arc-en-Ciel.

ISAIYA, MASTER—a Master of the Deryni Inner Order at the University of Rhanamé.

JAMES OF TENDAL, SIR—hereditary Chancellor of Corwyn.

JAMYL ARILAN, MASTER—nephew of Sir Seisyll Arilan, Deryni; a squire to King Donal and Prince Brion.

JÁNOS SOKRAT, COUNT—a Torenthi courtier.

JARED MCLAIN, EARL OF KIERNEY—only son and heir of Andrew Duke of Cassan; husband of Vera, father of Kevin and Duncan.

*JASHER HALDANE, KING—younger brother of King Nygel and elder of King Cluim, who helped repel the armored infantry of Duchad Mor in 985.

JASKA COLLINS, SIR—a new-made knight of Gwynedd, known for his horsemanship.

JATHAN, PRINCE—youngest son of King Donal and Queen Richeldis.

*JERNIAN, DUKE—fifth Duke of Corwyn, a comrade of Kings Nygel, Jasher, and Cluim; father of Stíofan Anthony.

*JESSAMY FERCH LEWYS MACATHAN, LADY—deceased daughter of Lewys ap Norfal and wife of Sir Sief MacAthan, all of them Deryni; mother of the murdered Krispin MacAthan by Donal Haldane.

JIRI REDFEARN, SIR—an aide to King Donal.

JORIS TALBOT, SIR—eldest son of Sir Lucien Talbot, royal governor of Meara at Ratharkin.

JOVETT CHANDOS, SIR—childhood friend of Alyce de Corwyn, secretly Deryni; close friend of Sir Sé Trelawney; marries Lady Zoë Morgan.

JUDIANA, MOTHER—see Iris Judiana, Mother.

JULIAN TALBOT, SIR—second son of Sir Lucien Talbot, royal governor of Meara at Ratharkin.

KAILAN PETER CHANDOS, MASTER—infant son of Zoë Morgan and Sir Jovett Chandos.

KÁROLY FURSTÁN, PRINCE—third son of King Nimur of Torenth; later, Crown Prince.

KENNETH KAI MORGAN, SIR—an aide to King Donal; husband of Lady Alyce de Corwyn, father of Alaric and Bronwyn, plus Zoë and two more daughters by a first marriage; created Earl of Lendour for life, in right of his wife.

*KERYELL OF LENDOUR, EARL—Deryni Earl of Lendour and husband of Stevana de Corwyn, Heiress of Corwyn; father of Alyce and Vera.

KEVIN DOUGLAS MCLAIN, MASTER—son of Jared Earl of Kierney by his first wife, Elaine MacInnis; Master of Kierney.

KHOREN VASTOUNI, PRINCE—brother of the Prince of Andelon, member of the Camberian Council.

*KITRON—an ancient Deryni mage-scholar.

*KRISPIN SIEF MACATHAN—murdered son of Jessamy MacAthan by King Donal, secretly sired to be a Deryni protector for the royal princes.

LAURENZ UDAUT, SIR—father of Sir Trevor and special counsel to the Duchy of Corwyn.

LEONARD—a guard in the service of King Donal, who accompanied him to Morganhall.

LEOPOLD, MASTER—steward of Morganhall.

*LEWYS AP NORFAL—infamous Deryni who died in a forbidden magical experiment; father of Jessamy and Morian.

LLION FARQUAHAR, SIR—a young knight of Corwyn, selected to be Alaric's governor and companion.

LUCIEN TALBOT, BARON—a baron of the Purple March, permanent royal governor of Meara at Ratharkin replacing the murdered Iolo Melandry.

*MARCUS FURSTÁN, PRINCE—father of Prince Hogan and brother to Camille.

*MARIE STEPHANIA DE CORWYN—younger daughter of Keryell Earl of Lendour and Stevana de Corwyn; murdered younger sister of Alyce and twin to Ahern de Corwyn.

MELISSA—a maid to Alyce.

MICHAEL, ARCHANGEL—guardian of the element of fire.

MICHAEL O'FLYNN, EARL OF DERRY—special counsel to the Duchy of Corwyn; father of Sir Seamus O'Flynn.

MICHON DE COURCY, LORD—member of the Camberian Council.

MIKHAIL VASTOUNI, PRINCE—sovereign Prince of Andelon, father of Sofiana, brother of Khoren; Deryni.

MILES CHOPARD, SIR—secretary to Corwyn's council of regents.

MILO GUTHRIE—Haldane lancer killed in Valoret.

MORAG FURSTÁNA, PRINCESS—daughter of the King of Torenth, sister of Princes Károly, Wencit, Festil, and Torval.

MORIAN DU JOUX (AP LEWYS), SIR—son of Lewys ap Norfal and brother of Jessamy, and Deryni.

NESTA MCLAIN, LADY—sister of Sir Kenneth Morgan's first wife, and aunt to his three daughters.

NIGEL CLUIM GWYDION RHYS HALDANE, PRINCE—younger son of King Donal and Queen Richeldis; later, heir presumptive to King Brion.

NIMUR FURSTÁN, CROWN PRINCE—eldest son of Nimur King of Torenth.

NIMUR (NIMOUROS HO PHOURSTANOS PADISHAH)—King of Torenth.

O'BEIRNE, BISHOP (NEIL)—Bishop of Dhassa.

OISÍN ADAIR—a horse breeder, member of the Camberian Council.

OLIVER DE NORE, BISHOP—itinerant bishop in Carthane, elder brother of the late Father Septimus; later, Bishop of Nyford.

ORBAN HOWARD, SIR—"father" of Vera (de Corwyn) Howard.

PASCHAL DIDIER, FATHER—R'Kassan-trained former chaplain to Keryell Earl of Lendour and tutor to his children; Deryni.

PATRICK CORRIGAN, BISHOP—auxiliary bishop in Rhemuth.

PAUL TOLLENDAL, BISHOP—Bishop of Marbury, elected Archbishop of Valoret in succession to William MacCartney.

PEDUR CHANDOS, SIR—a Lendouri knight, father of Sir Jovett.

*PHARAÏLDE NÍ PADRAMOS—author of a treatise on Deryni magic.

PHARES DONOVAN, SIR—a new-made knight from Marley, former squire to Prince Brion, a keen archer.

PHELIM—magical name given to Duncan McLain by his mother.

RAPHAEL, ARCHANGEL—guardian of the element of air.

RATHER DE CORBIE, LORD—an emissary of the Hort of Orsal.

RATHOLD, LORD—counsel to the Duchy of Corwyn.

REYHAN OF JÁCA—future consort of Princess Sofiana of Andelon.

*RHETICE—wife to Corwyn's second duke.

RHYDON SASILLION, SIR—junior member of the Camberian Council.

RICHARD BEARAND RHUPERT CINHIL HALDANE, PRINCE—unmarried half-brother of King Donal, Duke of Carthmoor and Earl of Culdi.

*RICHARD DU JOUX, LORD—father of Dominic, died fighting at the side of Prince Festil of Torenth in the conquest of Gwynedd; husband of Princess Tayce Furstána, a cousin of the new King of Gwynedd.

RICHELDIS, QUEEN—second wife of King Donal and mother of his children, a princess of Howicce and Llannedd.

ROBERT OF TENDAL, SIR—son of Sir James, the hereditary chancellor of Corwyn, whom he serves as an aide.

RODDER GILLESPIE, FATHER—a priest of the Diocese of Nyford, and secretary to Bishop Oliver de Nore.

RORIK HOWELL, LORD—Earl of Eastmarch.

*ROSMERTA—third wife of Keryell of Lendour, and stepmother to Alyce, Marie, and Ahern, returned to her own family after Keryell's death.

SEAMUS O'FLYNN, SIR—son of Michael O'Flynn Earl of Derry.

SEISYLL ARILAN, LORD—member of King Donal's council of state and also the Camberian Council; uncle of Jamyl and Denis Arilan.

*SEPTIMUS (SEPP) DE NORE, FATHER—late brother of Bishop Oliver de Nore, executed for his part in the murder of Krispin MacAthan.

SERAFINA, SISTER/MOTHER—see Camille, Princess.

SÉ TRELAWNEY, SIR—childhood friend of Alyce, secretly Deryni; formerly in the service of Lendour, but now a fully vowed Knight of the Anvil, *Incus Domini*, the Anvil of the Lord.

SEVALLA—the bloodred R'Kassan mare acquired for Prince Brion for his coming of age by Master Oisín Adair.

*SIEF MACATHAN—deceased husband of Jessamy; a former member of King Donal's council of state and also the Camberian Council.

SILKE HALDANE, PRINCESS—second daughter of Donal King of Gwynedd and Queen Richeldis.

SÍODA KUSHANNAN, LORD—Earl of Airnis, who served Duke Stíofan, Alyce's grandfather; a Grecotha scholar, and special counsel to the Duchy of Corwyn.

SOBBON, PRINCE—sovereign Prince of Tralia, also known as the Hort of Orsal.

*SOFFRID—an ancient Deryni sage.

SOFIANA VASTOUNI, PRINCESS—elder daughter of Prince Mikhail of Andelon and Princess Ysabeau; niece of Prince Khoren.

*STEVANA DE CORWYN, LADY—deceased heiress of Corwyn, granddaughter of Stíofan Duke of Corwyn; second wife of Keryell Earl of Lendour, mother of Alyce, Vera, Ahern, and Marie.

*STÍOFAN ANTHONY, DUKE—Duke of Corwyn, and Alyce's grandfather.

SWITHUN, FATHER—chaplain at Morganhall.

SYLVAN—a squire at Castle Coroth.

*TAYCE FURSTÁNA, LADY—first cousin of Festil I King of Gwynedd, wife of Lord Richard du Joux; their son was Dominic du Joux, first Duke of Corwyn.

THOMAS, SIR—a senior Kierney knight, captain of the guard escort that accompanied Countess Vera McLain to Zoë Morgan's wedding in Cynfyn.

THOMAS DE MAIN, SIR—a new-made knight, non-identical twin to Geoffrey, noted for his swordsmanship.

TIARNÁN MACRAE, SIR—a senior aide to King Donal.

TIVADAN, FATHER—Chancellor of the Exchequer of Corwyn.

TORVAL, PRINCE—second son of the King of Torenth.

TREVOR UDAUT, SIR—a young knight of Corwyn, son of Sir Laurenz Udaut; assigned to Sir Kenneth Morgan's service.

ULF CAREY, SIR—a new-made knight of Gwynedd, known for his keen horsemanship.

URIEL, ARCHANGEL—guardian of the element of earth.

VERA LAURELA (DE CORWYN) HOWARD MCLAIN, COUNTESS—younger twin sister of Alyce, but raised by and believed to be the daughter of Lord Orban Howard and Lady Laurela; wife of Jared Earl of Kierney and mother of Duncan.

VIVIENNE DE JORDANET, LADY—member of the Camberian Council.

WALTER, SIR—a knight of Kierney, husband of Geill Morgan.

WENCIT, PRINCE—fourth son of King Nimur of Torenth.

WILLIAM MACCARTNEY, ARCHBISHOP—Archbishop of Rhemuth.

XANDER OF TORRYLIN, SIR—a young knight of Lendour.

XENIA, PRINCESS—first daughter and third child of Donal King of Gwynedd and Richeldis.

YVES DE TREMELAN, SIR—a young knight of Lendour.

ZACHRIS POMEROY—Deryni foster brother of Hogan Furstán, and also a student of Mother Serafina, holding lands adjacent to those of Rhydon's father.

ZAIZIE—family pet-name of Alazais Morgan, Kenneth's youngest daughter by his first marriage.

*ZEFIRYN—an ancient Deryni sage of Caeriesse.

ZOË BRONWYN MORGAN, LADY—eldest daughter of Sir Kenneth Morgan, a former student at Arc-en-Ciel; heart-sister (and stepdaughter!) to Alyce de Corwyn.

APPENDIX II

Index of Places

AIRNIS—small earldom in southwestern Corwyn.

ANDELON—sovereign principality adjacent to the Forcinn Buffer States.

ARC-EN-CIEL, CONVENT OF NOTRE DAME DE L'—convent school of Our Lady of the Rainbow, where Alyce and Zoë studied.

ARRANAL VALLEY—part of a strategic pass between Torenth and the Earldom of Marley.

ARX FIDEI SEMINARY—one of the principal seminaries in Gwynedd, north of Rhemuth.

BELDOUR—capital city of Torenth.

BREMAGNE—kingdom across the Southern Sea from Gwynedd, whose king has marriageable daughters.

CAERIESSE—legendary land that sank beneath the sea.

CARDOSA—strategic city on the Gwynedd-Torenth border in the Rheljan Mountains; location of St. Mary's Cathedral.

CARTHMOOR—former subsidiary princedom in the former Principality of Mooryn, the holding of Prince Richard Duke of Carthmoor.

CASSAN—duchy in northwest Gwynedd.

CASTLE CYNFYN—seat of the Earl of Lendour, in the town of Cynfyn.

CASTLE RUNDEL—an hour's ride from Culdi.

CLAIBOURNE—northernmost and most senior duchy in Gwynedd, principal part of the ancient principality of Kheldour.

COAMER MOUNTAINS—mountain range marking part of the southernmost border between Gwynedd and Torenth.

COROTH—capital of the Duchy of Corwyn; location of Cathedral of St. Matthew.

CORWYN—ancient duchy in southeast Gwynedd, part of the ancient Principality of Mooryn; seat of the Deryni dukes of Corwyn.

CULDI—earldom and town in the Purple March formerly held by Camber MacRorie; currently a holding of Jared Earl of Kierney.

CYNFYN—capital of the earldom of Lendour.

DELLARD'S LANDING—ford on the Duncapall River, north of Coroth.

DESSE—northernmost navigable point on the River Eirian, several hours' ride south of Rhemuth.

DHASSA—free holy city in the Lendour Mountains; seat of the prince-bishops of Dhassa, presiding from Cathedral of St. Andrew.

EASTMARCH—county in northeast Gwynedd.

EIRIAN RIVER—principal river of Gwynedd, extending northward from the sea to Rhemuth and beyond.

FORCINN BUFFER STATES—loosely confederated group of independent principalities, nominally under the overlordship of the Hort of Orsal (who is also Prince of Tralia), the others being the Duchy of Joux, the Grand Duchy of Vezaire, and the Principalities of Logreine, Thuria, and Andelon.

FURSTÁNAN—Torenthi port town at the mouth of the Beldour River, and location of the Deryni Abbey of Saint-Sasile.

GRECOTHA—site of Gwynedd's great university, and also St. Luke's Cathedral.

GWYNEDD—principal kingdom of the Eleven Kingdoms, seat of the Haldane kings.

HALLOWDALE—village on the Molling River, scene of the burning of Deryni.

HAUT EMERAUD—equestrian stud facility of Oisín Adair.

HORTHÁNTHY—summer residence of the Hort of Orsal.

HOWICCE—kingdom linked with the Kingdom of Llannedd, southwest of Gwynedd.

INCUS DOMINI—the Anvil of the Lord, headquarters of the Knights of the Anvil, a Deryni order partially derived from fled Knights of St. Michael after the dissolution of that order.

JÁCA—sovereign principality, one of the Forcinn States.

JOUX—Torenthi duchy.

KHELDOUR—ancient principality in northern Gwynedd.

KIERNEY—earldom in northwest of Gwynedd, a secondary holding of the Dukes of Cassan.

KING'S LANDING—barge station on the River Eirian, just north of Rhemuth.

LAAS—ancient capital of Meara.

LENDOUR—earldom north of Corwyn.

LLANNEDD—kingdom linked with the Kingdom of Howicce, southwest of Gwynedd.

LORSÖL—duchy in Torenth, famous for its carpets.

MARLEY—earldom in northeast Gwynedd.

MEARA—formerly independent principality west of Gwynedd, now a province of Gwynedd.

MOLLING RIVER—eastern tributary of the River Eirian, joining it at Rhemuth.

MOLLINGFORD—market town on the Molling River, near Hallowdale.

MOORYN—former sovereign principality in the southeast of Gwynedd, divided by Festil I into the Duchies of Corwyn, Carthmoor, and numerous smaller earldoms and baronies.

MORGANHALL—manorial seat of the Morgan family.

NUR HALLAJ—sovereign principality sometimes regarded as one of the Forcinn Buffer States.

NUR SAYYID—great university in R'Kassi.

NYFORD—capital of Carthmoor; ancient market town and port; site of St. Joseph's Cathedral.

ORSALIA—ancient name of part of Trailia, whence derives the title "Hort of Orsal."

PLADDA—manor house of Coroth, nestled in a curve of the Duncapall River, bordering Tendal lands.

PURPLE MARCH—vast plain in the north-central part of Gwynedd.

RATHARKIN—provincial capital of Meara.

RHANAMÉ—great Deryni university and seminary in R'Kassi.

RHEMUTH—capital of Gwynedd.

RHEMUTH CASTLE—seat of the Haldane Kings, and center of Gwynedd's government.

RHENDALL—earldom in northeast Gwynedd.

RHENDALL MOUNTAINS—mountain chain encompassing Rhendall.

R'KASSI—kingdom east of Gwynedd and south of Torenth, famous for its horses.

RUNDEL CASTLE—an hour's ride from Culdi.

SAINT-SASILE, ABBEY OF—all-Deryni monastic establishment in Furstánan, at the mouth of Torenth's River Beldour.

TENDAL—barony of Corwyn.

TORENTH—principal kingdom east of Gwynedd.

TORTUÑA—Tralian port across the straits from Horthánthy.

TRALIA—more recent name of the sovereign principality ruled by the Hort of Orsal.

TRANSHA—small border earldom in northwest Gwynedd.

TRE-ARILAN—country seat of the Arilan family.

TRURILL—earldom between Gwynedd and Meara.

VALORET—former capital of Gwynedd; seat of the Archbishop of Valoret, Primate of All Gwynedd, at All Saints' Cathedral.

VEZAIRE—one of the Forcinn Buffer States.

◇◇◇◇◇◇◇◇◇◇◇◇◇◇ Don't miss ◇◇◇◇◇◇◇◇◇◇◇◇◇◇

"A vital continuation to the saga." —*Booklist*

In the King's Service

A Novel of the Deryni
from *New York Times* bestselling author

Katherine Kurtz

This is a tale of an earlier time in the kingdom of Gwynedd, a time before the magical Deryni were persecuted as evil beings, before they were hounded nearly out of existence. There were Deryni at court and some of the lords of the land claimed Deryni heritage.

But the king, Donal Haldane, ruled over all with a casual ruthlessness. He expected much of himself, as a ruler, as a warrior, and as the father of future kings. And he expected the same of those in his service—human and Deryni alike—in spite of the web of royal intrigue that threatened to ensnare them all...

"Kurtz's love of history lets her do things with her characters and their world that no nonhistorian could hope to do." —*Chicago Sun-Times*

"Exquisitely detailed." —*Publishers Weekly*